THREE DAYS

TO

FOREVER

A MAC FARADAY MYSTERY

BY

LAUREN CARR

THREE DAYS TO FOREVER

Published by Acorn Book Services

For information call: 304-995-1295
or Email: writerlaurencarr@gmail.com

This book is a work of fiction. Names, characters, places, and incidents are products of the author's imagination or are used fictitiously. Any resemblance to actual events or locales or persons, living or dead, is entirely coincidental.

Designed by Acorn Book Services

Publication Managed by Acorn Book Services
www.acornbookservices.com
acornbookservices@gmail.com
304-995-1295

Cover designed by Todd Aune
Spokane, Washington
www.projetoonline.com

ISBN-13: 978-0692353844
ISBN-10: 0692353844

Published in the United States of America

NOTE FROM THE AUTHOR

Fans of past Mac Faraday and Lovers in Crime mysteries are in for a treat with *Three Days to Forever*. I have chosen to take a different path with the latest Mac Faraday Mystery. Don't worry. We have plenty of dead bodies and lots of mystery—as well as intrigue, suspense, and page turning twists.

The key job of a fiction writer is to look at a situation, make observations about how things are and how they work, and then ask, "What if …" Then, the writer twists, turns, and manipulates, while maintaining believability, to make for a thrilling plot.

This is what I have done with *Three Days to Forever*.

Mac Faraday's latest adventure plunges him, Archie, David, Gnarly, and the gang head first into a case that brings the war on terror right into Deep Creek Lake. Current political issues will be raised and discussed by the characters involved.

Keep this in mind while you turn the pages—***Three Days to Forever** is fiction.* It is not the author's commentary on politics, the media, the military, or Islam. While actual current events have inspired this adventure in mystery and suspense, this fictional work is not meant to point an accusatory finger at anyone in our nation's government.

If, however, future events prove that circumstances in Washington are as I have depicted them in *Three Days to Forever* … well, keep in mind that you read it here first.

Happy Reading!

Lauren Carr

To the Men and Women of the United States Military—

All Gave Some, Some Gave All

Three Days

to

Forever

A Mac Faraday Mystery

CAST OF CHARACTERS

(in order of appearance)

David O'Callaghan: Spencer police chief. Son of the late police chief, Patrick O'Callaghan. Mac Faraday's best friend and half-brother. He is also a major in the United States Marine Reserves. Leads a team in special operations.

Jassem al-Baghdadi: High-ranking official of Islamic terrorist group in the Middle East. Leader of their military council. Top of Homeland Security's most wanted list. David O'Callaghan kills him during a mission.

Colonel Glen Frost: David O'Callaghan's commanding officer when on active duty.

Mac Faraday: Retired homicide detective. On the day his divorce became final, he inherited $270 million and an estate on Deep Creek Lake from his birth mother, Robin Spencer.

Robin Spencer: Mac Faraday's late birth mother and world-famous mystery author. As an unwed teenager, she gave him up for adoption. After becoming America's queen of mystery, she found her son and made him her heir. Her ancestors founded Spencer, Maryland, located on the shore of Deep Creek Lake, a resort area in Western Maryland.

Police Chief Patrick O'Callaghan: David's late father. Spencer's legendary police chief. The love of Robin Spencer's life and Mac Faraday's birth father.

Gnarly: Mac Faraday's German shepherd. Another part of his inheritance from Robin Spencer. Gnarly used to belong to the United States Army, who refuses to talk about him.

Archie Monday: Former editor and research assistant to world-famous mystery author Robin Spencer. She is now Mac Faraday's fiancée.

Russell Dooley: Husband of the late Leigh Ann Dooley, who Mac had arrested for murder many years ago. Blames Mac for his wife's suicide.

Joshua Thornton: Hancock County, West Virginia, Prosecuting Attorney. Retired Navy JAG officer. One of Mac's groomsmen. Recently married to Cameron Gates.

Abdul Kochar: Best-selling novelist who had immigrated from Afghanistan.

Donny Thornton: Joshua Thornton's seventeen-year-old son. He's in Spencer for the skiing.

Cameron Gates: Homicide detective with the Pennsylvania State Police. Recently married Joshua Thornton. She turned down an invitation to Mac and Archie's wedding because she doesn't do weddings or funerals.

Reginald Crane: Murder victim in Pennsylvania. He was tortured to death. Cameron Gates is on the case.

Ethan Bonner: Reginald Crane's assistant. Found the body. Now he is in the wind.

Chelsea Adams: Paralegal for Ben Fleming. First and current love of David O'Callaghan. Suffering from epilepsy, she has Molly, a service dog trained to sense and warn of seizures.

Deputy Chief Arthur Bogart (Bogie): Spencer's Deputy Police Chief. David's godfather. Don't let his gray hair and weathered face fool you.

Gil Sherrard: Lives at the Beaver Dam Motel where Russell Dooley's body was found. He spends a lot of time in jail.

Agnes Douglas: Mother of the bride. She raised seven children alone, six boys and one girl. She is proud to tell how she put food on the table by cleaning homes for rich folks.

Sheriff Christopher Turow: Garrett County Sheriff. Retired Army Officer. He's one of the good guys.

Dr. Dora Washington: Garrett County Medical Examiner.

Officers Fletcher, Brewster, and **Zigler:** Officers with the Spencer Police Department. They serve under Police Chief David O'Callaghan.

Hector Langford: Chief of Security at the Spencer Inn. A lean, gray-haired Australian, Hector has been with the Inn for over twenty-five years.

Jeff Ingles: Manager of the Spencer Inn, the five-star resort owned by Mac Faraday, who likes to keep Ingles' life interesting.

Leland Elder: Special Agent with the FBI. He and his partner Neal Black take over the Reginald Crane murder case from Cameron Gates.

Neal Black: Special Agent with the FBI. He and his partner Leland Elder take over the Reginald Crane murder case from Cameron Gates.

Tonya: Spencer Police Department Desk Sergeant. She runs things at the police station.

Murphy Thornton: Second Lieutenant in the United States Navy. Naval Academy graduate. He's not your average navy officer. Joshua Thornton's son. His identical twin brother, Joshua Junior, is older by seven minutes. Like father, like son.

Nathaniel Bauman: CEO of NOH Bauman Technologies, a billion-dollar company that has been selling weapons to both America and her enemies. He also owns multiple news organizations.

Tristan Faraday: Mac Faraday's son. In his third year of college at George Washington University. Studying natural science. He's an intellectual and proud of it.

Jessica Faraday: Mac Faraday's lovely daughter. Graduated with honors from the College of William and Mary with a master's degree in behavioral and cognitive neuroscience. Her inheritance from Robin Spencer thrust her into high society.

Spencer/Candi: Jessica Faraday's blue merle Shetland sheep-dog. She has a long way to go in training.

Colt Fitzgerald: Former underwear model turned actor. He may or may not be Jessica's boyfriend. Depends on who you ask.

Jan Martin-MacMillan: Joshua Thornton's childhood friend and neighbor. Married to Dr. Tad MacMillan.

Dr. Tad MacMillan: Joshua Thornton's cousin and next door neighbor. He's the town doctor in Chester, West Virginia.

Ra'ees Sims: Owner of Sims Security in Texas. Very active in a Muslim mosque. Supports Islamic extremists. The ATF has been watching his company.

Muhammad Muiz: Special advisor to the President of the United States on Islamic affairs.

Ismail Kochar: Abdul Kochar's brother. Islamic extremist. Leader of a terrorist group in Iraq.

Freedom lies in being bold.

Robert Frost

Prologue

Eighteen Months Ago – Desert outside Tehran, Iraq

"Don't you do this kind of backwards, Major?" Marine First Lieutenant Oliver Dean asked as he kept his eyes trained through the night-vision binoculars. He was peering down the mountainside to the terrorist training camp hidden in the valley among the desert caves.

"How is that, Lieutenant?" Major David O'Callaghan pressed the earbud to his ear. He didn't want to miss any confirmations from the members of his special operations team sent out to surround the camp.

"Rubbing elbows with the rich and famous in Deep Creek Lake for eleven months. Then, in the summer, just when the weather gets great and the sexy young things in their barely there bikinis arrive, you come out here in the desert with us smelly, ugly—"

"Who you calling ugly, Dean?" Bates objected from the other side of David. Second Lieutenant Hallie Bates puffed out her abundant bosom, which was crammed in under her bulletproof vest and desert fatigues. Raised in a tough neighborhood in Baltimore, Maryland, the African-American woman's street attitude flared. "Take any of those rich pampered hos from that fancy-dancy Spencer, strip her of her acrylic nails, shove her into desert fatigues and eighty pounds of gear, and slap a helmet on her prissy head. Then see just how pretty she is."

"They do smell better," David confessed.

Hallie wagged her head back and forth while asking, "Who would you rather have out here watching your lily white butt, Major? Me and Matilda"—she held up her assault rifle and patted its barrel—"or a sweet smelling deb?"

The Delta team saved David from having to answer. They were in position on the opposite side of the camp.

"Roger that," David said into his mouthpiece. "Charlie, do you read me?"

"Loud and clear, Major. Just waiting for the word."

"Still haven't heard from Foxtrot and Gamma," David noted more to himself than to his team of three men and a woman. They all kept their eyes and ears focused on what was supposed to be a sleepy terrorist training camp. "But they have further to go," he said to soothe his nerves.

Seeing lights moving down among the camp, he eased across the makeshift rocky clearing toward the telescope. "What's going on down there? Have we been blown?"

"It looks like everyone in that camp is awake," Lieutenant Dean said. "Maybe they're practicing nighttime maneuvers."

"Too many lights and movement to be business as usual," David said while studying three guards running toward the main entrance. The only road leading into the camp cut through a break in the rocky hillsides surrounding it. He thanked God that the members of his team had managed to get across the road before attention had been drawn in that direction.

"Gamma in place and ready, sir," his radio announced.

The last team followed to tell him, "Foxtrot is set up."

I don't like all this activity, David thought, too busy thinking to acknowledge receipt of the transmission.

"Do you copy, sir?" Foxtrot asked.

David hit the button on his mouthpiece. "Copy. Charlie, Delta, Foxtrot, and Gamma, do you all have visuals?"

All four teams reported that they had their equipment and weapons set up for their attack on the camp.

"Three vehicles arriving," Lieutenant Dean said with excitement in his voice. "Looks like they're having a party."

Taking in a deep breath, David focused his blue eyes through the telescope at the two trucks and a Humvee that were making their way across the rocky road into the camp.

"Talk about timing," Lieutenant Hallie Bates moved in to take a closer look through her night binoculars. "They just got two truckloads of weapons."

"Are you sure?" Lieutenant Dean placed his binoculars back up onto his face.

Their answer came when one of the men below yanked the lid off a crate to reveal a box full of automatic assault rifles.

"That's what it looks like." David could hear his team around the camp chattering into the radio. "Everyone hold their positions. I need to report this to command."

"Yeah," Hallie said with a note of sarcasm. "I can already tell you what they'll say."

"Stand-down," Dean replied before sticking his pinkie finger into his mouth to chew on a ragged fingernail.

"I've been at this a little bit longer than you," David said. "They may tell us to wait for backup—"

"With all due respect, sir," Hallie said, "You guys in the reserves. You haven't seen what we've been seeing. Sometimes, I wonder whose side Washington is on anymore."

Even in the darkness, David could catch the frustration in her eyes. Since arriving in Tehran five days earlier, he had noticed a significantly low level of morale in the fourteen-person special operations team of which he had been put in charge.

"Major!" the Charlie leader uttered a harsh whisper across the radio. "Check out the dude that got out of the back of the Humvee. It's Jassem al-Baghdadi!" David could hear him asking the rest of his team. "Isn't that Jassem al-Baghdadi? He's like the leader of their military council."

David was already peering through the telescope on his sniper rifle. He had memorized the lead terrorist's face the year before, when intelligence information given to the marines special operations units revealed that Jassem al-Baghdadi was the chief coordinator of a jihad attack on a marine base in Afghanistan. Nineteen marines, all relatively new and on their first overseas tours, had been killed when an enlisted marine drove onto the base in a military truck filled with explosives. Then, he had rammed it into a barracks of his fellow comrades.

A deeper investigation of the marine's background discovered that the Muslim was also a devoted member of Jassem al-Baghdadi's terrorist network. The attack had been planned for months with numerous communications between the marine and al-Baghdadi.

The official cause of the attack was listed as workplace violence by a disgruntled soldier. In-depth investigative reports from the few journalists who had uncovered proof of the direct communication between al-Baghdadi and the careful coordination of the attack had been unable to gain any traction within the mainstream media.

But all of the branches of the military, and especially the soldiers serving in the Middle East, knew the facts that had successfully been kept under wrap.

At the moment, Jassem al-Baghdadi was in Major David O'Callaghans crosshairs. The terrorist leader was proudly directing their freshly trained terrorists, who were gazing up at him in awe of his accomplishments—masterminding the death of innocent westerners.

In contrast to the excitement that David felt building up in the pit of his stomach and working its way to his beating heart, Hallie and Dean were apprehensive.

"Hundred bucks says we're told to let him go," Dean grumbled to Hallie.

"I'll take that bet." David thumbed the button to connect with Colonel Glen Frost at their base.

"How many times has ops had al-Baghdadi in their sites and been told to stand-down?" Hallie asked Dean.

"Twice that I know of," the lieutenant answered. "In Somalia, they were told that there were too many civilians around. Those civilians were confirmed to be pirates holding thousands of westerners hostage."

"Then there was Syria, when he was on the road home from a party—"

"I get your point," David said while covering his ear so he could hear the colonel picking up the call.

"What's your status, Major?" Colonel Frost said in a tone that concealed his concern for his team's safety.

"The camp just received two truckloads of weapons, sir," David reported, "delivered personally by Jassem al-Baghdadi."

"Are you kidding me?" The colonel sounded as excited as a schoolboy about to take down the playground bully with his secret weapon.

David peered through the scope on his rifle. "I have him in my sights right now. Permission to use lethal force to terminate the target, sir?"

"Here it comes," Dean muttered.

The colonel grumbled. "I need to contact central command."

David sat up from behind the rifle. "Excuse me, sir? Jassem al-Baghdadi is on the list of terror—"

"Protocol, Major," the colonel explained with increasing agitation about the situation. "We have been given orders to check with central command in Washington before using lethal force against any of our targets, even one identified as a high-ranking enemy target who killed innocent marines while they were sleeping."

Rubbing the back of his neck, David bit his lip to keep from saying what he was thinking.

"Told you, sir," Dean whispered.

"I'll have to contact command," Colonel Frost said into David's ear. "If they give me the go-ahead, use lethal force at will on my word. Code word Zombie."

"Zombie," David repeated. "I roger that. Zombie."

"Hold on tight, Major."

David continued peering through the scope on his rifle and reporting to each member of his team, some of whom were around him, and some of whom were at their posts around the perimeter. "Okay, team, here's the plan. If we get the go-ahead, I'm going to take out the head of this dragon. Once I take him down, you're all going to need to be ready. Gamma and Charlie, use the grenade launchers."

"Aim for the trucks," Gamma said.

"Got to take them both out," David said. "I want all snipers ready. Identify the leaders. These pawns aren't anything without someone to give them orders. Take out the instructors and those in command first."

"*If* Washington gives us the go-ahead," Hallie said.

"They will," David said with as much confidence as he could muster to pass on to his team. "We're at war. We can't win it if we don't neutralize the enemy, no matter how nasty killing might be. I don't like shooting people, but in situations like this, there are two options. Kill, or have my brothers and sisters in arms—or even innocent civilians like

22

those in the World Trade Center, the Pentagon, and flight ninety-three—murdered."

"*We* may not have forgotten," Lieutenant Dean said, "but *Washington* sure has."

"Not *everyone* in Washington," Hallie said. "Not the *Phantoms*."

"Phantoms?" David chuckled while cocking his head and pressing his radio to his ear to make sure he got the order when it came.

"It's a myth." Dean was laughing as well. "You know how people in the military talk."

Hallie was shaking her head. "A friend of mine who works on the top floors at the Pentagon says it ain't."

"What's a Phantom?" David asked with a grin. "Do they run around wearing black capes?"

"According to what I was told—do you remember the untouchables from Al Capone days?"

"That was before my time, but yes," David said. "A group of federal agents and cops who banded together to take down organized crime in Chicago. They couldn't be bribed or intimidated. They were untouchable."

"Well, this is the military version," Hallie said over Dean's quiet laughter. They were all aware of the camp full of men who would think nothing of torturing and killing all of them if they were discovered.

"This team is made up of members of each branch of the government and military, more highly trained than special ops and Navy SEALs," Hallie said. "You don't apply to be a Phantom. You're hand-picked. They have the top equipment and training, and their sole mission is to protect our country and citizens without the influence and intimidation of politicians and deal-makers with their own personal and political agendas."

She jerked her chin at the chief terrorist down at the bottom of the mountain. "Twice we've had that man in our sites, and twice we've been told by someone high up in Washington to let him go. Why?" She scoffed. "Because killing him would hurt those poor terrorists' feelings. Like he didn't care about hurting our feelings when he planned and coordinated the jihad attack in Afghanistan?" With a knowing expression on her face, she said, "It's going to take a Phantom to terminate him."

"They're a myth," Dean said.

"Do you remember that mansion that al-Baghdadi had in Syria?" Hallie asked.

"I wasn't there."

"Huge mansion," Hallie said. "They say that the downstairs was a command center for ISIS. Well, that mansion is no more. It's an eighteen-foot crater in the desert."

"Caused by an accidental explosion from their own weapons," Dean said.

Hallie whispered to David. "That's the hallmark of the Phantoms. When they strike, it's *never* traced back to us. You'd be surprised by what I heard—"

"Major O'Callaghan …"

Sucking in a deep breath, David pressed the button on his radio. "Yes, sir?"

"Zombie, O'Callaghan. Zombie," he heard the colonel say with a smile in his voice. "Terminate target at will. Wipe that camp off the face of this earth. See you when you arrive safely back home."

"Thank you, sir!" Chuckling, David bumped fists with the two lieutenants. "You owe me a hundred bucks. We've got zombies." Into the radio, he directed, "Everyone into positions. This is for our brothers and sisters in Afghanistan."

He focused in on Jassem al-Baghdadi, lining up his broad chest in the middle of the crosshairs in his scope. Even if al-Baghdadi was wearing a vest, the armor piercing bullet would still end his reign of terror.

"I'm putting the first shot right through his black little heart," David said while waiting for his heartbeat to slow. "Second one is going right between his black eyes."

Between the beats of his heart, he pulled the trigger.

"Drinks are on me tonight, ladies and gentlemen!" David announced after his team hopped off the helicopter that had returned them to the camp.

The sun was rising on what promised to be another blistering day. Amid fist bumps and high-fives, the special ops team woke up the camp with their celebratory cheers of success. They had not only taken out the whole terrorist camp and two fresh truckloads of weapons meant to be used against them and their allies, but they had also taken out the number-two man, the leader of the terrorists' military council who had successfully engineered the murders of their brothers and sisters in arms.

"O'Callaghan!" a voice rose above the cheers.

When David turned around, he saw that Colonel Glen Frost was not jubilant like his other comrades were. The hard look on the older man's face was not what he had expected to see. His face was red all the way up his forehead and across his bald head. His white mustache was stretched taunt across his upper lip.

"Yes, sir!" David stood at attention and raised his hand in a salute.

"My tent immediately, Major O'Callaghan!" The colonel turned around and disappeared into his tent.

The noise of excitement immediately ceased.

"What's going on?" a member of David's team asked. "You'd think al-Baghdadi rose from the dead."

"Maybe we were supposed to read him his rights before the major put that bullet through his chest," Lieutenant Dean said.

"Put our equipment away and get some breakfast," David ordered before stepping away. After taking a few steps, he turned back to his team, who was watching him with concern on their faces. "You all did great out there. I'm proud of each one of you."

When David arrived at his commanding officer's tent, he found the colonel pacing around his desk instead of sitting behind it. Immediately, David stood at attention and rose his hand in a salute. "Major O'Callaghan reporting as ordered, sir."

The colonel returned the salute before closing the door.

David sensed Colonel Frost circling behind him. Compared to the marines who served under him, Colonel Glen Frost was short. The top of his head came up to David's chin. But he made up for what he lacked in height with his commanding presence.

Having known the colonel for more than a dozen years, David was both at an advantage and a disadvantage. He knew how Colonel Frost operated, so he was rarely caught off guard by his actions. David knew what was expected of him. The disadvantage was that the colonel knew David equally well and set his expectations for the young officer very high.

Suddenly, Colonel Frost stepped into David's space. David felt his hot breath on his neck when he asked, "What happened out there?"

The colonel's anger confused him, and David responded while staring straight ahead. "Target was terminated as ordered, sir. We wiped the whole camp off the face of the earth as you directed."

Colonel Frost's blood shot eyes grew wide. "Ordered? Directed?"

"Yes, sir, as ordered."

"Whose orders, Major?"

"Yours, sir."

Colonel Frost stepped back and peered closely into David's face. "Major O'Callaghan, when did I give the zombie order, and to whom?"

"Me, sir," David answered. "After I requested permission to terminate the target using lethal force, you reported that you needed to contact central command. A few minutes later, I received a radio call from you stating that permission had been granted—using the code word 'zombie,' sir."

"I said 'zombie,' Major?"

"Twice, sir." Standing at attention, David wished the colonel would give him permission to stand at rest. His feet and shoulders were getting tired after a night of hiding on the rocky mountainside. "Is there a problem, sir?"

"Yes, Major O'Callaghan, there is a *big problem*," the colonel said. "The order was to *stand-down!*"

David felt his stomach drop to the floor. It took all of his control to not drop his jaw in a gasp. His whole body broke into a cold sweat. "With all due respect, sir, I did not receive a stand-down order."

"And I did not issue the code word to terminate the target," the colonel said through gritted teeth.

Beads of sweat forming on his forehead and rolling down his cheek to his neck, David searched his mind for a solution. "Could the radio signals have gotten mixed up, sir? Your message went to a different team, and I received my message from someone else?"

"Using our code word of zombie?" the colonel scoffed. "I referred to you by name, Major. I requested a confirmation from you—Major O'Callaghan—that you understood the order was to stand-down, and you and your team were to return to base ASAP. You rogered that you understood."

"That is not the order I received, sir," David replied. "Sir, I have worked under you for years. Have you ever known me to disobey an order, sir? *If I had received a stand-down order, I would have stood down and directed my team to do likewise, sir.*"

"Yes, O'Callaghan, I know that." The colonel turned to go back to his desk. "That is why I am so confused by what has happened."

"What now, sir?" David swallowed.

"General Thurston Affleck at central command went through the roof at the news that Jassem al-Baghdadi had been killed and the camp had been destroyed." The colonel allowed a slight smile to form at the corner of his lips. "Good job, by the way."

"I expect an inquiry, sir," David said.

"Of course," the colonel said. "You and I are both ordered back to the states immediately on military transport for an inquiry as soon as we arrive. Then, they will make their recommendations about disciplinary action." He added in a low voice, "Dishonorable discharge is the least of your problems. Court-martial for disobeying a direct order is on the table."

David blinked. "I understand, sir. What about my team, sir?"

"Captain Fellows will take over as team leader."

"I mean as far as disciplinary action towards them, sir?" David said. "They were following my orders."

"I'll do my best to keep them out of this mess," Colonel Frost said. "You are dismissed, Major. Go to your tent to pack. We are leaving in one hour."

"Yes, sir." David turned around on his heel and stepped toward the door. He stopped. "Permission to speak, sir?"

"Yes, O'Callaghan."

David turned back to him. "I know what I heard, sir."

"And I know what I said."

It was a long, physically tiring and emotionally exhausting flight back to the United States on a military transport, which was not made for comfort. The short time he was given to pack did not give David time to shower and change out of his desert fatigues.

Colonel Glen Frost barely spoke to David, who had considered his commanding officer a mentor and friend. During the long flight across the ocean, David would steal glances over at the Colonel—when he was not replaying the radio conversation over and over again in his mind.

"Zombie, O'Callaghan. Zombie. Terminate target at will. Wipe that camp off the face of this earth. See you when you arrive safely back home."

Could I have misunderstood? How could I have mixed up "zombie" and "terminate at will" with "stand-down" and "return to base?"

"Liquid courage?" Colonel Glen Frost held the flask out in front of David's face.

Grateful for the good will gesture, David took the flask, wiped off the mouth of it, and took a large gulp of the scotch. "Thank you, sir."

"You're going to need it." The colonel pushed the flask back to him. "Just because I'm PO about this whole thing is no reason for you and I to stop being friends. I do consider you a friend, O'Callaghan."

"I'm still trying to figure out what this thing is," David said. "I know I'm not imagining—"

"Forget that," Colonel Frost said. "Forget about what happened out there."

"That's what the inquiry is about," David said. "I need to know what happened."

"Like they're going to believe that *I told you* to *stand-down* and *you heard zombie?*" Colonel Frost chuckled. "We might as well tell them that aliens from outer space gained control of our radio waves."

He grabbed the flask out of David's hand. "Here's what we're going to tell them. I *did* tell you zombie. I *did* order you to terminate the target." He took a drink from the flask. "I disobeyed that idiot Affleck's orders to stand-down. You were following my orders."

"But you're only three years from retirement," David said. "They'll court-martial you. You'll lose your commission."

"General Affleck is looking for a scapegoat," Colonel Frost said. "Better me than you. You're young, David. You have so much to offer to this country—if they'll let you. I don't know what's happened to this country." He took a drink from the flask. "Actually, I do, but don't get me started. I told Affleck exactly what was out there. I told him exactly what had to be done. He knew as well as all of us what Jassem's history was, what he had done, and to whom. You had him right in your sites. He was on Homeland Security's list, damn it. But Affleck ordered you not just to stand-down, but also to scrub your whole operation. Leave all those weapons that were going to be aimed at us next—do you know why?"

"Why?"

"Because Affleck's loyalty is not to the military or his country," Frost was on a roll. "He may be a Marine General, but he's not military. He's a suck-up. He's been kissing butt and playing political games since his first day in boot camp." The colonel gritted his teeth. "Last night, before I hung up from talking to Affleck, I ended up saying something to him that I have never said to any commanding officer before in my life."

"What's that?" David asked.

"Whose side are you on?" He turned to David. "He didn't answer me." After nudging David in the arm, he handed him the flask. "So they'll buy that I gave you the zombie order—no problem. The best leaders are willing to take a bullet for their team."

His heart pounding, David took a drink from the flask. The scotch burned all the way down his throat and to his stomach.

"Repeat after me," Colonel Frost said into his ear, "My commanding officer gave me the order to terminate the target. I was obeying his orders."

By the time they returned to Camp Lejeune, North Carolina, David was wishing that he had refused the flask of scotch. Physical and emotional exhaustion—encased in what felt like two layers of dried sweat—accompanied by alcohol made him feel physically ill.

Following Colonel Glen Frost down the stairs to the runway, David noticed a limousine resting on the tarmac. A statuesque woman dressed in a black skirted suit with stiletto heels stepped up to Colonel Frost. On his way down the stairs, David noticed that she possessed the longest, sexiest legs he had ever seen in his life—and he had seen more than his share of women's legs. A black fedora hat covered her hair so that David couldn't tell its length or color. Her eyes were concealed behind dark sunglasses. She held a leather binder under her elbow like a clutch bag.

She offered a long slender hand to the commanding officer. "Colonel Frost," she said in a sultry voice, "it's a pleasure to meet you. I was sent to meet you and Major O'Callaghan."

When David shook her hand in a firm grip, he noticed that she was almost as tall as he was, six feet two inches, in her high heels. While she was not dressed in a military uniform, the way she stood with her shoulders back and her back straight indicated that she certainly had a military officer's training.

"Commandant Amos asked that I escort you to your hotel where you can rest after your long flight."

The color drained from Colonel Frost's face, starting at the top of his bald head. "General James Amos? Commandant of the Marine Corps? Joint Chief of Staff?"

"Yes, sir." With a gesture of her hand, the limousine driver hurried forward to take David's duffle bag. "I hope your flight was pleasant. You will have a day to rest before boarding the private jet tomorrow morning to take you on to Washington for a debriefing before the Joint Chiefs of Staff. They are all very anxious to meet you. By close of business tomorrow, the rest of your special ops team will arrive for the ceremony and reception on Friday."

"Friday?" David asked.

The driver had taken both of their duffel bags and placed them in the trunk. He then opened the rear door of the limousine and waited for them to climb in.

"I know," she said with a crooked grin. "Usually these type of things take forever—red tape and blah-blah-blah. But the commandant was so impressed by the report that General Affleck filed with his recommendation that he has personally rushed it through."

Feeling his stomach lurch, David hoped he could keep from throwing up on her black stilettos.

"Of course, considering the sensitive nature of the operation, we can't publicize the award and why you and your team are getting it. If the terrorist network ever got the names of those who executed Jassem al-Baghdadi, they wouldn't hesitate to come over here to the states to administer payback."

Even though her dark glasses blocked his view of her eyes, David could feel her gaze directed at him. *Not only am I going to be court-martialed, but now I'm on the terrorists' hit list.*

"Still," she went on, "we can't deny your friends and family from sharing in this honor with you. You are more than welcome to invite them to the awards ceremony and the reception afterwards. Many of the military's highest ranking officials will be there."

Colonel Frost's question came out as a squawk. "Honor? Award? Reception?"

"Why, of course," she replied with complete innocence while she climbed into the back of the limousine.

David followed the colonel. Not forward enough to sit next to the woman who had chosen to sit with her back to the driver, they took the seat facing the front. Still, in the dim light of the limousine, she continued to conceal her eyes with the dark glasses. David didn't care. He was more focused on the long pair of bare legs beckoning for his touch.

She waited for David and Colonel Frost to get comfortable before continuing. "General Affleck recommended that you and each member of your team be award the Bronze Star for taking out Jassem al-Baghdadi." She cocked her head at them. "What did you think all this was about?"

His grin encompassing even his white mustache, Colonel Frost nudged David in a sign to be silent. "We're just surprised by all of the fuss. After all, Major O'Callaghan and his team were only doing what they had been trained to do to defend our country."

"Exactly. They had the courage that, unfortunately, others have lacked."

After the limousine had started to move away from the airfield, David asked, "What did General Affleck say in his recommendation?"

"I'll be sure to give you both copies of it," she said. "You may be interested in knowing that General Affleck's recommendation on your behalf was his last official act before his death."

"General Affleck is dead?" Colonel Frost asked. "When? How?"

"His body was found yesterday morning," she replied in a tone devoid of emotion. "I guess you were traveling at the time—"

"How did he die?" David asked.

Ensuring that the window between the back and the driver was closed, she whispered, "It's embarrassing for the current administration, but ... it was auto-erotic asphyxiation."

"Are you serious?" David had never met the general, but he knew that he was a man of strict discipline who expected the same of everyone around him.

She was nodding her head. "Yesterday morning, a cleaning woman found him hanging in the closet at the Ritz across from the Pentagon. All he was wearing was his white skull cap—"

"White skull cap? He was Muslim?" Colonel Frost asked. "I've known the man for years and I never knew he was Muslim."

"Yes," she answered with a nod of her head. "The clerk at the hotel desk remembers him checking in with a very ugly transvestite who is known to be a prostitute. NCIS is looking for him, but the ME has already placed the cause of death as accidental. It's very embarrassing for a lot of people, from his wife and family to the president—especially because Affleck was appointed to that position by the secretary of state. Everyone in Washington has been flailing since extensive evidence was found on his computer proving that he has had a long history of leaking government secrets to Islamic terrorist branches throughout the Middle East."

"Leaking secrets to Islamic terrorists?" Colonel Frost practically jumped out of his seat. "No wonder Affleck repeatedly ordered special ops to stand-down when we'd get prime terrorist targets in our crosshairs."

"Like I said, it's embarrassing," she said. "The Joint Chiefs of Staff and Congress are already ordering a full investigation of what General Affleck knew and where that information went."

Unable to read her face due to the dark glasses, David studied her body language in an attempt to read how much she truly knew beyond what she was saying. She gave him nothing. "If General Affleck was working for Islam instead of for us," he said, "why would he give the order for us to terminate the target, and then put our team in for the Bronze Star?"

"Guess we'll never know for sure," she replied.

"I know one thing," Colonel Frost said, "dirty traitor got what he had coming. Feeding information to our enemies and ordering us to sit by and twiddle our thumbs while they were out there killing us and our people. Now everyone is going to know General Affleck for what he really was—a twisted perverted traitor to his own country."

David still had his blue eyes locked on her. "I'm sorry," he said, "it's been a long last few days. I didn't catch your name."

"That's because I didn't give it," she replied.

PART ONE

THREE DAYS TO FOREVER
THURSDAY, DECEMBER 29

CHAPTER ONE

Spencer Manor, Deep Creek Lake, resort area in Western Maryland

In the heart of Maryland, a cedar-and-stone home rested at the end of the most expensive piece of real estate on Deep Creek Lake. The peninsula housed a half-dozen lake houses that grew in size and grandeur along the stretch of Spencer Court. The road ended at the stone pillars marking the multi-million dollar estate that had been the birthplace and home of the late Robin Spencer, one of the world's most famous authors.

Cautious of the boiling hot coffee, Robin Spencer's son, Mac Faraday, took a sip from the mug and cringed. Not only was it too hot, but it was also too strong. Screwing up his nose, he set the mug on the bed stand and turned to glare at the deep brown eyes peering up at him from the pillow on the other side of the bed. "Why don't you start earning your keep and learn to brew a decent pot of coffee?"

The German shepherd's ears stood up. As if to inspect what had caused his master's displeasure, he lifted his head and looked across Mac's bare chest in the direction of the bed stand.

"I may have to make an emergency stop up at the Inn just to get a cup of coffee." Mac sighed. "Archie's been gone only four days and I already miss her."

With a whine, Gnarly dropped back down onto her pillow and buried his snout in an effort to take in her scent.

Mac stroked the top of Gnarly's head. "Yeah, I can see you miss her, too."

Knocking Mac's hand out of the way, Gnarly sprung from the bed with a series of loud barks. The eruption caused Mac to almost knock over his coffee cup. The action would have normally sent Mac reaching for the gun he kept in the night table, except for the fact that he heard the familiar roar of the delivery van's engine over the barks.

Yet another delivery of wedding presents.

Climbing out of bed, Mac threw on his bathrobe and slippers before following Gnarly, who kept running back to urge him to hurry, down the stairs to Spencer Manor's two-story foyer. By the time he arrived, the driver was waiting on the other side of the cut-glass door. Tightening the belt of his robe and closing it across his chest to block out the freezing morning wind whipping off the snow, Mac yanked open the door. Gnarly rushed outside to give the delivery man a nasal pat-down, which concluded with sniffing the oversized box he was delivering.

After handing the German shepherd a dog biscuit, the delivery man greeted Mac. "Good morning, Mr. Faraday. Are you ready for the big day? Saturday, isn't it?" He handed Mac the tablet to sign for the box.

"I've been ready." Mac signed the tablet and handed it back to him. "All I have to do is show up at the church. Archie's the one doing all the work."

He took the box and read the return address.

Celeste Danford.

He recognized the name as that of an elderly actor who, twenty-five years earlier, had starred in a movie based on one of Mac's birth mother's books. She had won a couple of Academy Awards. Like many of the famous folks sending wedding presents, Mac had never met her.

After thanking the driver, Mac put his hand on the door to close it, but first he paused to call Gnarly back inside.

"It looks like someone left you something else, Mr. Faraday." The driver knelt to retrieve an envelope that Gnarly was sniffing next to the door. It was anchored down with a rock to prevent it from blowing away in the wintry wind. "Maybe it's a card." Holding it up to keep Gnarly from snatching it out of his hand, the delivery man handed it to Mac.

After thanking him, Mac closed the door and carried the package and envelope into the drop-down dining room to add them to the massive collection of wedding presents that were growing on a daily basis. Curious, Gnarly pranced at his side.

After setting down the package, Mac studied the address on the oversized brown envelope left at the front door. It was too lightweight to be a card. The only writing on the front of it was "Lieutenant Mac Faraday." That had been his rank when he had left the police department in Washington, DC. The only other writing was a stamped return address in the upper left corner:

Beaver Dam Motel
Route 340
Accident, Maryland

His blue eyes narrowing with suspicion, Mac slipped his finger under the seal, tore the envelope open, and slid the contents out to view. It contained one color picture with a yellow note stuck to the front. The picture was of Mac's bride-to-be, Archie Monday, standing at a bar holding up a margarita glass. She was beaming with joy and surrounded by her friends and sisters-in-laws, most of whom were her bridesmaids for their upcoming wedding.

A single man was among the group. A flabby middle-aged man wearing thick glasses and slightly worn clothes beamed at the camera. His arm was slipped around Archie's waist.

Mac's blood ran cold as recognition set in.

Russell Dooley.

Mac recalled the note mailed to his home shortly after Thanksgiving. It was a "thinking of you" greeting card. Inside was a newspaper clipping announcing the prison suicide of Leigh Ann Dooley, the convicted murderer of Harris Tyler. The homicide detective who had broken the case? Mac Faraday.

The greeting card contained two sentences:

"You took my happiness away. Now, I'm going to take away yours."

The yellow note stuck to the picture was written in the same handwriting.

"I got this close."

Spencer Inn

Mac Faraday's ancestors had founded Spencer back in the 1800s. By the 1920s the electric company had put in the dam and built Deep Creek Lake, and they became millionaires. After that, Spencer, Maryland, became a resort town.

One of the most luxurious resort hotels in the country was the Spencer Inn, another part of Mac's inheritance from his birth mother. Mac's grandfather had built the resort and passed it down to his daughter, who preferred writing murder mysteries to hotel management.

The front of the Inn offered a view of the lake below and the mountains off in the distance. A wrap-around porch furnished with cane rocking chairs provided outside areas for guests to enjoy the mountain breeze while taking in a magnificent view in any direction. If there wasn't a foot and a half of snow on the ground like there usually was during ski season, guests could enjoy a light meal or refreshment at the outdoor café on a multi-leveled deck that looked out across tennis courts, a golf course, and a ski lift with trails down the mountain. During the summer season, the Inn also offered guests meals and refreshments at tables or in gazeboes lost among the flora of an elaborate maze.

Joshua Thornton was enjoying his third cup of coffee and the last of his Eggs Benedict in the restaurant. The view of the Spencer Inn's ski trails leading down to Deep Creek Lake at the bottom of the mountain was so spectacular that he hardly noticed how delicious his breakfast tasted.

He wished the view was not quite so spectacular. He found it difficult to concentrate on his target, Abdul Kochar, a best-selling novelist who had originated from Afghanistan.

Clad in a brown tweed jacket, a red sweater, and slacks, the heavy-set author had just completed his breakfast of steak and eggs. While sipping his coffee, he stared across the restaurant at the roaring fire in the stone fireplace behind Joshua. Occasionally, his dark eyes would flick over to the hard-cover book resting next to Joshua's plate, and then to Joshua. Then, the author would turn his head to look out the window at the falling snow. He scratched his thick beard while glancing around.

Be cool, Abdul, Joshua tried to tell him telepathically.

The server arrived at Abdul's table with the check.

Joshua's phone buzzed on top of the book. A picture of the pretty woman with auburn hair and brown-green eyes popped up across the screen. The ID read "Cameron."

Not now. Joshua glanced across the restaurant to where Abdul was signing the check for his breakfast. Fighting to keep from looking in Joshua's direction, he picked up his tablet and phone.

Damn. Joshua fingered the button on his phone to reject the call. Picking up the book, he slid out of his seat and hurried across the restaurant to catch up to the author just as he went into the lobby.

"Mr. Kochar …" Joshua called out to him. "Abdul Kochar?"

A muscle-bound African-American threw out his arm to block Joshua's access to the novelist. The bodyguard's demeanor dared Joshua to move so much as a step closer to Abdul Kochar.

The novelist stopped and turned to face Joshua.

Joshua Thornton may have been approaching middle-age, but he still had the slender athletic build of a former military officer. His auburn ultra-short jawline beard and mustache were in contrast with the wavy silver hair that touched the top of the collar of his sweater.

Holding up the back of the book for the author to see, Joshua compared the man standing before him to the author's image on the back of the book.

"I thought that was you," Joshua said with a sheepish grin. "Excuse me. You must have seen me staring at you while you were eating. I've been reading your novel." He showed him the book. "My wife gave it to me for Christmas and I have to admit, I haven't been able to put it down." He thrust the book at the author. "Would you mind autographing it for me?"

Abdul Kochar stared wide-eyed at him long enough for Joshua to worry that the author would lose his nerve and bolt.

"Just your name and the date will do," Joshua urged him.

"It is okay, Frederick," the novelist ordered the bodyguard to allow Joshua through.

Patting the pockets in his own jacket, Joshua stepped forward. "I'm afraid I don't have a pen on me. Do you?"

With a stiff movement, Abdul reached into the inside breast pocket of his jacket and took out a blue and gold pen. After opening the book to the first page, Joshua handed it to him. Abdul quickly scribbled his name before handing the book back to him. In the process, the author dropped the pen to the floor. "I am so sorry. Clumsy of me."

"No problem," Joshua said. "Let me." Book in hand, he knelt down to the floor, swept the pen into the book, and snapped it shut. At the same time, and with a quick jerk of his right arm, a pen identical to the one that the author had used to sign the novel slipped into his palm. The transfer took only a matter of seconds. Then, Joshua stood up and handed the duplicate pen to the author. "Thank you so much, Mr. Kochar. It was a pleasure meeting you."

"You are most welcome, sir." Quickly, the novelist turned on his heels. With his bodyguard by his side, he hurried across the lobby toward the elevators.

Clutching the book shut to prevent losing his prize, Joshua returned to the restaurant to find that his empty plate was gone. The check rested next to the cell phone and tablet he had left behind in his hurry to catch up to the author.

After glancing around to ensure he was not being watched, he slipped the pen into the inside breast pocket of his jacket.

"What's up?"

Joshua jumped when he heard the voice behind him, which was followed by a firm clasp on his shoulder. After realizing that it was only his seventeen-year-old son, Donny, he let out his breath. "Why do you have to always sneak up on me?"

"It's good for your heart to get a jolt once in a while." The muscular six-foot-four teenager slipped into the seat across from Joshua. He was dressed in his ski suit and boots, but, judging by how he was glancing around for the server, he intended to eat breakfast before hitting the sloops. "I thought you were going to see Mac."

"I'm on my way." Joshua thumbed through the log on his phone to find Cameron's call. "I assume you're on your way to go skiing."

"That's why I came," Donny said. "That, snowboarding, and the snow bunnies." He cast an eye in the direction of a table of young women clad in tight snowsuits.

"Well, order whatever you want for breakfast." Joshua signed the check to charge his breakfast to the suite Mac had reserved for him and Donny. "I may be having lunch with Mac, so plan on having lunch without me."

"Charge it to the room?"

"Yes, but don't go crazy," Joshua warned. "I don't want to take advantage of Mac and Archie's generosity." He clasped his son on the shoulder. "Have fun, but most of all, be careful."

"What fun is there in that?" Donny grinned before taking the menu the server brought him.

Taking note of the time, Joshua quickened his pace when he went into the lobby. He had to hurry to get to Mac Faraday's home on Spencer Point in order to pick up the groom-to-be and Gnarly, deliver the dog to the groomer, and make it to the tailor in Oakland, Maryland, to be fitted for his tuxedo.

While mentally making the list of what he had to do, he listened to the ringing on the other end of the phone line before Cameron Gates, his own bride of less than a year, answered. "Hey, Silver Fox, did I wake you up when I called earlier?"

"No," Joshua said, "I was talking to Donny and didn't get to the phone in time. How did you sleep last night?"

"Not well," she replied. "That bed is cold without you there."

Joshua took advantage of being alone in the elevator to tell her. "Same here. I missed you."

"I should have come," she said.

"Maybe you can."

"Too late," she said. "I'm on my way to a crime scene. Dead body in Fairfield Hills."

Making note that Fairfield Hills was a rural area outside of Pittsburgh that catered to luxurious homes with plenty of acreage, Joshua asked, "Murder or suicide?"

The doors in the back of the elevator opened to the parking garage. Joshua stepped out to see that every space was filled with vehicles. The Spencer Inn was filled with holiday and wedding guests. Hoping he could remember where he had parked when they had arrived the night before, Joshua made his way around to the far corner of the garage.

"I haven't gotten to the scene yet," Cameron was telling him. "First responders said it's an older gentleman. Lives in a big mansion. His assistant found him this morning when he came in for work." She sighed. "I have a bad feeling, Josh."

Recalling Cameron's anxiety the day before when he and Donny were packing to leave, Joshua stopped when he got to his SUV. "Honey, we talked about this yesterday. What you're feeling is not about me. It's Nick. Donny and me coming here in the winter, right after Christmas—it's bringing back all the grief from when your first husband was killed right after the holidays." He paused to choose his words carefully. "I'm not Nick, Cam. Nothing is going to happen to me."

"I'm sure if Nick had had the opportunity to talk to me before he was killed he would have said the same thing."

"I wish you had decided to come with us," Joshua said. "I wish you could turn your cruiser onto the interstate and come down here right now. It'd be great. The weather is perfect for skiing, the suite is fabulous, and the food is fantastic. We'd have a great time."

"Would've, could've, should've," she replied. "Too late now. You can't go back into the past to change things."

"But you can change the way things are now," Joshua said. "The wedding is three days away. Maybe we'll get lucky and this murder will be an open-and-shut case. Be real nice to your lieutenant, and do paperwork for the rest of the day. Then go home, pop Irving into the cruiser, and you can be down here by dinner."

"I don't do weddings."

"I'll do the wedding," Joshua said. "You go skiing and play the drunken stripper who pops out of the cake at the bachelor party."

"I thought Mac wasn't having a bachelor party," she said.

"You come down here to join me, my love, and we'll have our own party."

CHAPTER TWO

Fairfield Hills, Pennsylvania

Christmas holidays are tough on those who work for the police, fire department, or hospitals. When most people want time off to spend with their families, the emergency calls increase in volume. It's a given. It comes with the job.

Dreading the holiday season, Pennsylvania State Police Homicide Detective Cameron Gates always volunteered to work in order to allow those who had families to take off.

It had started the Christmas after her first husband had passed away.

She and Nicholas Gates, a Pennsylvania state trooper, had exchanged their vows in a lavish Catholic wedding in October. After four months of wedded bliss, Cameron found herself back in the same Catholic Church in January— burying her husband, who had been run down in a hit and run during a routine traffic stop.

Even though she now had a new family who wanted to spend time with her, this year was no different.

It was Cameron and Joshua's first Christmas as a married couple. To the Thornton family's surprise, she volunteered to work Christmas day, while almost all of Joshua's children had managed to come home for Christmas. Moreover, she had also refused to request time off to attend Archie Monday and Mac Faraday's wedding, which was turning into a major social event that famous authors, movie producers, politicians, and celebrities—all friends of the late Robin Spencer—would attend.

Weddings were the last thing Cameron wanted to think about during the holiday season. Christmas brought memories of Nick crashing back. Their only Christmas together was filled with joy and dreams of their married life together—and then those dreams had been crushed two weeks into the New Year.

A decade later, it was another Christmas with another new husband and his family. Instead of embracing the joy of their first season together, Cameron embarked on an emotional tug of war. She could feel herself pulling away from Joshua and his children for fear of getting too close—for fear of opening herself up only to have her heart ripped out of her chest and crushed as it had been before.

Forcing herself to push the pain and memories away, she would reach out to them by jumping into a family gathering of games or movies or a splendid dinner prepared by Tracy, Joshua's older daughter.

Just as the familial moment would start to seem perfect, Cameron would feel a cold sweat bead up on her back and chest, and then the fear of losing them all in a matter of an instant would swallow her up.

In a panic, she would retreat to the master bedroom she shared with Joshua to curl up with Irving, her twenty-five pound Maine Coon cat.

Irving loved those moments together.

Joshua—not so much.

Understanding the root of Cameron's anxiety, he instructed everyone to give their new stepmother her space.

She'd come around.

He hoped.

Three days after Christmas, it was with mixed feelings that Cameron kissed her husband and stepson Donny goodbye as they prepared to go to Deep Creek Lake.

Christmas was over. Three of Joshua's five children were returning to their homes. Tracy left for New York to finish her last year of culinary school. Joshua Junior, Joshua's oldest son, returned to Pennsylvania State University, where he was a first-year law student and an associate professor in pre-law. Sarah was going back to Annapolis, where she was a second-year cadet at the United States Naval Academy.

The only child who had not made it home was Murphy Thornton, Joshua Junior's identical twin brother. A Naval Academy graduate, Murphy was assigned to the Pentagon in Washington, DC, but couldn't make it home because he was on a temporary assignment overseas. However, Joshua and Donny were planning to make a side trip to Washington to visit with Murphy after the wedding in Deep Creek Lake for a small, late Christmas celebration.

Joshua's departure the day before brought back memories of that last morning Cameron had kissed Nick good-bye and waved to him while he pulled away in his cruiser. The snow was blowing around on the freezing wind, chapping her cheeks and sending chills down her neck—exactly like it had been that morning so long ago.

Forget it, Cameron.

She pushed the memory and the sense of dread from her mind.

Josh and Donny will be fine. Now focus on this case. Before you know it, they'll be home. You'll see.

With effort, Cameron pressed her foot on the gas pedal of her cruiser to speed along the rural country road that would take her into the countryside of Fairfield Hills. The heavy woods, which would break into landscaped properties all containing mansions, some renovated from old farmhouses, were coated in six inches of snow from Christmas day and the day before. Another two inches had fallen since midnight.

Luckily, a plow had made it through to clear the road for the emergency vehicles that were answering the call.

Cameron was one of the last of the crime scene personnel to arrive. As the detective assigned to the murder case that fell into state police jurisdiction, she would take the lead in the investigation. She also lived the furthest away. Since she was traveling in from Chester, West Virginia, it was more than an hour drive for her to arrive at the white mansion, complete with white pillars on the porch that stretched across the front. The mansion looked like a min-iature White House plopped down in the middle of a Pennsylvania gentleman's farm.

Cameron was climbing out of her white SUV cruiser when a uniformed officer came out onto the porch. "I'm surprised to see you here," the older officer called to her. "I heard your hubby was in the wedding of the year. Why aren't you there rubbing elbows with all the hoity-toidy people in Deep Creek Lake? Not that I'm complaining. It's good to see that the state police cared enough to send only their very best."

Cameron climbed up onto the porch. "Can you really see me hanging out with the rich and famous, Stan?"

Stan peered down at her windblown auburn hair, cut into wispy waves that fell to the bottom of her neck, and her greenish-brown eyes. She wore a brown leather jacket, black slacks, a form-fitting sweater, and black boots. "With the right hair and make-up ..."

"Give me a break," she muttered. "Where's the victim?"

"In the study in the back of the house," Stan answered with a jerk of his head.

Cameron showed her badge to the state police officer posted at the front door before ducking under the yellow police tape to go inside.

Leading the way through the two-story-tall foyer and down a hallway past a country kitchen, Stan continued, "He's some sort of consultant for the government. I'm still not sure what he does. His assistant isn't much help."

"Consultants usually charge a lot of money for doing nothing but offering worthless advice." Cameron noted that the rooms they were going through were ornately decorated in very expensive artifacts from various countries, which re-minded her a little of the house she now shared with Joshua. The Thornton home contained souvenirs from many coun-tries Joshua and his family had traveled to while he was in the navy.

"He's spent time overseas." In a short corridor, Cameron stopped in front of a hand-painted papyrus encased in a gold frame.

Stan turned from in front of a door leading into the study. Cameron could see bookcases lining the walls inside the room. "Usually these government contractors spend a lot of time working for the defense agencies before retiring and then becoming contractors. After that, they make two paychecks. Their retirement checks, plus the checks for the consulting. Sweet."

Cameron stepped inside to see the bloody body of a man duct taped to a chair. "I don't think he'd agree."

The medical examiner, Dr. Thomas Higgins, was in the midst of examining the body.

"Reginald Crane," Stan recited from his notes. "According to his driver's license, he's sixty-three years old."

Cameron noticed the dead man's firm and muscular build. "Pretty good shape for someone who's over sixty."

"Except for being dead," Dr. Higgins said.

"Point taken," Cameron agreed with a nod of her head. "Can you determine a cause of death?"

"I'll have to open him up," the doctor said. "In my preliminary exam, I see no knife wounds or gunshots. His fingers are broken. He's been tortured. He's been dead at least twenty-four hours."

Cameron looked around the study to see that books had been taken down from the bookshelves, drawers had been opened, and the contents of the drawers had been spilled onto the floor. The wall displayed framed diplomas and awards. One, Cameron noted, was a diploma from West Point Military Academy. *Ex-Military Officer.*

"Someone was looking for something." She turned to Stan. "What type of government agencies was Mr. Crane contracting with?"

"We'll have to ask his assistant," Stan said. "His name is Ethan Bonner."

"Where is Mr. Bonner?"

Stan led her from the study and back to the front of the house to the living room. When they stepped inside, they found it empty. "Where's Ethan Bonner?" Stan demanded of the uniformed officer who was standing guard outside the living room.

"He got nauseous," the officer explained, "so I let him use the bathroom."

"Bathroom where?" Cameron asked.

"Off the kitchen." He pointed back down the hallway to the country kitchen.

Cameron led the way back to the kitchen. The bathroom was down a short hallway leading to the garage. She threw open the door to reveal an empty half-bath. Pushing Stan out of the way, she rushed back out and continued to the door at the end of the hall. It led to the two-car garage, which was occupied by a silver Mercedes-Benz and a black SUV. In addition to the two garage doors, there was a door leading to the backyard, which had deep woods behind it.

With a curse, Cameron turned back to the two officers. "Looks like our witness just became a suspect."

Spencer Manor

Mac was in such a hurry that he didn't bother dressing. Gnarly leapt and barked as he led the way to the doors that lined the far wall of the drop-down dining room. Mac yanked open the doors and ran out into the snowy deck that was still packed with a foot and a half of Christmas snow.

With his slippered feet sliding under him, he ran the length of the deck and through the rose garden to the stone guest cottage where his half-brother, Police Chief David O'Callaghan, resided.

The cozy cabin's one bedroom was located up in the loft on the far side of the great room. The big windows in the cottage provided a tree-top view of the lake from the queen-sized bed. The galley kitchen was located directly beneath the loft.

The special Christmas present from David's girlfriend, Chelsea, a smart television took up most of the wall in the living area of the great room. David appeared to still be making discoveries about the television's host of special features. While racing across the great room, Mac noted the dog-eared instruction manual resting in the center of the coffee table.

Without pausing to knock on the door, Mac ran inside. "David!" The only response he heard was the shower running in the bathroom up in the loft.

Slipping in directly behind Mac, Gnarly raided a basket of dog toys that David kept for him in the corner. Selecting a stuffed mallard duck with a squeak toy inside, Gnarly jumped up onto the sofa and proceeded to chew it. The duck quacked with each gnaw.

Mac raced up the circular stairs to the bedroom.

"David!" Mac threw open the bathroom door. "I need your help!"

Startled by the abrupt intrusion, David almost slipped and fell inside the wet shower stall. After the first instant of shock, he recognized Mac's voice. "What are you doing in my bathroom?"

"Calling in favors!" Mac tossed a towel over the shower door for him.

Instead of drying himself, David clutched the towel against his chest while turning off the water. "What kind of favors?"

"I need protection for Archie," Mac said.

"You got it." David blinked away the water dripping into his eyes before wiping his face. "Now can I get dressed?"

Mac stepped back to allow David out of the shower. Realizing that the bathroom was not quite big enough for two grown men to move around freely, Mac backed into the bedroom, but left the door open so that they could talk.

"What is this about?" David demanded to know while drying himself off.

"A little less than three weeks ago I got a card in the mail from a man saying that since I had taken away his happiness, he was going to take away mine."

Naked, David stepped into the doorway. "Why? Who is this person?"

"Russell Dooley."

"How did you take away his happiness? Did you send him to prison?"

"No, his wife," Mac said. "I arrested her about eight years ago. Three weeks ago, she committed suicide in prison after her last appeal was denied." He handed David the photograph with the note. "I can't believe I actually felt sorry for the guy."

"I don't." Studying the picture, David came into the room and stood in front of Mac. "While he doesn't actually say the words, this is definitely an implied threat."

"Implied," Mac said. "But not enough for a restraining order. I already checked with Willingham. It's not enough. This guy knows what he's doing."

"Is there any chance that his wife was innocent?" David asked.

"No way," Mac said. "Leigh Ann was a number-one manipulative little witch. Russell Dooley is one of those pitiful men who you look at and wonder how he could ever get a date. He considered himself lucky to get this attractive woman. She was thrilled to have a man so blind with love that he couldn't see what a sociopath she was."

"Sounds like they were made for each other."

"How these people find each other, I don't know," Mac said with a shrug of his shoulders. "Dooley believed every single lie. They were married for fifteen years and had a daughter. Well, one day, Leigh Ann decided to stop watching daytime television and hit the gym, where she hired a private trainer."

David held up his hand. "Don't tell me."

Mac nodded his head. "His name was Harris Tyler. He was as bad a liar as Leigh Ann."

David took his police uniform out of the closet and draped it across a chair. "I guess things didn't end well."

"Compared to Russell, Harris Tyler was Brad Pitt." Mac shrugged his shoulders. "Leigh Ann became very possessive of her lover."

David took a pair of boxer shorts from a dresser drawer and put them on. "She didn't want to share?"

"Exactly," Mac said. "Tyler was a player. From what I found out, he seduced practically every woman he trained. For him, it was all a game. Leigh Ann found out about his long line of other women, and she stabbed him twenty-nine times while he was taking a shower. We got her blood on the floor, in the shower, and in the sink where she cleaned up. She had left the murder weapon with her blood on the handle at the scene. She had a cut from the knife on her hand. We got her DNA—everything. No question about it."

Seeing where Mac was going, David nodded his head. He had seen it so many times. "But since Russell was blindly devoted to her, he couldn't blame her for what she did. He had to blame you for catching her." He took his black uniform pants from the hanger and stepped into them.

"She told Russell that I framed her," Mac said, "and he believed her. Three weeks ago, when it became clear that she was going to spend the rest of her life in jail, she killed herself and Russell blames me for her death."

After zipping up his pants, David sat on the bed next to him. "Now he wants to give you payback by taking Archie from you."

"I can't lose Archie," Mac said in a low voice brimming with determination.

Mac's tone made David fear what would happen if he failed to stop Russell Dooley in whatever he may have planned. "I promise I won't let that happen." He patted Mac on the shoulder. "Why am I finding out about this now? You should have come to me three weeks ago."

"I was hoping the card was an idle threat made in the heat of his grief."

"Obviously, it's not."

Mac showed him the picture as a reminder. "He got this close to Archie."

David stood up. "Does she know?"

Mac stood up. "No, and I don't want her to know."

"She has a right—"

"This is the huge fairy tale wedding that her family has always dreamed about," Mac said. "She is the baby of the family and the only girl. I'm not going to have it ruined by everyone being afraid that some psychopath is going to wreak his revenge by destroying it." He grasped David's shoulders. "I'll pay whatever it takes. Do you think some of your officers who have taken off for the holiday would be willing to earn some extra money by working security up through the wedding?"

"I'll ask them." David took a white long-sleeved shirt off the hanger, shouldered into it, and buttoned it up while forming his plan of attack. "I'll let Bogie know what's going on. Since he's walking Archie down the aisle, he'll consider it his duty to act as her bodyguard. She won't even be suspicious about him hanging around."

David took the picture from Mac. "In the meantime, I'll find Russell Dooley and have a man-to-man talk with him."

Mac was pleased with the police chief's plan of action. "I think he's staying at the Beaver Dam Motel in Accident."

Startled, David turned to him.

"Do you know the place?" Mac asked. "I never heard of it."

"It's an old run-down motel in the woods along the creek, located way back off the main road," David said. "It's usually used by hunters. It makes the Bates Motel in *Psycho* look like the Spencer Inn. Why would he stay there? Are you sure? How do you know?"

"The picture he left had that return address," Mac said. "I'm thinking he wants me to know where he is so that I'll go see him … at which point he will jack me up to throw a punch at him so he can charge me with assault."

"Good for you, Mac." David smiled at him. "I'm glad you're not so emotional about all this that you can't see what he's doing. Most men in your position would think with their fists and end up on the wrong end of an assault charge and a civil suit."

"I was a police officer and detective for over twenty-five years," Mac said. "I've seen most of the tricks."

David took the picture and slapped it into his own hand. "Well, this is one trick that won't work. I'll go see Dooley and suggest in a nice calm manner that it would be wise for him to shake off his grief and walk away from all this before anyone else gets hurt."

"That's what I was hoping for," Mac said with a sigh of relief. "I'll be so glad when this week is over."

"All I care about is everyone getting through this wedding alive and safe." David buckled his utility belt with his service weapon around his hips.

Chapter Three

Accident, Maryland

David wasn't certain, but he suspected that the hollow along the creek where the Beaver Dam Motel rested wasn't part of McHenry because the town didn't want it.

The run-down establishment couldn't be considered a roadside motel. The road along which it rested had practically been abandoned since traffic had taken to the interstate back in the 1950s and 60s.

Settled next to a stream that fed into Deep Creek Lake five miles away, Beaver Dam Motel was made up of eight run-down cottages and a main cabin for guests to register in—when they had guests. As David pulled up to the registration office, he could see evidence that five of the cabins appeared to have become permanent residences for a host of seedy looking characters who resembled something out of a movie about the Hatfields and McCoys.

Even in a foot and a half of snow, and with the temperature dipping into the single digits, four men who were dressed in snow camouflage and bearing hunting rifles were sitting on the porch of the main cabin. Two young boys who didn't look old enough to be teenagers were target shooting with new crossbows. Both were slightly built. Exceedingly tall and lanky, one boy resembled a string puppet with his long bony arms and legs. Two women who resembled Russian refugees in their layers of heavy mismatched clothes and thick boots served their men hot egg sandwiches on paper plates.

Kind of cold outside for a picnic, isn't it?

Seeing the police cruiser, the men rose to their feet. The women stopped in mid-motion to regard the man climbing out of the driver's seat in a police chief uniform and coat.

The boys stopped shooting and turned to face David, who kept his hand on the gun he had unclipped from its holster. Then, he saw them both lower the arrows that had been pointed in the police chief's general direction.

"Good morning," David called out to them in a cheerful tone, which he did not feel. "How are you this chilly wintry morning?"

As if they didn't know the answer to his question, the women and children regarded the men, who said nothing.

David directed his attention to the youngsters. "Was Santa Claus good to you this year?"

"There's no such thing as Santa Claus," one of the boys replied in a jeering tone.

"A little out of your jurisdiction, ain't you, Officer?" A tall, scrawny man with a weathered face called from the porch. With both hands, he held his hunting rifle across his chest while moving to the porch railing.

"Chief," David corrected him. "I'm David O'Callaghan, the chief of police for Spencer, Maryland."

"So you're the sheriff of Nottingham for the five percent who look down their noses at the rest of us," the scrawny man chuckled.

"I'm not here to make any trouble." David held up his hands in submission. "I'm here to look for someone who had sent a package with a return address of this motel. Russell Dooley. If you could please tell me where I could find him, I'll just have a word with him, and then I'll leave and you can all go about your business. That's all."

Wordlessly, the women regarded the men. The three men who had said nothing seemed to relax, while the loud one continued to eye David with suspicion. His grip on the rifle seemed to tighten.

Keeping a close eye on him, David laid his hand on his own service weapon.

"Russell Dooley has been staying here for the last week," one of the women blurted out. "He's really weird, but he keeps to himself. He paid us in cash—up front for a month." She pointed to the cabin located far to the rear of the row of cabins. "He's in cabin number eight." She then added, "I hope that money wasn't stolen. You're not going to want it back if it is, are you? We bought Christmas presents for the kids with it."

Clutching the crossbows tighter, the boys' eyes widened in fright.

"Thank you, ma'am," David said with a nod of his head. "I don't think you have anything to worry about." He offered a reassuring smile to the youngsters.

"Do you have a warrant?" The skinny guy raised his rifle up to his chest.

"Don't be a jackass, Gil," one of the men answered before David could reply. "He don't need no warrant just to talk to the guy. Now put that rifle down before you shoot yourself in the ass."

To add fuel to the suggestion, one of the other men grabbed the rifle out of Gil's hands and shoved him into a chair.

While making his way down the row of cabins, David heard one of the women ordering Gil to eat his sandwich and shut up. "Do you *want* to spend New Year's Eve in jail *again*?"

Noting that Russell Dooley was from Washington DC, where Mac had been a detective until he had retired, David found his current location odd. If he wanted to be out of the way, there were half a dozen other motels that were nicer and more easily accessible.

How did Russell Dooley ever find this place?

At the end of the road on which the Beaver Dam Motel rested, David found cabin number eight. The path leading up to the tiny porch and front door was covered with freshly fallen snow, as was the old faded sedan parked in front of the cabin.

David waded through the several inches of snow to the cabin door and knocked. Over his shoulder, he could see the two boys, wielding their crossbows, watching him with wide-eyed curiosity. He shot them a smile and nodded his head. "Be careful with those crossbows, boys. Hate for there to be an accident."

Unsure if they wanted to challenge the armed police chief, they backed away.

"Do you think he's a serial killer?" David heard the shorter boy asked the other in what was supposed to be a whisper.

"He does keep to himself," the lanky one answered with the air of knowing about such things. "All serial killers are loners. Everyone knows that." He lowered his voice to an eerie-sounding whisper. "Last night, I heard screaming—probably his latest victim."

"Who? There's no one out here for him to kill."

"Some guy came to visit him last night," the older boy said. "After dark. I saw him. I'll bet they find his body buried under the cabin."

They went back to hide behind the cabin next door in order to watch the police chief who had come to question one of their guests.

Visitor? Screaming? With a shake of his head, David recalled an older childhood friend who used to spin stories to scare him. Smiling at how it worked, too, he knocked once more and waited for an answer. "Mr. Dooley, this is Police Chief David O'Callaghan with the Spencer Police Department. I'd like to speak to you for a moment, if you please?"

The only sound from inside the cabin was the television blaring one of the morning talk shows offering recipes for holiday leftovers.

David knocked once more. "I know you're in there, Mr. Dooley. Can you please answer the door?"

No answer.

Glancing around to see if anyone besides the boys was watching, David tried the doorknob. With one twist of his hand, the door swung open.

"Mr. Dooley, are you in here?" David stepped into the darkened cabin. "Chief David O'Callaghan from the Spencer Police. Could I have a word with you, please? I'm coming in."

The blankets were twisted and ripped from the bed to expose a sheet that looked like it had not been changed in months, if ever. The television was on full blast, and two women on it were shrieking with laughter while offering advice on how to cover up a bulging tummy while dressing scantily for New Year's Eve.

The only light in the cabin was provided by a lamp resting on its side on the floor next to the overturned nightstand.

65

Squatting down to examine the lamp, David saw that there was a bloody handprint on the base.

Laying his hand on his gun, David rose to his feet. "Mr. Dooley?" He turned around to see that the light was on in the bathroom. A brown smear on the wall seemed to act as an arrow for the police chief to follow.

"Is he a killer? Did you find a dead body?" The boy who had claimed to hear screaming the night before was peering inside through the open doorway. Scared but curious, his friend was hiding behind him.

Throwing up his hand in a signal to stop, David whirled around. "Don't come in here! Go out to the road and stay away from the cabin."

He didn't have to ask a second time. Both boys ran like they were being chased by the killer himself.

After taking his gun out of its holster and aiming it to the floor, David eased to the bathroom, careful not to step on any potential evidence. Dried spots of blood led the way.

With his finger on the trigger, David slowly opened the door to reveal a tiny bathroom that was barely big enough for an obese motel guest. It was constructed to accommodate nothing more than a small shower/tub, a toilet, and a sink.

The bathtub rested behind the open door.

The floor was covered in blood that had overflowed from the tub. The white sink was pink with splotches of blood.

Stepping carefully so as to not disturb the blood evidence, David tiptoed in to peer around the door into the tub, which contained the body of a man.

David recognized his face from the picture of the man with his arm around Archie Monday's waist.

Russell Dooley.

Naked, he rested in a tub filled with water stained with his blood. His body was riddled with stab wounds from his neck to his hips and on both arms and legs.

A steak knife rested on his bare bloody chest.

David recognized the weapon as one that he had used many times. Its distinctive insignia was stamped on the wooden handle: SI.

Spencer Inn—the five-star resort owned by Mac Faraday, the man whose wedding Russell Dooley had sworn to ruin.

CHAPTER FOUR

How many years have I lived here, and I still don't know where Archie puts the scissors?

After closing the drawer in the nightstand on his side of the bed, Mac gave up and twisted around to grasp the designer tag hanging from under his armpit. Hoping to not tear a hole in the new blue sweater that his daughter, Jessica, had given him for Christmas, he gave it a sharp tug.

The tag gave way, but the plastic "do-hickey" that kept it attached to the sweater didn't.

Rats!

From where he was sprawled out in the center of the bed, Gnarly cocked his head at him.

"I don't suppose you could bite it off without putting a hole in this sweater, huh, Gnarly?"

Mac studied the label he had torn off. *Dolce & Gabbana. Never heard of them. But if Jessica bought it, it has to be expensive, and she'll have a fit if I put a hole in it.* Mac went into the master bathroom in search of nail clippers.

Gnarly's bark, and then his jump between the bed and the door, prompted Mac to forget the do-hickey hanging under his armpit. After grabbing his gun from the drawer in the nightstand, he followed Gnarly down the stairs to the two-story foyer, out the cut-glass front door, and onto the front porch. Mac clutched his weapon behind his back. When Gnarly, sitting at his side, uttered a low growl, Mac tightened his grip and watched the sedan slowly make its way around the circular driveway before coming to a halt at the bottom of the porch steps.

When the elderly driver stepped out of the car, Mac placed her and the car.

Agnes Douglas. Archie's mother.

No wonder Gnarly had growled. He never had liked her very much … and the feeling was mutual.

Shoving aside his fears about the safety of Archie, his family, and their friends, Mac forced a wide grin onto his face. After shoving the gun into the back waistband of his pants and covering it up with his sweater, he hurried down the steps to take the white-haired woman into his arms. Like her only daughter, she was petite. She fell two inches short of five feet tall, and Mac had to bend over to hug her. In her heavy dark blue winter coat and thick snow boots, she resembled a blue snow man.

Shouldn't she be with Archie and the bridesmaids getting their hair done at the salon? Oh well, Agnes goes and does what she wants when she wants. Best not to question.

"Agnes, I'm so glad to see you." Mac clasped her arm, slipped his other arm around her waist, and guided her across the slick ice, up the steps, and inside.

At the top of the steps, Gnarly backed away. Agnes had made it quite clear to Gnarly that he was only allowed to look at, but not touch, her.

"I told her that I had one of my headaches." At the top of the porch steps, she turned to Mac. She tilted her head back to peer up at him from over the top of her glasses. She paused to look him up and then down, and then she noticed that he was wearing only his bedroom slippers without any socks. "What are you doing outside in two feet of snow and ice without boots on?"

"I heard you coming and didn't want you to slip on the ice."

Agnes' head bobbed up and down while she chastised him. "Do I look like I need your help? I haven't broken a hip yet. Archie depends on you. What good are you going to do her dropping dead from pneumonia?"

Unable to come up with an answer, Mac shrugged.

Willing Gnarly out of her way, she opened the front door. "I hope you have the tea ready." Grabbing him by the elbow, she ushered him inside. Gnarly was barely able to slip inside before she slammed the door.

"Actually," Mac said as gently as possible, "I was on my way out."

Her head snapped up to glare at him. "What do you mean you were on your way out?"

"One of my groomsmen and I have an appointment with the tailor." Mac looked down at the tiny elderly woman who stood before him in the middle of the living room. She clasped her handbag with both hands in front of her.

Like a referee at a boxing match, Gnarly sat between them, looking from one to the other.

"Did I do something to upset you, Agnes?"

"I think it's best if we lay out our ground rules *before* you marry Archie," she said.

Sensing a battle, Mac folded his arms across his chest. He was physically setting up a barrier. "Okay, Agnes. Shoot."

"To be blunt," Agnes said in a tone devoid of emotion, "I'm giving this marriage five years. Archie refuses to tell me how much you're paying for this huge three-ring circus, but I hope you'll think it's worth it when you only get five years on your investment."

"Five years? Investment?" Mac chuckled. "With all due respect—"

Agnes' hand shot up. She shook her head. "Don't give me that all-due-respect crap. I've had seven children, six boys. Archie's daddy keeled over with a heart attack when she was only five years old. Since that time, I've been 'round the block so much that I wore a rut in it and"—she shook her finger at him—"I learned ages ago that when someone says to me 'with all due respect,' they're not giving me an ounce of it."

"I don't consider Archie to be an investment," Mac said through gritted teeth. "And to be *blunt*, I don't think you know enough about our relationship to be in a position to make any sort of prediction about the success or lack of success of our marriage."

"Archie has spent the last dozen years of her life hiding out in this mansion, taking care of your mother," Agnes said. "Then, she's spent the last few years in your bed. Now," she glanced him up and down, "you're a very attractive man, and I'm sure Archie wouldn't want to marry you if you weren't good in bed. I'm sure all of that money adds to your appeal, but there's more to lifelong happiness than sex and money. There's character, and marriage with a man who has no character—"

Mac stepped toward her. "What gives you the right to comment on my character?"

As if to voice his agreement, Gnarly barked.

She moved in until she was toe to toe with him. Coming only up to his chest, she peered up into his blue eyes. "You're marrying my daughter. *That* gives me the right."

"You don't even know me," Mac said down to her.

"I've known dozens of men like you," Agnes said. "I've been in the shadows, watching them for the last thirty years. After my husband passed away, I had to put food on the table, and I did it well by cleaning the mansions of some of the

71

richest, and even famous, people in and around Pittsburgh."
She shook her finger at him. "Men who didn't know the
meaning of the word 'integrity.'"

"We're not all like that."

"I know," Agnes said. "I've seen that first hand. I'm lucky
to have a very fine position right now. I'm working for a man
with integrity coming out of his ears. Mr. Crane is a self-
made gentleman. He's worked hard his whole life to gain the
benefits of his wealth."

"And I haven't?"

She scoffed. "Where did you get all of your money,
Mac?"

Knowing that she knew the answer, Mac glared at her.

"You're living off the sweat of your mother and ancestors,"
she said.

"I was raised in a middle-class home by an Irish-American
father and an Italian-American mother," Mac said. "They
taught me the value of good hard work as soon as I could
carry my dinner plate to the sink without dropping and
breaking it. They also taught me about truth and justice. So
don't you stand there telling me that I'm not good enough
for your daughter, because you know nothing about me."

The front door flew open so abruptly that Mac reached
for his gun behind his back. He gripped the handle until
he saw Joshua Thornton cross the threshold. It took Mac a
moment to recognize Joshua in his beard and mustache.

"Am I interrupting?" Sensing the tension, Joshua looked
from Mac to Agnes and then to Gnarly, who spun around to
charge down into the dining room. Barking and whining, he
jumped up onto the windows and peered out.

Fighting a losing battle, Mac tried to sound casual. "We
were just talking." Stepping away from her, Mac ran his hand
over the top of his head while gesturing to Agnes with the
other. "Josh, this is Archie's mother. Agnes."

"Mother of the bride." Joshua clasped her hand in his gloved hand.

"Joshua Thornton is one of my groomsmen," Mac said before saying to him, "You grew a beard."

"Very observant," Joshua said with a grin while rubbing his facial hair. "I decided to take advantage of my rural roots." He turned to Agnes. "I understand most of the groomsmen are made up of your children. Six sons. That's a lot."

"All big strapping men like their father," Agnes said with pride. "Every one of them has a fine job and a nice family. I've got twenty-three grandchildren."

"And you're getting two more," Joshua pointed out. "Saturday night when Mac and Archie get married, she'll become a stepmother to Jessica and Tristan."

With a sudden thought, Agnes whirled around to Mac. "How do your children feel about you starting a new family with Archie?"

"Starting a new family?" Mac stalled. "Tristan and Jessica love Archie, and she loves them. Tristan is my best man, and Archie asked Jessica to be her maid of honor. We consider ourselves a family."

"And what about when you and Archie have your own children?"

"My children are her children."

Agnes laughed. "That's nice to say—"

Not wanting any piece of the conversation, Joshua went down into the dining room to see what had Gnarly's attention.

"It's the truth," Mac said.

"Will they still love Archie when she has your baby?"

"That's not going to happen."

"How can you be so sure?"

"Because I had a vasectomy years ago." Agnes' jaw dropped, and she fell back while Mac held up his hand

73

to silence her. "And Archie knew about it before we ever started dating."

"How could you do that to her?"

"To her?" Mac replied. "I had it done before I even met Archie—while I was married to my first wife."

"Why?"

"Because my first wife wanted me to," Mac said. "We had two children, and when my daughter entered puberty she ceased to be human anymore—"

"I know what you mean," Joshua called from the dining room where he was peering out the window. "Some kids are worse than others. My twins—when they hit twelve, Murphy turned into Mr. Hyde. Most ill-tempered kid you ever saw— until my daughter Sarah came along. Meanwhile, Murphy's identical twin, J.J., was as calm and steady as they come— still is. Nothing gets a rile out of that young man."

Something had Gnarly's attention. The German shepherd was growling and pawing at the window.

Is there something moving among the rose bushes?

"Well, Christine couldn't stand it," Mac said. "So she told me that if I loved her, I'd get a vasectomy to make sure she never had to go through that ever again."

Agnes' wrinkled face screwed up. "Your daughter was a handful, so your wife made you go under the knife?"

Mac shook his head. "I did it because I loved her. You won't believe the things I've done for the people that I love."

Is that a spark—what did the sun just reflect off of? "Mac," Joshua called out, "there's no hunting allowed around here, is there?"

"It's residential. Why do you ask?"

"Gun!" Joshua cried out while driving Gnarly down to the floor.

Several gunshots took out the windows and doors across the length of the dining room while Mac body slammed Agnes to the floor behind the sofa.

"Wh-what's—" Agnes sputtered out while Mac dragged her across the floor toward the wall. When she tried to climb up to her knees, he shoved her back down to the floor.

"Josh!" Mac cried out. "Are you okay?"

"We're fine!" Joshua and Gnarly were crawling across the floor toward the living room.

Mac had gotten Agnes up against the wall. "How many shooters?" He took his gun out and raised up to peer out the window to the front driveway.

"Is that a gun?" Agnes squawked.

"Yes."

"Were you carrying that the whole time we were talking?"

"As a matter of fact—" Mac replied. "Great self-control I have, don't you think?"

"There are two shooters in the back, Mac!" Joshua called out as a series of shots took out the front windows. "Plus some in the front."

"They have us surrounded?" Agnes yelled. "Why?" She hissed at Mac. "What are you into?'

"Mac," Joshua called out from where he and Gnarly were crouching at the stairs leading up to the living room, "cover me and Gnarly. They have us outgunned with automatic weapons. If we can get to my SUV, I'll grab some additional weapons to even things up."

Seeing that Joshua had a gun in a shoulder holster under his coat, Agnes shrieked. "What type of people is my daughter mixed up with?"

Nodding his approval to Joshua's plan, Mac crawled to the end table in the corner and opened the drawer. He took out a semi-automatic. "There's a Colt nine-millimeter in the bottom drawer of that cabinet at the top of the stairs, Josh. Can you make it to it?"

"I'll have to."

"On the count of three, you make a break for it."

Joshua said, "Gnarly and I will head for the SUV. I'll get in the back and cover you and Agnes. When you get there, Mac, you drive, and I'll cover us on the way out."

"What am I supposed to do?" Agnes asked Mac as he crawled along the floor toward the front door.

"You stay behind me," Mac said. "When I give the signal to run, you run for Joshua's SUV as hard and as fast as you can. Don't stop for anything—no matter what. Josh and I will cover you."

The shooting outside stopped.

With a sigh, Agnes said, "Maybe—"

"No," Joshua said, "they're getting ready to move in."

"Now!" Mac yelled.

With a slap on Gnarly's back, Joshua raced up the stairs and across the living room.

At the same time, Mac jumped up and shot with one gun out the front window while shooting across the dining room and out onto the deck. He shot at anything that moved.

Covering her ears, Agnes screamed at the top of her lungs.

Instead of heading for the front door, Gnarly leapt over the old woman and out through the broken-out front window.

A horrified scream and a series of gun shots erupted from the other side of the wall.

Agnes' screams reach an even higher octave when a man tried to run in through the broken-out dining room doors, only to have Mac riddle his body with bullets.

The gun shots were punctuated by an explosion that shook the floor around them.

Mac dared to glance out through the window. His eyes widened. "I don't believe it."

"They have a bomb, too," Agnes said with heavy breaths.

"Grenade launcher." Mac tucked one of the guns into the front waistband of his slacks. "But it's on our side." He dragged her to her feet by the arm. "Time for us to move, Agnes."

They dove out the front door. When they stepped out onto the porch, Agnes stopped when she almost tripped over the blood-soaked body of a man. Blood and tissue hung from where his neck had once been. The sleeves of his camouflage coat were shredded.

"Oh, dear—"

"We don't have time to sightsee, Agnes!" Slipping and sliding on the ice, Mac fought to stay on his own feet while pulling Agnes down the steps and across the driveway to where Joshua was shooting at two men he had pinned down between the garage and the house.

Racing past her blue sedan, Agnes noticed that it had been the victim of numerous bullet holes, and that several of the windows had been shattered. "That's my car!"

"Forget your car!" Mac dragged her along as fast as he could in his slippers.

Enraged, she seemed to be yelling at the gunmen when she demanded to know who was going to pay for it.

"Be serious!"

When Agnes' feet went out from under her, Mac picked her up and tossed her over his shoulder like a heavy sack of dog food.

"What are you doing?" she objected while beating on his back with her purse.

"Getting you out of here alive!" he said while dodging bullets that flew over their heads. Joshua was doing a good job of keeping them pinned so that they could not get a clear shot.

Joshua had planned well enough to leave the side door to the SUV open so Mac only had to toss Agnes into the back seat next to Gnarly before diving into the driver's seat and slamming the door shut.

The keys were already in the ignition.

"Let's give them something to remember us by!" Joshua called out right before Mac heard a *swoosh*.

Seconds later, he heard an explosion and saw the row of rhododendron bushes that lined the walkway between the garage and the house go up in a great explosion.

Oh my, he blew up Archie's rhododendrons!

Mac hit the gas pedal. The tires spun. The SUV was still gaining traction when Mac heard a shot ping off the back side panel.

"Hit it, Mac!" Joshua fired off another round of shots.

"I'm trying!"

When the SUV gained traction, it shot like a cannonball across the driveway and out onto the road.

Lured by the gunfire and explosions, neighbors were cautiously peering out their windows when the SUV raced down Spencer Point and crossed the bridge to head up the mountain.

"Are they following us?" Mac called back to ask Joshua.

"Not yet!" Grabbing his side, Joshua dropped down onto his back in the rear compartment.

The SUV swerved when it hit a patch of ice.

"Slow down!" Agnes yelled up at Mac. "Haven't you ever heard of black ice? Are you trying to get us all killed?"

"Josh, what are you doing with a grenade launcher?" Mac demanded while trying to maneuver on the snowy road. He was looking for a particular side road that would take them off the busy lakeside trail and up the mountain.

"I used to be a boy scout. I learned at an early age to always be prepared." Joshua went through the contents of the black canvas bag he had spread open in the back and reloaded his guns.

Seeing all the guns, Agnes asked, "What do you do, Josh?"

He answered while snapping a fresh clip into his handgun. "I'm a lawyer."

Agnes' eyes grew wide.

"That was a professional hit squad," Mac called out. "It was a thought-out attack. We need to find someplace out of the way and get in touch with David to let him know what we're dealing with."

"Disengage my GPS and get rid of your cell phone!" Joshua hurled his cell phone out the broken-out rear window. "Find some secluded place for us to stop. I've got burner phones for us to use." He held out his hand to Agnes. "Give me your cell phone!"

"I don't have *a cell phone*!" Agnes' tone said she was insulted that he would even suggest she carried such an instrument. She noticed blood all over Joshua's hand. "Are you bleeding?" She rose up in her seat to gaze at him in the rear compartment. What she saw made her scream.

Chapter Five

The wind had kicked up and shoved the single-digit temperature below zero, which made investigating a murder crime scene completely miserable.

David's best friend and half-brother had motive to seriously hurt, and maybe even to kill, the victim, and the apparent murder weapon was a steak knife from the resort said suspect owned. Otherwise, David would have been more than thrilled to leave the whole investigation in the more-than-capable hands of Garrett County Sheriff Christopher Turow and return to the Spencer Police Station, where he could get some hot coffee.

Such was not the case. David had a stake in this investigation, and he suspected that the first place the sheriff would look would be the Spencer Inn—and Mac Faraday.

After containing the crime scene and keeping the other residents of the cabins—including the two youngsters—away, David waited for the sheriff, his deputies, the state crime scene investigators, and the medical examiner, Dr. Dora Washington, to arrive. As soon as they went to work, David enjoyed the warmth of his cruiser—until Sheriff Turow jumped into the passenger seat with his notepad and pen ready.

"Tell me again what Spencer's chief of police is doing slumming at this back-roads motel in Accident?" the sheriff asked.

"You heard me the first time," David replied. "Russell Dooley had made some threats toward Archie Monday. He sent Mac Faraday a photograph of him with his arm around her, and a note that contained a veiled threat about getting that close." He gestured at the picture that the sheriff had slipped into an evidence bag and had pinned under the notepad on his clipboard. "I came to have a chat with him about the virtue of letting bygones be bygones and walking away, but someone killed him before I could offer him that advice."

"Wish they hadn't," the sheriff said with a shiver. "The motel owners should be arrested for lying about that cabin having heat. If you had gotten to Dooley sooner, we'd all be nice and warm and comfortable right now."

"I'm sure Dooley feels bad about ruining your day," David said with sarcasm.

"What did Dooley say when Mac Faraday told him to stay away?"

"Mac Faraday never talked to Dooley," David said. "He sent Mac a card with a note threatening to ruin his wedding—as revenge for ruining his life by framing his wife for murder. Mac told me that he ignored the threat, thinking that the guy was venting. But then this morning, he got that picture. Mac's no fool. He did the right thing. He brought it to me, and I decided to be proactive—let Dooley know he was on my radar, and that, if he were smart, he'd leave." David insisted, "Mac has never been here or in that cabin, and, to my knowledge, he told no one except his lawyer about Dooley's threat. You're not going to find any evidence to place him or any of his associates at this scene."

"Except the steak knife from the Spencer Inn, which Mac owns and frequents."

David shook his head with a laugh. "All of the china, dinnerware, glasses, and silverware, including the steak knives, at the Spencer Inn are special ordered to have the Inn's logo. There's no others like them in the whole world. Mac was a homicide detective for twenty years before he retired. Seriously? Do you really think he would make such a stupid mistake by using a one-of-the-kind murder weapon that would lead you directly to him? Just to kill a man for sending him a threatening picture?"

Turow cocked his head and arched an eyebrow in David's direction. "Maybe that's what Mac wants us to think."

"You know Mac didn't do this," David said in a low threatening tone.

"Based on that knife and the threats Dooley made, I would be negligent to not put him at the top of the suspect list," Turow said. "You know what it's like, O'Callaghan. What if this murder had been in your jurisdiction? What if you were me? Would you just check Faraday's name off the suspect list and go on to the next guy without at least questioning him?"

Hanging his head, David sighed. "No."

"Now for the good news," Turow said. "Doc says Dooley died shortly after midnight. It would have been dark, but one of those kids said he saw a man go into Dooley's cabin last night shortly before he heard screaming coming from it."

"I don't think these kids have bedtimes."

"The kid was kind of cagey about what he was doing out so late." The sheriff turned around and pointed to the cabin next to the cottage where Russell Dooley had died. "That cabin is empty. One of my deputies looked inside for evidence of someone who may have been hiding in it. He found cigarettes, empty beer cans, and porno magazines."

"Now we know what they were doing out so late," David said with a wicked grin.

Turow pointed at the end of the road where the motel's last cabin rested at the end of the woods. "There's a path leading to the creek where guests can go picnic and fish. The boy supposedly saw someone coming out of the woods and going up to the cabin—"

"The killer came on foot in all this snow?" David said.

"According to the kid," Turow said. "My deputies have found evidence of footprints that were made before the snow last night. They also found some evidence of blood drops. Forensics says that they may be able to get DNA from them since they've been frozen. The kid says he saw the killer go up to the porch on Dooley's cabin, and he got a look at his face in the porch light."

David grinned. "If he saw the killer, then you can get a sketch of him, and that will eliminate Mac."

Sheriff Turow's smile did not match David's. "The boy's aunt also confided that her nephew is a pathological liar and is most likely making it all up, so we need to take what he tells us with a grain of salt."

"Can I come with you to interview him?" David asked.

Before the sheriff could answer, David's radio squawked. Turow waited while David took the call.

Shots fired. Multiple victims reported by witnesses.

Both law officers' eyes jaws dropped when the address was reported. It was One Spencer Court.

"That's Mac's house." David shifted the cruiser into reverse while Sheriff Turow jumped out.

"I'll meet you there!" the sheriff called out to him as David sped down the ice-covered road toward Spencer.

"I don't understand why we can't just drive to the police station," Agnes was carping into Mac's ear while he dug through Joshua's black canvas bag to see what he had. "Those people tried to kill us. When someone tries to kill you, you go to the police. That's what Archie did, and it worked out very well for her."

"Until she met me," Mac said with heavy sarcasm.

"This is no time to be sensitive, Mac," she chastised him.

He had sped up the mountain and deep into the woods to a trail that David had shown him when he had first moved to Spencer. Originally used for mining cars to carry copper down to the lake, the trail was wide and smooth enough for a vehicle, until it became too steep to ascend further up the mountain. The abandoned copper mine was located at the very end of the trail.

Known only by die-hard hikers, Mac hoped that whoever was trying to kill them would not know about the trail.

Seizing what he recognized to be a combat first-aid kit, he eased the elderly woman out of his way so that he could climb out of the back of the SUV. He went around the side to where Joshua was stretched out across the back seat.

While Mac was searching for the first aid kit, Joshua had pulled up his sweater and undershirt to reveal a bullet hole that had gone through his side. His stomach and clothes were soaked with blood.

"Oh, dear!" Agnes clasped her hand over her mouth. Her dismay turned to fury when she saw that Joshua was digging through her purse. After reading the title on the cover of her paperback novel, which featured a scantily cladded couple, he shoved it back into the bag and continued digging. "What are you doing?" She snatched the purse out of his hand, which came out holding a red thumb drive. "Hasn't anyone ever told you to never go through a woman's things?" Snarling, she grabbed the thumb drive out of Joshua's hand and hurled it back into her purse. Clutching it to her chest with both arms, she said, "I should expect as much from a *lawyer.*"

"I was looking to make sure you didn't have a cell phone."

"I told you I don't have any cell or smart or any phone," she said. "I don't use computers or laptops or those little square techno books that people use instead of books anymore. I'm low-tech and proud of it."

When she backed away, Agnes almost tripped over Gnarly, who was trying to follow Mac into the back of the SUV. "Why did we have to bring that filthy beast?"

"That filthy beast saved my life," Joshua said.

"Well he's a mobile germ palace, and you've been injured."

In the cramped space of the backseat, Mac crouched down in order to examine Joshua's wounds.

Joshua stifled a groan when Mac touched the bullet wounds in his side. "Did you find the quikclot?"

Mac held up the brown package. "Got it right here."

"That will stop the bleeding," Joshua said.

"We need to take him to a hospital," Agnes told Mac. "Have you ever treated someone who's been shot before?"

"As a matter of fact, I have," Mac replied. "It looks like a through and through."

"Apply the quikclot and then wrap it up," Joshua said, "and I should be ready to go."

"You need to sterilize it first." Agnes crowded into the back of SUV and shoved Mac out of the way. "Let me. You're doing that all wrong. He's going to get an infection."

"Agnes—"

"I'm completely certified in first aid," she said while cleaning Joshua's wounds. "I have children and twenty-three grandchildren. So I make sure I know everything there is to know about taking care of emergencies, from poisoning to burns to choking to extracting pen caps stuck up little noses."

"How about a gun shot?" Joshua asked with a grimace.

"You're my first gun shot," Agnes said. "But it should be no different from a stabbing, and I did handle that."

"Who got stabbed?" Mac asked.

Agnes shot Mac a sidelong glance. "You haven't gotten Archie really mad yet, have you?"

The stinging from the antiseptic made Joshua throw back his head and clench his jaw.

"I made darn sure I knew how to treat a wound when someone got hurt." She tore open the quikclot package with her teeth and spit out the plastic corner.

Joshua grabbed Mac's arm while she pressed the gauze to his stomach. "Did you find the burn phone in my bag?"

"Yeah, Josh." Mac met his gaze. "I'm impressed. You take being prepared to a whole new level."

Joshua's eyes met his. "I'm sorry you got dragged into this, Mac."

"We'll talk about it later." Mac examined Agnes' work. He was impressed with how quickly and efficiently she had taken care of the wound. With her tending to Joshua, he was free to climb out of the SUV and call for help. "You need to stay still to make sure the bleeding stops before we move you. That will give us time to figure out our next move."

"Our next move should be to the police," Agnes said. "Aren't you friends with that cute young chief of police?"

Grinning at her noticing how attractive David O'Callaghan was, Mac confirmed that he was. "But they have a small police force, and these guys had us outgunned. We need to figure out exactly what we're dealing with"—he shot a glance in Joshua's direction— "so that we'll know how best to go up against them."

Mac climbed out of the back of the SUV.

"And how are we going to do that without asking for help?" she demanded to know.

Mac held up the disposable phone that he took out of the black bag. "Call them." He yelled back to Joshua. "Is this thing activated?"

"Yes," Joshua answered with a moan.

Gnarly had climbed up into the back of the SUV. Laying on the floor, the German shepherd rested his head on Joshua's hand. With his ears laid back flat on his head, he gazed up at him.

"Thank you, Gnarly." Joshua stroked the dog's snout. "You did good."

Stepping away from the SUV, Mac punched in a number on the phone. Stomping his slippered feet to keep warm, he listened to the ringing on the other end of the line. With the adrenaline wearing off, he realized that he had made his retreat so fast he didn't have boots or a coat. Checking his pockets, he discovered he didn't have his wallet either.

Oh, man! This can't be happening now.

"Hello …" Hector Langford's voice came across the phone line when he picked up the call. Hector was the chief of security at the Spencer Inn.

"Is Pat there?" Mac asked.

There was a slight pause before Hector replied. "Sorry, bloke, there's no one here by that name. You must have the wrong number."

"I'm sorry. I must have misdialed." Mac hung up the phone.

"You called the wrong number!" Agnes' voice directly behind him made Mac jump so quickly that he grabbed the gun he had tucked in the waistband of his pants before he remembered that she was Archie's mother.

"Yes, I misdialed." Mac stomped back to the SUV to check on Joshua. Bending over him, he saw a slight smile come to Joshua's lips. "Are you feeling better?"

"I was just remembering something my cousin told me when I was younger and had my first serious girlfriend."

"Oh?" Mac asked while patting Joshua on the shoulder.

"He said, 'Before you marry the daughter, take a *good long look* at the mother.'" With a wink, Joshua jerked his head in the direction of where Agnes was standing with her arms folded across her bosom while glaring at the SUV where they were huddled.

In his corner office at the Spencer Inn, Hector Langford hung up his phone on which he had taken the call made to his private line.

A lean, gray-haired Australian, Hector had been with the Inn for over twenty-five years, which was longer than Jeff Ingle, the Inn's manager, had worked there. Hector knew Spencer and the mountaintop resort inside and out. When he'd first met Mac, the security chief took great delight in revealing that Robin Spencer had often asked for his help in planning the murders for her books.

After grabbing a notepad and a pen, Hector picked up the receiver again and punched star-six-nine.

The phone number that Mac had called him from filled the screen. Hector wrote down the number. After taking his cell phone from his belt, he sent off a text to David O'Callaghan. Then before closing the door to his office, he removed a disposable phone that he had stashed away in the bottom drawer of his desk.

CHAPTER SIX

Spencer Manor resembled a war zone.

With sirens blaring and lights flashing, David drove as fast as he could risk on the icy roads along the shores of Deep Creek Lake to Spencer Point. Every local, county, and state police officer on call seemed to be on the scene of the bullet-riddled mansion.

David felt his mouth hanging open when he climbed out of the cruiser and saw no less than three sheets covering dead bodies. Two were where there had once been a rhododendron bush, next to the path leading to the rear of the mansion and the lake. Another was on the porch in front of the bay window. David spotted another sheet covering a body at the other corner of the house.

"We've got five dead bodies," Spencer Police Officer Fletcher trotted down from the porch to tell his police chief. Before David could ask, he grasped his arm. "None of them are Mac or Archie, Chief."

Sighing with relief, David noticed the bullet-riddled blue sedan in front of the house. It had Pennsylvania tags. "Who does the sedan belong to?"

"It's registered to an Agnes Douglas," Spencer Officer Zigler said. "Do you know her?"

"That's Archie's mother." David swallowed.

"The mother of the bride?"

"I need to call Bogie," David said at the same time that his phone buzzed. The caller ID read 'Bogie.' He brought the phone to his ear. "Yeah, Bogie."

"What's going on? I heard a call from dispatch that there's been a shooting, and it's Mac's address. I'm at the hair salon with Archie and her bridal party. What's going on? Do you need me to come in?"

David turned around to take in the bodies covered with white tarps. The medical examiner's van pulled up to the yellow crime scene tape that they had stretched across the two stone pillars marking the estate entrance. "It's bad, Bogie," he said with a choke in his voice.

"Mac …" Bogie's voice was barely above a whisper. "Do you think I should take Archie and the ladies back to the Inn?"

"Yes," David answered. "Mac's not here. Has Archie talked to him?"

"Not since I've been with her."

"We don't know where he is, Bogie. Archie's mother's car is here, but she's gone, too."

"What do you want me to do?"

"Stay with Archie. Make some sort of excuse to get her back to the Inn. But don't tell her anything. I want to know some answers before I talk to her."

"Will do, Chief." Bogie hung up.

Sucking in all his strength. David sent a quick text to Mac's phone. "Call me ASAP!"

"Chief O'Callaghan," Sheriff Turow called out as soon as he climbed out of his cruiser. Two more sheriff's deputy cruisers pulled in behind him. "How can we help?" He squatted to take a look under one of the tarps. "Are any of the victims Mac Faraday or Archie Monday?"

"No," David replied. "Archie Monday is with my deputy chief. She knows nothing about this yet. We're looking for Mac."

"Anything you need from me or my deputies, you got it," the sheriff said. "I guess we need to take a deeper look into Dooley's background. We can't eliminate the possibility that this is connected to Dooley's murder."

"No, we can't," David said with a nod of his head.

"What do you know?" the sheriff asked.

"Neighbors say it was sudden," Officer Brewster reported. "They were all heavily armed with automatic weapons. One minute all was quiet, and the next minute all hell broke loose. The two guys and the bush over near the garage, and the guy over at the corner of the house—all got taken out by what looks like grenades."

"I don't think Mac uses grenades," David said with a shake of his head.

"Then on whose side were these guys who got hit with grenades?" the sheriff asked. "Mac or whoever was shooting at him?"

David shrugged his shoulders.

Officer Brewster continued his report. "The guy inside got it in the chest as he came in through the deck windows. As soon as it was over, witnesses saw a black SUV with West Virginia tags flying out of here."

"West Virginia?" Deciding to get all of the information that he was going to need to answer Archie's questions, David slipped his cell phone back into the case. "Joshua ..."

"Joshua?" the sheriff repeated.

"Joshua Thornton is one of Mac's groomsmen," David said. "He and Mac were going to the tailor this morning for a fitting for Josh's tux. He's the county prosecutor in West

Virginia. He drives a black SUV and it has West Virginia tags."

"Sheriff," one of the deputies waved for the sheriff to meet him over in the driveway. "We got a blood spatter over here."

Seeing that the deputy was pointing to a place in the driveway that was far from any of the fatalities, David rushed over. In the red spray that dotted the snow and ice, there was a straight line across which the blood splatter stopped. It was a void that indicated something else on the scene, something that had left before the police arrived. Tire marks that fishtailed around the circular drive indicated that it belonged to the vehicle that had left.

"The neighbors say they only saw one vehicle leave the scene," Officer Fletcher said.

"This void spatter tells us that someone at the rear of the vehicle was shot," David said, "and they must have left in the vehicle—the SUV with West Virginia plates, which probably belongs to Joshua Thornton. Let's get Thornton's tag numbers and put out a BOLO."

"What about the gunmen?" Sheriff Turow asked Brewster and Fletcher. "How did they get here? Have you found their vehicle?'

"We sent a cruiser to search the side roads deep in the woods," Officer Fletcher said.

"Good." David called over every officer within hearing distance. "I want IDs on these guys ASAP." He gestured to one of his officers. "Brewster, make sure their fingerprints are run through the federal database of known paid assassins. The rest of you, fan out into the woods. These guys had to have come in a vehicle. As heavily armed as they were, they couldn't have traveled far on foot."

"What about Faraday?" Officer Brewster asked David with a note of concern in his voice.

"Call Tonya to contact all of the hospitals and put a BOLO out on him, Joshua Thornton, and Agnes Douglas," David said. "One of them's hurt."

"It could have been Gnarly," Fletcher suggested. "In which case, they could be at an animal hospital."

The vibrating on David's hip indicated a text message coming in. "Good idea, Fletcher. Tell Tonya to check with the animal hospitals." Praying for a text from Mac, David snatched up the phone to read the text.

"Come 2 Inn ASAP. Alone. Important. Hector."

CHAPTER SEVEN

By the time David reached the top of Spencer Mountain, the sheriff's deputies had located the gunmen's van parked in the driveway of a summer residence across the cove from Spencer Manor. Shut up for the winter season, no one was around to see the assailants.

"We're running a make on the plates, but based on how they made their assault, I'm betting money they covered their tracks," the sheriff radioed to Spencer's police chief.

"Most likely the plates are stolen," David said.

"We'll have our forensics people go over it inch by inch," Sheriff Turow said. "But so far, it looks clean. They were all carrying burn phones, so we can't trace any of their accounts."

"Maybe Dooley hired them, and for some reason they decided to kill him to cover their tracks," David said.

"You're not really buying that, O'Callaghan," Turow said. "You know as well as I do that Dooley's murder was not committed by a pro."

"Nor was it committed by an experienced homicide detective." David tried to sound optimistic, which he was not. As many men as there were, and as heavily armed as they had been, they had to have cost a lot of money. Money that David didn't feel like Russell Dooley had. Unless he had cashed in all of his chips. Maybe he had drained his accounts to have Mac taken out.

Still, that left the question of who had killed Russell Dooley.

Elbowing his way through the throng of holiday vacationers scurrying about in the hotel foyer and lobby, David felt his cell phone buzz on his hip. Hoping that it would be Mac answering his text, he picked up the phone and read the caller ID. It was Archie.

Rats! David forced an upbeat tone into his voice when he answered. "How's the bride?"

"Terrible," she replied with tears in her voice. "Where's Mac?"

In an effort to get out of the way of heavy human traffic, David ducked into the small corridor leading to the restrooms. "Why are you asking me?"

"Because my calls to him are going straight to voice-mail," she replied. "Misty called. Gnarly missed his appointment with his stylist and my stylist—oh, David, you're never going to believe what she did to my hair! It's awful!"

"Archie," David said in a gentle tone, "calm down. I'm sure it's not that bad. Isn't Mac with Josh Thornton?"

"I don't have Josh's number." Archie sniffed.

"They probably got hung up at the tailor. Maybe something didn't fit. You know how those things go."

"Boy, do I ever," she said. "But, David, they didn't show at the tailor. I'm worried. Were they in a car accident? The roads are slippery. I heard of a bride who was killed in a car accident just days—"

"Archie, you have to believe me," David interjected, "I'm going to do everything I can to make sure nothing happens to you or Mac—"

"Then where were you when my stylist was ruining my hair?"

"I can only control so much," David said. "Let me make a few phone calls. Come back to the Inn and have a wonderful lunch with your bridesmaids, enjoy yourself, and let me take care of everything. Can you trust me to do that?"

Tears seeped into her voice. "What's going on, David?"

"I can't tell you right now, hon."

"Why not?"

"Because I don't know." Unable to hear anymore of her questions, David pressed the button to disconnect the call and rushed toward the Spencer Inn's business wing. When he pressed through the door of the security offices, the receptionist directed him back to Hector Langford's office.

David could see that the security chief was expecting him. He was standing at the open door, beckoning the police chief to hurry. As soon as David stepped into his corner office, Hector closed the door.

"I heard from Mac," the bald-headed Australian said in a low voice. He gestured for David to sit down next to his desk. "What's going on?"

"If you heard from Mac, didn't he tell you?" David noticed the cell phone resting on top of a notepad with a phone number written on it in the middle of Hector's desk. He went on to explain about the shooting at Spencer Manor. "What did Mac say?"

"I was waiting for you to get here before calling him back. I thought it was best for both of us to talk to him."

"You didn't talk to him?" David tried to remain calm.

Hector explained. "Back in the days of your father and Robin Spencer, the Inn would sometimes be asked to help out with special types of guests by certain government agencies that we won't mention by name."

In spite of his rising anxiety, David chuckled and shook his head. "Okay, I'm following you. Get to where Mac fits into this."

"Sometimes, certain people would fear, for good reason, that their phones were being tapped. So if they wanted us to call them on a secure line, they would call me on my private line and ask for someone like Pat or Robin, and I would say they had the wrong number. Then, after they hung up, I would check to see where they were calling from, get the number, and then call them back using a secure line." He tapped the notepad. "That's what Mac did, and I got his phone number. I already checked out the number. It's a burn phone that was activated just last week."

"And his registered phone is turned off," David said. "We're still trying to check the GPS on Joshua Thornton's SUV. I'm assuming that's disengaged. They've gone off the grid. Do you know if Thornton has been in contact with his son?"

"He's been on the slopes all morning," Hector said. "If he knew something was happening with his father, he'd be in here. From what we can see, those two are tight. I'll put a couple of my people on him to make sure whoever it is doesn't go after him. If these guys are pros, which it sounds like they are, they may try to flush out Mac or Thornton, whichever one is their target, by nabbing a member of their family."

"So Josh Thornton is off the grid, too." David grabbed the cell phone from the middle of Hector's desk and dialed the phone number.

"Hector …" Mac answered the phone on the first ring.

"Mac, it's David. What's going on? Is everyone okay?"

David held his breath when Mac hesitated before answering in a low voice, "Josh has been shot. I think we stopped the bleeding, but he needs to see a doctor."

David heard a commotion on the other end of the line. "What's going on, Mac? Where are you?"

Mac returned to the line. "Josh doesn't want you to tell Cameron."

"I can't keep this from his wife," David said. "She's going to be trying to get in touch with him, and when she doesn't reach him, she's going to be calling me."

"Donny's going to be looking for him," Hector added in a whisper.

"What about Josh's son?" David asked Mac.

"You can tell Donny, but not Josh's wife," Mac said. "Don't tell her about Josh getting hit. David, I can't go into it now, but just tell Cameron that Josh is fine."

"She's going to know I'm lying the first time he takes off his clothes and she sees a bullet hole," David said. "Where are you?"

"We're in Josh's SUV, parked at the top of the Spencer Mine trail," Mac said. "David, these guys were organized. They had us outgunned until Joshua got to his grenade launcher."

"What's a small-town county prosecutor doing with a grenade launcher?" David asked.

Hector's eyebrows went up to the top of his forehead.

"I have the same question," Mac said. "Right now, we need to get out of the snow. Can someone bring me some boots and a winter coat? And I left without my wallet. I have no ID or cash."

Hector leaned over to the phone. "I got just the place for you. It's a safe house that the CIA used back in the sixties during the Cold War. It's not even on the map. It's got a garage for you to park the SUV so it will be out of sight. I'll get the restaurant's chef to make you some food and meet you there."

David said, "And I'll get Doc Washington to go up and check on Josh."

They were about to hang up when they heard a commotion in the background.

"No, I'm not going to tell them that!" Mac snapped.

"Tell us what?" David asked.

"If you don't tell them, I will!" they heard an elderly woman insist.

"What?" Hector asked.

"Agnes, now is not the time!" Mac yelled.

David and Hector heard Agnes' sharp tone coming through the phone. "If we're going to be on the lam, then bring me my knitting so I have something to do while waiting to get back on the grid."

"I don't feel comfortable treating a gunshot victim on the sly like this." Dr. Dora Washington clutched the police cruiser's door handle while David sped around a corner to make a sharp turn onto an icy dirt road. The road, which was only minimally plowed, would take him halfway up the mountain to the secluded three-bedroom log cabin.

It was hard to believe that the forty-year-old woman, who always wore her blue-black hair in a silky ponytail that spilled down to the middle of her back, made her living dissecting dead people. With her flawless figure, she looked like she would have belonged more on the cover of a fashion magazine. It was even more unbelievable that the beauty was dating sixty-five year old Deputy Chief Art Bogart.

After talking to Mac, David practically abducted the medical examiner from Spencer Manor, where she was still conducting on-scene examinations of the five bodies that littered the estate.

"Why have they gone underground?" she wanted to know. "What has Mac gotten himself into now?"

"That's what I want to find out."

"I thought they got all of the shooters," she said. "The sheriff's people found their vehicle."

"They're professionals, Doc," David said. "They didn't decide to do this on their own. They were sent. With this type of attack, whoever hired them isn't going to quit. That's who we need to identify. Archie's mother was there. They didn't care one bit about shooting at a seventy-year-old woman. She would have been no more than collateral damage."

They broke through the heavy woods to enter a clearing in the center of which rested a sprawling one-level ranch-style log house. Off to the edge of the clearing was a single-car garage. Hector's van, marked with the Spencer Inn insignia, rested next to the garage. David came to an abrupt halt near the front door of the cabin.

Gnarly's barks inside the house broke the quiet of the mountain landscape.

After gathering up Mac's coat, gloves, and boots, David trotted to the door and knocked.

Poised to fire his gun if the situation called for it, before opening the door Mac peered out through the shutter that had been pulled shut. David rushed the doctor inside, and Mac closed and locked the door behind them.

Dark and dusty, it was evident that the cabin had not had any visitors for several years. The television was an old analogue type that took up a heavy entertainment center containing an old VCR. David could smell the hot food that Hector had delivered from the Spencer Inn. A large black canvas bag occupied the coffee table. From across the room, David could see that it was filled with guns, ammunition clips, passports, identification, and a wad of cash.

Doc got right to business. "Where is he?"

Mac pointed down the bedroom hallway. "The room down at the end of the hall. Hector is with him."

Handing the coat and boots to Mac, David strolled over to peer into the bag. "You look good for a man who just got attacked by a death squad."

"IDs on any of them yet?" Mac dropped into a chair to slip on his boots.

"None." David handed Mac his wallet, which he had retrieved from the manor when he picked up the medical examiner. "It looks like you and Josh took out the whole team. Tonya and Fletcher are checking their fingerprints in AFIS."

He lowered his voice when he noticed Agnes come into the great room from the bedrooms. Gnarly was directly behind her. She stopped to regard the two of them with a note of suspicion before moving on to the kitchen. "Tea, David?" she offered.

"No, thank you, Mrs. Douglas," David said. "I can't stay long."

She stopped short. "Where's your hat?"

"Hat?" David wondered if he misunderstood her.

Like a woman on a mission, Agnes rummaged through the cabinets while chastising the police chief. "It's freezing outside. You should be wearing a hat on your head. You're going to catch cold, and then what are we going to do with a stricken police chief?"

David glanced at Mac, who turned his full attention to his boots. "I just remembered. I left it in my cruiser."

"It's not doing you any good there." Spotting a fire extinguisher clamped in a holder on the wall, she rose up to inspect it. "Has this been tested lately to make sure it still works?" For her answer, she checked the date. "This is going to expire in the next six months. Mac, you should tell your people to check on the fire alarms and extinguishers to make sure they're all current. You don't want any horrible accidents to happen, do you?"

"No, ma'am." Sighing, Mac shook his head in his hands.

Agnes returned the fire extinguisher to the holder and resumed her search until she extracted a bin of cleaning supplies and a sponge from under the sink. She turned on the sputtering faucet and waited for the water to run clear.

"Agnes, what are you doing?" Mac called across the room to ask.

"We have an injured man back there in the bedroom, and this place is a breeding place for germs." Agnes wrung out the sponge under the water. "It needs to be cleaned."

With the wet sponge in her hand, she turned around and almost tripped over Gnarly. "Will you get away from me, you filthy beast?" She glared at Mac. "Everywhere I go, he goes. He hasn't let me out of his sight since we got here. I went to the bathroom and he sat right outside the door."

"He's guarding you," Mac said. "That's what Gnarly does. He considers it his job to protect you, and he's very good at it. Be glad."

"I wouldn't mind it so much if he didn't smell and have dried blood on him," she said. "I guess as long as he's stalking me, he's staying away from Josh. Do you know how many germs dogs have? He could *kill* Josh!"

"Aren't you exaggerating just a bit?" Mac was doubtful.

"Mr. Crane has no pets. Unlike most men who I've cleaned for, he's very clean." With a hand on her hip, Agnes shook her finger at them. "You know why? Discipline. Mr. Crane doesn't get all wrapped up in people and animals and pets. That's why he's so successful. He's got important responsibilities—"

"What does Mr. Crane do?" Mac asked.

"He helps people."

"How?" Mac asked. "You keep talking about him like he's some sort of Superman."

"He *helps* people," she replied while wiping down the kitchen counter. "My point is that Mr. Crane doesn't let himself get distracted with frivolous things like furry mammals. That's the type of people who have dogs." She gestured with disdain at Gnarly. "They have big brown eyes and they're all soft and furry—totally covers up what burdens they are to take care of, and for what? So they can kill you with all of the diseases that they carry." She ticked off on her fingers. "They carry bacteria, viruses, parasites, and fungi." She glared down at the German shepherd sitting in front of her. "A lot of *good* you do protecting me from a hit man, only to *kill* me with Ebola."

With a whine, Gnarly hung his head.

"I'm going to go check on Josh," David said.

Mac jumped to his feet, then encased in warm boots. "I'm coming with you."

"Wash your hands first!" Agnes called out.

Seeing David's glare shot in his direction, Mac muttered, "She's ... going to be ... my m-mother-in-law ... I'm marrying ... her daughter. I'm really marrying her daughter."

"I think Archie was adopted," David said.

Mac was hopeful. "Do you think?"

When David turned to open the bedroom door, Mac stopped him with his hand on his arm. "Can I ask you a question?"

"About what?"

"Archie," Mac said. "Does she want children?"

"Isn't that a question you need to be asking *her*?" David replied with a hint of impatience. "Like maybe back *before* you asked her to marry you?"

"I did, and she said she didn't. Agnes insists Archie does want children and that she lied."

David chuckled. "Archie doesn't lie." He tilted his chin in the direction of the kitchen. "I'd believe Archie before I'd believe the Wicked Witch of the West." He went into the bedroom.

His hand on his weapon, Hector turned around when David and Mac came into the bedroom. "It's only Mac and me," David announced to the jumpy security chief.

David observed that Joshua had been stripped down to the waist so that Doc could examine him. He was heavily bandaged around the mid-section. His complexion was as gray as his silver hair.

While Doc finished her examination, David strolled up to the bed, where Joshua held what appeared to be his jacket tucked under his arm, close to his body on the opposite side of where he had been shot in the side. "How are you feeling?" David asked him.

"I'll be okay." Joshua grinned through a grimace. "Has anyone checked on Donny?"

"Donny is fine," Hector said. "Members of my security team have eyes on him as we speak."

"Are you sure none of the perps got away?" Mac asked.

David said. "We found their van parked at a summer residence across the cove from the manor. It had stolen plates. If someone had escaped, we would assume they would have returned to the van to make their getaway."

"Do you have Russell Dooley in custody?" Mac asked.

"He's dead," David said.

Stunned, Mac was still staring at David when Joshua asked, "Who's Russell Dooley?"

"Husband of a murderer I arrested," Mac said. "She killed herself. In retaliation for her suicide, he threatened to ruin the wedding." He turned back to David, "How'd he die?"

"Murdered at his motel," David said. "Turow wants to talk to you."

"Does this Dooley guy have the resources to hire a hit squad?" Joshua asked.

"No," Mac said. "But if he was murdered—was it a professional hit on Dooley?" he asked David. "Maybe this whole thing is a setup."

"It didn't look like it," David said. "But then, it's not my case. The murder was in Accident, Sheriff Turow's jurisdiction. Who would kill Russell Dooley and send a hit squad after you?"

"Maybe the victim of this murder that you put this Dooley guy's wife in jail for was connected," Joshua said. "Maybe she was framed."

"She did it!" Realizing the harshness of his tone, Mac apologized.

Softly, Joshua replied, "I'm only suggesting that if her victim was connected in some way to drugs or organized crime …"

"But why come after me years later?" Mac asked.

"Maybe Dooley uncovered something," Joshua replied. "They killed him to keep him quiet and came after you to tie up any possible lose ends."

Slowly, Mac shook his head and then nodded. "That's a thought." Then, he shook his head again. "But I found no evidence in that case of Tyler being connected to drugs or organized crime."

"It's worth looking into," David said.

Mac turned his attention back to the police chief. "Tell me what happened to Dooley."

"You need to talk to Sheriff Turow."

"What's the time of death?" when David didn't answer, Mac turned to Doc.

"Shortly after midnight last night," she replied. "That's all I'm telling you."

"Damn!" Mac pounded his fist on the foot of the bed.

"What's wrong?" Joshua asked.

"I don't have any alibi," Mac said. "I was home in bed alone … unless you want to count Gnarly."

David agreed. "I was at the Inn with Chelsea, so I can't say if you were home or not."

Doc proceeded to pack up her medical bag. "The bleeding has stopped for now. Agnes did a good job. But even though the quikclok did stop the bleeding, he does need to go to the hospital for treatment. The wound could get infected. He could have a perforated intestine, which could lead to peritonitis, which could kill him."

"We just need some time to figure out who is behind this," David said.

"They had military combat training," Joshua said. "If their target goes to the hospital, they would not hesitate to kill innocent people to get what they want."

"Okay," Doc said. "I've done all I can do for now. I suggest moving him as little as possible until you can get him to a hospital. Keep him warm, and keep the wound clean."

"Warm and clean," Mac said with a nod of his head. "Will do."

Doc glanced at each one of the men. Sensing by their silence and by their gaze on Joshua that they did not want to talk in front of her, she said, "I'm going to go check on Gnarly." She picked up her bag. "Hector, can you take me back to my van?"

"Yes, ma'am."

Out in the hallway, she announced, "I'll be waiting." She closed the door behind her.

Mac moved around to the other side of the bed. Folding his arms across his chest, David peered down at Joshua. Sensing an interrogation coming, Joshua pulled the covers up over his chest and tucked his coat under his arm.

"I'm interested in your thoughts, Josh," Mac began. "My first impression when the shooting started was the same as yours. To send a death squad after me was overkill for Russell Dooley. My sense from his note threatening me was that he would want to be on hand to see my pain. This attack was calculated. Like men on a mission with an objective to fulfill. Don't you agree?"

"A military mission," Joshua said.

"This is my town," David said. "I have a need to know if you're involved in something that's going to threaten the people who live, work, and visit here."

"I'm a county prosecutor. I took the same type of vow and have the same responsibility for the people in my county." Joshua avoided their gaze. "But I can't tell you anything," he said with a sigh.

"What do you mean you can't tell us?" Mac bent over him. "I got shot at. We all got shot at. My home was invaded and looks like something out of a warzone now. Archie's mother was in the line of fire and ... *you can't tell us anything!*"

"Mac ..." David said in a soft voice.

"David is the chief of police," Mac told Joshua. "If you can't tell him, then who can you tell? Is this someone you put away? Someone from organized crime? Maybe a terrorist you had arrested when you were in the navy?"

"I can't say, Mac," Joshua said. "All I can say is that I'm sorry this happened."

"Sorry isn't enough!" Mac clenched his fists. "I have a right to know who is trying to kill me!"

"Mac has a *need* to know," David said. "He *needs* to know what he's fighting. I *need* to know what I'm protecting you from."

Mac leaned over the bed to tell him, "If I'm going to get killed right before my wedding, Archie has a right to know why it happened."

"Stand down, Mac!" David roared in a voice so loud and harsh that the walls seemed to echo.

Instinctively, Joshua sat up straight in spite of his pain. Hector stood up straight to gaze straight at David, whose eyes were on Mac. The police chief's expression was firm. He dared Mac to challenge him.

The bedroom was filled with silence.

"Hector …" David's eyes did not leave Mac's face.

"Yes, sir."

"Take Doc back to her van. Return Agnes to the Inn. Make sure Donny Thornton is taken care of."

"He's a minor," Hector reminded David. "We can't let him stay at the Inn by himself."

"I will come to the Inn and stay with him tonight," David said. "Just make sure he is taken care of. I'll talk to him when I get back to let him know what's going on."

"He's going to be looking for his father. What should I tell him about the situation?"

David looked down at Joshua. "Tell him his father got hung up working on a case, but he's fine."

"Yes, sir." Hector practically saluted David before rushing from the room.

After Hector was gone, David gestured with a toss of his head for Mac to leave.

"I'm not leaving." Mac folded his arms across his chest. "I know all about national security-type operations. This is a case where I have a need to know." He tapped his chest. "I was getting shot at."

"And I have top-secret security clearance," David said.

Joshua looked up at David.

"So we have a man who has become a target, and you have a police chief with top secret clearance," David said. "Start talking."

"How do I know you're telling me the truth about your clearance?" Joshua asked.

"I'm a major in the United States Marine Reserves," David said. "Special Operations. I've served tours in Afghanistan and Iraq. Once a year, I get sent out on another mission—usually overseas on highly classified assignments. So I know exactly what you're not talking about." He relaxed his stance. "You?"

"Captain in the naval reserves."

"And you're on an assignment right now?" Mac asked.

"Special assignment," Joshua said. "But I didn't agree to be a groomsman in your wedding for this. The timing and the place worked out for the exchange."

"What was your mission?" David asked.

"Pick-up and delivery of classified information," Joshua said.

"From who and to whom?"

"I can't tell you," Joshua said.

"You can tell me who we're dealing with, Captain." It was an order. "Mac is right. We have a right to know who's trying to kill us."

"How can we fight an enemy we don't know?" Mac asked.

"It's the same people who've been trying to kill us," Joshua said. "Islamic terrorist groups. Despite what Washington wants us to believe, they're here in America, and they don't all have dark skin and wear rags on their heads."

"You don't have to tell me what it is." Seeing Joshua clutching his coat, David reached for it. "Just give it to me and I'll—"

Joshua pulled the coat tighter. "Don't, David. You have no idea how sensitive this information is. A lot of people would kill to keep it from reaching its final destination."

"Who are you supposed to deliver it to? What am I supposed to do if you die? Who am I supposed to call?"

Anticipating the question, Joshua was searching through the pockets of his coat until he found his wallet. He extracted a business card from it and handed it to David. "I answer to my commanding officer. Call this number and tell her exactly who you are and your social security number. She answers directly to the Joint Chiefs of Staff. Tell her to send Murphy. If I can't deliver it to her myself, then Murphy will have to complete the assignment."

"Your son?" Mac asked.

"Isn't he just an ensign?" David inquired.

"He's a lieutenant now," Joshua said. "He's got the highest security clearances available—just like me. If I can't complete my assignment, Murphy will be able to."

David read the phone number on the card. There was no name. No government or military insignia. Only a phone number. Wordlessly, he handed the business card across the bed to Mac.

"There's nothing but a phone number on this card," Mac said. "What's her name?"

"Just call that number," Joshua said. "She'll contact Murphy."

"This stinks," Mac whispered to David once they were outside in the hallway with the bedroom door closed. "A phone number without a name. Spies. Mysterious women with no names. Secret assignments. Hit squads. It's like something out of a bad movie."

The pain killer that Doc had given Joshua was starting to work. In spite of the desperation of the situation, he had finally managed to drift off to sleep. The last thing he asked David before falling asleep was to call Cameron to tell her about the situation, but to keep it from her that he had been shot. "If I talk to her, she'll be able to tell by my voice that something has happened." He gave David a phone number to a burn phone that she had for just such emergencies.

"You're always prepared," Mac noted with a small grin.

"I was an Eagle Scout," Joshua uttered before drifting off.

"Where there's smoke there's fire," David said in the hallway while tucking Cameron's phone number into the inside pocket of his coat. "The summer before last when I was in Iraq with my unit, I heard a rumor about a very elite and highly secret team that supposedly the Joint Chiefs of Staff had put together. Each member of the team was hand-picked. It was made up of top members of every military branch, and they were sent on the most highly classified missions."

"Black ops?"

"They were referred to as Phantoms."

"Military is just like the police." Mac shook his head with a laugh. "There're always rumors going around, and more than half of them aren't true."

"I thought the same thing when I first heard the rumors," David said in a low tone, "but something very weird happened in that desert—weird enough to make me wonder."

"What happened?"

"You'll never believe me." The corner of his lip kicked up in a smile at the memory of the stunning woman with no name and fabulous legs.

"Who are we dealing with?" Mac murmured. "Terrorists? That does fit. Military types. Professional hit squad."

Clenching his jaw, David suppressed a shudder.

Mac saw the blood drain from his face and his complexion turn pale. "Are you okay?"

"Just tired," David murmured. "Josh may very well have been the target."

Mac shook his head. "But they hit at Spencer Manor. How did they know he was going to be there?"

111

"You two did have an appointment at the tailor," David pointed out. "You'd be surprised at the sophisticated technology these guys have. People see dirty smelly looking men dressed in rags and skull caps out in the desert living in mud huts with these radical barbaric beliefs and they think they don't know anything. Truth is, some of these groups have big financial backing to get them top-notch support, both in technology and espionage. And they have a lot of political backing as well." He shook his head. "If Josh's cover got blown, then there's no telling how they got that, and if he has something they want, they won't stop at Spencer Manor."

"You need to get Archie's mother out of here," Mac said.

David was already jogging down the hallway to the great room. "She's on her way back to the Spencer Inn *now*. I'm going to try to get some of my men up here to back you up."

In the great room, they found Doc writing out instructions on a notepad. "There's usually a thirty to fifty percent rate of success after surgery."

"That high?" Agnes replied. "I am always amazed at what medical science can do nowadays. It's like magic."

"Doc, Agnes, what are you two still doing here?" David turned to Hector, who was standing at the door with his coat on. "I told you to get them back to the Inn."

"Have you ever tried to get two women moving when they don't want to?" Hector replied. "I've *been* ready to go, but they've been yapping."

"About what?" Mac asked.

"Having your vasectomy reversed," Doc answered.

His jaw dropping, Mac backed up several steps while involuntarily covering his crotch with his hand. "What!" He whirled around to his future mother-in-law.

"Good news, Mac." Agnes' smile spread across her wrinkled face. "Doc here says that they can reverse your vasectomy, and you won't even have to spend the night in the hospital."

"It's outpatient surgery done with a local anesthetic," the medical examiner explained in a matter-of-fact manner. She could very well have been talking about his tonsils. "How long ago did you have the vasectomy done?"

Stunned, Mac could only gaze at Doc, a woman he had known for years. But he didn't know her well enough to discuss his sexual reproductive organs with her.

When Mac didn't answer, Agnes did. "It was when his daughter hit puberty."

"Jessica's in her early twenties now, isn't she?" Doc asked Mac, who narrowed his eyes before turning to Agnes. "There's less chance for success after ten years. You're cutting it kind of close."

"I can't believe you'd discuss my *vasectomy* with *her*," Mac finally managed to sputter. "I *know* this woman. She's a friend and a colleague. The last thing I want to discuss with her is my …" He found it difficult to form the words.

"Do you or do you not love Archie?" Agnes asked firmly.

"Loving Archie has nothing to do with you violating my privacy and discussing my sex organs with other people!"

"If you really loved Archie, you'd do whatever you have to do to give her a baby!" Agnes slammed her hand down on the kitchen counter. "It isn't like you don't have the money to have the surgery done by the best doctors money can buy! So the only reason you wouldn't have it done is because you're just plain too selfish to do it!"

His eyes wide and his face pale, Hector had backed up to the door.

His tail tucked between his legs, Gnarly scurried to hide in the corner behind a recliner.

113

Afraid Mac was going to grab for his gun, David rushed around the kitchen counter and took the elderly woman by the elbow. "Agnes, it's time to go."

She shook David's hand off her arm. "Go where?"

"Back to the hotel," David said. "It isn't safe for you here …" Taking note of the fury on Mac's face, he added in a mutter, "on more than one front."

Doc tore the top sheet of paper from her notepad. "Well, Mac, if you decide to have the surgery reversed, here's the name of a colleague of mine. Dr. Maura Monroe. She'll fix you right up." Her tone was as casual as if she were referring him to a barber for a good clean shave.

When Mac refused to take the note, Doc slapped it down on the counter, snapped her medical case shut, and strode over to the door. "Let's go, Hector."

"Agnes, we need to go." David made another attempt to grab Agnes by the elbow.

"I'm not going anywhere!" She slapped David in the arm with her purse.

"Agnes, it's dangerous for you to stay here." David clutched her elbow and kept tight hold of it.

"David is right." Mac laid his hands flat on the kitchen counter and bit off each word. "It would be dangerous for you to stay here."

"Archie and your sons are going to be worried about you," David said.

"Joshua is injured." Agnes stomped on David's foot to force him to release his hold on her. "Doc says he has to rest and keep quiet. He needs me to take care of him."

"Mac will take care of him," David said.

Agnes laughed. "Be serious. Mac can't even take care of himself."

"I take care of myself just fine," Mac insisted.

"Archie has been taking care of you ever since you moved to Spencer."

"That's not true!"

"What brand of coffee do you like?" Agnes shot at him.

"Black," Mac replied.

"That's not the *brand*," Agnes said. "That's the way you *take* it. What brand and flavor do you like?"

Confused by the question, Mac stared at her and then at David, who was waiting for his response. Even Hector and Doc were waiting. Gnarly peered out from behind the recliner.

"You have no idea how much my daughter does for you," Agnes said with her arms crossed. "Just like every other pampered rich man. She takes such good care of you that you can't even see it—until it's not done. Believe me, if you got the wrong type of coffee served to you, you'd know it in a heartbeat. That's how devoted she's been to you."

Taking her hand off her hip, she wagged an arthritic finger at him. "The thing is, Joshua is hurt bad. He needs someone who knows how to take care of him here, because if not, he's going to die."

"She's right," Doc's voice came from the door. "It's preferable that Josh go to a hospital, but if he can't, then have someone here who knows advanced first aid."

"I'm certified," Agnes said.

Mac gritted his teeth.

Agnes glared back at him.

"Doc has a point," David said in a low voice, "as much as I hate to leave her here."

"You have no choice," Agnes said, "because I'm not going."

With a sigh, David headed for the door. As he passed Mac, he paused to whisper, "I'll send a couple of officers up here to guard the place." With a glance back at Agnes, who was matching Mac's glare at her, he added, "I'll be back first thing in the morning to check on the survivors."

Chapter Eight

Evening: State Police Barracks, Pittsburgh, Pennsylvania

"Josh, I know you're probably busy with wedding stuff," Cameron said into her cell phone. Her tone was heavy with worry. "I've left you three messages today already, and it's not like you to not return my calls." Conscious of her fellow detectives busily working at their desks, she kept her head bowed and her voice low. "I'm starting to get worried. I know it's just me, but can you please call me back? I need to hear your voice." Forcing a confident expression on her face, she sat up tall in her seat while thumbing to disconnect the call.

Maybe Mac Faraday dragged Josh into a case. A reassuring grin crossed her face. *Josh never has to be dragged into a murder investigation.*

She picked up the phone and thumbed through her contact list to Chief David O'Callaghan's direct line at the Spencer Police Department. She recognized Desk Sergeant Tonya's voice when she answered.

"Hey, Tonya, this is Detective Cameron Gates with the Pennsylvania State Police," she said, "I guess Chief O'Callaghan isn't in his office."

"He's on his way to a meeting, *Detective Gates,*" the desk sergeant replied. "Let me see if he has a minute to talk to you."

Cameron waited on hold.

"Talking to your hubby?" Detective Butch Howard, a man with a beer belly of which he was very proud and a gray buzz cut and flat top, had sauntered up to her desk. An older man, Butch had never adjusted to women becoming detectives—especially homicide detectives.

Cameron was torn between hanging up or telling Butch to come back later. Before she could decide, Tonya came back onto the line. "Chief said he'll call you right back, Detective Gates."

Click!

Perplexed, Cameron looked at the phone and hung up. Tonya hadn't asked for her phone number. *Must be going by the caller ID.*

"Yes, Butch, I was talking to my hubby." Even though she had not actually talked to Joshua, she didn't want to bother with the full explanation. "This is the first time Josh and Donny have been away since we got married, and I miss them. Don't you miss any of your ex-wives?"

"Every month when I have to write the alimony checks." With his knees unable to handle holding up his poundage for very long, Butch plopped down into the chair next to her desk. "I ran a background check on your vic."

"What did you find out?"

"Nothing." Butch's smug expression was begging for her to ask for more.

"No arrests?"

"Nothing as in nothing," Butch said. "Your vic is a ghost. Reginald Crane does not exist."

"We found his wallet with his driver's license—"

"All bogus," Butch said.

Recalling the West Point Military Academy diploma hanging on his wall, Cameron asked, "Did you check the military database?"

Butch was shaking his head. "VA has no record of him, and his social security number isn't in the system. This guy does not exist and never did."

"He must be in the Witness Protection Program," Cameron said. "Though I never heard of someone in the program being put up in such fancy digs before. They usually want them to blend in with the rest of society."

"If he's in the program, the US Marshals office is denying it on every front," Butch said. "Usually when we end up with one of their witnesses, they swoop in to chase us away like vultures staking their claim on a carcass. Not this time."

"That must have something to do with why his assistant, Ethan Bonner, took off."

"He's a ghost, too."

Cameron stared at Butch, who enjoyed a good chuckle at her confusion.

"Fingerprints?" Cameron asked.

"Place was wiped down," Butch said, "but we did get a hit on prints that they managed to lift off some picture frames." He slapped a folder down on her desk. "Agnes Douglas from Hopewell, Pennsylvania."

Cameron picked up the folder and opened it. "Any priors?"

"Not in all of her seventy years," Butch said with a chuckle. "She's got a bunch of kids."

Cameron nodded while reading over the background information. "Six sons—all with clean records. A daughter who died over twelve years ago." She read. "Kendra Douglas? Where do I know that name?"

"According to Douglas' driver's license, she weighs a whole one hundred and ten pounds. Yep, I can see her duct taping your vic to a chair to torture him."

"What were her prints doing at the scene?" Cameron found the answer in her listed occupation. Housekeeping. "She cleaned his house. Maybe one of her sons did it. It was a big house, and he was an older man. They could have been after money or valuables."

"He'd have to know we'd be talking to Mommy," Butch said. "Was anything stolen?"

"I'm not coming up with anything." Dismissing the information as not much of a lead, she closed the folder and dropped it back onto her desk. "What about the computers? I saw a laptop and two desktops."

"Hard drives had been wiped clean before we got there," Butch said. "Forensics claims that whoever did it was a professional. He knew what he was doing. Not much hope of retrieving anything."

"We have a body," Cameron said. "That dead man in that mansion was somebody, and someone killed him. There's somebody out there who knows and cares about him." She picked up the folder with Agnes Douglas' information. "Let's check out the housekeeper. Maybe this Crane guy, or whatever his name is, talked to her. I'll give her a call to see what she knows."

"Well, good luck with that, Gates." Chuckling at delivering her an impossible case that he would enjoy seeing her fail at solving, Detective Butch Howard pried himself up out of her chair and sauntered away.

"I hate this case." Cameron dropped back into her seat with a moan.

The hair on the back of her neck stood up on end. She had been feeling like she was being watched on and off ever since she had left Reginald Crane's home. On a hunch, she turned around to look out the window. It was dark outside, but she narrowed her eyes and peered through the falling snow and the dim parking lights to see a white Mini Cooper with black stripes parked in the corner of the visitor's lot.

Didn't I see that car when I pulled out of the burger place for lunch? Nah, there are millions of Mini Coopers in the big city, and they all look alike. Forcing the thought of being followed from her mind, she pulled away from the window. *You're getting paranoid, Gates.*

"Gates," Lieutenant Miles Dugan called to her from his office door, "can I see you in my office?"

Cameron sat up in her seat and looked over her shoulder to her squad leader's corner office. Beyond him, she saw two men with heavy coats over suits waiting for her. She was rising from her chair when she heard the cell phone she had in her handbag, which she kept in the bottom drawer of her desk, ring.

Not instantly recognizing the ring, she had to pause to determine from where the sound was coming and what it meant.

My burn phone. It has to be Josh. He's in trouble.

The phone rang again.

Yanking open her desk drawer, she dug into the pocket and down to the bottom to extract the phone. The caller ID didn't read Joshua. It read a phone number she didn't recognize.

For a split second she was disappointed, until she realized it could be Joshua calling from a different phone. She waved her thumb over the answer button.

"Gates, did you hear me?" her lieutenant called to her again.

Cameron felt her body break out in a cold sweat. *I'll need to call him back. Please, God, let him be okay.* "Coming."

After setting the phone down in the center of her desk, she hurried across the detective squad room to her chief's office.

Lieutenant Miles Dugan's workspace may have been an office, but it was still small. Between the two visitors, dressed in heavy coats and wearing shoulder holsters, and the police lieutenant, the room felt overcrowded when Cameron entered it.

Immediately, one of the men jumped up from his chair in front of the desk to offer her his seat.

"This is Detective Cameron Gates," the lieutenant introduced her. "She's the detective taking the lead in the Reginald Crane homicide." He then went on to introduce his visitors. "Gates, these are Special Agents Leland Elder—" the larger of the two agents, who had remained seated, nodded his head to acknowledge her, "and Neal Black. They're with the FBI."

Both agents displayed their badges for Cameron to examine.

Yep, FBI all right.

Both agents were broad shouldered. Square shaped, Elder looked like he was the same size as a refrigerator. With thick reddish-blond hair that was combed with every strand in place and green eyes, Agent Neal Black was an attractive man. Judging by the way he grinned at her, Cameron could see that he knew it, too.

"Your background search on Reginald Crane brought up all sorts of flags in our department, Detective Gates," Special Agent Black said.

"Not on our end," Cameron replied. "We got nothing. Not even an ID on him. According to our records, Reginald Crane does not exist."

Special Agent Black looked over his shoulder at his partner. Special Agent Elder cocked a dark heavy eyebrow back at him.

"Well," Agent Black drawled, "that's because he doesn't exist. You see, Reginald Crane was one of our agents. He's been working deep undercover on a case for quite some time, and we thought he was about to finally get a break. Obviously, he must have, since someone tortured him to death."

"What kind of case was he working on?" Cameron asked.

"We can't tell you that," Elder said. His voice was so low that it sounded like a disembodied voice from a demon in a movie—devoid of any human compassion.

"The case is much too sensitive to discuss," Special Agent Black said. "The fact is, I'm afraid the FBI is going to have to take over this investigation. We're here to ask that you turn over everything that you have gathered on it so far, including any leads you may have. Possible suspects."

"Or other agents involved in the case?" Cameron asked. "Like Ethan Bonner? Am I correct in assuming he was working with your man Crane? He's probably the one who scrubbed the place down and wiped all of the hard drives."

Special Agent Black grinned at her. "You're good, Gates. That's exactly what happened."

"Why didn't he just identify himself as an FBI agent?" Cameron asked.

"Because he was working deep undercover," Agent Black countered. "His partner had just been killed." He laid his hand on her shoulder. "I'm sure you understand how the sudden death of someone you are close to can make you not think straight, Detective Gates. It can even make you unsure of who you can trust."

Cameron leaned away from his touch. "What division of the FBI are you with, Special Agent Black?"

"Detective Gates," Lieutenant Dugan interjected before the agents could respond. "The fact of the matter is that the FBI is now taking the lead on this case, which will free you up to take a few days off to go meet Josh and attend the Faraday wedding."

"Faraday wedding?" Special Agent Black's green eyes brightened. "As in Mac Faraday, the multi-millionaire? I had no idea that we were in the midst of high society." He made a big display of bowing in front of Cameron, who felt her cheeks turn pink. "How do you know Mac Faraday?"

"We've worked together on a couple of cases," Cameron said.

"Her husband is one of Faraday's groomsmen," Lieutenant Dugan tossed out. "Joshua Thornton."

"Thornton?" Special Agent Elder croaked out. "Where have we heard of him?" he asked his partner.

"He's the prosecuting attorney in Hancock County in West Virginia," the lieutenant said. "He was also a JAG lawyer in the navy and prosecuted some very heavy-duty cases before retiring."

While her chief spoke, Cameron was feeling increasingly uncomfortable with how Special Agent Black was eying her. She felt like a piece of meat. Meanwhile, Special Agent Elder's dark eyes looked menacing. She had met some unsavory characters who worked for the FBI and other federal agencies. As a matter of fact, she had discovered that being slightly unsavory yourself gave you an edge in solving a case. You had an easier time getting into the killer's head.

"I'll get you everything we have." Cameron stood up from the chair.

"Wonderful," Special Agent Black said.

"Then I'll approve your leave starting tomorrow," Lieutenant Dugan said. "I'm sure Josh will be thrilled to see you."

"And I'll be thrilled to see him."

Spencer Police Department

Located along the shore of Deep Creek Lake, Spencer's small police department sported a dock with a dozen jet skis and four speed boats. For patrolling the deep woods and up the mountain trails, they had eight ATVs. Their fleet of SUV cruisers was painted black with gold lettering on the side that read "SPENCER POLICE."

Hurrying through the front door and out of the cold, Police Chief David O'Callaghan fingered the business card in his pocket that Joshua Thornton had handed him. He dreaded the thought of calling and speaking to the unnamed woman.

He felt like making the call would be on par with opening a Pandora's Box to let all the demons of his past escape to wreak havoc all over again. As long as he didn't dial the phone number, then he could pretend they didn't exist.

But not making the call did not make reality disappear. It was still there.

Terrorists. Who else would Joshua Thornton be working against? David had had his fill of terrorists on his tours in the Middle East. But if Joshua's assignment was so important that it involved the Phantoms—if they really existed—then failure was not an option. Failure would be a major casualty that could be catastrophic for many lives—and possibly the nation.

"Chelsea called," Tonya, the desk sergeant announced upon his entrance. "I didn't know what to tell her."

"I'll call her." David took a stack of message forms from her. "And I'll call Archie, too. Have you explained things to Bogie?"

"Bogie has been briefed," Tonya said. "He's waiting for your orders about what to tell Archie. He says he'll talk to her if you want."

125

"I have to go to the Spencer Inn anyway," David said. "Joshua Thornton's teenage son is by himself. So you'll be able to reach me there tonight."

She placed several disposable cell phones across the top of the counter. "They're all activated and have the numbers for Mac's and Hector Langford's burners already input in them. I also put your phone number on each of them. You're all connected." She touched each one as she rattled off names. "One for each of our officers. One for you, Bogie, me, Archie, and Donny Thornton."

David grinned when he saw that she was way ahead of him. "Thank you, Tonya. You're a peach." He picked up the phone on which she had written "Chief."

"I know." With a jerk of her thumb, she gestured up the stairs to his office. "Sheriff Turow has been waiting for you."

Reminded of the Russell Dooley murder, David suppressed a groan. He'd been so busy thinking about Joshua Thornton's possible role in the hit squad that had attacked Spencer Manor that he had actually forgotten about Russell Dooley's murder and the knife with the Spencer Inn's insignia.

"Do I need to call Mac's lawyer?" David asked Tonya in a low voice.

"Ask him." She gestured toward the office door at the top of stairs. "He's not talking to me."

She touched his arm when he slumped. "You and I both know that Sheriff Turow is a fair man. He's only doing his job. He's not going to railroad Mac into jail. If anything, he'll go out of his way to make sure Mac gets a fair shake."

"Someone is trying to frame Mac for Russell Dooley's murder," David said. "But if they're trying to frame him, then why send a hit squad to kill him?"

"Good question," she replied. "Maybe it's a coincidence?"

"I don't believe in coincidences."

"I do," she said at the same time that the phone rang on her desk. "That's your direct line," she noted before picking up the receiver.

The office door at the top of the stairs opened, and the sheriff stepped into the doorway. "I don't have all day, O'Callaghan." He had a leather binder tucked under his arm.

When David turned to leave, Tonya gestured for him to stay with a wave of her arm. "He's on his way to a meeting, *Detective Gates*. Let me see if he has a minute to talk to you." She pressed the button to put the call on hold.

David slumped.

"I can't keep dodging these people, Chief," Tonya said. "Cameron sounds frantic."

"I know," David said, "but I can't talk to her on that line. They could be monitoring the police calls." He took the phone number that Joshua had given him for Cameron's burner phone and his burn phone. "Tell her that I'm in a meeting and will call her right back."

"They?" Sheriff Turow asked about who could be monitoring their phones.

"I'm coming, Turow." Slowly, David made his way up the stairs.

Before he reached the top, the sheriff said, "Rumor tells me that you've located Faraday."

"We don't deal in rumors here in Spencer." David gestured for the sheriff to step into the office ahead of him. He then followed him inside and closed the door.

David slid into his chair behind his desk. The corner office provided a magnificent view of Deep Creek Lake and the police department's docks, which had been closed for the winter season.

"Does Faraday know about Dooley's murder?" Sheriff Turow lowered himself into the chair across from David's desk. He laid the leather binder across his lap.

"I told him," David said. "But I didn't give him any specifics. I only said that Dooley had been murdered. Someone else told him the time of death."

"Doc Washington?" Turow asked. "My people saw you pick her up at Spencer Manor and take her to an undisclosed location. Who got injured in the shootout?"

"Thornton," David said. "He needs a doctor."

"Then you need to bring him and Faraday in."

"We need to identify who was behind this hit squad," David said. *"This* squad got killed, but there could be more who will make another hit with bigger and badder arms. They clearly don't care who gets caught in the crossfire. Are your people equipped to deal with that type of fire power?" He shook his head. "My department isn't."

"My people may have uncovered a lead on that." Sheriff Turow sat up in his seat and extracted a printout from the binder. He handed the paper across the desk to David. "We found a paper trail on Dooley. Now these types of hit squads don't come cheap, and you have to be connected to find one."

"That's what I've heard."

"Well …" Turow pointed at a section of the printout. "Dooley could have hired them. He sold his house to a real estate company the week after his wife killed herself, and he didn't give a forwarding address either. There's no current address for this guy. At closing, he was handed a cashier's check for one hundred twenty thousand dollars, which was way below the tax assessor's estimate. He cashed it in. There's no record of him putting that money into any account." He chuckled. "Where did all that cash go?"

David cocked an eyebrow at him. "Where indeed? One hundred twenty thousand dollars would buy a pretty good hit squad."

"That's what I think," Turow said. "But that still leaves the matter of who killed Dooley. Does Faraday have an alibi?"

"Unless you want to count Gnarly."

"Prosecutor Fleming has intimate knowledge of Gnarly's conniving nature," Turow said with a grin.

"What about the kid who saw someone going into the cabin last night?" David asked with an air of hope.

"You mean this dude?" The sheriff took a sketch out of the binder and tossed it across the desk in David's direction.

David studied the picture of a bloated round face with eyes that appeared to be bloodshot. He had thick eyebrows and flabby jowls. It was definitely not Mac Faraday. But he did look familiar.

"Recognize that guy?" Sheriff Turow asked while David tried to place the face.

"I have seen him before."

"Of course you have." The sheriff took the sketch out of David's hands. "At the cabin. In the bathtub. That's Russell Dooley. That's who the kid saw, if he saw him. His aunt says the kid is a compulsive liar. Now Dooley did keep to himself, according to the people at the motel. The kid may have seen him a couple of times and not known that the man he saw go into the cabin was in fact the murder victim. But since he's the victim, he certainly isn't the killer."

"If the kid is telling the truth," David said, "Dooley did go out last night before he was killed. The killer could have been waiting for him inside the cabin when he came back."

"You mean Mac, who the kid did not see?" The corners of the sheriff's lips turned up in a grin.

"No." David slammed his hand down on the desktop.

Sheriff Turow winked at him. "I know Mac didn't do this, O'Callaghan."

David failed to suppress his sigh of relief.

"But I have to do my job. There are people out there who will jump down my throat if they even think I'm cutting Faraday any special favors because he's a friend of the police."

"I know, Turow," David replied.

"That's why I'm not asking you where he is," Turow said. "Because if I know where he's hiding, then those same people will be asking why I don't go drag him in for an interrogation about Dooley's murder."

"That's why I'm not telling you."

"It's the holidays." The sheriff stood up. "You and I are both shorthanded. If you need anything from my people, don't be afraid of calling. We're all on the same side here."

David rose to his feet and shook the sheriff's hand. "Once I know what's going on, you'll be the first one I call."

"I'll be sure to let you know if I hear anything else."

David watched the sheriff leave before taking the business cards out of his pocket. Sucking in as much courage as he could, he dialed the first phone number, only to listen to it ring repeatedly until it came to an automated voice mail.

"Cameron, this is Police Chief David O'Callaghan. Josh gave me this number to call you. *He's okay.* But we need to talk. Call me back at this number as soon as you get this message."

Hanging up, David gritted his teeth with determination. Looking down at the cell phone and Cameron's phone number, David spotted the plain white business card that contained only a phone number.

If anyone can help us, it has to be her—if she is indeed the team leader for the Phantoms. Nah! Maybe.

David dialed the phone number into the burner phone and listened to it ring twice before a sultry feminine voice answered.

"Hello …"

David sat up straight in his chair. He felt the air sucked out of his lungs, and his head swam as the memory of that voice came crashing back to him.

He was in the back of the limousine. Her hair and face concealed by the black fedora and dark glasses, he studied her body language for a clue of who she might be. She gave him nothing to go on. "I'm sorry, it's been a long last few days. I didn't catch your name."

"That's because I didn't give it."

"Hello?" the sexy feminine tone came again from the speaker of the burner phone. "Who is this?"

David swallowed and licked his lips. "This is Major David O'Callaghan. I'm with the United States Marine Reserves. I'm currently the police chief in Spencer, Maryland."

"David … O'Callaghan?" There was a pause. "How did you get this number?"

"From Joshua Thornton," David said. "He's in trouble."

Concern flooded her tone. "What kind of trouble, Major?"

"He's been shot."

"How badly?"

"He's been seen by a doctor, but he needs to be hospitalized," he reported. "We have him in a safe house. He's asking that you send his son Murphy to complete his mission."

"He talked to you about the mission?"

"No details," David said. "Look, I'm the chief of police in Spencer—"

"I know exactly who you are, Major O'Callaghan," she interjected. "I will send Lieutenant Murphy Thornton to complete his father's mission. He'll brief you about what you need to know."

"We've met," he said.

Instead of confirming or denying his statement, she replied in a brisk tone. "Lieutenant Murphy Thornton of the United States Navy will be calling you on this phone to coordinate his arrival in Spencer. After he briefs you on the mission, he will be instructed to follow your orders since you are the ranking officer."

"Then this is a military operation?"

"It is a matter of national security," she replied. "Top secret clearance." After a slight pause, she added in a pleasant tone, "It was nice talking to you again, Major."

Click.

CHAPTER NINE

Cameron had mixed feelings about packing up the few files and what little evidence they had collected in the Reginald Crane—or, rather, John Doe—murder case.

Because she hadn't heard anything from Joshua since breakfast, she was desperate to get to Deep Creek Lake to see him. *I hope Donny is okay. If anything was really wrong, he would have called me ... unless Josh told him not to.*

But then, there was something about Special Agent Elder and Black that made her skin crawl. Even so, her supervisor ordered her to turn over the case to the FBI. If Reginald Crane had been a federal agent working deep undercover, it was their case.

The fact that she was creeped out was no excuse for her to fight it.

Cameron welcomed the opportunity to take the stairs down to the forensics office to gather up the physical evidence. While waiting at the reception desk, she wished she had thought to bring her burn phone with her to check to see if Josh had left her a message after she had failed to answer his call. She could have eased her mind during the fifteen-minute wait for the lab personnel to gather the evidence, sort through it, and do up the paperwork for her to sign. By the time they gave her the white evidence box, she was anxious to get to her desk, hand over everything to the creepy FBI guys, and call Joshua with the news that she was on her way.

Maybe I'll even get Tad and Jan to watch Irving and Admiral right away so that I can leave tonight.

Special Agents Black and Elder were waiting at her desk in the squad room. Cameron handed them the box and the forms releasing the case to them. Part of the protocol was for them to write down their badge numbers on the forms as well.

"How does it feel to get invited to the social event of the year?" Special Agent Black asked her while his partner signed his section of the release forms.

"I doubt if I'll be going to the wedding." A split second after saying the words, Cameron wished she hadn't. That was an invitation for a conversation.

"Why not?" Black chuckled. "Your husband is in it."

"I'm not into weddings," she replied. "I'll probably be hitting the slopes or waiting for Josh in the hot tub."

"We've had a couple of cases out at Deep Creek Lake," Black said. "Elder and I were talking about it while you were gone. We were trying to remember the name of the police chief there. Real nice guy …"

"David O'Callaghan," Cameron answered.

"That's right." With a laugh, Black turned to his partner. "We were close. I was saying O'Connell. David O'Callaghan."

Elder's dark eyes narrowed, and he nodded his head. "Wasn't he in the marines?"

"Still in the reserves," Cameron cocked her head at the disdain on his face.

Black was laughing. "Elder here is an army guy."

"Ah, rivalry," Cameron said. "I can understand. But we can't lose touch with the fact that we're all on the same side."

"Very true." Black shoved the box into his partner's arms and turned back to Cameron. "Nice to meet you, Detective Gates." He stuck out his hand. "Have a grand time at the social event of the season. Happy New Year."

When Cameron shook his hand, he grabbed her extended elbow with his hand and squeezed it. She felt that cold sweat wash over her again.

With a grumble, Elder followed his partner out the door. Watching them leave, Cameron had an odd feeling that she had just made a big mistake, even if she had technically done the right thing.

Once they were out of sight, she whirled around to grab her phone and check for a voicemail from Josh. To her dismay, it wasn't in the center of the desk where she had left it. The thin folder that contained Agnes Douglas' background information was still resting in the middle of the desk, but her cell phone was gone.

Dropping down into her chair, Cameron scratched her head and started thinking.

The phone had been ringing. She checked the caller ID, but it had not been Josh. It was a phone number she had not recognized. She had been about to answer it when the lieutenant called her to his office. She had set it in the middle of the desk.

Maybe I only thought I did.

She opened the desk drawer to check her purse. As she was about to dig into it, she saw the phone resting in the top drawer of her inbox.

How did it end up there?

Recalling that she had been carrying the box back from forensics, and that the two agents had been waiting, she realized that they must have moved the phone to the inbox to make room in the middle of the desk for her to set the box down. *Boy, Cameron, you're really getting paranoid. Just because you didn't like those guys—*

David stretched out on the sofa in his office. With his arm, he covered his eyes to block out the dim light from the office—and to block out as many of his thoughts as possible.

David felt like practically everything in the case was spinning around him.

Russell Dooley had made one hundred and twenty thousand dollars disappear—enough money to hire a hit squad to kill Mac. He had sworn to ruin Mac's wedding. Killing him would certainly have done that.

Joshua Thornton was on some top-secret mission that most likely involved terrorists. The attack had all the earmarks of professionals with military training—which was exactly how terrorists or a hit squad for hire would attack.

Who was the target? If we can figure out who the target was, then we can figure out who is behind it.

The ringing of the burn phone sounded unfamiliar. Grasping it, David checked the number, which was also unfamiliar to him.

"David O'Callaghan here," he said into it.

"David, this is Cameron. What's going on? I haven't heard from Josh all afternoon. Is he okay?"

David sat up on the sofa. "He's okay," he lied.

Her voice went up an octave. "Donny?"

"Donny's okay, too," David said. "It's … a hit squad attacked Spencer Manor today while Josh was there."

"Mac? Archie? Was anyone hurt?"

"No one was hurt," David said. "Mac and Josh, and Gnarly, too, got out. They were pros, Cam. No IDs. Burn phones that we can't trace. We don't know who hired them."

"I guess Archie wasn't there," Cameron said.

"She's staying in the penthouse at the Spencer Inn," David said. "But her mother was at the manor when the attack happened. Right now, until we can figure out who is behind this, they're off the grid. We have them stashed in a safe house up here on the mountain."

"Josh has a burn phone."

"You can call him on that," David said, "but I would suggest waiting until morning. They all went through a lot today—"

"They have to have protection."

"We've got a couple of police officers guarding the place," David said.

"I'm coming out there."

"I'm sure you are," he replied.

After working out the details for Cameron's arrival at the Spencer Inn first thing in the morning, David hung up the phone with a sigh.

Now to go to the Spencer Inn to tell Archie, Tristan, and Donny Thornton.

Spencer Inn - Mac Faraday's Private Penthouse Suite

"David, will you stop looking at my hair and tell me what's going on with Mac?" Archie Monday demanded in a tone devoid of any nonsense.

No matter how hard he tried, David O'Callaghan could not tear his attention from the blonde beauty's shorn locks.

For the decade that David O'Callaghan had known Archie Monday—which was longer than Mac had known her—she had worn her light blonde hair in an ultra-short pixie style. With her delicate facial features, high cheekbones, emerald green eyes, and petite build, she had resembled Peter Pan's Tinker Bell.

David was amazed by how a switch in hair color from blonde to midnight black could change a woman's whole appearance—especially when she was mad and frantic with worry.

"Weren't you a blonde last night?" David made the mistake of muttering.

His deputy chief, Art Bogart, cleared his throat. "That's the wrong response, Chief."

Deputy Chief Art Bogart, known as Bogie, may have been sixty-five years old, with gray hair and a bushy mustache to match, but he had the build of a wrestler half his age. More than one young man who had challenged him had ended up eating the floor within seconds.

"I have *always* been a *blonde*," Archie replied. "Where's Mac?"

"There was an incident at the salon," Bogie whispered while rubbing the back of his neck. "She's still a little sensitive about it."

"Actually, *a lot* sensitive," Chelsea Adams added.

David took in Chelsea's naturally platinum locks that fell in soft layers to her shoulders and thanked God that she had opted only for a trim. Laying on the floor next to the kitchen counter, Molly, Chelsea's service dog trained to detect signs of her master's epileptic attacks, appeared to be equally appalled by the change in Archie's appearance.

"Maybe if we put a hat on Archie we can concentrate on Dad and when he can come home." Tristan, Mac's son, said as he pushed his dark-framed glasses up on his nose. "If they killed all of the hit men who came after them, then they should be safe now, shouldn't they?"

"We don't know that for certain," David replied.

Tristan Faraday, who was perched at the counter that divided the penthouse's kitchenette from the dining area, bore only a slight resemblance to his father. With his blond hair, dark-framed eyeglasses, and thick sweater on his tall slender frame, he resembled the stereotype of the intellectual he was. His laptop and tablets were his constant companions. Not to play games, but to keep on top of the latest developments in a host of scientific areas and news. Tristan Faraday was in his third year of undergraduate studies at George Washington University.

One would never guess that the twenty-one-year-old student was a multi-millionaire. Tristan certainly didn't live the lifestyle. He owned a brownstone in Georgetown, which he shared with two fellow students and lifelong friends. A city dweller, he didn't own a car. Except for an occasional beer, he didn't drink and avoided parties. He didn't date—that anyone knew of.

Deputy Chief Art Bogart was sitting in on the meeting in Mac's private penthouse on the top floor of the Spencer Inn to offer his support. He said, "These hit men could very well have been working for a boss guy, who, since they're dead, will send out another squad to finish the job."

"Was it Russell Dooley who hired them?" Archie asked.

David shot a glance in Bogie's direction.

Bogie was as puzzled as David was. Holding up his hands in surrender, he shook his head. "I didn't say a word."

"Bogie didn't have to," Archie said. "I could smell something funny when that man came up to us at the Santa Fe Grill claiming to be a huge Robin Spencer fan and wanting to have his picture taken with me. There was something just not right about him. So," she arched a lovely blonde eyebrow, which did not match her black bangs, "I got his name and ran a background check on him. Mac arrested his wife for murdering her lover, and she killed herself three weeks ago." She pointed a long French manicured finger at the deputy police chief. "That's why Mac sent Bogie to shadow me."

"Actually, I was the one who sent Bogie," David said.

Clint, Archie's oldest brother, said, "Then arrest this Dooley guy, and that will be that. Mac and Mom can come back to the Inn, and we can get this wedding over with." Clint Douglas, a mountain of a man with reddish-brown hair and a thick beard, clutched his only sister's hand. He was pretty big, but compared to Archie he resembled a bear.

"I wish it was that easy," David said with a sad shake of his head. "Russell Dooley is dead."

"Did he commit suicide?" Tristan asked. In response to the cock of David's head, he added, "He's attempted suicide six times since his wife was convicted of murder."

"Where did you learn that?" Archie asked.

"It's in his medical records at George Washington University Hospital," Tristan said.

"Which are classified," David said in a low tone. "You can't search that without a warrant."

"How did you get in to get that information?" Chelsea asked.

His cheeks turning pink, Tristan turned back to his laptop. "It was only a little difficult, but then most medical record sites are."

"I don't think Dooley committed suicide," David said.

"Yeah, he was stabbed twenty-nine times," Bogie said.

"How do you know how many times he was stabbed?" David asked his deputy chief.

"I asked Doc," Bogie said. "Nothing as fancy as what Tristan did. I simply asked and she answered."

David gestured at the people gathered in the suite. "Do any of you have other information that I don't have yet?"

"How badly was Dad shot?" Donny asked. "You said that he's seen a doctor. How bad is it?"

"He's okay," David said. "I want him to go to a hospital, but he's refusing. Mac and Archie's mother are there to take care of him. If it gets more serious, then we're going to bring them in, even if he does object."

Archie gasped. "Mom is there … with Mac … alone?"

"What was Mom doing there?" Clint asked Archie.

"I don't know," she replied. "She was supposed to go to the salon with all of us, but she told Mona that she had a headache and didn't want to go."

"If she was having one of her headaches, why did she go see Mac?" Clint asked.

The question caught David's interest. "That's a good question. Why was she at the manor when she was supposed to be with you and the bridesmaids?"

Archie felt all eyes on her in search of an answer. Unable to come up with one, she shrugged and shook her head. "I've got nothing."

CHAPTER TEN

Istanbul, Turkey - Night

Straddling his black motorcycle in the remote countryside, Second Lieutenant Murphy Thornton, United States Navy, checked the time on his watch. It was 11:56 p.m.

Murphy Thornton did not bare any resemblance to a prestigious navy officer who was little more than a year out of the Naval Academy in Annapolis, Maryland. Instead of a navy uniform, he was clad in black—from his helmet to his slacks to his leather gloves. Even his utility belt on which he wore two sidearms and other tools for his mission were black to conceal him in the darkness of the night.

He sat perched on the bike with a pair of night-vision binoculars parked in front of his blue eyes.

Confident that their terrorist training camp was safe on the Turkish mountainside, the extremist group wasn't on alert. Removed from the hot spots of Syria, Pakistan, Afghanistan, Iran, and Iraq, and under the protection of the Turkish government, they had hoped to escape detection from the United States and Britain.

At least, they had hoped they would.

From what Murphy could see, intelligence had been correct about the training camp being the base of operations for an upcoming attack on a Western target. He had counted two trucks loaded with explosives arriving during the course of the day. Since the arrival of the explosives, the group had doubled their guards around the main building to twelve men armed with automatic weapons.

Murphy checked his watch again. 11:57 p.m.

In less than twenty minutes the warehouse would be blown sky high, the terrorists would be with their black-eyed virgins in their twisted version of heaven, and he'd be down the road on his way to the helicopter transport that would take him out to an aircraft carrier and then back to civilization.

Careful not to make any noise, Murphy eased up off the bike.

His smart phone vibrated on his hip.

Seriously?

Only one person had the number for that phone.

Ducking into the bushes, and careful to keep his voice as low as possible, Murphy answered the phone. "Yes, ma'am."

"Thornton, I need you to come in ASAP," the deep sultry voice said.

"With all due respect, ma'am, you can't pull me out now," Murphy said. "I'm in the middle of an operation."

"This case takes precedent, Lieutenant." His commanding officer's calm smooth tone took on a hint of emotion. "Your father has been shot. You need to get back to the States now."

Murphy swallowed. "Please hold, ma'am?"

Okay, change in plan. Delete stealth. Insert speed.

Careful to hit the hold button so as nit to lose her, Murphy slid down the hill to the camp. With his slender build and the agility that comes from extensive training, he was able to move gracefully without being noticed.

Keeping low, he trotted up to the back of the warehouse and kicked open the door. When he slipped inside, the guard who came around the corner warehouse shelving units was surprised to see an intruder bold enough to make such a brazen attack on such a volatile target. Before the guard could utter a sound, Murphy rolled the tear gas canister in his direction. It went off at his feet.

Murphy then rounded a corner to encounter two guards. Instead of running away, he went into a slide to sweep their feet out from under them. Before either could get up, he took them down. As a fourth guard came running in, Murphy hurdled one of the downed guards and kicked him in the head. With his weapon firing, the guard fell down with a broken neck.

So much for being silent.

Whipping both sidearms from their holsters, Murphy spun around on his heels and shot both of the guards who were scrambling for their automatic weapons to shoot the intruder.

Hearing more guards coming, Murphy didn't have time to wait.

Two more guards came running in.

Murphy was ready.

As they charged through the door, Murphy took one down with a kick to the knee. When his partner paused to determine where the attack had come from, Murphy wrapped the garrote around his neck and silently strangled him.

Around the warehouse, he could hear the remaining guards still trying to determine where the threat was.

Taking the bomb out of his backpack, Murphy yanked off the adhesive on the back, and clamped it to the latest shipment of weapons that were still in their packaging emblazoned with the manufacturer label. The label read:

NOH Bauman Technologies
San Francisco, California
Made in the United States of America

"Well, how about that?" Murphy breathed. With no time to spare, he whipped his cell phone from its case and snapped a picture of the label and barcode on the shipment.

Murphy pressed the button to activate the bomb with the pre-set settings.

The time read 00:02:00.

It immediately started the count down.

He had less than two minutes to get out and down the road.

He then pressed an adhesive label over the slender bomb to conceal it from the guards during their search.

He hid behind the door he had entered through. The guards didn't see him when they ran in. Silently, he slipped out when they broke up to search for the intruder.

He scrambled up the hill, jumped on his motorcycle, and revved the engine.

Kicking up dirt on the trail that ran along the top of the hillside surrounding the camp, the bike raced for the trail leading up to the dirt road that would take him to the meeting point for the military airlift out. As he broke through the bushes, a young man brandishing an automatic assault rifle broke out onto the road.

"Allah!" He aimed the gun directly at Murphy.

It was not a warning to stop or be shot. There was no attempt at mercy.

Without hesitation, Murphy gunned the engine and swung the bike around to crash the rear into the young killer in training. As the terrorist toppled over the back of the bike,

Murphy could sense that he was slightly built—he was not much more than an adolescent.

Hitting the ground, the young man scrambled to get a firmer hold on his rifle to shoot at his enemy, but Murphy was too quick for him. While keeping control of the bike, Murphy kicked him in the head with his boot.

The young man fell flat.

Murphy didn't know if he was still alive or not. He didn't have time to check. With the amount of explosives in the warehouse where he had set the bomb, the kid was going to be dead anyway. If he lived, then there was no telling how many Westerners he'd kill after completing his training.

Whirling the bike back around, Murphy revved the engine and hit the ramp at top speed to take to the air.

The bike was airborne when the bomb detonated.

Murphy could feel the heat and pressure of the blast on his back when the bike hit the road, rear wheel first.

Three miles down the road, Murphy pulled his bike in behind a grove of trees. The sound of sirens and racing vehicles and subsequent explosions caused by the bomb in the warehouse packed with explosives filled the night air.

Murphy checked the time on his phone.

She had been on hold for four minutes and fifty-three seconds.

"What happened to my father, ma'am? Who shot him?" Murphy asked her when he took her off hold. "He's still alive, isn't he?"

"My last report says he's still alive," she replied. "Did you terminate the target?"

"Target terminated." Murphy thumbed the screen on his phone. "I'm sending you a picture from inside the warehouse. It's a label on a shipment of heavy-duty weapons that I just blew."

After a beat, she replied, "Got it ... well, well, well. That explains a few things ... that explains a lot of things."

"What kind of things?" Murphy asked, even though he suspected he knew the answer.

"Agendas, Lieutenant," she replied in a husky voice. "When you put people with agendas in positions of leadership to make life and death decisions, Americans die. That's why our country needs Phantoms." A smile came to her voice. "Thank you for taking this picture. You did well, Lieutenant. Now come home."

Murphy checked the supplies on his utility belt. "So I'm coming home to go on emergency leave?"

"No, Lieutenant, you're coming home to go on your next assignment," she said. "You need to find your father, bring him in safely, and complete his mission for him."

"Complete his mission?" Murphy asked. "My father is retired, ma'am."

A sexy laugh came from the other end of the line. "Lieutenant, once you're a Phantom, you're *always* a Phantom."

PART TWO

Two Days to Forever
Friday, December 30

Chapter Eleven

Shortly After Midnight

"You should be asleep." With her hands on her hips, Agnes stood beside the bed where Joshua Thornton was vacillating between trying to sleep to keep his strength up and staying awake in case they were attacked.

The two police officers that David had sent had checked in. They were taking turns patrolling outside in the blustery, snowy night, and making the rounds of the doors and windows inside the cabin.

"You didn't eat your dinner either. When was the last time you ate?" Agnes asked him.

"Breakfast," Joshua said. "I'm not hungry." He pushed up from the pillows, and with effort he tried to sit up, only to find the old woman pushing him back down onto the bed.

"Doc said for you to stay in bed."

"I need to go to the bathroom."

She reached under the bed and plopped an old dusty bedpan onto the mattress next to his leg.

"No way." With all the strength he had, Joshua pushed her away and climbed out of the bed.

"Mac," Agnes called out, "we need you."

Thinking that Joshua was having an attack of some sort, Mac came running down the hall. He threw open the door as Joshua was going out. "What's going on?"

"I have to go to the bathroom." Holding himself up against the wall, Joshua pushed by him to go out into the hall.

Agnes threw up her arm to point at Joshua. "Help him, Mac!" she ordered.

Mac turned to Joshua, who had opened the door and was shuffling into the bathroom. "Do you need help?"

"No, I've got this covered."

Mac turned back to Agnes. "He's got it covered."

"A lot of help you are," she grumbled.

"There are certain things that men insist on doing themselves," Mac said. "It's a matter of pride. Think about how you feel about Gnarly shadowing you. Josh is probably feeling the same way. Just let him get some sleep, and he should be ready to go tomorrow." He went back down the hall to the great room.

"Go where?" Agnes asked with her hands on her hips.

"Hopefully back to the hotel."

The safe house had three bedrooms, but Mac chose to sleep on the sofa in front of the door. It may have been called a safe house, but it certainly had not been built with the intention of being one. The heavy woods surrounding the house served as a double-edged sword. While they concealed the house from the road a quarter a mile away, and were thick enough to provide some camouflage from the air, they also provided cover for any threats making its way toward the house.

The great room alone had three doors. Why one room would have three doors, Mac did not know. The front door led into the living room. The back door led to the small porch and the wood pile at the edge of the woods. There was also a side door directly across from the hallway leading back to the bedrooms between the dining area and the living room.

The two officers and Mac had to watch them all.

At the insistence of the two officers, Mac allowed himself to finally doze off long enough to worry about how Archie was handling the situation. This week was supposed to be the happiest days of their lives—filled with the excitement of their big wedding day—and here they were, separated by what? Whom?

The wind whistled outside.

"That snow is really coming down now," Mac heard one of the officers say to the other.

Mac felt a cold paw on his hand. Stirring, he turned his head in the direction of the whine, which was accompanied by claws scratching the top of his hand. Mac opened his eyes slightly. Through the fog of sleepiness, he could make out the tall dark ears trimmed in bronze, the black face, the almond-shaped brown eyes, and the white square covering his black snout.

Mac blinked until his vision cleared.

What? Is he ... seriously?

Gnarly whined and pawed at Mac again to ask for help.

"Agnes?" Mac sat up. "Really? You put a facemask on my dog?"

Agnes came out of the bedroom to announce, "That filthy beast won't stop breathing on Josh."

Gnarly hung his head.

Unable to take it, Mac slipped the mask off and tossed it on the floor. In a gesture of thanks, Gnarly climbed up onto the sofa and buried his head under Mac's arm. "I know. No one appreciates you anymore. I do, buddy." Laying back down, Mac drifted off to sleep with Gnarly stretched out next to him.

Listening to Agnes continue her talk of Gnarly being a breeding ground for germs that would kill him, Joshua laid back against the pillows in his bed with a sigh. His thoughts gradually turned to his grandmother, who had passed away two decades before.

What a feisty woman. She would have liked Cameron.

"Are you asleep?" Agnes' whisper next to his ear startled him out of the sleep he had started to drift into.

"Not anymore." Recalling how his grandmother used to do the same thing to him when he was sick, a smile came to his lips. "It's hard getting out of the caretaking mode once you're dragged into it, isn't it, Agnes?"

With a weary sigh, she plopped down into the chair next to his bed. "I think I could adapt to being a lone wolf very easily."

"Wanna bet?" He struggled to sit up. Seeing that it was too hard, he dropped back down. "I have five children. Their mother died when Donny was only ten years old."

He saw Agnes' demeanor soften. "They were older than my batch."

"Still needed me, full time," he explained. "So I retired from the navy, moved them all back to the small town where I had grown up and had family for emotional support, and became the county prosecutor." He sighed. "Now four of them are grown and gone. But it's hard to quit being the care-taker ... it's like ..." His eyes met hers. "If your role in the re-lationship is not that of caretaker, of the protector, then what role do you have?"

They stared at each other in silence.

"My grandmother was one smart cookie," he said in a light tone. "She raised me after my parents died in a car accident. As soon as I was old enough to make decisions, she insisted on my making them myself—and paying the consequences for my own mistakes. When I went off to the Naval Academy, she welcomed her freedom with open arms. Started bowling, working at the library. She said that she was done taking care of others. Now it was her turn to be taken care of." A note of sadness came to his tone. "Unfortunately, she died before that could really happen."

A shadow moved on the wall behind her. Clutching the gun he had hidden under his blanket, Joshua turned to see Mac's reflection in the mirror. He was listening in the hallway.

"I guess," Joshua said, in a quiet tone, "it's hard for some people to adjust to taking on new roles after a lifetime of playing a particular one."

He saw that Agnes was staring across the room with wide eyes. "Agnes …" Placing his hand on hers, he broke her from her stare. He smiled softly at her. "Can you do me a favor?"

"What would you like, Joshua?" Her voice sounded choked.

Joshua jerked his head to the water glass on the bed stand. It was three-fourths full. "Can you get me some fresh water, please?"

A smile came to her thin wrinkled lips. "Of course, Joshua."

David pulled the white comforter that covered the king-sized bed up to his chin and shivered. Donny had the suite's temperature set at seventy degrees, but David didn't think it felt that warm. A cold chill washing over him, he concluded that it was a combination of the unsettling howl of the wind outside, sleeping in a strange bed, and adrenaline.

His nerves on edge, he was sitting straight up in the bed and reaching for his gun on the nightstand when he heard footsteps outside his bedroom door.

It wasn't actually *his* door—he was in Joshua Thornton's bedroom in the suite that Mac and Archie had reserved for him and Donny. Mac and Archie had reserved suites for every member of the wedding party. In hopes that Cameron would attend with her husband, they had reserved a two-bedroom suite. Donny had his own bedroom.

Upon arriving at the hotel to stay with Donny, David had taken Joshua's room. If David had gone by regulations, he would have called children's services. But, knowing Joshua, David vowed that the circumstances would be easier if Donny was with a friend of his father's rather than a stranger—even if David had not met Donny until Hector had introduced them in the lobby.

When David heard the television turn on, he climbed out of the bed, slipped into the hotel bathrobe hanging in the closet, and went out into the sitting room where he found Donny slumped on the sofa with his feet propped up on the coffee table. He was channel surfing.

"You should try to get some sleep," David said.

"Can't."

David sat down in the chair across from him. "Your dad is going to be fine. This time tomorrow, he'll be back here."

Donny glanced over at him. "You don't know that."

David peered over at the teenager. In many ways, Donny was not an average teenager. He was taller and more muscular than Joshua. David had to remind himself that while he looked like a grown man, he was still a child on the verge of becoming a man. In less than two years, he could be overseas fighting for his country.

"My dad was an officer in the navy," Donny said. "I was really young when he retired, but I still remember hearing about the stuff that he'd get into. Even now, as a prosecutor. So I know the score. One day, he's going to leave home to go do something to help someone, and he's not going to come back." He shrugged. "He'll be gone." His attempt to cover up his emotion failed. Swallowing, Donny resumed surfing.

"I know how you feel, Donny," David said.

"My dad isn't like other dads," Donny said. "When he was in the navy, he prosecuted some heavy-duty dirt bags. We moved to Chester because Dad wanted us kids to have a normal life, but that didn't happen. My dad busted a preacher moonlighting as a major drug lord. He had committed a whole string of murders going back over fifty years. From then on, Dad was a prosecutor, and if there's a murder mystery out there, somehow, some way, he gets pulled into it." He shook his head. "I have a lot of friends, and none of their dads exposed a senator for being a serial rapist." He concluded, "So don't tell me you know how I feel, because unless your dad busted killers for a living, you don't."

David leaned forward and placed his elbows on his knees. A sly grin crossed his face. "Donny, I do know how you feel, because my dad busted killers for a living. He was Spencer's Chief of Police for over thirty years."

Donny stopped channel surfing. He looked directly at David. "Seriously?"

"Seriously," David said. "I don't know how many nights he'd get a call and leave home, and I'd know it was something bad, and all I could do was pray that he'd be okay. As a child, I felt helpless and scared. By the time I was your age, I felt like there had to be something that I could or should do to help him—but I had no idea what."

"Is your dad ..."

"He passed away several years ago," David said in a quiet voice before adding, "He didn't die on the job. He had cancer."

"I'm sorry."

"But my dad did what he loved to do," David said. "The same as your father, and Mac, and Cameron, and me. We do this type of work because it's important that people stand up and uphold the law, no matter what the cost—even if that cost may be our lives."

"Yeah, I know." Donny swallowed.

David reached across for Donny's hand. "Your dad's going to be fine. You're going to be fine. I called your brother Murphy's CO, and he's on his way."

"Why?" Donny asked.

"Your father asked that I send for him."

Sensing something more, Donny yanked his hand away and shot a glare that demanded the truth be told. "What does the navy have to do with this?"

"Nothing," David lied. "It's just that your dad wanted Murphy to come take care of you."

"Cameron is closer than Murphy. Why didn't you call her?"

"Cameron is working on a murder case right now," David said, "but she'll be here tomorrow morning."

Donny wasn't buying the explanation. Before the teen-ager could fire off another question, David shifted the conversation in another direction. "I imagine that since your brothers and sisters live away from home, you have more time to spend with your father. What do you two like to do?"

After a beat during which Donny studied him with narrow eyes that were piercing blue and in contrast to his dark auburn hair, he answered, "Dad likes to fish."

"We have some great fishing here on Deep Creek Lake."

"We go fishing at Tomlinson Run Park," Donny said.

"So you like fishing?"

"Not really," Donny said. "But I like going with Dad. The fishing is boring, but what I really like is that we talk about a lot of stuff. I really have him one on one then, and he'll tell some really great stories." His expression changed to sad. "Dad's got lots of stories."

"And I bet he'll have a great story to tell you after this is over," David assured him.

"Did your dad take you fishing?"

"Always," David said. "He loved to fish. That was his thing." He offered a weak grin. "I was like you. I wasn't crazy about the fishing, but I liked going with him. But not all of the conversations were that great. He'd take me fishing when he wanted to talk about something serious and really wanted my attention."

"Like what kind of things," Donny asked, "would he take you fishing to grill you about?"

"Girls," David said. "I've had a lot of girlfriends."

"Lucky you!" Donny said with a wide grin.

"Not really," David said. "I've gotten into trouble more than once because of my weakness for the wrong type of woman."

"Isn't Chelsea Adams, one of the bridesmaids, your girlfriend?"

"Yes."

"So is she trouble like the women your father warned you about?"

"No," David said.

Donny refused to let up. "Then what type of women did your dad want to talk to you about?"

David tried to think of how to change the subject.

Donny continued peering at him with the same probing eyes that his father, a lawyer, used to force the answer to a question.

"It's private," David finally said.

"Did it have anything to do with Robin Spencer?"

David looked at Donny, who was gazing back at him with an expression of complete curiosity. Not malevolent, but totally innocent curiosity. "Why would my father talk to me about Robin Spencer?"

"She was a big famous author," Donny said. "She had Mac Faraday back when she was a teenager and put him up for adoption. So, since Dad and Cameron became friends with him, I asked who Mac Faraday's father was or if he had ever met him. They didn't know. So I decided to go hunting, and I found on one of those gossip websites where this Internet journalist speculated that it was the police chief of Spencer, Maryland, back before he was police chief. He was a couple of years older than Robin Spencer. I mean, like, he was legal age, and she was only sixteen years old when he got her pregnant. The blogger said that it was legally statutory rape. How ironic that he raped Robin Spencer and then became the chief of police."

"Dad was not a rapist," David said in a firm tone.

"So Mac Faraday *is* really your brother!" Now Donny was grinning. "That's so cool."

Befuddled by how easily Donny had drawn the family secret from him, David murmured, "I guess so."

"And he invited you to be a groomsman at his wedding," Donny said. "I guess he knows you two are brothers and you two are both okay with it? I mean, obviously, you two are friends."

"We would prefer that you don't go spreading that around, Donny," David said.

"Sure, I'll be cool about it." Donny sat back on the sofa and tucked his legs under him. "It's weird, really."

"Not really."

Once again, Donny's expression was sad. "Think about it. You grew up with your dad. You went fishing with him.

You really spent time with him. And now, you have taken his place as chief of police. I bet he taught you a lot."

"Yes, he did." David wondered where Donny was going.

"And then, Robin Spencer dies and leaves this huge fortune, everything, to Mac Faraday, your brother, who was put up for adoption as soon as he was born." Donny cocked his head at him. "Mac Faraday can do and have anything he wants, except one thing." Donny held up his finger to show David.

"What?"

"Spend time with his father, which you got to do. Don't you see? He got the fame and fortune, but you got his dad. And that's something he can never buy, no matter how rich he is." Pleased with himself for his observation, Donny fell back onto the sofa and shook his head. "Makes you wonder who the rich man really is."

Chapter Twelve

"Shouldn't you be breaking out your high heels and dancing down south to Deep Creek Lake?" Lieutenant Dugan almost spilt his coffee when he arrived at the police station to see Detective Cameron Gates at her desk.

"I don't wear high heels," she said with a moan. "Josh's cousin Tad and his wife are visiting her mother in Florida. They took the baby. When they fly in later on this morning, I'll go hand over Irving and Admiral and get on the road. I should be there by early afternoon."

"Josh's big ole dog can't babysit your psycho cat until this afternoon?"

Cameron flicked her eyes from the computer monitor to her chief and then back again. "I'm usually a better liar, but that is true. Tad and Jan won't be back until later, but Admiral has become pretty good at keeping Irving in line."

Dugan crossed his arms. "What's up, Gates? Is it this whole wedding thing? Josh will be cool about you waiting back in the room wearing nothing but a smile while he's doing his groomsman's thing."

Ignoring his comment, she asked, "Did you check out those two FBI guys?"

"You mean Black and Elder?" Dugan scoffed. "Is that what this is about? You've got a stick up your craw because that agent made a pass at you. So now you want to play junk-yard dog and keep the Crane case for yourself ... even if it means missing out on an all-expenses paid vacation?"

"Something is not right about those two," Cameron said.

"If something is not right, it's you and your territorial ways, Gates." Dugan leaned over and placed his hands on her desk. "Yes, I checked them out. I logged into the same FBI database that I always do to confirm their IDs and their badge numbers. It's a match. They are Special Agents Black and Elder."

Unintimidated, she asked, "Photo IDs?"

"Their photos popped right up," Dugan said. "They are FBI, and they staked their claim on this case." He pushed up from the desk. "Now go be with your husband."

Cameron stood up and took her coat from where she had it slung across the back of her chair. "Right after I go talk to Agnes Douglas."

Dugan called after her on her way out the door. "Then you are officially on leave. I don't want to see your face back in this office until Tuesday morning!" With a roll of his eyes, the lieutenant stomped back into his office and slammed the door.

It's over.

Jessica Faraday repeated the statement in her head over and over again until she could visualize herself saying those words to Colt Fitzgerald.

"It's over?" His dark brown eyes would get big and round in confusion. How could she, Jessica Faraday, dump him, Colt Fitzgerald, former underwear model and television star lusted after by sex-crazed women everywhere? "What are you talking about?"

The vision was so clear that she almost lost sight of the interstate on which she was speeding toward Deep Creek Lake.

The thought of Spencer Manor turned her thoughts from her soon-to-be-ex-boyfriend to her father and the tearful phone call she had received from Archie.

Dad has to be okay. Of course he's okay. He's a rock. He can out-think and out-maneuver anyone he's up against. He's been cornered by cold-blooded killers and has walked away without a scratch. He'll certainly get through this and make it to the church in time for the wedding.

In search of comfort, she reached across the driver's compartment of her purple Ferrari 458 Spider for her constant companion in the passenger seat. Spencer. Jessica had named the Shetland sheepdog after the grandmother she had never met, Robin Spencer.

She had been in her second year of college and on the verge of dropping out due to financial difficulties when she was informed of her multi-million dollar inheritance.

Like Cinderella, the penniless college student had become the lovely heiress overnight. She was the only granddaughter of Robin Spencer, and the daughter of that brilliant retired homicide detective Mac Faraday. Suddenly, she received party invitations from people she didn't know … but didn't mind meeting.

The pursuing of her by dashing young men had increased in the last year after her father had been approached by a Hollywood producer seeking the movie rights for three Mickey Forsythe movies that would feature Robin Spencer's most famous literary detective.

After over a year of negotiations, Mac Faraday had signed the deal for an obscene amount of money. Contrary to how they do things in Hollywood, the producer had agreed to give Mac Faraday script and cast approval, which had opened the doors for unknown actors vying for the role of Mickey Forsythe in the big budget movie series.

How better to get to the father for an audition than through his daughter? Twenty years earlier, the last series of Mickey Forsythe movies had made a star of an unknown actor who had actually won an Academy Award.

Jessica half-believed some of the men chasing her sincerely wanted to be with the beauty with striking eyes that were the same violet hue as her grandmother's. Jessica's slender figure had curves in all the right places. That, combined with her long legs and biting wit, had made her a socialite in no time. Her busy social schedule made it a miracle that she was able to graduate at the top of her class from William and Mary University with a masters in behavioral and cognitive neuroscience.

Jessica Faraday had the luxury of learning first hand that life in high society can get old fast. It got old especially fast when she was sitting across the table in a five-star restaurant with a fame-obsessed actor tweeting about having dinner with Mac Faraday's daughter while his publicist was paying paparazzi to snap their picture to post on celebrity blogs.

Four months after inviting her then-boyfriend to her father's wedding, Jessica looked forward to a weekend with Colt Fitzgerald as much as she looked forward to having her impacted wisdom teeth extracted after the holiday wedding. According to "unnamed sources" across the Internet, the couple were head over heels in love. It was not hard for Jessica to deduct who the infamous "unnamed source" was.

By the time she got Archie's tearful call, Jessica welcomed the excuse to escape to go to Deep Creek Lake ahead of her planned arrival. Less than an hour later, she had tossed her suitcase into the trunk and plopped Spencer in the front passenger seat. With a wicked grin, she sent a text to her best friend, Penny.

"Wake Colt up. Tell him my father needs me. I'll C U 2 later."

That should be good for causing some high anxiety between the little cheaters.

If she cared, Jessica would have been upset about her best friend sleeping with her boyfriend. Instead, Jessica was relieved to know that when she dumped Colt, he would have someone else's arms to fall into.

If I'm lucky, he'll dump me before the wedding. Jessica sighed. *I should be so lucky. As long as the role of Mickey Forsythe isn't cast, Colt Fitzgerald will be hanging onto me for all its worth.*

When it came to relationships, Jessica Faraday felt like a woman dying of thirst in an ocean. *Water, water everywhere, but not one drop to drink.*

"What I wouldn't give for a man of substance." With one hand, she stroked the top of Spencer's head. "Someone with enough brains that I can have a conversation with him about something other than *his* tight butt and his ranking on the A list." With a shrug, she grinned. "But do I really have to give up the sexy butt, too?" She sighed. "I am spoiled, aren't I? I just can't give up having my beefcake and eating it, too."

Like her master, Spencer had descended from a long line of blue bloods. The champion Shetland sheepdog was called a blue-merle. Her lush black and white coat had a dusting of long white fur that created a white filmy effect over the black spots. The overall result was a bluish cast to her coat. Her blue eyes made her as striking as her master.

At nine months old, Spencer had the disposition of a toddler. Riding in the passenger seat, Spencer sat up with her paws on the door, peering out at the passing scenery.

Occasionally, when something caught her attention, she would yap her high-pitched bark. It was almost as if she sensed that she was on her way to see her "Uncle Gnarly," as Jessica had come to dub her father's German shepherd. Surprisingly, Spencer was such a bundle of energy that she exhausted even Gnarly with her antics.

When Jessica had visited at Christmas, Spencer had nipped at Gnarly's back legs so much that the German shepherd had resorted to hiding under Mac's bed to escape the young pup, who stood guard at the edge of the bed and barked at him non-stop in a plea for him to come out to play.

Jessica felt a pang in her heart thinking about Gnarly. *He's with Dad. I hope he's okay.* No matter how much Mac denied it, he loved Gnarly. David O'Callaghan referred to him as Mac's partner.

After driving through Cumberland, Maryland, Jessica eased her Ferrari convertible onto Interstate 68 to head toward Deep Creek Lake, Maryland. She had to tap the brakes to keep from skidding on black ice, which was a serious threat during the winter morning hours. Traveling up and down the mountain roads in the freezing weather was dangerous.

A check of the gas gauge told her that she was running low on gas.

"You probably need a bathroom break," she told Spencer, who turned from the passenger side window. The pup's ears perked up and she wagged her tail.

"Okay," Jessica said. "We'll stop at the truck stop in Grantsville to fill up and let you stretch your little legs."

The thought of a bathroom break made Jessica's body remember the extra-large coffee she had drunk after filling up her gas tank shortly after leaving Williamsburg. Anxious about her father, she hadn't eaten breakfast, and it was almost lunchtime.

167

When Jessica got to Grantsville, she left Spencer strapped in the passenger seat while she raced into the truck stop and rounded the corner to the restaurant section. *Spencer's just going to have to wait. She doesn't have a pot of coffee sitting on her bladder.*

The truck stop smelled of burgers on the griddle and fries in the deep fryer. Many of the tables were filled with drivers who had stopped to gas up their rigs and chow down before continuing east or west across the mountains.

A middle-aged woman in a server's uniform carrying a full coffee pot shot Jessica a grin. "Looking for the ladies' room, honey?" The name plate she wore clipped to her bosom read "Madge."

The burly and rough-looking truck driver dressed in a hunting jacket who she was serving chuckled. They weren't the only two to do a double take upon Jessica's entrance.

Among the men dressed in heavy, worn driving clothes and gear, Jessica Faraday looked out of place in her brown suede ensemble. Her ankle-length skirt revealed her high-heeled brown suede boots. The ensemble was topped off with a fitted winter jacket that showed off her trim waist, which also served to accentuate her abundant bosom encased in a light brown fitted sweater with a plunging V-neck.

Clearly the best dressed customer in the restaurant, Jessica was accustomed to attracting attention when entering a room. Accentuated by her thick raven-black hair that fell in a single wave to touch her shoulders, Jessica's striking violet eyes grabbed attention not only from men, but also from women.

As a child, Jessica had been teased by cruel classmates for her odd-colored eyes, and she had called her mother a liar when she tried to console her by saying that one day she would love the striking color. Jessica's violet eyes were one more blessing from Robin Spencer. Now, she proudly accentuated them with her dark hair and cool-colored clothes.

Madge pointed to a small hallway off to Jessica's left. The sign overhead read "Restrooms."

With a quick 'thank you,' Jessica practically ran down the hallway and through the door on the right that had a sign with a silhouette of a stick figure wearing a shirt. All four stalls were empty.

I guess trucking is still a men's world.

She rushed into the corner stall and hung her handbag on the hook inside the door. After finishing, flushing, and redressing, she heard the door opening and the heavy footsteps of more than one person entering.

The stall door next to hers swung open, but no one entered.

Peering through the crack between the door and the stall's panel, she saw two men waiting outside her stall. They were clad in dark heavy clothes and leather jackets. A police officer's daughter, she recognized the bulge under one of their coats.

Shoulder holster.

She saw the man outside her door motion to the other that she was inside.

This is not good. Not good at all.

Jessica thrust her hand inside the handbag just as the stall door was kicked in.

After grasping the handle of her thirty-eight caliber Colt Mustang Pocketlite, a small handy semi-automatic that she carried inside her bag, she was propelled by the force of the blow back against the far wall of the stall. With both hands gripping the weapon inside her bag, she aimed it, bag and all, at her attacker and pulled the trigger while falling to the floor.

The first man coming through the door took two bullets to the chest before collapsing on top of her and pinning her to the floor with his dead weight.

Struggling to crawl out from under him, Jessica fought to keep hold of the gun in order to fire on the second man, who raced into the stall and dropped down to the floor to press a white cloth against her face.

The sweet scent filling her head, Jessica jerked her head away while he pressed the cloth to her face.

"Get your filthy hands off me!" She delivered a kick with her high-heeled boot to his knee.

"Bitch!" He backhanded her across the face and pressed the cloth hard to her nose and mouth.

Jessica fought to hold her breath while fighting him.

"We need you to deliver a message to your father," she heard as darkness enveloped her.

Murphy Thornton had been on the road on his motorcycle for over two hours. His plan had been to get some sleep after flying in on a military charter from Germany, but he was too keyed up to sleep—especially after his commanding officer told him that his father had been shot and was on the run.

Donny is all alone at that ski resort and doesn't know if Dad is going to make it. Dad has to make it. He's tough. It takes more than a death squad to take out a Thornton. I need to get to Dad. Get him home safely. Kill the slimy devils behind this. And deliver the package, whatever it is, to—oh yeah, and keep Donny with his raging hormones away from the snow bunnies at the Spencer Inn.

As soon as he got back to the states, Murphy had called Donny to see how he was holding up at the Spencer Inn without their father. He felt some relief to learn that Police Chief David O'Callaghan was spending the night in the suite with him.

This Chief O'Callaghan sounds like a nice enough guy. Donny said he was one of the groomsmen in the wedding. Close friends with Mac Faraday. Still, I'll feel better seeing Donny myself and getting the lowdown from O'Callaghan about finding whoever hired that team of hit men. The sooner I get to Dad, the better we will all be.

Murphy pressed on the accelerator to kick up the speed a notch on his black BMW motorcycle.

After more than two hours of riding on his BMW K 1300 sports motorcycle over the mountains, Murphy opted to stop in Grantsville to get a drink of organic orange juice and to hit the men's room.

Nearing noon, the truck stop was littered with semis warming up and drivers milling around. The gumball purple Ferrari 458 Spider sports car with the young sheltie sitting in the passenger seat looked out of place among the men and some women dressed in worn winter clothes shivering in the cold and drinking hot steaming coffee.

"Well, hello, beautiful," Murphy greeted the young dog after taking off his motorcycle helmet and placing it in the traveling compartment on the back of his bike. The sheltie jumped up and planted her front paws on the window. Yapping, she wagged her tail.

Rubbing his rear end, sore after hours of riding his bike, Murphy strolled into the truck stop. The scent of burgers, hot dogs, brats, and greasy fries filled the diner.

Among the truck drivers and travelers waiting for their lunches, Murphy spotted six men in heavy dark coats, black slacks, and military-style combat boots waiting at the entrance to the short hallway, which was marked "Restrooms."

Murphy wasn't the only one who noticed the men. Most of the patrons in the diner were eying them, as was a buxom middle-aged server who was going from table to table filling up coffee mugs.

"Men's room, sweetie?" she called out to him. Before Murphy could answer, she nodded toward the hallway behind the thug barricade.

"Thank you, ma'am," Murphy replied.

The six men eyed the young man when he approached them to go down the hallway.

The silence in the truck stop thickened when the sea of men refused to budge to allow him to pass.

Wordlessly, Murphy returned their glare. After a long moment of silence, he stepped forward into their space. His sheer will parted them to allow him through the barricade.

Moments later, he was washing his hands when he heard two gunshots.

Dropping to his knee, he grabbed the gun from his ankle holster and braced himself at the door. It was best to ascertain what the situation was rather than rush out blindly into a fire-fight. He could tell that the sounds of fighting and screaming were not coming from outside the door or in the diner. They were coming from across the hall in the ladies' restroom.

"What's going on?" Murphy heard one of the truckers demand in a firm tone from out in the diner.

Opening the men's room door a crack, he could see one of the remaining four brutes at the end of the hallway open his coat to show the truck drivers what had to be a weapon. "Everything is fine," the gunman declared. "Go back to your lunch and mind your own business."

The door across the hallway opened. A muscle bound man emerged carrying the unconscious body of a young woman clad in a long skirt and boots.

Murphy closed the door before they could see him. When he stepped from the door, he almost tripped over a bucket with a mop inside.

"Where's Sid?" he heard one of the men ask.

"Dead," another man answered. "She shot him."

"I thought this was supposed to be an easy snatch," the third man replied. "Pampered daddy's girl."

"How was I supposed to know she was packing and not afraid to use it? Let's get out of here before the police show up."

Kidnapping! Murphy thought again.

The diner was littered with drivers and employees. With the young woman and the drivers, there were too many potential hostages and possible victims. He tucked his weapon into waistband behind his back.

Six, now five, of them. All armed. They already have one hostage. I need to free her and take down five armed men without getting anyone hurt.

Placing his hand on the door, Murphy's eyes fell on the mop.

Having heard the shots, every trucker in the diner was looking toward the restrooms when the four thugs guarding the hallway stepped aside to allow their leader, who was carrying Jessica's limp body, to step out.

"What did you do to her?" Madge had to fight to keep from dropping the full fresh pot of coffee that she had just carried in from the kitchen.

"The young lady isn't feeling well," the thug carrying her announced. "She'll be better once we get her out of here."

Those who might have thought of confronting them paused when they saw that all five of them were armed with guns on their belts. Even the two cashiers behind the counter in the restaurant were frozen in fear.

The brutes chuckled at the collected panic.

"Rog-Roger ..." Madge nudged the burly trucker who had chuckled at Jessica when she came in.

"I'm not stupid," Roger said.

"Right answer," the thug carrying Jessica said while nodding in the direction of the door where one of his cohorts had cleared the way for their escape. "We'll be leaving now. If all of you are smart, you'll forget you ever saw us."

Everyone seemed to be holding their breath.

The door at the end of the hallway abruptly opened. Murphy charged out so fast that he resembled a black blur in his black leather chaps and leather jacket. Like a ball player diving for home plate, he slid across the floor, swinging the mop handle to swipe the brute's legs out from under him.

Dropping Jessica, the thug tumbled backwards to the floor. He landed on his back so hard that his breath was knocked out of him.

Roger and another trucker rushed to pull Jessica out of the way of the chaos that followed.

Splashing hot coffee on her hand, Madge slammed the coffee pot on a nearby table to help protect Jessica. Grimacing at burning herself, she pulled out a chair for them to place Jessica in.

The customers took full advantage of Murphy's distraction.

Seizing on the remaining gunmen's surprise, one trucker charged like a linebacker. Lunging right out of his chair, he grabbed the gunman around the middle and drove him backwards into a shelving unit containing chips and other snacks. He was moving so fast that they slid all the way across the floor and body slammed into the wall. Once they stopped, the trucker proceeded to punch the gunman in the face repeatedly until he was unconscious.

One of the clerks behind the counter raced out to grab the weapon that the gunman had dropped and ran back behind the counter to take cover with his coworker.

"Do you even know how to use a gun?" the clerk behind the counter asked the one who had grabbed it.

"No, but as long as *we* have it, *they* can't use it on us."

A trucker who was waiting by the door rammed his full three hundred pounds of muscle into the assailant by the door, causing him to drop his gun. The impact was so powerful that the gunman broke through the glass door and dropped onto his back in the shattered glass. Pulling up his sleeves, the truck driver stepped through the broken door to finish the job.

Murphy didn't stop moving after toppling the first man. With the mop handle still in hand, he jumped to his feet and drove its end into the diaphragm of one gunman. When the gunman doubled over, two truckers descended on him to take him face-down to the floor.

Seeing out of the corner of his eye that the ringleader had recovered enough to make a grab for his weapon, Murphy delivered a kick to his head and sent him flying over a table. As the gunman went down, Roger slugged him in the face to make him stay down before snatching the gun out of his hand.

"Go ahead, punk," Roger said with a growl while aiming the weapon at the unconscious man. "Make my day."

"Roger," Madge pointed out, "he's out cold. He's not going to be making anyone's day for a while."

"What's happening?" As Jessica was coming to, she realized that her head felt numb. Her hands were shaking.

"Looks like some knight has come to rescue the damsel in distress," she heard Madge say. "Some ladies have all the luck."

His gun gone, the last gunman came back up with a hunting knife. He lunged at Murphy who blocked each thrust with the mop handle. Through her blurred vision, Jessica could only see a young man in a black jacket sparring with an ugly brute wielding a knife.

175

"H-help him," she said, but found that her words came out as an unintelligible stutter. She was still feeling the effects of the chloroform that had knocked her out.

Behind her rescuer, the brute who had carried Jessica out of the restroom was climbing to his feet and reaching for the gun in his holster. He had his eye on Murphy.

Spotting a full pot of coffee resting on a table where she was sitting, Jessica grabbed the hot pot with trembling hands. Lunging forward, she poured the whole pot of scalding coffee over the head of the man who had tried to kidnap her. Screaming, he grabbed his burning face and collapsed down to his knees.

His cohort turned at the sound of the scream, which distracted him long enough for Murphy to strike the assailant's wrist with the mop handle. In spite of the pain from the blow, the hoodlum refused to release his weapon.

Murphy was ready to take full advantage of the small window of opportunity Jessica had given him. He grabbed his opponent by the arm and wrapped it around the mop handle. Pinning both the stick and arm against his side, Murphy whirled around into the gunman's body and elbowed him in the nose, breaking it. Then, Murphy hooked his foot behind his opponent's and yanked his feet out from under him.

After the gunman fell to the floor, Murphy stepped on the hand still clutching the knife and pressed the end of the stick against his throat. "Drop it!" he ordered.

The doors at every entrance and exit busted open, and some Maryland State Police Officers came running in with their guns drawn. "Don't anybody move!"

Seeing the rough-looking truckers standing over the downed well-dressed assailants, the police officers paused. "Some of you are under arrest."

CHAPTER THIRTEEN

"Just to be clear," the Maryland State Trooper asked his sergeant, "the scruffy looking ruffians are the good guys ..."

The sergeant nodded his head. "The well-dressed guys are the bad guys, and the rednecks are the good guys. Arrest the suits, and then get the smelly ruffians' statements and send them on their way."

Looking over to the back of an ambulance where an injured gunman was being loaded, the trooper said, "Looks like the bad guys got the worst of it."

The sergeant agreed. "Every call should go down like this."

It was only after the emergency crews had arrived and one of the EMTs had started checking Jessica Faraday for bullet wounds that she realized her clothes were covered in blood. Then she remembered shooting the first attacker and him landing on top of her.

Now her clothes were evidence, and the Maryland state police needed them. A female forensics officer was willing to accompany Jessica to the hospital to be checked over by an emergency room doctor.

Determined to get to Spencer, Maryland, as quickly as possible, Jessica took her suitcase from the Ferrari's trunk.

The manager of the truck stop consented to her and the forensics investigator using his office for Jessica to change out of her bloody clothes. Aware that allowing her dog to accompany her, even if only to offer mutual comfort, would contaminate the evidence she was wearing, Jessica had left Spencer in the front seat of the car.

When Murphy and the state police officer who had taken his statement stepped outside the truck stop restaurant, Murphy heard Spencer whining from where she was waiting in the front seat of the Ferrari. "Hey, beautiful, are you worried about your master?"

"How is she?" the officer who had questioned Murphy asked one of his colleagues. "Which hospital are you taking her to?"

"None," his colleague replied. "Ms. Faraday has refused a hospital examination. She's hell-bent on getting to Spencer, Maryland. She's taking off her clothes in the manager's office for the forensics people to take into evidence."

Hearing the last name, Murphy whirled around to them. "Did you say Faraday?"

"As in Mac Faraday?" the senior officer asked.

"Her first name is Jessica." He shrugged his shoulders. "I guess she could be related to him."

The senior officer regarded Murphy. "Have you met Ms. Faraday before?"

"No," Murphy said. "It's a huge coincidence that those men tried to abduct her when a hit squad tried to off her father just yesterday."

"What are you talking about?" the junior officer asked.

"This guy," the senior officer jerked his thumb in Murphy's direction, "is Murphy Thornton. *His* father is the guy who disappeared along with Faraday yesterday—" He jerked his thumb toward the inside of the truck stop. "*Her* father."

Both officers turned to Murphy, who had opened the passenger door to the Ferrari and was attaching the leash to a squirming Spencer. The sheltie was so grateful that she covered Murphy's face with licks.

"I guess she likes you," the senior officer noted.

"She likes everybody." Murphy set her down. "Come along, Candi. I think you need a break." He led her to a grassy area at the end of the parking lot to allow the pup to squat and pee, something she was very anxious and grateful to do. During the walk across the parking lot, Murphy took a cell phone from the inside pocket of his leather jacket and thumbed a phone number.

The senior officer followed him. "Jessica Faraday is the daughter of a rich man. It was in the news a few months ago that he sold the movie rights for Mickey Forsythe to Holly. The amount was undisclosed, but you know it was several million dollars. That's a lot of motive for someone trying to kidnap her for ransom."

"These guys were organized," Murphy said. "I heard them in the bathroom. They assumed that she was a pampered diva who wouldn't put up a fight. They were quite surprised when she did, but they were prepared."

Murphy held up his finger to motion for the trooper to hold his thoughts. "Chief David O'Callaghan, this is Lieutenant Murphy Thornton. I believe you spoke to my CO last night."

"Yes, Lieutenant," David replied with an edge of irritation in his voice. "What's your ETA?"

Murphy took note of the police chief's tone. The message between the lines was, "I'm in charge of this operation." He followed the police chief's lead. "Forty-five minutes, sir. We've had a complication that you should be aware of, sir. There was an attempted kidnapping here in

Grantsville. The target was Jessica Faraday, Mac Faraday's daughter."

The irritation shifted instantly to worry. "Is Jessie okay?"

"She's fine, sir," Murphy reported. "The kidnappers were thwarted by civilians and are now in police custody. One is dead, shot by Ms. Faraday. Four are on their way to the hospital. One with second- and third-degree burns, attributed to Ms. Faraday. The other has a concussion. Two with multiple broken bones. The sixth is just badly bruised and in a state of great disappointment."

"He's on his way to the state police barracks for processing," the state trooper told Murphy to report, which he did. "All of them are screaming for a lawyer, except the dead guy. None have any identification." After Murphy relayed this information, the trooper grasped his arm. "Tell him about the black van that we saw tearing out of here when we pulled in."

"Chief O'Callaghan," Murphy reported, "the police saw a black van with Washington, DC, plates leaving the truck stop when they arrived. The truck stop does have security cameras and they are checking to identify the van."

"Jessica is a rich woman ..." David said thoughtfully.

"I don't believe this is a coincidence, sir," Murphy told him. "I could tell by how they handled themselves that they had military or law enforcement training. Ms. Faraday is here now, being processed for evidence. I'll await your instructions about how you would like me to proceed, sir."

There was a slight pause from the other end of the line during which Murphy knelt to pet the pup. By the time David replied, all annoyance in his tone had evaporated. "Can you escort Ms. Faraday to Deep Creek Lake, Lieutenant?"

Out of the corner of his eye, Murphy saw the entrance doors open across the parking lot. A uniformed state trooper wheeled out an oversized suitcase and held the door open for the raven-haired beauty to exit.

In the heat of the abduction, Murphy hadn't had time to get a clear look at the woman being carried out of the restroom. But now, after his heartbeat had slowed down to normal, the sight of her slender figure clad in black faux leather pants with over-the-knee black boots that revealed long, shapely legs, Murphy felt his heartbeat kick up until it was roaring in his ears. The top half of her lovely body was clad in a loose-fitting purple sweater with a plunging V-neckline.

"Lieutenant Thornton?" David's voice came across the line again. "Are you still there? Can you stay with Jessica Faraday to make sure she is safe and personally deliver her to me at the police station here in Spencer?"

"No problem, sir," Murphy said while taking in her silky alabaster skin. "It would be my honor."

Through it all, she did not lose sight of her knight. More than one trucker, a server, and even the clerks behind the counter made sure she knew that she owed her life to the guy in the black leather jacket and chaps who knew how to swing a mop handle like a pro.

Well, I wasn't completely helpless. I did take out two of them.

The kidnappers who were in a condition to speak refused to talk, except to say they wanted a lawyer. But they had said enough to her.

We need you to deliver a message to your father. Jessica recalled the one saying. *This has to do with Dad. I need to find Dad.*

"Ma'am," one of the state troopers stopped her when she stepped out of the manager's office after dressing in fresh clothes from her suitcase. "I thought you might like to meet the gentleman who saved you." He took the handle of her suitcase to wheel it out for her.

Having acquired friends who lived in a variety of places, Jessica had learned how to pack. With her clothes ruined by the blood, she made an easy change. Seemingly unaware of how the sweater and leather pants hugged every slender curve of her body, Jessica followed the trooper through the truck stop and out the front door into the snowy weather.

How she wished she hadn't gotten evidence on her coat. *Note to self—pack two winter coats next time.*

Jessica stepped outside to see the most dashing smile she had ever seen. He held out his hand from where he was holding her dog. Jessica felt the blood rushing in her ears while he stared at her with blue eyes that sparkled like sapphire jewels.

The state trooper cleared his throat. "His name is Murphy Thornton. He's an officer in the navy."

Murphy continued to stare at her.

The senior trooper said, "And her name is Jessica Faraday."

Blinking, Murphy stuck out his hand. "I'm Murphy Thornton."

"I already told her that," the trooper whispered.

Before Jessica could take Murphy's hand, Spencer proceeded to lick his fingers and wag her whole body. He patted Spencer on the head.

"Th-thornton?" she stuttered out. She stopped to swallow. "I'm sorry, I'm still lightheaded from the chloroform."

"I understand." He reached around Spencer to take her hand. "Your father is Mac Faraday?"

"Y-yes," she said through chattering teeth.

Murphy glanced around to the man with the knife who was being loaded into the back of a police car. "I don't want to frighten you, but these guys were not your average kidnappers of opportunity. I know your father is missing. Mine is, too. My dad is Joshua Thornton."

Jessica gazed up at him. "Our fathers are friends," she said in barely a whisper.

He gazed into her deep violet eyes. He had to fight to keep from being pulled into the desire he felt as he gazed at her lovely face, framed by raven waves and her alabaster skin. He was dying to touch it.

He had to concentrate on the matter at hand. Here was Mac Faraday's daughter, and whoever was chasing their fathers had gone after her.

Why?

"Why do you have my dog?" she asked him, interrupting his attempt to take his focus off her gorgeous violet eyes.

"Candi needed a bathroom break," he replied.

"Her name is Spencer," she said.

"I call her Candi." He stroked the sheltie's head while she continued to lick his jaw.

She took her dog back into her arms. "You *renamed* my dog?" To her surprise, Spencer struggled against her.

"Because she reminds me of a girl I knew in high school," he replied with a crooked grin. "She liked to kiss all the guys, too."

With dimples in both cheeks, his smile is as sexy as his eyes. A shiver ran through her that made her feel weak in her knees.

"You must be freezing," she heard him say. Before she knew it, his leather jacket was draped across her shoulders. She became lost in his blue eyes when he stood before her to pull the collar together in the front to block the cold wind.

"Feel better now?" He flashed that killer smile at her.

"Totally," she murmured.

Taking her by the shoulders, he stepped in close to her. "You and I are going to be close friends." She took in the warmth of his hand on her elbow while he led her to her car.

"I'll drive you to Spencer." He held open the passenger door and eased her into the seat with the care of someone handling a delicate piece of glass. Once she was sitting in the car with Spencer in her lap, he knelt in front of her.

What's he doing? Proposing? I wish.

To her surprise, he gently lifted her feet from where they rested outside the car and placed them inside.

"What about your car?" she asked.

He gestured at the black BMW motorcycle parked next to her sports car. "I'll send someone to pick it up." He went around to the travel compartment at the rear of the bike, opened it, and took out a black canvas bag, which he tossed behind the driver's seat of her Ferrari.

"That's all you've got?" She noted how easily he tossed his bag around while her suitcase practically filled the whole car trunk.

"I travel light." He knelt down beside where she was sitting in the passenger seat of her car. "I'm going inside to see if I can get your keys and wallet from the crime scene investigators."

"Don't bother with the purse," she said. "I shot out the bottom of it. I've only had that Chanel handbag one month. I bought it for an obscenely low discount on Cyber Monday."

"Better your purse takes two bullets than you." Murphy laid his hand on hers. His touch sent a wave of warmth through her body that instantly comforted her.

"You're absolutely right."

His eyes met hers. She didn't know or care how long he held her gaze. It felt as if her problems—and the problem of their missing fathers—were somewhere far away in the background. At the moment, it was only the two of them.

He abruptly released his hold on her hand to break the wonderful spell and stood up. "Well, I'll go inside to see if they'll release your keys and wallet so you won't be completely handicapped." He flashed her that brilliant smile filled with white teeth and partnered with twinkling blue eyes.

She grasped his hand before he could step away. "If they'll let you do that, then can you convince them to release my compact and lipstick?"

"I'll ask. No guarantees."

He turned away only to find her grasping his hand again with slender soft fingers tipped in fingernails that had been designed with white snowflakes dancing over a sky-blue background. "Can you get my cell phone, too? I have my life on that phone."

"I don't know if they'll let me take that, but I'll ask them."

"Can you please ask?" Her violet eyes were pleading.

Murphy felt a pang in his heart. *Oh yeah, I'd kill if I had to just to kiss those lips of yours, lady.* "Sure, buttercup, anything you ask."

Buttercup? She melted. *He called me buttercup. Certainly a term of endearment.*

"Anything else?" he asked.

"How about a café mocha with double cream and sugar?"

"Is that in your purse, too?"

"No, but they sell it inside, and that's what I had stopped here for in the first place. That and gas."

"I don't think they have gas inside," he replied.

"At the pump, silly. We need to stop for gas before we leave."

"You got it, buttercup." Touching the tip of her nose, he flashed her a grin and went inside.

With a deep sigh, she watched him walk away into the truck stop to retrieve her keys. The rear view was just as impressive as the front. When Spencer whined at his departure, she hugged her pup tightly. "Don't worry, Spencer. He'll be back."

185

Brave, handsome, and gentlemanly to boot. Oh, yeah, I'm going to stick to you like glue, Mr. Murphy Thornton.

The emotions were crashing through her body like waves. She was shaking because of the cold and the fear. Yet the comforting warmth of where he had placed his hand on her elbow washed away her anxiety.

To Jessica's pleasure, he had returned with everything that she had asked for, including the café mocha coffee with double cream and sugar and her cell phone, which had all been photographed and processed by the police. They were kind enough to drop the contents of her purse into freezer bags for her to carry them in. Each item, including her Lancôme cosmetics, still had fingerprint powder on them.

Murphy gassed up the Ferrari and backed out of the space to fall in behind a Maryland State cruiser. A second cruiser fell in behind the Ferrari, and the small convoy pulled out of the truck stop parking lot and onto the freeway. Jessica waited until they were on the freeway before asking him why he hadn't gotten any coffee for himself.

Murphy cringed before glancing over in her direction. "I don't drink coffee. But thanks for asking."

"Tea drinker, huh?" she asked before taking a cautious sip of the hot coffee while being careful not to spill any on Spencer, who had laid down in her lap. The dog was gazing in total adoration at Murphy in the driver's seat.

"Herbal tea." Murphy paused before adding, "I'm a vegetarian. I do eat fish, but—"

"Coffee isn't meat."

"It's the caffeine, buttercup," he explained. "I also don't eat dairy or eggs. Occasionally I will eat cheese, but generally, I'm a pescetarian." He sighed. "You're going to think I'm weird."

"You saved my life, darling," she said. "How could I think you're weird?"

Murphy said, "Normal people don't go after half a dozen armed kidnappers."

"I'm glad you did," she said. "Though I should note that I killed one, and I did save you from the guy who was about to pull his gun on you by dumping the hot coffee on him."

"Which proves coffee can be hazardous to your health." Murphy shot her a broad smile.

She tried not to melt in front of him at the sight of his dimples.

"So where was Colt Fitzgerald while you were being kidnapped?"

"You checked me out on your smartphone while you were inside the truck stop." She fought the blush coming to her cheeks. "He's not my boyfriend."

"That's not what he says on Twitter. He is *so* looking forward to being your date for your father's wedding. Sounds to me like you're dating, buttercup."

"Not for long, darling," she said.

CHAPTER FOURTEEN

Cameron maneuvered her white, unmarked cruiser down a two-lane country road, past a row of neat modular homes, until she found the number she was looking for: one hundred seventy-three. The name on the mailbox read "Douglas."

Through the six inches of snow, Cameron could see a neatly trimmed hedge. Around the corner, she saw an elaborate swing set in the spacious backyard that contained a willow tree and bird feeders.

According to Cameron's background check, Reginald Crane's maid, Agnes Douglas, was seventy years old. *Play set must be for grandchildren.*

She pulled her cruiser into the empty driveway and climbed out. As she rounded the fender of the cruiser, she glanced up and down the street. The homes were modest and neat in a middle-class, family neighborhood. Most of the vehicles were SUVs for mothers to carry their children from school to soccer games and dance recitals, which was what made the black and white Mini Cooper parked halfway down the block and across the street stand out.

Narrowing her eyes, Cameron tried to focus on the car's driver, whom she could not clearly make out through the windshield. She turned her attention to the license plate. It had Pennsylvania tags. She only read the first three letters, FDS, before the driver turned on the engine, raced down the street, turned the corner, and roared out of sight.

"Can I help you?" Cameron heard an elderly woman call to her from her front door in her home across the yard and driveway.

Startled out of her thoughts of who might be following her and why, Cameron turned around in the driveway to respond. "I'm looking for Agnes Douglas." She wasn't comfortable questioning potential witnesses via screaming across suburban front yards.

"And who are you?"

While Cameron made her way up the neighbor's icy steps to the door, the elderly woman with a dark wig squinted through her dark glasses at her. "You aren't one of her granddaughters."

"No, I'm not." Once she made it to the door, Cameron presented her police detective shield to the woman. "I'm Detective Cameron Gates with the Pennsylvania State Police."

"State police?" the elderly neighbor clutched her chest. "Does this have to do with her grandson?"

"What grandson?"

"The one with the marines," she said. "I forget his name. He's stateside right now. But I guess his security clearances are coming due, so the federals have to reinvestigate him. Is that why you're here? To do another background check on Freddie?"

"No," Cameron said. "I'm not with the feds. This has to do with another matter. I need to talk to Agnes. Do you know when she'll be back?"

"Not until next week." The elderly neighbor smiled broadly to reveal her yellowed dentures. "Agnes is at her daughter's wedding."

"Daughter?" Recalling that Agnes' daughter had passed away over a dozen years earlier, Cameron's head snapped up. Grasping for her memory of the background check, she asked, "Do you mean Kendra?"

"That used to be her name," the woman said. "She changed it. Agnes said it was a real complicated story. Anyway, she goes by Archie now—"

"Archie Monday!" It came out as a gasp.

"She's marrying Robin Spencer's son," the woman said with pride. "Now that I do remember because I love all of Robin Spencer's books. I sent my copy of her very first one and asked Agnes to get this man, Robin's son, to sign it." Her hands went to her hips. "I told those FBI agents all of this the other day. You would think you all would check with each other."

"What FBI agents?"

"Two of them," the neighbor said. "I guess they travel in pairs. One was young and had this big grin like Satan—"

"Black."

"That was his name," she nodded her head. "And the other was real sour. A real bump on a log."

Cameron was trying to keep calm. "And they were here yesterday."

"No, day before yesterday," the elderly woman said. "I know because they came in the afternoon only a few hours after Agnes had left to go to the big fancy wedding."

Cameron couldn't get away fast enough. She almost fell twice racing to her car in the driveway.

Day before yesterday! They were here looking for Agnes before Crane's body was even found. Before the shootout at Mac Faraday's place—and Agnes was there!

190

At her car, Cameron whipped out her burner phone and hit the redial button for David O'Callaghan. As soon as he picked up, she blurted out, "Agnes is the target!"

"What?" David replied. "Agnes? Archie's *mother!*"

Cameron saw a dark shadow reflected in the snow on the opposite side of the driveway. Grabbing her gun, she whirled around, but not fast enough.

The prongs from the Taser shot through her coat and connected with her side, sending a shock through her body. Her whole body jerked wildly while she fell to the ground.

"You women just don't know when to stop asking questions," she heard Elder grunt before blackness overtook her.

Spencer Police Department

"That's not possible." David tried to maintain a respectable tone when he responded to Sheriff Christopher Turow's latest development in the Russell Dooley murder.

Mac Faraday's blood and DNA had been found at the murder scene.

"I had them run the results through twice," the sheriff said in a low voice even though they were in the privacy of his office. "Mac's blood is on the knife, in drops leading to the sink, and in it."

"Which means he got cut while stabbing Dooley," David said. "But I saw Mac with my own two eyes yesterday—*after* the murder. He doesn't have a mark on him."

"Sorry, O'Callaghan," the sheriff said with a shake of his head, "but I know how tight you two are. You're in his wedding, damn it. I need to see Mac myself and document that he has no cuts on him, and I need to interrogate him. You

191

need to bring him in. We'll protect him and Thornton from whoever it is that's after them."

"Yeah, by slapping Mac in a cell," David said.

"Don't tell me that you wouldn't do the same if our positions were reversed."

Even though it was true, David wanted to deny Turow's statement so badly that he welcomed the call on his burner phone. Fearing it was Mac, he grabbed it from the case and brought it to his ear.

"What?"

"Agnes is the target!" Cameron shouted into the phone.

"What?" David covered his other ear. "Agnes? Archie's *mother!*"

Instead of repeating herself, Cameron screamed.

"Cameron!" David shouted into the phone. "What's going on?"

He heard a loud crackle sound before the phone went dead.

"What is it?" Sheriff Turow asked with his hand on his radio.

"Thornton's wife just called." David threw open his office door. "She says Agnes Douglas is the target."

"The old woman?" Sheriff Turow was behind him. "How? Why would anyone send a hit squad after an old woman?"

"I don't know!" David was trying to redial the number, which went straight to a voicemail box. "Cameron, call me! I'm taking my men out to get Agnes Douglas and bring Mac and Josh in, but I need answers about what you've uncovered."

Gesturing at his officers in the squad room, David snapped orders while grabbing a ballistics vest. "We're going to the safe house to bring in Faraday and Thornton. I just got information that the target is Agnes Douglas."

"The old woman?" Tonya gasped.

"Tonya, Gates and I got cut off," David said. "Call the Pennsylvania State Police to make sure she's okay. She's obviously happened onto something big."

Turow was already on his radio calling in back-up. "Me and my people are coming with you."

"You won't get any argument from me," David replied on his way out the door.

While running for his cruiser, David pulled out his cell phone and thumbed the number for Joshua's burner phone. The call was still connecting when he saw the purple Ferrari pull into the parking lot.

Seeing the police swarming out of the police station, Murphy and Jessica, who was clutching her sheltie pup, jumped out.

"What's going on?" Murphy demanded to know. "Is it another attack?'

Recognizing the purple sports car, David stopped before climbing into his cruiser. "We got a lead on who's the target. Are you Lieutenant Thornton?"

"Yes, sir! Permission to offer my assistance, Major!"

"Major?" Jessica murmured.

David hesitated a moment before gesturing at the passenger door of his cruiser. "Get in."

On the other side of the cruiser, David pressed the phone to his ear. "Mac! David! Agnes is the target. I don't have time to explain. We're on our way up to get you. You're coming in."

Murphy turned to Jessica. "I'm going with them." He grabbed his canvas bag out of the backseat of the car. "You go up to the Spencer Inn, and I'll meet you there."

"I'm going with you." Still clutching Spencer in her arms, she rushed around to stop him with her hand on his arm. "My dad's in trouble."

Uttering a whine, Spencer licked his arm.

"And how are you going to help him?" Murphy argued.

"Move your ass, Lieutenant!" David snapped from the driver's seat. "Or I'm leaving you behind."

Murphy clasped his hands on her shoulders and stared into her eyes. "Go straight to the Spencer Inn and leave your room number at the front desk. I'm bringing your dad and mine back home."

"Okay," she said reluctantly. "Be careful."

As if to urge them along, David started the cruiser's engine. Fearing the police chief would leave him behind, Murphy turned to grab the door handle.

Before he could pull away, Jessica kissed him on the cheek. When he jerked back to look at her, she smiled softly. "For luck."

He kissed his fingertip and touched the tip of her nose. "Same to you, buttercup."

"Today, Lieutenant!" David yelled.

Murphy threw open the cruiser's door and tossed his bag inside on the floor.

"You better be careful, honey buns," she shouted. "I'm planning on kissing you New Year's Eve."

"You can count on it." Murphy turned around to climb into the front seat.

Struck with a sudden thought, Jessica whirled around and shouted over the cruiser's engine to Murphy inside the front passenger seat. "You don't have a girlfriend, do you?"

David's head snapped around, and he stopped trying to back up.

A wide, wicked grin crossed Murphy's face before he closed the door and lowered the window. "No, but if you're interested, I'll be glad to discuss the *position* with you later in your room at the hotel."

"Oh, I love it when a man talks dirty to me," she oozed while David backed the cruiser out of the parking space, turned on the sirens and lights, and sped out of the police parking lot with two cruisers behind him.

While David fought to keep the cruiser on the road at this news, Murphy bent over and opened up the canvas bag to reveal his utility belt, which contained a host of weapons, some of which David recognized. Trying to maneuver on the icy roads, he tried to conceal his shock at seeing that the utility belt had two guns on it, one for each hip.

"Twice the firepower." Murphy fastened the belt on. He also removed a black, light-weight and form-fitting bullet-proof vest.

"FYI, Lieutenant Thornton, Jessica Faraday's father, Mac Faraday, is my best friend."

Murphy sat straight up in his seat while David flicked his eyes in his direction.

"You break her heart, and I'll personally rip yours out."

"That's never going to happen, sir," Murphy replied.

"Good." David's lips curled to hear the sincerity in the young navy officer's tone.

"I'm in love with her, sir."

"What in the world are you talking about saying *I'm* the target?" Agnes said in a tone that was a mixture of outrage and laughter while Mac paced from one end of the cabin to the other.

The two Spencer Police Officers, Officers Fletcher and Zigler, trusted members of David's police force, had split up to watch at different vantage points of the house. At the end of the bedroom hallway, Joshua was peering out the side door to the woods.

Whining, Gnarly was pacing from one door to the other and then the other. His snout was twitching. After years of working with Gnarly, Mac sensed that Gnarly was picking up on scents that were threatening.

"David didn't have time to explain." Mac threw Joshua's coat at him. "We need to be ready to move. They're on their way. We need to go."

"Well, your police chief friend has a whole lot of explaining to do when he gets here," Agnes grumbled while putting her coat on. She clutched her purse to her chest. "You say these guys are killers for hire. Who would want to send hit men after *me?*" She pounded her fist to her chest. "Me? I haven't done anything to anyone. All I do is clean houses and take care of my grandkids. I read my books. I keep to myself—"

"Like most lunatics." Mac rolled his eyes in Joshua's direction.

Agnes continued, "I don't even get into any of that social media type mumbo-jumbo that brings in cyberstalkers—"

Joshua turned to her. "Because you don't have a computer," he said in a low voice.

"That's right." Agnes hitched her chin up at him. "I'm low-tech and proud of it."

Joshua stared at her.

Seeing Joshua's blue eyes boring at the elderly woman, Mac stood up straight. "What's wrong, Josh?"

"If Agnes has no computer," he said slowly while directing his eyes at her purse, "why does she have a thumb drive?"

"A what?" Agnes squawked while clutching the bag, which had both of their attention, closer to her chest.

They moved in closer to her.

"A flash drive!" Joshua pointed at her purse. "When I was searching your purse yesterday, you had a thumb drive in it. A red one. I actually held it in my hand."

"But you have no computer," Mac said. "Then what are you doing with a flash drive?"

"What's on it?" Joshua demanded to know.

Mac snatched the bag out of Agnes' hands.

"How dare you!"

Turning the purse upside down, Mac held it open and dumped all of the contents onto the floor. Everything from candy to pens to tissues to store receipts to earrings to paper clips to bandages to a small sewing kit to lipstick to hairbrushes—everything imaginable scattered across the floor. "You got everything in here but the kitchen sink, Agnes!" He knelt down to dig through the mess.

"You never know when someone will need a bandage."

Holding his wounded side, Joshua eased down to his knees to paw through the contents. "It was red."

They could hear the police sirens in the background.

"What's a thumb drive?" Agnes demanded to know. "What does a thumb have to do with a computer, and why would I have one when I don't have a computer?"

"Good question," Joshua replied.

"I've got it!" Mac held it up.

With her hands on her hips, Agnes shook her head. "That doesn't even look like a thumb!"

"It's a thumb *drive*," Mac said while climbing to his feet. "You *stick* it into a computer, and then you can retrieve data and other information from it."

Her voice was low as she glared up at him. "I know where I'd like to stick it."

"What's on it?" Joshua asked.

"What are you not telling us, Agnes?" Mac asked. "Does this have something to do with your boss, Crane? What are you really into?"

"I'm into cleaning his toilet and taking out his garbage, that's what I'm into!"

197

Gnarly ran up to Mac and jumped up to tag him in the back with his paws. The dog let out a loud anxious bark.

"They're almost here!" Officer Fletcher announced. "ETA less than one minute."

As if to announce that no one was leaving, a gunshot blast broke out the kitchen windows. Grabbing his neck, Fletcher dropped to the floor behind the kitchen counter.

"Fletcher!" Mac yelled.

Seeing blood seeping through the officer's fingers, Agnes screamed.

Shoving the thumb drive into his pants pocket with one hand, Mac grabbed Agnes by the back of the neck and drove her down to the floor.

"No!" the old woman screamed, "He needs help!"

Clutching his gun, Officer Fletcher rose up onto his knees and shot out the broken window.

"Stay down!" Mac yelled while taking the officer's place.

"I'm okay." Fletcher grimaced while attempting to tighten the grip on his bleeding neck.

Seeing movement through the window on the other side of the house, Joshua warned Officer Zigler. "Ten o'clock!"

While the officer ducked, Joshua fired off three shots over his head through the window. They heard a scream, and then the bush outside the window shook when the body fell into it.

Agnes grabbed an old discolored dishtowel and rolled it up. "Now you listen to me, young man, we're all going to get out of here alive," she said in a no-nonsense tone. "So don't you go giving up on me. I'll hold this to your neck." She moved over to give him a view out the kitchen window. "You keep on shooting those bunch of good-for-nothing so-and-sos. You hear me?"

"Yes, ma'am."

CHAPTER FIFTEEN

Spencer Inn

As much as she hated to admit it, Jessica Faraday couldn't deny that Murphy had been right. How could she help her dad escape whoever was after him? She had seen Murphy in action with her own chloroformed eyes.

And he looked so good while doing it. She had to pause to watch him climb into David's cruiser. *Hmmm. What a nice pair of buns. Honey buns. Yeah, that's what I'll call him. My honey buns.*

The memory of the dimples on both of his cheeks made a giggle bubble to the surface when she pulled her purple Ferrari into the valet parking at the Spencer Inn. Recognizing the Inn owner's daughter, the doorman opened the driver's door for her almost before she came to a complete stop.

He offered his hand to help her out of the car. "A pleasure to see you again, Ms. Faraday." Taking the leash from her, he attached it to the squirming sheltie and handed the other end of the leash back to her. "I see you brought Spencer for the wedding."

"Oh, I take Spencer everywhere with me."

A chuckle escaped the doorman's lips while he held open the door for her to pass through. "The inn's manager, Mr. Ingles, will be thrilled to see her. Any luck in her housebreaking?"

"She's much better. Thank you for asking."

Even though the doorman's tone was devoid of sarcasm, Jessica sensed the humor in his comment. The Spencer Inn's manager wasn't fond of Gnarly, who was reasonably trained. How could he possibly be fond of Spencer, who had had an accident under his desk when the sheltie was still a puppy? At least Gnarly never peed under his desk. But then Spencer had never dove into the swimming pool from the penthouse suite balcony on the top floor.

Jessica had barely reached the top of the steps leading down to the lobby when she heard her name called from three directions.

Jeff Ingles was racing with as much dignity as possible behind Hector Langford, the chief of security. Before Jessica could descend the stairs, the security manager had her by one arm while Jeff had her by the other.

"Thank God you're okay, Jessica," Hector said. "Chief O'Callaghan called ahead with orders for me to personally escort you to your suite and make sure you are under watch the whole time until we find out who's behind this."

"Have you heard any word from Dad yet?" Jessica made her way down the steps while being careful to not get tangled up in Spencer's leash.

Taking an immediate interest in Jeff Ingles, the pup was jumping on his leg and begging to be picked up. Conscious of the fact that Spencer belonged to Jessica, his boss's daughter, Jeff was trying to discourage the dog as politely as possible, even though he wanted to give her a swift kick across the lobby. "We have your suite ready and waiting for you, Ms. Faraday."

"Hey, Jessie!" a call came from the lounge area in front of the fireplace. Tucking his tablet under his arm, Tristan Faraday unfolded his tall frame from a chair and rose to his feet.

Before he could race across the lobby to his sister, a shriek came from the registration desk. A slender blonde scurried across the granite floor in her high heeled boots. Her bosom bounced in her red sweater, which she had paired with black leggings. "Jessie! My BFF! I was so hoping I'd run into you! You wouldn't believe who I ran into while checking in!" She took Jessica into a hug and kissed her on the cheek.

Penny turned around and waved over to the firmly built man leaning against the reception desk. "Hey, Colt, here's Jessie!" She whirled back to Jessica. "Cute text you sent this morning by the way." She uttered a nervous giggle. "Roll over and wake Colt up ..."

"It wasn't a joke," Jessica said.

Penny's brown eyes clouded over as fear sent a lightning bolt through her heart.

Hector touched Jessica on the elbow. "I would feel better if you just invited your friends up to your suite, Jessica. There are way too many people down here for us to keep you safe." He gestured at Tristan. "You, too. Since they failed in nabbing Jessica, they may come after you."

"I'll be going upstairs with you," he replied before adding to Jessica in a low voice, "I really need to talk to you. It's important."

"This will only take a minute," Jessica said in a firm tone that prompted an expression from Penny not unlike that of a deer spotting a hunter with his weapon aimed at her.

As Colt sauntered across the lobby, Spencer lost all interest in Jeff and turned her attention to the young man. Running to the end of her leash, the sheltie barked in an angry tone at the approaching human.

"Spencer! Stop!" When Jessica knelt to pick her up, Spencer raced out of her reach while trying to reach Colt, who stood frozen in place. Finally, Tristan snatched up the dog and held her in his arms. When Tristan almost dropped his tablet, Hector took possession of the pup.

"I don't know why that dog doesn't like me," Colt said to each of them. "She must be a lesbian." He stepped forward to hug and kiss Jessica, who turned her head away so that his lips brushed her cheek. Sensing that he was in trouble, the actor stepped back and flashed his most charming smile at her. "I think there's a mistake. The clerk refuses to give me a keycard to your suite or to allow the bellhop to take my luggage up."

"No," Jessica said, "there's no mistake."

"Jessie," Penny uttered a nervous giggle again, "now let's not cause a scene right before your father's wedding. Somewhere, somehow, you've got it in your head that Colt and I have been having an affair behind your back ..."

"Uh-oh." Jeff pushed his way through them to run off to the reception desk. "Hector, I assume you will control all of this."

Hector took note of Jessica's calm demeanor.

"I got it in my head because it is fact," Jessica said. "In the last five weeks, Colt has taken to wearing Clive Christian men's cologne. Your favorite, Penny. All of your men wear it because you buy it for them."

His face turning red from the top of his head to his V-neck sweater, Colt chuckled.

"Sorry, Colt," Jessica said. "Your fantasy of two women getting into a catfight ain't happening. Not today. Fact is, this is the best thing that could have happened to me now, because I'm in love with another man. That's why I called the registration desk to tell them not to let you in my suite."

"Another man?" Colt's eyes grew wide. "What other man? How could you fall in love with another man?"

Penny's eyes teared up. "Jessie, you're positively glowing."

Jessica giggled. "I know. Isn't it wonderful?"

The two women hugged. As she pulled away, Penny asked, "So you're not mad at me for sneaking around with Colt behind your back?"

Jessica shook her head. "It's absolutely perfect. Now I can dump Colt, and he can go running into your arms for you to tend to his wounded ego. You two can still come to the wedding together, and I'll go with the man I love."

Clapping her hands, Penny squealed with delight. "Then we're still friends."

"Of course."

"Man ... she ... loves?" Colt was still putting it all together. "But not me?" He raised his hand. "I have a question."

"You're staying in my room," Penny said.

Colt pointed at Jessica. "Are you still going to talk to your father about my auditioning for the part of Mickey Forsythe?"

"Of course I will, Colt," Jessica said. "I can't promise anything, but I will put in a good word for you."

Colt nodded. "Then I'm good." Struck with a sudden thought, he asked, "Who's paying for my room?"

"I am." Penny whirled around on her high heels and headed for the elevator. "Come, Colt," she ordered with a wave of her hand. "Let's go up to my room where I can lick your wounds."

"Cool." Aware of feminine eyes on him, Colt turned around and followed his lady. With a gesture at the bellhop, he ordered his luggage to follow him onto the elevator.

The corners of Jessica's mouth curled when she took her phone from her purse and whisked her thumb across the touch screen.

Hector sighed with relief. "That had to be the most congenial catfight I've ever witnessed."

"Shallow people heal fast," Jessica said. "Think about it. When you're shallow, how deeply can you be wounded?"

"Are you really going to put in a good word for Colt playing Mickey Forsythe?" Tristan asked.

Her attention directed at the various screens flashing on her phone while she thumbed through the applications, Jessica giggled. "Sure. I'll put in a good word and Dad will fall out his chair laughing. But hey, I kept my promise."

Tristan leaned over to see what had her attention. "What are you doing?"

"Deleting those two cheaters from my address book and blocking them from my social media sites." A wide smile crossed her face. Her violet eyes sparkled. She dropped the phone back into her purse and grasped her brother's arm. "That chapter of my life is now over. Time to move on."

"Now tell me about this other man you're in love with?" Tristan took note of the men's black leather jacket she was wearing. "I'm assuming that jacket is his."

David's cruiser broke through the clearing to find the perimeter of the log house surrounded by gunmen taking shots with high-powered rifles at the occupants inside the house.

"How many're inside?" Murphy grasped the door to fly out.

"Your father, Faraday, Agnes Douglas, and two of my officers, Zigler and Fletcher," David said. "Plus Gnarly."

"What's a Gnarly?"

Instead of answering, David was on his radio. "Three gunmen are in the back making their way inside," Sheriff Turow reported.

"I've got five in the front." Throwing open the door and rolling out into the snow, Murphy jumped up behind a snow bank with both guns blazing. One shot took out a gunman by the garage, while the other took out the one who was approaching from David's side of the cruiser. "Now we have a total of six—counting those in the back."

David was issuing orders. "Sheriff Turow and his people will secure the perimeter. He's called in a helicopter. ETA three minutes. My men will provide cover while you and I will go in to get our people out."

Leaving Murphy behind the cover of the snow bank, David pulled the cruiser up as close to the house as he could. Because of the foot and a half of snow, the vehicle was too far away from the side kitchen door. The shooters had a clear view.

While surveying the layout between the cruiser and the side entrance to the house, Murphy scurried up alongside the driver's side of cruiser. "They've got a kill zone," he hissed while they crouched behind the vehicle. "Even if the targets don't get inside, they have time and space to nab our people when they come out. We're going to need cover between here and the door for when they evacuate."

"Turow just said they are down to two shooters in the back, but that they are moving in to the back side door," David said. "The chopper can take care of all them—"

"Two minutes is a long time when people are shooting at you."

"I know." Reminded of when he had fought in the Middle East, David felt his voice shake. It was all too familiar. He cleared his throat.

Murphy jerked his head over at a snow-covered barbeque resting next to the back door. "Does that thing work?"

"I have no idea," David said.

"I'm going in," Murphy said. "I'll provide cover for them when they come out. Keep the engine running and be ready to gun it. If I'm not out in thirty seconds after they load up, you go without me."

"I told you that I was giving the orders," David told him.

"Yes, sir. I'm prepared to follow your plan." Murphy casually fired a shot over his shoulder, and it took out a gunman who had been creeping around the corner of the house. He had barely even looked in that direction. "Now we're down to three shooters." It was like he had eyes in the back of his head.

When a shot flew over his head, David replied, "We'll go with your plan."

"Order your people to cover me while I go in," Murphy said. "FYI," he added with a grin, "I saw that guy's reflection in the car window. *I don't have eyes in the back of my head.*"

"I never said you did." David tapped his radio button. "Lieutenant Thornton is going in. Everyone cover him. Fletcher, Zigler, prepare to cover Thornton. He's coming in the side kitchen door."

The back door opened from the inside. Murphy sprinted across the snow- and ice-covered walkway past the abandoned barbeque. As soon as he crossed the threshold, he slid across the floor to hit the kitchen counter.

Mac slammed the side door behind him.

"Who's that?" Agnes squawked.

"That's my son," Joshua said with pride while Murphy quickly checked him over.

"Why isn't he wearing a coat?" Agnes asked.

"A beautiful woman charmed it right off my back." Murphy knelt next to his father. "Are you okay?"

"Of course, I'm not okay. I've been shot." Joshua shoved the pen into Murphy's hand. "You need to take care of this."

Murphy slipped the pen into a pocket on his thigh and sealed it shut. "I'm going to give you all cover to make a run for Major O'Callaghan's cruiser." He gestured for Agnes to help Officer Fletcher to his feet.

"They're moving in," Officer Zigler reported over his shoulder while keeping an eye out the front window from behind the sofa. "They're more aggressive, too."

As if to confirm his statement, a shot rang out. Clutching his arm, Officer Zigler fell to his knees.

Murphy jumped to his feet. Moving steadily toward the window, he fired shot after shot until he was standing in front of the window, daring anyone to fire again. Behind him, Officer Zigler crawled toward the kitchen where Mac examined his arm.

"Who's the major?" Agnes asked.

"David." Mac gestured for Gnarly to join them.

Moving to the side next to the window, Murphy ejected the cartridge and snapped a full one into his gun. "Get everyone to the cruiser. The sheriff's deputies and the major's men, and I'll cover you."

"What about you?" Joshua asked.

"I'm going to do my job." Murphy took a smoke bomb out of his utility belt. "On the count of three, you all move it. Run straight through the smoke. The cruiser will be at the end of the walkway. I'll provide extra cover from this end."

With his good arm, Officer Zigler took Joshua on one side. Clutching the cloth to his bleeding neck, Officer Fletcher wrapped his arm around Agnes. His weapon ready to fire, Mac took a position in the front.

On the count of two, Murphy threw open the door and tossed the smoke bomb outside. He then took out both guns and fired simultaneously in both directions to cover the group running for the back of the cruiser.

"Fletcher! Zigler!" David's shock turned to fury when he saw his two wounded officers.

"It's like being back in Iraq," Zigler said.

David turned his eyes to the clock. Murphy said to give him thirty seconds, and there was still no sign of the chopper to back them up. Sheriff Turow's deputies were trying unsuccessfully to keep the two shooters in the back away from the safe house.

As soon as they jumped into the back of the cruiser, Murphy turned around to see the back door fly open and two gunmen run inside. A third kicked in the kitchen door and dove in.

While shots were flying in his direction, Murphy plunged out the door and hit the ice on his knees. Sliding down the walk, he twisted around to see the gunmen inside the log home running through the kitchen.

"Murphy!" he heard his father screaming at him from the cruiser.

Murphy hit the end of the walkway. Firing three shots with both guns, Murphy fired a shot beyond the gunmen into the house to take out the fire extinguisher while simultaneously taking out the propane tank just outside the doorway where they were perched. Any escape behind them was impossible due to the blinding smoke from the fire extinguisher.

The fireball from the propane quickly spread with the fuel from the fire in the fireplace inside the log cabin to take the roof off the safe house.

CHAPTER SIXTEEN

Spencer Inn

On the top floor at the Spencer Inn, Jessica took a moment to pinch herself at the classy style of the suite where she would be staying for the next week during and after her father's wedding. She never stopped letting herself forget that there was a time when she wasn't certain if she could finish college, let alone stay in such elegance.

Her stepmother-to-be, Archie Monday, was in the suite across the hall.

I wonder how she's holding up. She's tough, but weddings are stressful enough without all of this happening.

Tristan was staying in a suite next door. Because he was one who concentrated on the simple things in life, Jessica doubted if Tristan had even noticed the sunken Jacuzzi tub in the bathroom, the hot tub out on his balcony, or the view of the brightly lit ski slopes leading down to the lake at the bottom of the mountain.

"By the way," Tristan said upon entering the suite, "when you see Archie, don't say anything about her hair."

"Why?" Jessica turned from where she was admiring the view.

"You'll know as soon as you see it," Tristan said.

Tears of sympathy welling up inside her throat for Archie, Jessica swallowed. "How bad is it?"

"I don't think it's too bad." Tristan flopped down into a comfortable chair and propped his feet up on the coffee table.

"You wouldn't think a shaved head was too bad. You wouldn't even notice."

Unable to argue, Tristan shrugged his shoulders.

Hector came out of the bedroom. He had checked each room, door, and window in the suite. "Everything is clear and secured."

The scream out in the hallway suggested that Hector had spoken too soon. Yanking his weapon out of its holster, the security manager raced out. "Stay here!" he ordered.

They could hear the woman's hysterical scream fade away as she ran down the corridor and out of earshot either on the elevator or the stairwell.

When Jessica tried to run for the door, Tristan stood up to block her exit. "He said to stay here."

"But I can't just stand still—" Clutching Tristan's arm, Jessica noted Hector Langford's stern expression when he came back into the suite. "What's going on?"

"It was the cleaning woman assigned to service Tristan's suite." Hector leveled his gaze on Tristan. "You brought *her* with you."

Jessica backed away from her brother as if Hector had announced that Tristan was the mastermind behind their current situation. "Tristan! You didn't! You brought Monique."

"I couldn't leave her home alone," Tristan said in a miserable tone. "My roommates aren't the most responsible guys around and I was afraid they'd forget about her and she'd have a slow horrible death from starvation." Seeing Spencer trotting in from the bedroom after checking out the suite, he stood up tall. "Besides, you brought Spencer. At least we can count on Monique not peeing on the rug."

"Spencer doesn't have eight legs and isn't bigger than a dinner plate!" Jessica argued.

"Dinner plates are eleven inches," Tristan corrected her. "Monique is only eight. She's just a *little* bigger than a salad plate."

"Never mind, you two." Hector waved his hands. "One good thing about Monique being here, we know as soon as word gets out that Tristan is sharing his suite with a giant tarantula that we can be pretty certain that *his* room will be safe." He sighed. "As far as housekeeping, we're probably going to have to pay the maids hazard pay."

"She's in a tank," Tristan said. "As long as they don't take off the lid, she can't hurt them."

"She's still creepy," Jessica said with a shudder.

Tristan's lip curled. "You're such a girl."

"I'm telling Dad and he's going to kill you."

Hector stepped between them. "Chill out, you two, or I'm going to tell your father about both of you."

"What'd I do?" Jessica asked. "All I did was stop at a truck stop to pee—"

"And you hooked up with some guy who you don't even know." With a chuckle, Tristan dropped back down into his seat and picked up his tablet. "For all you know, he has a giant tarantula."

"Tristan does have a point," Hector said. "Who is this new guy, and will you be expecting him to come up here to your room?" He held up a hand. "Not being nosy. Safe. These guys who are after your father wouldn't be above luring you out with a hunky piece of beefcake."

"He's Joshua Thornton's son," Jessica said. "Murphy Thornton. He's a lieutenant in the navy. Right now, he's working with Chief O'Callaghan to rescue our dads."

"I'm still going to run a check on him," Hector said. "I promised your father that I'd keep you safe, and that's what I intend to do."

"He's a graduate of the United States Naval Academy," Tristan said while eying his computer tablet. "He played quarterback for two years on their football team. He was co-valedictorian at his high school with his twin brother Joshua Thornton Junior. Do you want me to check to see if he's got any restraining orders against him, Hector?"

"Wouldn't be a bad idea," Hector said. "I'll have a couple of my guys stationed out in the hall."

Jessica waited for the chief of security to leave before sitting down onto the sofa across from her brother. "I take it you don't have a date for the wedding."

Tristan grunted. "I don't have any big yearning for hooking up like you and Dad and everyone else." His eyes met hers. "And I'm not gay."

She held up her hands. "Hey, you don't have to tell me. I'm the one who caught you peeping in Meghan Dawson's window while she was changing out of her cheer-leading outfit. Remember?"

"How could I forget? You blackmailed me for four months over that."

Jessica gazed across at her brother. Tall and slender, he was an attractive young man. He had inherited their father's square jaw. With his dark-framed glasses, he looked studious, and geeky was "in."

To her, he was the perfect specimen to study when it came to sexual attraction. Her brother definitely put out the signal to women that he was not interested in any relationship. Therefore, women didn't even try. While they were not repelled, there was definitely a sense or scent that said he was not looking for a mate.

She could pinpoint the approximate time that she first sensed it in him. His senior year in high school, when that witch had broken his heart. First loves and losses are always the hardest.

"Dad's in trouble," Tristan's voice broke through her thoughts.

"I know." Jessica leaned forward to put her elbows on her knees. She cupped her chin on top of her hands. Between her long legs and the high heels of her boots, she was forced to spread her feet apart and bring her knees together to create a less-than-sophisticated pose.

"No," Tristan clarified while swiping his fingers across the screen on his tablet, "Dad is really, really in trouble. Meaning if he gets out of this alive, he could be in jail."

"How?"

Tristan pushed his glasses up on his nose. "Did Archie tell you about Russell Dooley and how he came to Spencer to make trouble for Dad?"

"She told me last night that he was murdered and that she thinks there has to be a connection between that and the hit squad going after Dad," she said. "Do you remember the Dooley case?"

"Do you know how many murder cases Dad's worked?"

"Well, I remember this case," Jessica said. "I got out of school to attend Leigh Ann Dooley's trial so that I could write a research paper on sociopaths. She was one—a big one. I even interviewed her daughter, who was my age. Most people could see through Leigh Ann, but not her husband. Guy was in complete denial about her."

"Love can be deaf, dumb, and blind," Tristan said.

"Luckily, Bianca, the daughter, was perceptive enough to see through her mother," Jessica said. "But Russell Dooley bought Leigh Ann's lies hook, line, and sinker."

"Which is why he blames Dad for framing his wife and for her suicide," Tristan said, "which gives Dad motive for killing him in self-defense."

Jessica stared down at the floor. "That murder case was the tipping point for the end of Dad and Mom's marriage."

With an edge in his voice, Tristan asked, "What are you talking about?"

"Since you never saw or met any of these people, you wouldn't know," Jessica said. "I saw Leigh Ann on the stand and studied her life—talked to her daughter. I saw a lot of similarities between how Leigh Ann worked people, especially those close to her, and how Mom treated people." She rose her eyes to meet her brother's. "Dad must have, too. After that case, things changed between him and Mom."

Tristan chuckled. "Their marriage broke up because of Mom's cheating."

"Why, after over fifteen years of marriage, did Mom suddenly decide to step out on Dad?" Jessica asked. "Could it be because Dad saw a little bit of himself in Russell Dooley and didn't want to end up as pathetic as him?"

"Dad has never been *pathetic* in his whole life," Tristan said. "Even when Mom kicked him out and took everything from him for that bastard, Dad still landed on his feet and did what he had to do to take care of us." He grumbled. "More than Mom ever did."

"You're absolutely right."

"I think Dad needs us now." Sitting up and placing his feet on the floor, Tristan handed the tablet across the table to her. "They found Dad's blood and DNA at the crime scene for Russell Dooley's murder."

Jessica studied the report that filled the tablet's screen. Reading the heading for the forensics report, she gasped, "You hacked into the county police department records!" As if she feared being accused as an accessory to the crime, she tossed the tablet back at him.

"Like if I asked they were going to tell me everything they had against Dad."

"Like they can trace the IP address directly to that tablet and to you and arrest you for hacking into classified government databases."

Tristan laughed. "The local police don't have the funds for that type of cyber security."

Jessica's violet eyes narrowed into slits. "Archie taught you how to do that, didn't she?"

"She started out teaching me," Tristan said with a grin. "Now I've been teaching her a thing or two."

Finished exploring the suite, Spencer scurried into the sitting area and leapt from halfway across the room to land in Jessica's lap. She continued to squirm while her master petted her.

"How did Dad's blood and DNA get in that crime scene?" Tristan asked his sister. "Not only is it at the scene, it's also on the knife, too. The murder weapon, Jessie. His blood is on the murder weapon. That puts him at the scene at the time of the murder."

"He was set up." Jessica dropped back against the sofa. "In order to plant Dad's blood and DNA, the killer had to have gotten access to it."

"Like a jury is going to believe that?"

"Before it can get to a jury, Dad has to be arrested first," Jessica said. "And I'm not going to let that happen."

"I'm with you there, Jess," he said. "We need to find out who set Dad up. He or she had to be close enough to Dad to gain access to his blood. Someone he trusted."

Leaping out of her lap, the pup ran to the door, sat down, and whined while looking from the door, back to Jessica, and then back again.

"Not necessarily," Jessica said. "You'd be surprised at how easily someone who knows what they are doing can pick up and plant someone else's DNA."

Spencer's whine at the door made her groan.

"Now? Really?" Jessica looked pleadingly at Tristan.

"She's your dog." Without mercy, he closed the cover over his tablet and stood up. "I've never heard you offer to clean Monique's tank." With a wicked grin, he left the room.

"I need to go check in with Archie anyway," Jessica said to Spencer. "I'll stop in after taking you outside in the freezing weather."

Zipping up the black leather jacket, Jessica recalled the feel of Murphy's hands on her when he pulled the collar close to cut out the cold wind. She melted when she recalled staring into his deep blue eyes.

With a bark, Spencer snapped her back into the present.

"Coming!" With a groan, she grabbed Spencer's leash.

One of Hector's security officers escorted Jessica and Spencer down the elevator and out into the lobby. Not trusting Spencer to not make a beeline for Jeff's office and under his desk, Jessica carried her outside and over to the courtyard to conduct her business. With the mountain wind kicking up, she shivered while Spencer sniffed and barked at the brightly colored lights on the Christmas trees.

"Hurry up, Spencer," she said through shattering teeth. "We need to go see Archie." She bent over to whisper to the pup. "Don't say anything about her hair. She's going through enough as it is."

"Jessie?"

216

For a split second, Jessica thought it was Spencer speaking to her. The dog was looking right up at her when she heard her name uttered behind her.

"Jessie Faraday?"

Jessica turned around to see a slender woman approximately the same age as she, peering at her from the sidewalk. Her jeans and brown suede jacket were worn. A red knit cap was pulled down to cover her ears, from which big earrings hung. Her long hair was a chestnut color.

Recognizing her, but not placing a name with the face, Jessica cocked her head at her.

"Bianca." The young woman patted her own chest. "Bianca Briggs. Used to be Dooley. We had met at my mother's murder trial." She stopped to swallow. "I remember how nice you were to me."

A grin came to Jessica's lips. "Of course, I remember you." She stepped forward to take Bianca into her arms in a sincere hug. Stepping back, she looked her up and down. "You look great."

The last time Jessica had seen her, Bianca had been a young anorexic teenager who exuded a gothic-punk style, complete with pierced lips and eyebrows.

"I grew up," she admitted. "Got loads of therapy." She uttered a nervous laugh. "Like *years*. Put on weight. Stopped drinking and smoking pot and met a great man who knows how to treat a lady."

"It's amazing how when a man treats you like a lady, you start to act like one." Jessica scooped down to pick up Spencer before she had a chance to jump on Bianca. "This is Spencer."

"Named after your grandmother." Bianca petted the dog, who wagged her tail.

"I'm sorry for your loss," Jessica said. "First your mother, and then …"

"Thank you, Jessie. You always were so nice to me." Bianca forced a smile onto her face and a lighter tone to her voice when she added, "I see things certainly changed for you, too."

Jessica asked, "Are you staying here at the Inn?"

"No," Bianca said. "I could never afford the Spencer Inn. I'm staying at a place in Oakland. I was hoping that your dad would talk to me … I wanted to apologize for my father."

Jessica grasped her hand. "Apologize? Why should *you* apologize to us? You're not responsible for your parents. You lost your dad—"

"He's been gone for years," Bianca said. "I really lost him the day that jury convicted Mom of killing Harris Tyler." She sighed. "He tried to kill himself six times since Mom's conviction."

"Suicide?" Jessica replied.

"As a matter of fact, when the sheriff called to say my father was dead, I thought it was because he killed himself. But then, the sheriff said he had died of multiple stab wounds."

"How did he try to kill himself?"

"Once he tried to shoot himself," Bianca said. "But the bullet only grazed his head. He flinched. He took pills the very first time he tried to kill himself. I found him. That was when I was still living at home. He got his stomach pumped. He drove his car into a tree. He was in the hospital for close to a week with that. Had broken both of his legs." She sighed. "He's tried hanging himself, but the knot slipped and he fell. Broke his ankle and three ribs."

"All because of your mother, huh?" Jessica concentrated on stroking Spencer's soft fur. Thinking of her own mother, she buried her face into the dog's warm, soft fur. "I know your dad blamed mine for arresting your mother, but you know something?"

"What?"

"Dad truly felt sorry for your father," Jessica said. "Being an outsider looking in, coming into the murder case, interviewing all of the suspects and witnesses, you get a perspective of things that those on the inside don't see." She swallowed. "Dad saw how she manipulated and lied to your father, and he felt so bad that he never realized—"

"Never *wanted* to realize," Bianca said. "To face what Mom really was meant having to admit that the state of their marriage was really only a fantasy."

"And since he couldn't blame your mother for all of their problems, he had to blame Dad."

Tears welled up in Bianca's eyes. "The thought actually crossed my mind that he came to Deep Creek Lake to kill your father. After they told me that Mom had hung herself in her cell, I thought he would kill himself."

She uttered a hollow laugh. "It's a sad thing to say, but … after Dad had tried suicide so many times, you get to the point that you think, 'Just do it, all ready. Just get it over with and stop screwing around.'" She looked up at Jessica. "But he didn't kill himself. I was shocked when he sold the house to a realtor. I found out from the lawyer that he updated his will."

"Putting his affairs in order," Jessica said. "That's a sign that he was getting ready to kill himself. Maybe those previous times were practice. Now he really meant business this time."

Bianca nodded her head. "Dad was in debt up to his eyeballs. He had put a second mortgage on the house and had massive legal bills for all of their appeals. Well, after Mom died, Dad sold the house for a hundred and twenty thousand dollars. After he paid off all of the legal bills, he had ten thousand dollars and the gold watch Mom had given him."

"Gold watch?" Jessica said.

Bianca nodded her head. "A gold one. Engraved. Mom gave it to him for a wedding present. That was the one thing he refused to sell when he was liquidating everything to pay off the lawyers. Now it's gone."

"Maybe he did sell it after all?" Jessica suggested.

"No way," Bianca said. "He wore it all the time, and he did have it on his wrist when Chuck and I went to confront him after we found out that he had met with the lawyer to make final adjustments to his will after Mom's death. We both thought he was putting his affairs in order and was going to try to kill himself again. But he claimed he wasn't. He was preparing for if something went wrong."

"What could go wrong with what?"

"He claimed that in Mom's things, he found proof that Mac Faraday framed her, and he said that he was going to come up here to confront your dad with the evidence and go public with it."

"What kind of evidence?"

Bianca was shaking her head.

Jessica stepped toward her. "He had to have told you."

"He said I would be safer if I didn't know."

"Dad did not frame your mother for murder," Jessica said. "He had everything he needed for the arrest. It was a good arrest."

Bianca reached out to touch her hand. "I know. You don't have to tell me that. I'm only telling you what Dad told me, and I had to tell Sheriff Turow that. But I know Mac Faraday didn't frame my mother, and he did not kill my dad."

"Then who would want to kill your father?"

"I think someone robbed him," she said. "The sheriff says the watch was not in his effects, and I know he had ten thousand dollars in cash when he left home to come here. That's gone, too." Bianca grasped Jessica's arm. "I'll tell you this. If things get bad and your dad needs me, I will testify on his behalf because something's not right." She let out a sad laugh. "I half-believe that Mom came back from the grave to kill my dad and manipulate things to get back at your father for being the first man who didn't fall for her lies."

"Maybe she did," Jessica muttered into Spencer's fur.

"Jessica!" Hector snapped out her name while running around the corner. He stopped when he saw Jessica talking to Bianca. Seeming to recognize the young woman, he paused. "You were inside asking for Mac Faraday a bit ago, weren't you?"

"Bianca is a friend," Jessica interjected before she could answer. "We were just talking."

"Well," Hector said, "I just got a call from your father. Archie and your brother are waiting for us to go meet him at the hospital."

Chapter Seventeen

Mercy Hospital, Oakland, Maryland

With no regard for appearances, Donny raced across the emergency room reception area and took Murphy into a bear hug, lifting him up off the floor. "The big navy man returns!"

Murphy delivered a playful karate chop to both of Donny's shoulders to make him release him. Finding himself looking up at his little brother, who was a couple of inches taller than he was, he said, "Guess those days of picking on you are long gone, huh, bro!"

"Long gone!" Donny laughed before looking around. "Dad's okay, right?"

Forcing a reassuring grin, Murphy nodded his head. "They're prepping him for surgery." Seeing worry cross Donny's face, he quickly added, "The gunshot was a through and through. It doesn't look like it hit any major organs. They just need to go in to clean it up and make sure all the bleeding has stopped and that he doesn't get an infection. That's all. He was conscious and chewing me out the whole way here."

"Chewing you out? What for?"

"I blew up a house," Murphy said with a roll of his eyes and a shrug of his shoulders.

Chuckling, Donny murmured, "Still a bad-ass."

Behind Donny, Murphy watched the police chief and Mac Faraday engaged in a conversation. The two men were huddled next to the coffee vending machine.

The situation was not good.

Two Spencer Police Officers had been shot. While their wounds were not life threatening, it was still a blow. It meant whoever was behind the attack was serious. They did not care who they shot and killed—even police.

In spite of the police chief and Mac Faraday's best efforts to appear casual, Murphy noticed their glances in his and Donny's direction.

Something is wrong. Very wrong. Officers Fletcher and Zigler have been listed as serious, but are expected to recover. It's not them. This is something else.

Replaying the events of the day, a question came to Murphy's mind. *Where did the police chief get the tip that the old woman was the real target? Agnes Douglas. Archie Monday's mother. Where did Archie come from originally? Pennsylvania! The same place where Cameron is a detective with the state police.*

Murphy asked Donny, "Have you heard from Cameron?"

With wide eyes, Donny shook his head while looking around. "She should be here by now. David said that she was leaving this morning, and it's only a few hour's drive. I expected her to be here by lunch."

Gently pushing Donny aside, Murphy stepped across the reception area to the vending machines. "Where's my stepmother?"

David and Mac exchanged quick glances.

Displeased with their hesitance, Murphy repeated his question. "Detective Cameron Gates with the Pennsylvania

State Police." He told David, "*She* gave you the tip that Agnes Douglas was the target. In what context did she give you that tip and where is she now? Why is she not here? You told my brother that she was on her way first thing this morning, and now it is mid-afternoon. Chester is only a few hours away. You're hiding something, and I want to know what it is."

David stood up to his full height. His eyes met Murphy's. "You're out of line, Lieutenant," he said in a low firm voice. "Stand down."

"Why are we all talking military-eeze?" Mac asked in an attempt at humor.

"Because this whole case revolves around national security." David kept his gaze locked with Murphy's. "I still don't know what's in that package that your dad was picking up and delivering in my jurisdiction. If you two can keep secrets, so can we."

"With all due respect, sir," Murphy said in a steady tone, "Secrets dealing with national security are one thing. It's a whole other ballgame when it comes to my family."

"Has something happened to Cameron?" Donny's tone betrayed his affection for his stepmother.

David's eyes flicked to the teenager's face.

"My dad was devastated when Mom died," Murphy said through clenched teeth. "*We all were*. We can't lose Cameron."

"Everyone is looking for her," David said. "The Pennsylvania State Police. The last person to see her was Agnes' neighbor. That was about the same time that she called me with the news that Agnes Douglas was the target."

"Who was this neighbor, and why is Faraday's future mother-in-law a target for a death squad?" Murphy asked.

"Agnes Douglas was the maid for a murder victim whose case Cameron was investigating," Mac said. "I believe the victim was killed by someone who was after this." He removed the red thumb drive from his pants pocket.

When Murphy tried to take the thumb drive, Mac closed his hand into a fist before he could grab it. "We found it in her purse. She claims to be low-tech. So what is she doing with a flash drive?"

"*Who* was this murder victim?" Murphy demanded to know. "*Where* is Ms. Douglas?"

"The sheriff has taken her into protective custody," David said. "They're escorting her up to the Spencer Inn to be with her family along with an army of sheriff's deputies."

"With six oversized sons, the sheriff's department, Hector's people, and Gnarly by her side, she should be safe," Mac said. "She claims to have no knowledge about this, and I believe her. I'm thinking the murder victim slipped it into her purse to keep whoever was after it from getting it."

"When they couldn't find it in the victim's home, they tracked it here somehow." Struck with a thought, David tapped Mac on the arm. "Why did Agnes go to see you yesterday morning?"

Mac shrugged his shoulders. "She just showed up."

"But the attack on Spencer Manor was planned." David recalled, "When I met with Archie and her family last night, they said she was supposed to go to the beauty salon with the bridal party, but she claimed she had a headache and stayed behind."

"And then she came to the manor to see me," Mac said. "Now that you mention it, she seemed disgusted when I told her that I was on my way out." He took his cell phone from his pocket.

"She's always disgusted," David said. "Are you calling Agnes?"

"She doesn't have a cell phone," Mac reminded him. "I'm following up a—Gene?" He turned his conversation to the phone. "This is Mac Faraday. How are you? ... Did you have a good Christmas? ... You're welcome. You really deserved that bonus. … Busy is good. It keeps you off the streets and out of trouble. Hey, can you check on something real quick for me? That message that I left for Agnes Douglas, Archie's mother—I can't remember when I left it—it would have been yesterday or the day before—yeah, that's right, I called it in. Did that get delivered to her?" Turning to David and Murphy, Mac arched an eyebrow. "You gave it to her personally, huh? … Well, thank you for being discrete like I asked. I certainly appreciate it, Gene. … No, no problem at all. Just checking."

Mac hung up the phone.

"What is it?" Donny asked about the significant expressions exchanged between the three men. "What's going on?"

"The front desk manager, who I know, and who knows me," Mac explained, "took a message Wednesday night *from me* to give to Agnes Douglas to come to Spencer Manor at ten o'clock Thursday morning. I had told him to make sure no one saw him give it to her."

"Did I hear you say you called him?" David asked.

"I did not call in to leave any message," Mac said.

David felt his breath taken away as if he had been kicked in the chest. *So I wasn't imagining things that night in Iraq. If Gene spoke to Mac when he didn't call, then I really did hear Colonel Frost say "zombie" to give the order for the hit.*

"How is that possible?' Mac was asking.

"They recorded your voice and edited it to call in to leave a message and lure their target to your home," Murphy said.

"It sounds like Gene had a full conversation with me," Mac argued. "He asked me things and said things and I responded—like a full conversation."

"The technology is available," Murphy said, "but you have to have people trained in how to use it to pull it off."

"They'd have to be listening in in order to get the voice recordings?" David asked more than said.

"One or two conversations will do it," Murphy said. "Plus, if that front desk clerk was busy—"

"They're very busy this week with the holidays and the wedding," Mac said.

"And he wasn't suspecting anything," Murphy explained, "then he wouldn't have been paying close enough attention to notice that it wasn't you."

"All that to lure her to my place," Mac said with doubt in his tone, "so that when they made the hit, everyone would assume *I* was the target."

"Or my dad," Murphy said. "I got a report from my CO. The delivery man who gave my father the package is safe and clear. Neither of their covers were blown. She's confident Dad wasn't the target."

"Does that mean international terrorists are out of the picture then?" David said with a hint of relief in his tone.

"Depends on what this dude in Pennsylvania was into," Murphy said. "Contrary to what our government and the media have been telling us, they're here in America already. You'd be surprised and sickened to know how much progress they've made in their war against us since those in power forgot about September Eleventh. But, not knowing anything about this guy Agnes was working for, there's no telling who or what we're dealing with."

Mac noticed the color drain from David's face. "There's at least a dozen things this Crane guy could have been into besides terrorism. If it has to do with computers, he very well could have been into drugs, illegal arms, or identity theft."

"We need to find out what's on this that's valuable enough to kill for." David took the thumb drive from Mac's hand. "I'm going to lock this up in the safe in my office until I can get it to our technical people to check it out." He slipped the flash drive into his breast pocket.

"Give me the name of this murder victim in Pennsylvania." Murphy took his phone out of its case.

"Crane," Mac answered. "Agnes kept talking about a Mr. Crane."

"First name?" Murphy asked.

"No idea," Mac replied. "Mr. Crane."

"Murdered in Pennsylvania?" Murphy asked while thumbing across the smart phone's screen.

"She's from around Pitts—"

"Got it. Reginald Crane," Murphy read from the screen. "Tortured to death earlier this week. Body discovered yesterday morning. COD is heart attack. Detective leading the case is Cameron Gates, Pennsylvania State Police, Homicide Division—aka my stepmother." One of his eyebrows arched. "She's forty-two. I never would have thought she was over forty."

"Did the murderers grab Cameron?" Donny asked with impatience in his voice. "If it's the same—"

"Does Dad know Cameron is missing?" Murphy asked. "What have you told him?"

"He was asking for her," Mac said. "We just told him that she's on her way. We didn't want him going into surgery not knowing whether she's okay."

"She has to be okay." Donny clutched his brother's arm. "Nothing is going to happen to Cameron, Murphy. Right?"

"Mac!"

Expecting his lady love to jump into his arms and give him a big hug, Mac turned around. The sight that met his eyes caused his jaw to drop. Instead of grabbing Archie and holding her tight, he stood straight in disbelief when the now dark-haired brunette threw her arms around him.

"Oh, Mac, I was so worried about you! Hector told me that the manor is in shambles, but when I think of what could have happened to you and Josh and Gnarly." She pulled away and gazed up into Mac's face with tears in her eyes. "How is Josh? Is he okay?"

As hard as he tried to concentrate on what Archie was saying to him, Mac couldn't piece the words together to understand what she was saying. They only sounded like noises, and they were drowned out by the question that kept repeating itself in his mind.

"Don't say it, Dad," he heard Tristan warn him in the background.

"Mac, are you okay?" Archie asked. "Say something."

The words spilled out of his mouth. "What in heaven's name happened to your hair?"

Tears spilled like a waterfall from Archie's lovely emerald green eyes. "Oh, Mac!"

"Now you did it." Jessica wrapped her arm around Archie. "It isn't her fault, you know."

"What?" Mac asked. "*I* didn't do that to her." Watching Jessica hugging the sobbing Archie, Mac realized how blunt he had been in his shock. "Archie," he pried her away from his daughter. Gently, he rocked his fiancée in his arms. "I'm sorry. I was just so shocked. You need to give a guy a warning when his little blonde pixie suddenly turns into I don't know what. I'm sure they can fix it—"

Archie choked. "Not before the wedding."

"That's okay." Mac stepped back to admire her pretty face. "I'm marrying you, not your hair. You're a beautiful woman and I love you … even if you do have ugly hair." Noticing that instead of peering down at her, they were eye to eye, Mac held her back and looked her up and down. "Are you taller?"

"It's my new boots." Archie lifted one of her feet to show him her high-heel, platform boots. With a flick of her eyes in Jessica's direction, she wordlessly sent the warning to Mac to remind him that they had been a Christmas present from his daughter.

With a small grin, Mac picked up the signal. Archie, who preferred to go barefoot, rarely wore such extravagant footwear. She had only put them on for the arrival of his daughter. "Very nice."

"I don't think her hair looks half bad," Murphy said to Jessica.

"Spoken like a man," Jessica said while shrugging out of the leather jacket he had lent to her earlier.

"I am a man." Murphy reached for the jacket. "What do you expect me to speak like? A giraffe?"

Keeping hold of the jacket, Jessica moved in closer to him. "How is your father, Murphy?"

"In surgery," he said. "But the prognosis is good."

"I'm glad." She lowered her head to peer at him from the top of her violet eyes. "I broke up with Colt Fitzgerald." She laid her hands on top of his where they grasped the jacket that hung between them.

Murphy tried to fight the smile that came to his lips. "Really?"

"Really."

"Would I be thinking too highly of myself if I thought you did that for me?"

"No."

"You didn't have to end it with Colt Fitzgerald, underwear hunk, just for me." A wide grin crossing his face, he pulled away to put on his jacket. "But I'm glad you did."

Jessica reached out to lay her fingers on his firm chest. "Are you doing anything tomorrow night, Murphy Thornton?"

With a quick motion, he zipped up the coat, almost catching her fingertips in the zipper. "Sounds like I'm going to a wedding, Jessica Faraday."

She tilted her head to gaze up into his eyes. "These lips will be reserved for yours at midnight."

It took all of his control to keep from pulling her into his arms.

"Jessie …" Tristan practically stepped in between the two of them. "Excuse me," he said to Murphy, who backed up a full step to break the sexual tension that had such a strong hold on the two of them. "I'm Tristan, Jessie's brother." He offered Murphy his hand.

With a sigh, Murphy shook the offered hand. "Nice to meet you, Tristan."

"Thank you for saving Jessie earlier," Tristan said, "and for what you did at the safe house. Chief O'Callaghan says you really put yourself in the line of fire to save everyone, including our dad."

Murphy warmed up to the young man in the eyeglasses standing before him. "You're welcome, Tristan."

"I admire men like you and my dad, who aren't afraid to put their own lives on the line every day."

"I'm sure if the situation called for it, you'd do the same, Tristan."

The young man's cheeks turned pink. "I'm not the physical sort."

Jessica wrapped her arms around her brother in an affectionate hug. "Tristan is an intellectual and proud of it."

"Do you know where our world would be today without the intellectuals?" Murphy asked. When Tristan hesitated, he answered, "The dark ages." He tapped Tristan on the chest. "It's men like you who keep the rest of us moving forward."

Turning to Jessica, Tristan whispered into her ear, "You have my permission to marry him."

Stepping out of the emergency room exit into the parking lot, David was praying for a second wind. He had barely slept the night before, even though he was staying at one of the luxurious suites at the Spencer Inn.

Something that Donny Thornton had said about Mac Faraday was nagging at the back of his mind.

Don't you see? He got the fame and fortune, but you got his dad. And that's something he can never buy, no matter how rich he is. Makes you wonder who the rich man really is.

Standing out in the freezing wind, David looked up at the darkening sky in an attempt to watch the snowflakes whirling down through the parking lot lights that had just turned on with the approach of evening.

Mac had never met Patrick O'Callaghan, his birth father. Yet, they were so very much alike. More than once since meeting Mac, becoming close friends with him, and working with him on murder cases, David had been taken aback by an expression that would cross his face, or even the tone of his voice in a particular circumstance.

Mac has no idea how much he takes after Dad.

And yet, Mac had never met him even once. It was all in his DNA.

Mac had inherited the Spencer birthright and all the wealth and respect that went with the name, but David inherited the memories of a lifetime growing up with his father.

Somehow, it just didn't seem right.

Who really is the rich man?

David was startled by the feeling of two arms wrapping around him from behind to take him into a warm hug. "You seem to be miles away," Chelsea whispered into his back.

David clasped her hands and pulled her around. Her light blue eyes looked translucent in the parking lot lights beaming down on them. "Don't tell me you came in for a medical reason." It had been more than a year since her last epileptic seizure. Seeing Molly sitting calmly next to her, he didn't think it was a possibility, but he wanted to ask.

"Bogie drove me in," she said. "I wanted to see if you all needed anything. Both Fletcher and Zigler got shot?"

David nodded. "They're okay. They'll be going home soon. Fletcher only got grazed on the neck. If the bullet had gone just a fraction of an inch to the right, he'd have been gone, though. It would have gone through his neck. Officer Zigler got a bullet in his arm. They've already removed it. He's happy on painkillers. His wife is here. She'll be taking him home."

"With everything that's happening, there's still going to be a wedding?"

David trapped her in his arms. "We need a celebration now more than ever. After the last few days …" He stopped to gaze down into her face.

The look on her face—it was total adoration and love. It reminded him of a time … fishing.

"Darling?" Her voice sounded far away. "Are you okay?"

David blinked.

"What's wrong?" Her adoration changed to concern.

"Tired," he muttered. With a sigh, he tightened his arms around her. "I was just … do you remember when we used to go fishing?"

She giggled. "Fishing? David, when we were kids, we used to go fishing all the time."

"Do you remember that time …" As the memory came back, his cheeks felt warm. "When I asked you to go steady. You said yes and we …" He bent over to kiss her on the forehead.

"Your father walked in and caught us in the boathouse." Her ivory-colored cheeks turned bright pink.

He lifted her face to gaze down into her eyes. Gently, he kissed her on the mouth.

"What brought that up?" she asked.

"You're very important to me, Chelsea."

"I know."

David sighed. "After all this is over, the wedding and Dooley's murder, and … everything, I want us to take some time off, you and me, and go someplace just the two of us."

As if to remind him of her, Molly touched her cold snout to his hand.

"The three of us."

While Chelsea was awed by his sudden display of affection for her, she was also confused. "Okay. Where do you want to go?"

"Wherever you want."

With a giggle, she replied, "Mac and Archie are going to Australia for their honeymoon."

"Within reason." He kissed her on the nose. "I'm going home to shower and change. See you at the church?"

"Try to avoid me." She kissed him on the lips.

His gaze on her was soft. "I love you, Chelsea. Don't you ever forget that."

His tone scared her. "I love you, too, David."

Before she could ask him the reason for his sudden declaration, he pulled up the collar to his coat and walked across the parking lot to his cruiser. She watched him climb into the front seat of the cruiser. Before turning to go inside, she caught his eye as he sat staring through the windshield.

Maybe he needs a nap before the rehearsal dinner.

He shot her a wave of his hand. Only slightly reassured, she turned around to go inside to check on everyone who was still there.

Staring at the car keys in his hands, David heard another voice, this one from Donny's brother, Murphy, in his head.

Contrary to what our government and the media has been telling us, they are here in America already. You'd be surprised and sickened to know how much progress they've made in their war against us since those in power forgot about September Eleventh.

They're here in America.

How naive could I be to think they would not come here? Like I really thought our government would put their own agendas and personal interests aside to protect me and my team?

David stared at the key ring in his hand.

Want to know a trick a buddy of mine taught me? It was Patrick O'Callaghan's voice speaking inside his head.

Narrowing his blue eyes, David focused in on the keys.

An undercover narc from Philadelphia taught me this.

They were two men sharing a beer at the kitchen table. David had a long weekend away from the police academy. After hearing his son's report on a class taught by a former FBI undercover agent, the police chief couldn't resist relaying a few tricks he had learned on his own.

Taking his key ring from the hook on the wall next to the kitchen table, Patrick O'Callaghan removed the hand cuff key. "If you ever get into a situation where you end up in a pair of cuffs, what are you going to do?"

David chuckled. "I happen to be flexible enough that I can slip the cuffs." He had practiced himself, bending over and slipping his cuffed hands down past his hips and under his feet.

"Suppose you're hog-tied, or zip-tied, or tied down flat?" Seeing that his son didn't have an answer, Patrick's eyes sparkled. "Always have a handcuff key stashed away where you can get it if you need it." He shook the key at David. "The bad guys do. So should you."

Standing up from his chair, the police chief went over to a kitchen drawer where they kept a small first aid kit. "I'm going to show you an old trick that I pray you never need to use."

Patrick O'Callaghan had been dead for many years, but David sat in the front seat of his cruiser remembering that night and how the police chief had made his son practice his little trick over and over again until he had it down.

When did I stop doing that? David looked up to see the snow blowing around his cruiser in the parking lot. *When did I get so comfortable ... and complacent?*

With a sense of urgency, he dug his hand into the breast pocket of his shirt until he found his spare hand cuff key. Throwing open the door to his cruiser, he climbed out and went around to the back in search of the first aid kit.

Time to stop being comfortable. If the enemy is here, then I need to be ready.

"Time to wake up and take your medicine, little lady."

The words bounced and echoed inside Cameron's head.

"Wake up." The harsh sounding words were partnered by a slap on her cheek. "I don't have all day."

With effort, Cameron fluttered her eyelids to look around. The dark room was blurry, and there was a white round figure in the middle.

"There. Are you awake? Open your mouth. It's time for your medicine."

Thick rough fingers grasped her jaw and pried her mouth open. The sting of the alcohol burned her tongue and throat where it went down. When she jerked her head away, the whiskey spilt across her face and down her throat, chest, and behind her shoulders to dribble down behind her neck. She felt her sweater cling to her chest.

"Get your hands off me!" she said between coughs. Attempting to sit up, she discovered that her hands were cuffed to the bedposts. Soft cloths were wrapped around her wrists to prevent telltale bruising.

Her vision clearing, she recognized the fat round face of Special Agent Leland Elder.

"You son of a bitch!" Even though she was tied down, she lunged for him. "I'm going to kill you!"

"I don't think so, Gates." A cocky grin crossed his face. "You wouldn't be in this position now if you had just minded your place. My partner and I took over the Crane murder case—"

"Who *you* killed!"

"That's irrelevant to your situation."

"Are you even real FBI agents?"

"Of course," Elder said. "Your boss checked us out. I've been with the bureau over twenty years. Black, close to twelve. Both of us have distinguished commendations. Sterling records."

"For a couple of killers."

"We do what we have to do for our nation." Bottle in hand, he bent over her. "Now lay back and have a few drinks, and then you can die happy—which is a lot better than how Crane went out."

With a snap of her teeth, Cameron attempted to bite him.

Elder threw back his hand as if to slap her, but then he thought better of it. "Nah, the police can't find you with any marks on you. Won't go with the scenario."

"What scenario?"

With a cocky laugh, Elder sat back on the bed. "Oh, you've been very depressed, Detective Gates. Your first husband died about this time several years ago, didn't he? With the holiday season, memories have come crashing back. Since your current husband left town, you've become increasingly depressed thinking about Nick. You've been calling your husband, but he's been busy and unable to comfort you. So you decided to check into this motel and drown your sorrows until, unable to take the pain and guilt any longer,"—he held up Cameron's phone and pressed a button—"you sent one last text to your hubby. 'I love you and I'm sorry. Good-bye.'"

"No!" Only when Cameron attempted to pull up her legs to kick him did she discover that her feet were also bound with handcuffs to the footboards.

Grabbing her by the jaw, Elder reached over to press the muzzle of the gun into her mouth, pry it open, and shove the gun in. "Time to eat your gun, little lady."

"You first," Cameron heard a male voice say before she heard the shot.

CHAPTER EIGHTEEN

Rock Springs Boulevard, Chester, West Virginia

Were the holidays always this exhausting?

Jan Martin-MacMillan wanted a nap. But she had to clean the house while the cleaning was good—while her eight-month-old son was sleeping. If she laid down, she knew she'd be asleep as soon as her head hit the pillow.

T.J. (Tad Junior) still wasn't cognizant about Christmas and New Year's Eve. If making the house special for the holidays was this exhausting, then what was she going to do next year when he'd be completely mobile?

She was tired just thinking about it.

Kneeling under the tree, Jan was smoothing the tree curtain when she sensed, rather than saw, her husband, Dr. Tad MacMillan, come into the room and sit down on the edge of the sofa next to her. He bent over to kiss her on the top of the head. "Alone at last," he breathed into her blonde hair.

Irving, Cameron's twenty-five pound Maine coon, leapt up onto the sofa and curled up to sit down, facing the two of them.

"Not quite," she replied.

He lifted her chin to face him. His green eyes sparkled. "Ignore him." He kissed her gently on the lips.

The doorbell rang.

"How about whoever is at the door?" she replied.

"Let's pretend no one is home."

"You're the town doctor," she said with a sigh while climbing to her feet. "Our vehicles are outside. If someone needs help and you don't answer …" She hurried from the living room to the foyer. Passing the bay window, she saw that Cameron's cruiser was in the driveway. "I thought Cameron left for Deep Creek Lake this morning."

"She did." Tad jumped to his feet and went to the window. He saw a tall, slender man with longish brown hair and dark-rimmed glasses on the porch. He was dressed in jeans and a military fatigue jacket. Cameron was nowhere in sight.

Concerned, Tad raced his wife toward the stairs. "Go upstairs."

"What?" Jan laughed.

"Something's not right. Go check on T.J. and don't come down until I call you." Insistent, Tad waited for her to head up the stairs of their red-brick colonial before opening the door a crack to regard the young man on the porch.

"Dr. Tad MacMillan?" the young man smiled politely at him.

"Yes …"

The young man gestured at the three-story stone home next door, on the corner of Rock Spring Boulevard. "You're cousins with Joshua Thornton, who lives next door, and his wife, Detective Gates."

"That's right," Tad said. "Who are you?"

"I'm Ethan Bonner," the young man said. "You'll find there's a warrant out for me on suspicion of murder, which is why I didn't go to the hospital. I have Detective Cameron Gates in the backseat of her cruiser here. She needs your help."

"Did you come to tell us something, Tristan?" Jessica asked her brother about the reason for his interrupting a very pleasant conversation with Murphy.

"Rehearsal dinner tonight," Tristan replied. "We need to be at the church in two hours."

When Jessica looked at Murphy with hope in her eyes, he sighed. "I think I need to stay with Donny. We should be here when Dad wakes up."

Understanding, Jessica nodded her head. "But I'll come back for you right after the rehearsal. I'll even bring you some dinner from the Spencer Inn if you'd like."

"I'd like that."

Sensing the electricity between them, Tristan backed away. "I'm going to go check to see if Dad and Archie are ready to go. Dad is riding back with us. Chief O'Callaghan went home to shower and get dressed. He'll be meeting us at the church." He gestured at them. "Go back to what you were doing."

"What do you like?" she asked Murphy, who gazed into her face.

"I like everything."

Blushing, she giggled. "I meant for dinner from the Spencer Inn."

"Just so long as it's vegetarian, no meat—"

"But you do eat fish." She took yet another opportunity to touch his firm chest, allowing her fingers to slide down the center to his stomach.

"You remembered that?"

Locking her eyes on his, she said, "I remember everything."

He flashed her a grin that encompassed the dimples in both cheeks. "Surprise me."

She reached for his hand. "Don't tempt me."

He brought her hand to his lips. She thought he was going to kiss the top of her hand. Instead, he turned her hand over and pressed his lips to the inside of her palm.

The touch of his lips on her flesh sent a sensuous shockwave through her body. Her breath caught. Every muscle from her throat down through her stomach tightened. She could hear her heart beating in her ears, drowning out the sound of a crash and a scream from somewhere behind them.

The shriek sounded strangely like Archie Monday.

From a hallway across from the reception desk, Tristan came running out.

Mac came rushing out of the waiting room at the sound of Archie's scream. "What happened?"

Speechless, Tristan pointed down the hallway. Mac and two orderlies ran in the direction he pointed.

Jessica raced up to her brother. "What happened?"

"She fell off her boots."

From down the hallway, Jessica could hear Archie Monday sobbing uncontrollably while Mac tried to comfort her. One of the orderlies came racing out into the reception area. "We need a gurney and a doctor. Get x-ray ready!"

"Honey, it's going to be okay," Jessica, Tristan, and Murphy heard Mac say from down the hall.

"Oh yeah, easy for you to say standing there on both feet, not a mark on you, and having a good hair day," Archie spat out. "The only thing that's happened to you this week was a bunch of hit men tried to kill you!"

"They're funny when they fight." Chuckling, Tristan turned to Jessica and Murphy. He saw that Jessica and Murphy were not laughing.

Murphy noticed a far-away look come to Jessica's violet eyes. She was looking beyond her father, kneeling next to his bride-to-be, trying to soothe her growing distress. "Buttercup?"

"Look at him," she said in a soft voice.

"Who?" Murphy asked.

"Dad." She nudged her brother with her elbow. "Look at Dad, Tristan."

"I see him."

The three of them peered down the hallway at the man dressed in slacks and a sweater. After two rough days without a shower or shave, he had a heavy five o'clock shadow across his lower face, and his hair was disheveled.

"Clue me in," Murphy said.

"He doesn't have a *mark* on him," Jessica said forcefully. "Yet, his DNA and blood are all over a murder crime scene from two days ago."

"You mean he's accused of murder?" Murphy shook his head. "I wonder ..."

"You're not the only one." Jessica grabbed Tristan by the elbow. "Bring up that case file on your tablet again."

"You said hacking into the sheriff's department files was *wrong*," Tristan said with mock innocence.

"I want to see the autopsy report," she ordered.

Tristan dug his computer tablet out of his case.

"Someone impersonated your father to leave a message for Archie's mother," Murphy said, "In order to lure her to his house to be killed. That takes some brains and planning."

Jessica said, "Like the kind of organizational skills needed to acquire my father's DNA and blood in order to frame him for murder."

"Possibly," Murphy asked. "Who's the murder victim?"

"Russell Dooley," Jessica said. "Dad arrested his wife for murder. She recently killed herself in prison."

They all stepped aside while the hospital orderlies, Mac, and Bogie wheeled Archie past them and the reception area to go into an examination room.

Murphy asked Jessica, "Did either this guy or his late wife have any ties to international terrorism?"

"I don't think so." With a cringe, Jessica shook her head. "Tristan, haven't you hacked into that database yet?" she snapped.

Murphy was chuckling. "Feisty. I like feisty women."

"You ain't seen nothing yet, honey buns."

Cameron could hear voices—fuzzy voices. Soft, tender, kind voices swirling around her.

"Is she going to be okay?" asked a feminine voice that sounded vaguely familiar.

"I think so," another friendly voice answered. This one was male.

"Josh …" Cameron fought to call out.

"Shhh …" She felt a touch on hers. "It's okay, Cameron," the male voice said. "You're safe. You're going to be fine."

With effort, she opened her eyes to the blurry image of a man leaning over her.

"Josh …" Her vision cleared. "Tad."

"That's right."

"I'm here, too, Cam." Jan eased down onto the bed on her other side. "You're here … at our house … in our guest room. Your prime murder suspect, Ethan Bonner, brought you to us."

Suddenly, Cameron's vision cleared as she focused in on the man standing at the foot of the bed with a cell phone to his ear. While she had never met or seen him before, he matched the description that had gone out on her notice to be on the look out for the suspect, who was tall with longish hair and dark-framed eyeglasses. A dozen questions came to her mind at once. "You …"

She tried to sit up, only to have Tad push her back down onto the bed. "Cameron, I suggest you don't try to say or do anything right now. Someone filled you up with alcohol. Right now you have a blood alcohol level of point one-four. So you're not thinking very clearly, hon."

"I've been sober—"

"It's not your fault, sweetie." A recovering alcoholic himself, Tad sympathized with the grief that Cameron had to have felt at having been purposely dragged down off the wagon of sobriety. "You have an injection mark in your abdomen. Not only did they pour it down your throat, but they injected it directly into your stomach—"

"Trying to stage your murder to look like a suicide after a binge," Ethan Bonner interjected.

"You killed him," Cameron recalled. "That FBI agent— Elder. What's this about? He said he was doing what he had to do for his nation."

"Why would they have to kill Cameron to protect our nation?" Jan twisted around on the bed to ask Bonner.

"Not *our* nation," Ethan corrected her. "*His* nation. The nation of Islam."

"But he was an FBI agent," Cameron argued. "My boss said he checked him and Black out. They've been with the FBI for—"

"Yes, they have," Ethan said. "They were both born in the good old U S of A. But the background check for these types of organizations don't check into people's religious loyalties or worldviews. I'm sure you've heard of separation of church and state. Good guys who never even had a parking ticket. No one would suspect that they have both been spending their free time working for Islam extremists for I don't know how many years."

"If they're so clean, how'd they end up on your radar?" Tad asked.

"And who are you?" Cameron wanted to know.

"My boss, Reginald Crane, worked for the federal government for several years," Ethan explained. "He retired with wonderful credentials. He was on the ground floor of cyber security when it was in its infancy. He taught me everything I know. After he retired, he offered his services to the private sector, and big corporations jumped into hiring him for consulting—especially when they had government contracts. We're talking huge bucks." Ethan rubbed his fingers together.

"A ghost making huge bucks?" Cameron asked.

"Huh?" Ethan replied.

"When we did a background check on Reginald Crane and you, nothing came up," Cameron explained. "Social security, driver's license—someone made both of you disappear off the grid."

"That would be me," Ethan said.

"Why?" Jan asked.

"I figured if they couldn't find anything on Crane or me, they wouldn't be able to find me," Ethan said. "These are some really bad dudes." He pointed at Cameron. "That guy was an FBI agent—he was supposed to be on her side!"

Tad held up his hands. "Okay, so you wiped you and your boss off the grid in order to hide from the people who killed Crane. Who exactly are these people? Start at the beginning."

"Six weeks ago, Crane was hired by a medical firm that was working on a cure for Ebola."

"Why would a medical firm hire a computer security specialist?" Jan asked.

"Because everything is computerized nowadays," Ethan said. "Their internal technical services were picking up some suspicious activities. Security breaches that could have been just flukes within the system—or they could have been real breaches of security. Considering what they were dealing with, they didn't want to take a chance, so they called us in. Crane and I narrowed down the security breach to one specific researcher. A background check on him revealed several trips over the last few years to Iraq and ties to an Islamic terrorist group."

"He was helping them make a dirty bomb," Tad said.

Ethan nodded his head. "In their research, the company, and this man was on the team, developed a man-made version of Ebola. This researcher had the recipe for it. Right before Christmas, our security team and the firm's private group caught him just before he was able to send the formula to his people in Iraq. He committed jihad in a car bomb right outside an Internet cafe in Philadelphia."

Uttering a hollow laugh, Ethan said, "You may have seen it on the news. Homeland Security was notified about it, but the official government statement claims it was an accidental explosion caused by a faulty electrical system in an old car." He winked at Jan, a newspaper journalist. "Have you ever heard of propaganda?"

"Yes," she said in a soft voice.

"It's alive and well," Ethan said. "Two members of that medical company's security division were injured with second- and third-degree burns in that 'accidental blast.'"

"Then why kill your boss and go after Cameron?" Tad gestured at Cameron, whose alcohol-fogged mind was still trying to keep track of what had happened. "Homeland Security was notified about this guy and the Ebola he was sending to Iraq to fuel a dirty bomb. You guys intercepted it before it went."

"Because they still want the man-made Ebola formula," Ethan answered. "When this researcher realized we were on to him, he smuggled it out of the facility on a thumb drive

247

to send through his own laptop. I shut off the Internet connection surrounding the cafe before it could go and intercepted the file he was sending before he blew himself up. Then, Crane was contacted by a couple of feds saying they were with Homeland Security and needed the copy of the file that we had intercepted. To Crane, that was fishy. The research facility had the file. Being an old fed, he decided to play them along to find out who they really were. He got enough to check them out and found out that they were really with the FBI—and they were also on annual leave."

"I'm sure my boss didn't check that far," Cameron said.

"So then Crane dug even further," Ethan said. "Whatever he found in their background convinced him that they were the last ones he wanted to turn over that flash drive to."

"Why didn't he destroy it?" Jan asked.

"Because he didn't have time," Ethan said. "The formula was already on our computers. Crane called me. I was out of town. He told me that they were on their way—and then he got spooked. He heard something on the line that told him that someone was listening. He told me that he was going to send the formula into the black hole."

"What's the black hole?" Tad asked.

Ethan laughed. "At first, I didn't get it either. But then I remembered that right after he said that, he turned and said something to Agnes, his cleaning lady. He always referred to her hand bag as the 'black hole' because she kept everything in it."

"But Agnes left to go to her daughter's wedding," Cameron said, "and took the black hole with her. As luck would have it, her son-in-law-to-be is Mac Faraday. So they launched their attack on her at his place to cover up who the real target was."

"And you refused to back down in your investigation," Bonner said. "So they cloned your phone." He took a phone out of his pocket. "I found this on Elder. I've been following you to find Agnes, and I saw them following you."

"So they know exactly where Agnes and *Josh* are?" Cameron sprang upright, only for Tad to gently push her back down. "I led them to them!"

"Did they get the thumb drive?" Jan asked.

Ethan held his phone. "I managed to get ahold of one of Crane's old colleagues. He had given me her business card before to call if he ever got into trouble. This has clearly been that time. Those two sleeper agents split up. One of them went on to meet up with a team to track down Agnes Douglas. Crane's old friend has been trying to get one step ahead of them."

If it was any other day, or any other event, David would have begged out to go to bed and sleep for twelve hours. But this was the day before Mac and Archie's wedding. It was their rehearsal, and he was honored that Mac had asked him to be one of his groomsmen.

There was no way he was going to miss it.

While driving back to Spencer Manor, David could smell the soot and sweat on his clothes. His coat was torn and covered with a mixture of blood from more than one person. Rubbing his aching shoulder, he could feel where the blood from one of the assassins had hardened when it dried into the fabric.

A long hot shower will make me a new man—at least new enough to make it through the rehearsal and the dinner. Then I'll take Chelsea up to her room, hold her soft body close to mine, and get a good long sleep.

The crime scene tape was still stretched across the front of Spencer Manor. If he hadn't been the chief of police, he would have been denied access to the property and the stone guest cottage where he lived. He would have stayed at the Spencer Inn, but the new suit he had bought for the rehearsal dinner was at the cottage. As long as he was there to get it, he'd take a shower and hopefully feel human again.

David parked his cruiser outside of the stone pillars marking the entrance to Spencer Manor. Realizing Mac and Archie hadn't been around to collect the mail, he went to the box at the end of the driveway and extracted a stack of cards, letters, bills, and advertisements. After tucking the stack under his arm, he ducked under the crime scene tape to jog up the icy driveway and travel the stone path between the garage and main house that would take him to the stone guest cottage where he lived.

Tucked in the corner of the rose garden at the end of the wrap-around deck of the main house, the guest cottage was cozy with a view of the lake provided by floor-to-ceiling windows. Once he turned the corner of the stone path to come out on the other side of the manor, a stiff, chilling breeze blew in off the lake to hit David with full frigid force. Shaking it off, he picked up his pace to the cottage door and stuck his key into the lock. With a twist of his wrist, he unlocked the door and hurried inside.

"Damn! It's cold," he said out loud with a shiver.

Hurrying across the great room, he stole a glance at the big screen smart television acting as the focal point for the living area. He was still getting used to not only seeing it in his home, but learning how to work all the special features that Chelsea claimed it had—like syncing it with his smart phone and email.

"Why would I want to check my email on my television?" he had asked Chelsea when she showed the feature on the extension control panel and remote.

"Because you can," was her reply.

"Where's the button to watch the game?"

He had yet to find it since she had shown it to him Christmas morning.

Oh, man, he thought while casting a glare at the monstrosity on his wall, *if I have to call Archie over here to turn on my television in front of the guys to watch the Super Bowl ...*

After tossing the mail in the middle of the table to land next to the bowl of fresh apples that he used for a centerpiece, David shrugged out of his coat and draped it across the back of a kitchen chair. Then, he unbuckled his utility belt with his service weapon and baton and hung it on the same chair on top of the coat before making his way to the fridge for a beer. After twisting off the cap, David uttered a heavy sigh while quickly recounting everything that had happened in the last two days.

Terrorists! David took a mouthful of the beer and held it in his mouth while thinking with narrowed eyes. *What does Murphy know that he's not telling? How much progress have they made in their mission?*

Feeling a rumble in his stomach, David tried to remember the last time he had eaten. He turned around to go back to the fridge and set the bottle of beer down on the counter while grasping the door handle with the other. Out of the corner of his eye, he saw a movement in the reflection of the stainless steel refrigerator door.

Whirling around one hundred and eighty degrees, David used his right hand to grab the butcher knife from the knife block on the counter from behind him. Holding the menacing knife with the blade outward, David flung the blade with a backward motion to slice the man who came charging out from the shadows of the hallway leading to the small den and office. The point and blade caught the muscle-bound brute in the throat. David continued slashing with the knife to severe his jugular vein, vocal box, and come out the other side of his neck.

David could feel the man's warm blood shoot out and shower his face and uniform as his attacker clutched his throat. Slipping on the blood that splattered everywhere, the attacker's feet went out from under him, and he landed flat on his back on the floor, his body jerking in death tremors.

"Allah!"

David sensed the second attacker before he heard him scream out. With the bloody knife still in his hand, David whirled around and ducked. Wrapping both arms around the man's midsection, David plunged the knife into his lower back.

As the assailant fell back against the kitchen counter, David heard the loud rattle of the beer bottle falling over and rolling across the counter. It landed with a clatter in the sink.

Damn! I wanted that beer.

David withdrew the knife and stabbed him again in the chest.

David had his arm raised to continue his defense when he felt a sharp pain in the back of his left thigh.

I've been shot!

His leg crumbling out from under him, David felt the pain shoot throughout his entire body. Arms and legs shaking uncontrollably, he slid down to the bloody kitchen floor between the two dead assailants.

Fighting against the numbness and his twitching limbs, David looked up to see a man coming around the corner of the kitchen counter and peering down at him. Through the fog, he could see that he had reddish-blond hair. As his face came closer, David squinted up into the face that appeared as all-American as his own.

What kind of terrorist ...

His voice sounded like it was coming to him from the end of a long tunnel. "Major David O'Callaghan, my friends are anxious to meet you."

CHAPTER NINETEEN

Sheriff Christopher Turow had not been looking forward to tracking down Mac Faraday at the hospital in Oakland to begin with—not with three of his friends being tended for gunshot wounds. The sheriff knew all three. Two were well-respected officers with the Spencer Police Force.

The fact that whoever it was came into Garrett County and shot two uniformed police officers had Turow's deputies on edge as much as he was.

It was all a big mess.

Mac Faraday was not your average murder suspect. The sheriff knew and respected the man.

Russell Dooley's murder had the earmarks of a crime of passion.

The crime scene did not fit in with how Mac operated at all. Mac was not a hothead. Police Chief O'Callaghan's claims that Mac had come to him and that the police chief had gone to speak to Dooley made sense. Mac Faraday had a cool head, and so did David O'Callaghan.

Having investigated so many deaths as a homicide detective, Mac knew better than to allow himself to get into such a situation. He would have sent someone—like Police Chief

David O'Callaghan—to give Dooley a calm cool talking-to while he stayed as far away as possible from the situation.

Then how did Mac Faraday's blood and DNA get at the scene?

Sheriff Christopher Turow didn't know the answer to that.

He didn't feel like he knew anything—especially when he stepped into the waiting room at the hospital and found himself face to face with Jessica Faraday, who was asking the same question. Her piercing violet eyes seemed to bore into his soul and demand an answer.

"I've got nothing, Ms. Faraday," the sheriff said with a sigh.

"Did you know that someone engineered a fake recording of Dad's voice to call the Spencer Inn and leave a message with the desk clerk? It was that message that lured Agnes Douglas to the manor in order to kill her—and made it look like a hit on Dad."

"I did not know that," Sheriff Turow replied.

Jessica gestured behind the sheriff. "Ask him yourself. He'll tell you."

The sheriff turned around to discover Mac coming into the waiting room. He was carrying a cup of coffee.

A pleasant grin crossed the murder suspect's face. "Sheriff Turow." Mac shifted the cup of coffee to the other hand and offered it to shake. "Thank you so much for your help out there."

The sheriff took his hand. "You're very welcome. I just wish none of your people were hurt."

"It could have been worse."

"How are you doing?" the sheriff asked.

"Better than Archie."

"What happened to Archie?" Sheriff Turow groaned. "Don't tell me that whoever it is—"

"She fell off her high-heeled boots," Jessica announced. "That tends to happen when you aren't used to high fashion."

Sheriff Turow looked down at Jessica's own thigh-high, high-heeled boots. "I guess you can't go from bare feet to stilettoes overnight."

"She broke two bones in her ankle and tore a tendon," Mac said. "She needs surgery and can't be on her feet for the next six weeks."

"What about the rehearsal dinner and wedding?"

"I have no idea," Mac said with a shake of his head and a sigh.

"If you want my advice," the sheriff said with braced breath, "I highly recommend putting this wedding and all of the events leading up to it on hold until we find out who is behind this. They shot two police officers. They're heavily armed. Spencer has a small police force, and my department is limited in the protection we can give—"

Mac held up his hand to halt the sheriff. "I hear you, and I've been thinking the same thing."

"Then what are you going to do?"

When Mac hesitated, Jessica asked, "How many tens of thousands of dollars have you put into this?"

"These people who are coming, most of whom I don't know, are friends and family," Mac said. "Even one of their lives is more valuable than the money." He groaned. "And it's sickening to me that I keep thinking about the money and the stroke Jeff Ingles will have if I cancel."

He gestured down the hallway to where Archie's ankle was still being examined and treated. "But look at Archie. I *really* don't think she is in the mood for a wedding right now."

Sheriff Turow felt genuinely sorry for the man. He was about to give his condolences, offer to help any way he could, and then beg off to go check on Officers Fletcher and Zigler when Mac interjected, "But you didn't come here to hear about our little social problems. You have a murder investigation to conduct, and you need to talk to me."

Relieved, Sheriff Turow chuckled. "I tried to talk to you at the safe house, but things got a little busy."

Mac gestured to the waiting room, and up and down the hallway. "I'll talk to you wherever you want."

The sheriff offered to wait for Mac's lawyer. "Maybe you'll want to have Willingham—"

"I know the drill, Turow," Mac said. "And I know my rights. As long as you aren't charging me, I'll answer any questions you have without a lawyer."

"Are you sure, Dad?" Jessica asked.

"I've been in his shoes," Mac said. "I'm not going to waste his time by playing games. I don't have anything to hide."

Sheriff Turow gestured down the hallway toward the cafeteria. "How about if we talk over coffee?"

When Jessica fell in to follow them, Mac turned around and pointed back to the waiting room. "I think it's best if you wait here until you can see Archie."

"I thought you had nothing to hide," she shot back.

With a gesture of his hand, Mac sent Jessica back to the sofa in the waiting room.

They had only started down the hallway before the sheriff said, "O'Callaghan told you about the blood and DNA."

"Yep." Mac took a cautious sip of the hot coffee. "I have no idea how it ended up there other than being planted, which I know sounds cliché, but that's the only thing I can come up with. I'd never even heard of that motel until I found the picture in the envelope on my doormat. It was marked with the motel's stamp."

Slowly nodding his head, the sheriff went into the cafeteria, which was almost empty. When he stepped up to the coffee machine, Mac took a five dollar bill out of his pocket. "Coffee's on me."

"Is this a bribe?" he asked while taking the money.

"No," Mac said with a chuckle. "I don't need to bribe you. I didn't do anything."

The sheriff eased the money into the machine while Mac took off his sweater and draped it across the back of a chair at one of the cafeteria tables.

After Turow pressed the buttons to order his coffee, he turned to Mac and examined his outstretched hands and arms. "Just like O'Callaghan told me. Not a mark on them."

Without direction from the sheriff, Mac pulled his white undershirt over his head to reveal his bare chest and back. "Look as much as you want."

His coffee was brewed, but the sheriff was more interested in getting this part of his investigation out of the way. He removed his cell phone from its case on his belt. "Do you mind if I take pictures?"

"As long as you don't post them on the Internet," Mac replied with a laugh while turning around to allow him to examine his back for any cuts or bruises that could indicate that he had been in a knife fight with Russell Dooley before stabbing him to death.

The handful of hospital employees in the cafeteria stopped eating to watch the man disrobing for the sheriff.

"I'm only going to send these to the sheriff's department to have them uploaded to the case file." The sheriff snapped a couple of pictures of Mac's back. One was a full shot to take in his whole back, and the other was a closer shot of his broad shoulders that revealed that they were free of any injuries.

After Turow tapped him on the shoulder, Mac turned around for him to take pictures of his smooth, muscular chest and stomach. Unlike many wealthy men who became soft in their middle age, Mac Faraday kept somewhat fit. Even in the middle of winter, his body was still tanned from the short winter getaways that he took with Archie.

He also noted that Mac had no bruises or marks on his face.

"Have you found any witnesses to contradict my statement that I have never been to that motel?" Mac asked him while redressing.

"Nope." The sheriff thumbed the button to forward the pictures. He carefully took the hot coffee cup from the machine.

"Other than the blood and DNA, can you place me at the scene?" Mac leaned against one of the tables and draped a leg over its corner.

"No." The sheriff took a cautious sip of the hot coffee. "But you're a wealthy man, Mac. You know how the system works. Look at you now. You're practically leading this interview, you've been through it so many times. Who's to say that you didn't stage all this? You hired someone to get rid of Dooley, who was threatening Archie. You had your man plant the blood and DNA at the scene, knowing that you've never been there and that the lack of wounds on your body contradicts your blood—"

"Blood and DNA is enough to arrest me," Mac said. "If I was going to set myself up, I would make real sure that I had an alibi for the time of the murder—which, with this being a holiday week, and right before my wedding, I could have very easily done. Why would I do that without establishing an alibi in order to clear myself? Right now, I can't."

"No," Sheriff Turow said. "While the lack of any cuts on you can clear you of being at the scene, we can't clear you of hiring someone to commit the murder. I imagine that right now you have a lot of money flying out of your accounts to pay for this wedding. Probably would have been pretty easy for you to have hidden a payoff to someone to eliminate Dooley in all that mess."

259

Mac folded his arms across his chest. "Listen, Turow, Dooley made threats against Archie, but like you said, I'm a wealthy man. I have a whole security staff at the Spencer Inn—all very highly trained. My best friend is the chief of police. Plus, I'm pretty handy when it comes to defending myself and those I care about. So, why would I risk losing everything to kill Russell Dooley?"

Without missing a beat, Sheriff Turow countered. "Because he had enough evidence to take it all away."

Blinking, Mac backed up a step. "What are you talking about?"

The sheriff was thumbing through images on his cell phone. "Dooley's lawyer photographed and forwarded a letter that his client had left with him to open and send to law enforcement in the event of his sudden death. He is sending the original to be put in the case file." He handed the cell phone to Mac. "It instructs us to consider you the prime suspect in the event of Dooley's murder."

Mac enlarged the image of the photograph to read the handwritten letter. Sheriff Turow's brief synopsis was correct.

The narrative explained that Russell Dooley had found a micro cassette tape that his wife had recorded of a conversation she had with the lead detective in Harris Tyler's murder, Lieutenant Mac Faraday. In the conversation, Mac Faraday accused her of killing her lover. Leigh Ann Dooley told him that he couldn't prove any such thing, to which he cockily admitted that he couldn't. That was why he planted her blood and DNA at the scene to ensure her arrest and conviction for murder.

"I never planted evidence at a crime scene," Mac gasped out to the sheriff. "And if she did have a recording like that, why didn't she give it to her defense attorney to have presented at her trial."

"Keep reading," he said.

Mac's heart raced. With effort, he found the place he had left off in the letter to continue reading.

Russell Dooley went on to say that he was taking the tape to Deep Creek Lake to confront Mac Faraday with the evidence even though he knew that he was putting his life in danger by doing so. In his concluding paragraph, he told the letter's reader that in the event of his sudden death and the disappearance of the tape to consider Mac Faraday the prime suspect in the case.

Mac thrust the cell phone back into Sheriff Turow's hand. "I assume you found no cassette tape at the scene."

"Nope."

"Has anyone heard this recording?"

The sheriff shook his head. "Not his lawyer nor his daughter. Neither of them had ever heard of Russell's wife getting you to admit to planting evidence."

"He had to have made all this up," Mac said. "If this was true—and I was him—I'd have made a dozen copies of that tape and released it on the Internet. I would not have come to confront me alone with the only copy."

"His daughter says Dooley was not quite stable."

"You're right there."

"The man was stabbed twenty-nine times with a knife from the Spencer Inn, Mac," the sheriff said. "This letter provides motive. You have no alibi for the time of the murder, and your blood was found at the scene. I hate to say it, but you have a big problem."

Mac slumped against the table. "You have to have other suspects on your radar," he said in a pleading tone.

Sheriff Turow peered into Mac's eyes. He could see the worry floating to the surface in their blue pools.

"Anyone?"

"One," Turow said with hesitance.

"Who?"

"Brother of the woman who owns the motel," Sheriff Turow said in a low voice. "Gil Sherrard. Been in and out of jail half a dozen times for drugs and petty theft. He's been staying with his sister since he got out of his second stint in rehab for heroin—ten days ago. His fingerprints were found in the cabin where Dooley was staying."

"But his sister owns the place," Mac said with regret.

"That's not all," the sheriff said with a sigh of disgust.

"What?"

Sheriff Turow growled. "Damn it, Mac, I should not be talking to you about this."

"Tell me."

"According to Dooley's daughter," the sheriff said in a low voice, "he had a Rolex watch that was a wedding present from his late wife. It was engraved on the back. He also had a little over ten thousand dollars in cash with him when he left Washington. We found neither the cash nor the watch in the cabin."

"But you found Sherrard's fingerprints in the cabin, and he's a petty thief," Mac said.

"Plus, his son was the kid who gave us a description of a man who came up to the cabin around eleven, shortly before the time of death."

"David told me." Mac was nodding his head. "But the description this kid gave did not match my description—it matched Russell Dooley."

"Or maybe the kid actually saw his father going inside and is covering for him," Turow said. "Or he saw nothing. The kid's aunt says he's a pathological liar."

"Or he could be telling the truth," Mac said. "Russell Dooley went out, and the kid saw him come back. It could or could not be connected to the murder."

"Could be he's covering for his father," Turow said. "Sherrard broke in to steal from Dooley, who caught him, and things got out of hand. Now, Sherrard's in the wind. His sister says he left right after the police finished at the crime scene. I have my people checking the fences and pawn shops right now."

Mac should have been happy, but he wasn't. "Even if you find that Sherrard stole the watch and the money, his defense attorney will point the finger at me during the trial because of that letter and my blood and DNA being at the crime scene."

"Exactly."

Out in the hall, Jessica mentally said the name over and over again. *Gil Sherrard. Gil Sherrard.* She had a suspect. Now all she needed to do was uncover how a petty thief was able to frame her father.

"Before you even say it, Mac," Sheriff Turow said with a shake of his head, "I myself have had more than one run in with Sherrard. He isn't smart enough to know how to frame you—certainly not this elaborately."

"Then it had to be someone else."

Deep in thought, Mac jumped when the burn phone that Joshua Thornton had given him vibrated on his hip. "Hello."

A smug voice spoke into Mac's ear. "You have something that doesn't belong to you."

"Cameron ..." Joshua murmured the name that kept running through his mind.

With effort, he opened his eyes, only to shut them again when the bright lights above pierced through his eyes and stabbed his brain.

"Murphy," he heard Donny's voice, "he's waking up."

Murphy.

Joshua had a dull memory of the safe house and Murphy ... giving the pen to his son. "Murphy?"

He felt a strong hand clasp his shoulder. "I'm here, Dad. You're safe. Donny's here, too."

Grasping Murphy's hand, he asked, "Where's Cameron?" He sucked in a deep breath from the tube of oxygen going up his nostrils.

"She's on her way, Dad," Murphy said. "She'll be here soon."

"Did everyone get out of the safe house okay?"

"Everyone is fine."

Joshua remembered Officer Zigler taking the shot to the arm. "Zigler?" Then, recalling Officer Fletcher, he added, "Fletcher?"

"They're both fine," Murphy said. "They're already on their way home."

Joshua was then struck with the memory of the explosion. "Murphy, did you blow up the safe house?"

Murphy grinned. "Yeah."

"You always were obnoxious."

"Mac is arranging for us to stay on longer at the Spencer Inn," Donny said. "More skiing."

Joshua shook his head. "I don't feel like skiing right now." Waking up, he clutched Murphy's hand. "Pen?"

"I got it." Patting his chest to indicate his inside breast pocket, Murphy winked at him.

"When will Cameron get here?"

"She just needed to finish up a few things with her murder investigation." Murphy was startled to feel his secure phone vibrating on his hip. "She got a late start, but she'll be here soon," he said while moving away from the bed and unclasping his vibrating cell phone from his belt.

He went over to a far corner of the hospital room before answering the phone. "Yes, ma'am?"

"Where's Major O'Callaghan?" she demanded to know.

Murphy didn't like the urgency in her tone. "He went home to shower and change for Mac Faraday and Archie Monday's wedding rehearsal dinner. Why?"

"Is anyone with him?"

Before Murphy could answer, Mac charged into the private room. "They have David."

Chapter Twenty

As far as Mac was concerned, the rehearsal dinner was off. At this point, he didn't even care about the wedding and the tens of thousands of dollars that he could see going down the drain if it was cancelled—or even rescheduled.

All he cared about was finding David O'Callaghan and bringing him home safely.

One of Sheriff Turow's deputies drove Jessica Faraday to the church to announce that the rehearsal was cancelled due to a family emergency, but that everyone was welcomed to return to the Spencer Inn to enjoy the rehearsal dinner. All she could do was offer a shrug of her shoulders when asked if the wedding was postponed as well. Since Archie was in the hospital with her leg propped up and scheduled for surgery on Monday morning, Jessica doubted that there was going to be a wedding.

The phone calls prompted Mac, Sheriff Turow, Bogie, and Murphy Thornton to descend upon David O'Callaghan's stone cottage next to Spencer Manor, where they found two men with their throats slashed behind the counter in the galley kitchen. One was bald with a generous mustache and goatee. The other had red hair.

"O'Callaghan put up a good fight," Sheriff Turow said.

Murphy knelt as close to the bodies as he could without disturbing the blood spatter evidence. "Whoever did this knew how to fight with a knife. Major O'Callaghan was special ops in the marines."

Mac peered over the counter at the two dead men. "Still is. In the reserves." He turned around to take in the dining area in front of the galley kitchen. A stack of mail rested in the middle of the table. Mac picked up the envelopes and read the mailing addresses. There were several wedding cards addressed to him and Archie. "He picked up the mail on the way in."

Murphy and Sheriff Turow rose to their feet.

Bogie peered at Mac from across the table. "Most people do pick up the mail on their way in."

"Some of this is mine. That means he picked it up today, right before they grabbed him." Deep in thought, Mac circled the table, taking time to touch each chair until he came to the chair at the head of the round table, the one the furthest from the counter and closest to the living room. "Something's not right."

"What are you thinking about, Mac?" Bogie asked.

In silence, Murphy watched Mac looking from the door to the counter and then back again.

Sheriff Turow said, "It's plain to see what happened. David picked up the mail. He came in." The sheriff went to the hallway leading to the spare room and bathroom. "They must have been hiding in the hallway. When David got to the kitchen, they surprised him. But David was too quick for them, and he grabbed the knife."

"That's right!" Mac snapped his fingers. "Why did he grab the knife? Why didn't he use his gun?"

Sheriff Turow sighed. "Mac, you were a cop and detective for over twenty years. You know as well as I do that when your gun is holstered and a guy is running at you from only a few feet away with a knife drawn and ready to stab you, you usually don't have time to draw your gun—contrary to what the media wants the public to believe. David was standing in the kitchen." He pointed at the darkened hallway that was only eight feet away. "He saw them coming. Knew he wouldn't have time to draw his gun, so he pulled the knife from the block and defended himself. He took out two, but there's no telling how many there were. They overpowered him."

Murphy and Bogie looked from the sheriff to Mac for his response.

"What's wrong with the sheriff's theory, Mr. Faraday?" Murphy asked.

"Call me Mac."

Murphy smiled slightly—enough to show one of his dimples. "Mac, something is bothering you."

"Only because I know David and his habits." With a sigh, Mac picked up the pile of envelopes. "This is today's mail. He didn't have time to sort through it. I have walked in here with David numerous times, so I know that when he comes in, he tosses the mail on the middle of the kitchen table." To demonstrate, Mac tossed the envelopes onto the middle of the table. "He takes off his coat, if he's wearing one." Mac unzipped his coat and shrugged out of it. "And then he puts it across the back of this chair." He draped his winter coat across the back of the chair nearest the living room. "Then," Mac held up a finger to silence any objections or suggestions. "David will take off his utility belt—gun and all—"

"Because it's heavy," Bogie said with a nod of his head.

"And hang that off the back of the chair on top of his coat," Mac said. "At which point David will go into the kitchen and take out a beer. Then, he will come back to the table and drink the beer while going through his mail."

Murphy pointed at the empty beer bottle laying on its side in the sink. "He got as far as the beer." He leaned over to study the countertop and sniffed it. "Beer all right. Most likely, the bottle got knocked over on the counter and spilt while rolling over into the sink."

"You're point being?" Sheriff Turow asked Mac.

"Those two dead men in the kitchen," Mac said. "I don't see any gunshot wounds."

"They were knifed but good," Murphy said.

"That tells me they attacked and overpowered David in the kitchen *after* he took off his gun." He patted the back of the empty chair at the table. "He wasn't wearing his coat and gun when they snatched him. Yet, they're missing. How many abduction cases have you worked where the kidnappers took the victim's coat and *weapon?*"

When no one had an answer, the four men exchanged worried glances.

"Maybe David managed to grab his coat and gun and escape," Murphy suggested, "but they grabbed him outside."

"There was no struggle on this side of the counter," Mac said. "And if David could get to his gun, he'd have fired it." He gestured at the walls. "I don't see evidence of any gunshots in here."

"And the neighbors didn't call in any reports of shots outside," Bogie said.

"Then I have nothing." Murphy joined Mac and Bogie in looking to the sheriff for a suggestion.

When the sheriff could only offer a shrug, Bogie turned to Mac for reassurance. "David is alive?"

"I didn't speak to him," Mac said. "The kidnapper just said that I had something that didn't belong to me, and that if I didn't want what happened to these two men to happen to David, then I would bring it to them. They'll call me to arrange the exchange later on tonight."

Sheriff Turow asked, "What is it that they want?"

"Has to be the thumb drive that this Crane guy slipped into Agnes Douglas' purse," Mac said. "When they failed to snatch Jessica earlier today, they grabbed David for leverage to make me turn it over."

Bogie said, "I called the station on the way here. David did stop there before coming home. He wasn't there long, but Tonya said he went upstairs—he was only there a few minutes and then left."

"He's got a safe in his office. That's where David said he was putting it," Mac said.

"What's on this thumb drive?" Sheriff Turow asked.

While Mac and Bogie shook their heads, Murphy answered, "A recipe for a dirty bomb to infect people with a man-made form of Ebola."

Mac, Bogie, and Sheriff Turow turned around to where Murphy had been studying the two dead men.

"We're dealing with an Islamic terrorist group from Iraq," Murphy said. "Reginald Crane, the murder victim in Pennsylvania, intercepted the recipe from a Muslim trying to send it to the Middle East. The terrorist group sent a couple of sleeper agents, who happened to be real bona fide FBI investigators, to get it from Crane. But he was too smart for them and put it in Agnes Douglas' purse. Once they get that formula, they're going to use it to build a dirty bomb. There's no cure for this form of Ebola."

"We have to give it to them," Mac said. "They have David."

"They're going to kill him after they get it," Murphy said. "He's too valuable to let go."

"What are you talking about?" Mac asked. "What makes him so valuable to them?"

"ISIS put a price on O'Callaghan's head," Murphy said. "They're going to pay the kidnappers a quarter of a million dollars upon delivery to their camp in Iraq."

"Are you serious?" Bogie asked. "Why—"

"Major O'Callaghan was the leader of the special ops team that took out one of their leaders," Murphy said. "Somehow they got his name. I told you"—he looked at Mac—"they're already here and working in America. They have people in positions of influence in our government working to change our policies in their favor. One of those people was able to get David's name, and ISIS put a price on his head. A quarter of a million dollars."

"I'll pay them a million to get David back," Mac said through gritted teeth.

Sadly, Murphy shook his head while holding up his cell phone. "That's why my CO called. We've intercepted chatter in Iraq. According to our information, he's on his way to a terrorist camp in the Middle East, and they're going to behead him in a big public ceremony on New Year's Day." He added, "This will be a big coup for them. Nabbing a US citizen here on our soil and taking him over there—it will be a big triumph for them, and a demoralizing blow for Westerners in this war. It will send a message that there is no place on this planet that terrorism can't reach you."

The burner phone in Mac's pocket rang.

All four men looked at each other before Mac finally took the phone from his pocket and connected the call. "Yes." He pressed the button to turn on the speakers.

"You see what I mean?" the smooth voice from the other end of the line asked.

"I know what you want," Mac said.

"And I have something you want," he replied. "I'm not unreasonable. We'll agree to a trade."

"But first," Mac replied. "I want to talk to David."

271

"Of course you do."

They heard muffled voices before David's voice came through.

"Mac?" he sounded weak.

"Are you okay, David?"

"Yes," David replied before hurriedly adding, "Stand down! No negotiations! Stand down, Mac!" His order was cut short with a slap and a loud curse followed by another slap.

Mac grabbed up the phone. "Now you listen to me, you—"

"No, you listen to me, Faraday!" The smooth voice no longer sounded so calm when he returned to the phone. "I'm in charge here, not you!"

Mac said in a low and steady tone, "You hurt David again—you so much as break a fingernail on his pinkie, and I'll hunt you down to the ends of the earth—there won't be a cave deep enough in whatever hell you've crawled out of where you can hide from me. And when—not if—when I find you, I will personally send you in a million little pieces on a one-way trip to meet your black-eyed virgins."

There was a strange silence on the other end of the line before the caller replied in a cool tone, "If you want O'Callaghan back alive—bruised a little but alive—then you better keep that phone charged up to take my call at eleven thirty. I'll give you the location for the drop then."

Click!

Mac slammed the phone down on the table and glared straight ahead at the bowl of apples as if they could give him the answer to saving David.

"They couldn't have gotten David out of the country yet," Bogie said. "We'll tear down every tree and overturn every rock until we find him and kill those slimy bastards!"

Mac showed no sign of hearing him.

"We're going to—" Sheriff Turow started to say before Mac cut him.

With a scream starting from deep in his gut, Mac grabbed one of the apples out of the bowl, whirled around, and hurled it across the great room. With a crash, the apple hit the television directly in the center of the screen, which shattered into several pieces.

Mac then expelled the rest of his pent up fury by sweeping his arm across the table to send the rest of the apples rolling and the mail flying off the table and in various directions to the floor.

When he had finished, Mac huffed and puffed deep breaths.

A stunned silence filled the cottage.

Dropping his face into his hands, Mac said in a quiet voice, "I'm sorry. I just …" He shook his head.

"I think you just killed David's fancy new TV," Bogie said.

"You mean the one that he invited us all over to watch the Super Bowl on?" Sheriff Turow asked.

"If we don't come up with a plan, David won't be alive to have a Super Bowl party," Murphy said.

Mac lifted his head from his hands. "We can't just go running off half-cocked. We need to be smart about this."

"Bogie's right," Sheriff Turow said. "David still has to be in the country. They'll need to file flight plans to get him out of the country."

"Not necessarily," Murphy said. "They've got heavy backers with deep pockets and private jets that don't go through customs. They can fly under the radar so we can't track them, or use a number of other tricks to stay off our radar."

"Point is, David is alive." A tinge of hope came into Mac's tone. "And they want that thumb drive bad. As long as they don't have it, we have some leverage."

"But if O'Callaghan is so valuable to them," Sheriff Turow pointed out, "they aren't going to risk losing him by bringing him along for the exchange."

"The sheriff is right, Mac," Murphy said. "He's worth more than money to them. They're not going to take any chances. They're going to have him stashed away safe. They may even be putting him on a plane to send him out of the country before the drop."

"I'll insist on seeing him there before I turn over the flash drive," Mac said. "They'll have to bring him with them."

"They'll just get you there and then kill you and take the thumb drive off your dead body," the sheriff said.

As the thought formed in Murphy's mind, a slow grin came to his lips.

"If what you're saying is true," Mac said to the sheriff, "then they're going to have to be ready to move out fast as soon as they get that flash drive."

"They're not going to make the drop too far away from their escape route out of the country," Bogie said. "So they have to be near the airport."

"Not the airport," Murphy said, "too easy for us to check. Are there any private airstrips in the area?" He had been in such deep thought that Mac was surprised he had been listening enough to hear them.

"A few," Bogie answered. "But there's more than a foot and a half of snow out there."

"So they'd have to plow the airstrip in order to land a plane and take off," Sheriff Turow said. "Unless they have equipment, they probably had to hire someone."

"I'll start making phone calls." Bogie whipped his cell phone out of its pouch.

"Now you look like your father," Mac noted the wicked grin on Murphy's lips. "What's going through your head?"

"They want a bomb," Murphy said. "Let's give 'em one."

CHAPTER TWENTY-ONE

Joshua felt like he was drifting on a cloud filled with painkillers for the wound on his side. On the brink of consciousness, he reached out for the familiar hand that he had grown used to being next to his side. The soft long fingers of his new wife entwined with his. "Cameron ..." he murmured.

Her lips touched his fingers. "I'm here, darling." He felt her lips on his neck and then his cheek.

He dragged his eyelids open and peered through the fog to the pleasant face surrounded by cinnamon-colored waves. Her brown eyes with green specks looked tired. "You're here." He reached up to touch her face to make sure she was real.

"Of course." Her voice turned firm. "You didn't tell me that you went and got yourself shot."

"And you didn't tell me that you've been messing around with international terrorists," he replied. "Are you okay?"

"No," she replied. "One of those lousy cretins poured whiskey down my throat and tried to kill me."

"But you're okay?" His vision clearing, Joshua searched her face for the answer.

"I don't like being drunk." Her voice was filled with remorse.

"Isn't that why you quit drinking?"

"Yeah."

"That's good." He pulled her down to lay next to him. "We're good."

With a sigh, she laid her head down on his shoulder. "My prime suspect blew away that lousy FBI agent slash international terrorist. Somehow, the world got turned upside down when we weren't looking."

"Isn't that always when it happens?" Joshua replied, "When we let our guard down?" He took her into his arms. "But you're here now. We're together. You and me against the world's insanity."

After breathing in his scent and taking in the comfort of his arms around her, she let out a sigh. "Now and forever."

Sanders Farm, located outside McHenry, Maryland

Strapped down onto a gurney under a blanket to give the impression that he was a medical patient, David could hear the wind whipping around the plane on the abandoned private airstrip. One would think a private luxury jet would have been more sound proof.

After he had been tasered, he regained consciousness in the back of a van already strapped down onto the ambulance gurney. His hands were cuffed behind his back. A hood draped over his head prevented him from seeing the men who had him captive until he was lifted out of the back of the van and moved into the back compartment of the plane.

The bag was then ripped off his head.

Lifting his head and shoulders up off the gurney, David tried to take in his surroundings, looking for any means of escape that he could make use of. Maybe not at that instant, but later.

Never give up.

"Easy, Major."

David recognized the face of the man who had tasered him when he shoved David forcibly back down onto the gurney.

"You're not going anywhere right now."

David looked down to see that under the blanket, his shirt was missing. They had taken his shirt and the ballistics vest he wore under it, leaving him in his undershirt and slacks. He was grateful that he still had on his boots. That would make it easier for him to run when he escaped. Without his ballistic vest, he would be unprotected if they shot at him. "Who are you? What do you want from me?"

"I guess it's only polite of me to tell you who I am, since I am the one who's going to execute you." He flashed a wide toothy smile. "Special Inspector Neal Black."

"Special Investigator?" David squinted up at him. "Of ..."

"FBI."

"This can't possibly ..." David glanced around at the other men in the room—there were six besides Neal Black. Dressed in dark coats and ski masks under heavy hats, they were all heavily armed with sidearms and automatic rifles.

"Justice," Black said. "It's time to avenge our comrades killed in Tehran."

David swallowed. The name he had called him came back to him. *Major. He knows who I am in my other life. But he— how could he possibly end up a special investigator with the FBI?* David noted his reddish-blond hair and Caucasian features. *He doesn't look—*

David glanced around at the other men in the room that he recognized as part of a plane—a private jet.

They're taking me back ... there. Somehow they found me.

David asked, "How could you do—"

"The same way you can go over there to kill good men who are simply doing Allah's will!" Black was in his face.

"By torturing, killing, and bombing whole families and towns—simply because they disagree with your twisted ideology?"

Suddenly, the blade of a bayonet was pressed across his throat.

David didn't even see one of the men yank the long knife out of its sheaf on his belt and press it against his throat. Fearful of the sharp blade cutting through his neck, David fell back onto the gurney. He stared up into the hard face of the man glaring down at him. The skin of his round, bloated face was blacker than black. The whites of his dark eyes were yellow and bloodshot.

"Easy, Ra'ees. This one's ours," Black said with a laugh. "We need him alive for the New Year's celebration. You wanted yours dead tonight—"

"Along with many others." Ra'ees grinned to reveal a mouth of brown teeth. He bent over to sneer into David's face. David swallowed when he got a whiff of the foul stench. "Soon your friends will be dead. Then, you will join them."

David tried to ease the sick feeling in his stomach. Not only was his shirt gone, but the police shield he wore clipped to the breast pocket was also gone. *They had to be sending a jihadist impersonating a police officer into a club or restaurant to blow the place up.*

"Go spread your men out around the plane to make sure no one gets too curious, Ra'ees," Black ordered. "Make sure one of your men monitors the police scanner—"

"We know our job," Ra'ees said. "Bauman wouldn't have recommended us if we didn't."

Black's cool exterior dropped slightly. "Then go do your job and leave my prisoner alone."

Ra'ees tore his hate-filled eyes from David and glanced over at Neal Black. With a jerk of his head, the agent ordered him to back away. As Ra'ees stepped back, Black took out his cell phone and pressed a button.

"You see what I mean?" Black asked into the cell phone. While he listened to the reply, an evil grin filled his face. "And I have something you want," he replied. "I'm not unreasonable. We'll agree to a trade."

He sauntered over to the gurney to stand over David. "Of course you do."

Covering the phone, he said, "Your friend Mac wants to talk to you." He pressed the phone to David's ear.

"Mac?" he was surprised by how weak his voice sounded.

"Are you okay, David?"

"Yes." He sucked in a deep breath. He only had one chance. "Stand down! No negotiations! Stand down, Mac!"

Black slapped him hard across the face.

The phone fell to the floor with a clatter.

Before David could recover, Black backhanded him across the other side.

The bitter taste of blood filling his mouth, David heard Mac's voice yelling from the phone's speaker. "Now you listen to me, you—"

Smoothing his hair, Black grabbed the phone from the floor. "No, you listen to me, Faraday! I'm in charge here, not you!" His cocky demeanor had been shaken.

Sucking in on his bottom lip, numb from the blows he had received, David watched a series of emotions cross his captor's face. First he saw a hint of fear, and it was followed by a return to his cocky demeanor.

"If you want O'Callaghan back alive—bruised a little but alive—then you better keep that phone charged up to take my call at eleven thirty. I'll give you the location for the drop then."

With the fury in his eyes directed at David, he disconnected the call and hurled the phone across the room.

Once more, Black was leaning over the gurney. David could not only smell his hot breath, but he could also feel it. "You have no idea how much I'm looking forward to sawing that blade across your throat." Pausing to lick his lips, Black eyed David's white flesh. "I'm going to do it slow and easy. I want to feel your hot blood pulse from your neck and hear you pleading for your life until the blade cuts through your larynx."

He raised his eyes to meet David's glaring up at him. "I'll bet I enjoy it more than you enjoyed it when you put that bullet between Jassem al-Baghdadi's eyes."

Saying nothing, David stared at him. *What connection does this American, a federal agent who has undergone psych exams and background checks, have with the second in command of such a high level terrorist group?*

"Or don't you remember shooting him from behind the safety of the cliff high above him—coward that you are?"

Refusing to blink first, David held his gaze.

"You were the one who pulled the trigger," Black said. "My source is very reliable." A crooked grin crossed his face. "Of course, you don't have to die alone. You may not even have to die, if you can offer up someone else to take your place … like your commanding officer. Someone who can provide us with information that can make it worth our while to keep you alive. Of course, you'll spend your days as a prisoner of war—until you are of no other value to us."

Involuntarily, David sucked in a breath when Black caressed his throat with his cold hands.

"We know you didn't do it alone," Black said. "There were many up in those cliffs firing down on our defenseless comrades."

"They had two truckloads of weapons," David said. "They weren't exactly *defenseless*."

"You killed Jassem," Black said. "Offer up your commanding officer, the one who gave you the order to murder Jassem, and maybe we can arrange to have him die in your place." He bent over to whisper into David's ear. "How badly do you want to live?"

David turned his head to meet Black's eyes. "Kill me now … because I'm not giving you *anything.*"

CHAPTER TWENTY-TWO

Spencer Inn

In contrast to the party atmosphere surrounding the long-awaited wedding and the New Year's Eve celebration, the penthouse elevator was filled with silence while Mac, Bogie, Sheriff Turow, and Murphy rode up to the top floor.

"I'm waiting for a call back from this buddy of mine who runs a snow plowing business," Bogie said in a soft voice to break the silence. "He's the only guy around with a plow big enough to handle a whole runway."

"If it's a small plane," Sheriff Turow said, "they wouldn't need that long of a runway. They're at least two men down."

Seeming not to hear the conversation, Mac said, "This isn't right."

"Of course it isn't," Sheriff Turow said.

"No." Mac turned to the sheriff. "How many kidnapping cases have you worked?"

"A few," the sheriff said, insulted. "What are you getting at, Mac? You're still fussing about David's coat and weapon being gone? So am I. I'm hoping he's got them."

"Yes, but that's not all. This whole thing is out of whack." Mac checked the time on his phone. "It is almost nine o'clock. They're going to call at eleven thirty to give us the drop-site for the flash drive. If the drop is right after that, then it's not happening until around midnight."

"That's at least *three* hours away." Bogie's tone turned suspicious.

Mac was nodding his head. "Three hours is a long time."

The elevator doors opened. Mac led them off to find three room service carts filled with food and four servers making their way into his suite. They could hear what sounded like pre-wedding festivities coming from inside.

Instead of investigating his daughter's activites, Mac held Murphy, Bogie, and the sheriff in the hallway. "It's been my experience that kidnappers want to keep control in abduction cases. The best way to do that is to keep the family of the victim and the police off balance."

"Keep things moving so fast that no one has time to think and figure out what's going down or what's coming next," Bogie explained.

"In three hours we could locate them and David and plan a rescue," Mac said. "These are supposed to be *terrorists*? Professional soldiers? They have to know that we have easy access to that thumb drive. Why not have us meet them now? What are they waiting for?"

Murphy sucked in a deep breath. "Abdul Kochar."

"Who?" Sheriff Turow asked.

Murphy punched the elevator down button. "Novelist. He's written about Afghanistan and life in that culture. He doesn't write favorably about Islamic extremists and is open about their terrorist activities, especially the ones against their own people. He gets death threats on a daily basis."

"Then what's he doing writing books?' Bogie asked.

"He's got a bodyguard, but I doubt that one bodyguard would be a match for these guys."

The elevator doors opened. Murphy jumped on.

Mac grabbed the doors to keep them from closing. "Was he your father's contact?"

"What's all this about?" Sheriff Turow demanded to know. "What does this novelist have to do with O'Callaghan? I thought they wanted some thumb drive that the old lady had in her purse."

"You want to know what they could be waiting for?" Murphy replied. "Maybe they're waiting to make a hit, or kidnap another victim to make an example of Kochar about what happens when you speak out against them. Kochar is staying *right here at this hotel.* How hard would it be for them to grab him, too, while they're in the neighborhood?"

"Make the beheading a double feature," Bogie said.

Mac, Sheriff Turow, and Bogie piled back onto the elevator to take them down to the lobby.

In the lobby, Murphy ran to the reservation desk. Since hotel policy did not permit the front desk to freely give out room numbers, Mac rushed up to use his authority to extract the information from the clerk.

Keeping a vigilant eye on the hotel guests in search of possible terrorists spying on them, Bogie and Sheriff Turow were making their way across the reception area when the hotel manager's call drew their attention.

"Hey, Bogie, I would have thought O'Callaghan would have dressed up a little for Faraday's rehearsal dinner, considering that he's one of the groomsmen and all." Jeff Ingles made his way through a throng of guests to join them.

"Huh?" Bogie asked.

285

"O'Callaghan? Chief of police." Seeing Mac in slacks and sporting almost two day's worth of a beard, Jeff furrowed his brow. "Why isn't Mac at the rehearsal dinner?"

"Business," Bogie replied. "What's this about the chief?"

"I assumed since he was on his way upstairs that he was going to the rehearsal dinner." Jeff paused when Mac came over to them.

"He's in room five twelve on the fifth floor," Mac said.

"No, the rehearsal dinner is on the second floor," Jeff said.

"When did you see the chief?" Bogie asked.

"He saw David?" Mac asked.

Bogie's hand shot up in a sign of silence so that they could hear Jeff's response. Under his gray bushy eyebrows meeting in the center of his forehead, Bogie's piercing eyes struck fear in the hotel manager's heart. He was afraid to answer.

"You said he wasn't dressed nice for the rehearsal dinner," Sheriff Turow reminded him.

Jeff stuttered. "He was in his uniform. At least I think it was his uniform. His black slacks and black heavy coat with his police chief badge. And I saw that he was wearing his gun, too … but then he always wears his gun."

"When?" Mac asked.

"A few minutes ago." Jeff pointed toward the elevators. "He went up the hotel elevators just as you guys came down the penthouse elevators."

"A few minutes ago?" Bogie gasped. "Maybe he escaped."

"He would have called us if he had escaped," Mac said.

"Not if he didn't have a phone," Bogie said.

Mac grabbed Jeff roughly by the arm. "Jeff, did you actually talk to David?"

"N-no," Jeff stuttered. "I was too far away." With a trembling finger, he pointed across the lobby. "I had just come out of the restaurant."

Mac dropped his arm. "So you didn't actually see *David*. You saw his *uniform*."

"That answers your question about his coat!" Murphy was already pressing the elevator button. "They're using David's police chief uniform to gain access into Kochar's room to assassinate him." He sprinted for the stairway. "I'll meet you up there!"

"Assassination!" Jeff called out. When all of the guests within hearing distance heard him, he covered his mouth with both hands. With wide eyes, he sucked in a deep breath. "Never mind." He waved his arms to encourage merriment. "Enjoy your holiday. Eat, drink, and be merry. The new year is right around the corner!"

The hotel corridor was busy with guests coming and going out of rooms. Three couples dressed in evening fare were getting on the elevator while Mac, Bogie, and Sheriff Turow waded through them to step into the hall.

"We don't know for certain that that was O'Callaghan," Sheriff Turow said.

"It was his uniform, not him," Mac said. "From across the lobby, Jeff thought he saw a police shield on the coat."

"They're using his uniform to get in to see this writer guy," Bogie argued.

"We're jumping to conclusions," Sheriff Turow said as they approached the room. "My advice to you right now is to remain calm and not to get excited." He knocked on the door. "Mr. Kochar, this is Sheriff Turow of the Garrett County Sheriff's Department. May I speak to you for a minute?"

There was a moment of silence.

The sheriff knocked on the door again. "Mr. Kochar, open the door please."

The answer from inside came in the form of a burst of automatic gunfire and the sound of glass breaking.

They dove on either side of the doorway for cover.

"Can we get excited now?" Mac asked the sheriff.

The sheriff, Bogie, and Mac drew their guns. Mac took his master keycard from his pocket and unlocked the door. Before he could push down on the handle, the door flew open.

Seeing three guns aimed at him, Murphy Thornton threw up his hands. "Easy guys, I'm on your side." He stepped back to allow them into the hotel suite, which looked like a bloodbath.

A few feet inside the door lay the sprawled-out body of a muscular African-American. He had three gunshot wounds to the chest. Mac assumed he was the author's bodyguard.

"How did you get in here?" Mac asked Murphy while stepping around the dead bodyguard.

A glance across the suite and the burst of freezing wind answered his question. Through the broken balcony doors, Mac saw a rope dangling from the floor above.

"You may want to send the couple in the suite on the next floor up a bottle of champagne on the house," Murphy told Mac.

Bogie rushed to a man in a sweater and slacks lying on the floor next to the writing desk on the other side of the suite. "This one is still alive." He got on his radio.

Anticipating Jeff's reaction to the shot-out door, Mac asked, "Couldn't you have opened the deck door before shooting him?"

"Not enough time." The corner of Murphy's lip curled upwards. "Besides, it wouldn't have been half as dramatic."

Sheriff Turow knelt next to another dead man sprawled out on the floor in the middle of the room. He was wearing the uniform of the Spencer Police Chief. The coat lay open to reveal a vest made up of explosives. There was not much left of his head. His body lay in a growing pool of blood and body tissue.

"Is that bomb deactivated?" Mac asked while holding his breath.

"Wires have been disconnected," Sheriff Turow noted while looking up at Murphy. "You did this?"

Murphy patted the knife resting in the sheath on his belt. "When I heard he was wearing O'Callaghan's coat when he got on the elevator, I realized there was probably a reason he didn't take it off once he was in the hotel."

"You assumed he was wearing a bomb under it," Mac said.

"Surmised," Murphy responded. "These guys want to take out as many infidels as possible. They wouldn't waste the perfect opportunity to bring down a seven-story five-star hotel filled with rich Americans. Take out someone on their hit list, plus a hundred or so Westerners—it would be a big score for their side. I was right. I had just dropped onto the balcony when I heard your knock. As soon as you announced yourself, he reached for the detonator." He gestured at the handheld switch lying on the floor a couple of feet from the body.

"You could have detonated the bomb when you shot him," Sheriff Turow said.

"That's why I made it a head shot and not a shot to the body."

"You were damn lucky," Sheriff Turow said. "We were all lucky."

"If I hadn't shot him, then he would have blown us all up anyway," Murphy argued. "You don't know—"

"I do know," Turow said. "I'm a retired army captain. Did three tours overseas fighting these morons. My wife died over there. So I know exactly what we're dealing with."

"EMTs are on their way," Bogie stepped between the two men to announce.

In an effort to break the tension, Murphy joined Mac kneeling next to the author, who had two bullet wounds to his chest.

"Ambulance is on the way," Mac said to the man gasping for breath. "You're going to be okay."

Gasping, the author uttered one word, "Ismail."

"Ismail?" Mac asked. "Who is that?"

"Brother."

Murphy knelt down close. "Mr. Kochar, I was sent to help you. Ismail is your brother? Correct?"

"Not ... his fault."

Murphy cast a glance in Mac's direction before saying, "Isn't your brother the leader of a major terrorist group in Iraq—"

"Yes," Kochar replied with gasping breaths. "He ordered ... he sent this jihadist to kill me because ..."

"Save your strength," Mac told him while grasping his hand.

"I know what you did," Murphy said. "We all know what a chance you took bringing information to us to help fight your brother's group."

"Not ..." he coughed up blood, "not his fault."

"Ismail has been ordering jihadists from all over the world—"

Kochar grasped Murphy's arm. "Yes, he has, because he ... and many like him ... they have all been fooled ... they have failed to see who is behind the mask."

"What mask?" Mac asked. "Who?"

"Mohammad," Kochar said. "The Quran. The archangel Gabriel showed himself to Muhammad, and he wrote the Quran." He held up a finger. "Islam was established as a religion of peace and understanding." Grabbing Murphy by the shirt, he coughed loudly.

"You need to rest," Mac said gently.

"No, you must tell them," Kochar said, "They have been betrayed … by Satan. It is not Allah who orders the murder and destruction of non-believers—"

"That's the basis of the extremists' beliefs," Murphy said.

Kochar slowly shook his head. He held up a bloody hand. "They fail to understand that those orders come from Satan wearing the mask of Allah." He spewed blood over his bottom lip. "They truly believe they are following Allah when in reality they are doing Satan's bidding." Blood dribbled down his chin.

The EMTs hurried into the room.

"Forgive them!" Kochar cried out in anguish. "Not their fault! It is Satan!"

CHAPTER TWENTY-THREE

"He's handcuffed and tied down. That's good enough," David heard Neal Black arguing outside the door of the small room at the back of the jet where they had him secured.

"He's a Marine Special Ops Officer," Ra'ees said in a low voice that David barely heard. "As long as he's alive and conscious, he's going to be looking for a way out. If he escapes, Ismail will still carry out the execution and celebration—but it will be your head they saw off." His voice dropped too low for David to hear what he added, but he could guess what it was—advice for Neal Black to think about his order.

Pressing against the strap holding him down on the gurney, David worked his fingers to insert the key he had taped inside his wrist into the hole on his cuffs. Black hadn't noticed it under the liquid bandage that David had used to conceal it.

It was bad enough feeling his way with the key and cuffs. Being strapped down so that he didn't have much room to work made the exercise more difficult.

"I want him fully awake and cognizant when we land in Tehran," Black was saying.

"This stuff will only knock him out for six to eight hours," Ra'ees said. "We'll be over the ocean when he wakes up." He chuckled. "He'll have plenty of time to think about what's going to happen to him when we land."

A cell phone rang in the room and interrupted their debate.

"It's Bauman," Ra'ees said.

Success. With his hands freed, David thrust his arm out from under his back and twisted it to grasp the catch on the latch of the strap. He made sure he loosened the one on the far side of the gurney away from the doorway so that they wouldn't notice it until they were standing over the gurney.

"José, go give our guest something to help him sleep," Ra'ees ordered.

"Si, señor."

Dropping back down onto the gurney, David tucked both arms under the blanket. He watched the brown-skinned young man come into the room. He was dressed in a heavy winter coat. He wore a knit cap on his head that was pulled down over his forehead and ears.

Upon seeing David eying him as he came toward him with the syringe, an evil grin crossed José's face. "Betcha wish there was something fun in this, si, piggy-wiggy?" Waving the syringe before David's eyes, he bent over and snorted like a pig. "Day after tomorrow, we're going to have a pig roast, and you're going to be the main course." He sniffed and wiped his nose with his sleeve. "Maybe if you're nice to me, I can give you a little something to help you go out with a bang."

José reached over to pull down the blanket and expose David's arm. Looking for where to make the injection, he was unprepared when David's other arm shot out, grabbed him by the back of the neck, and yanked his head down. At the

293

same time, David shot up to head butt him between the eyes.

David heard José's nose break under the force of the head butt.

His nose bleeding, José slid down to the floor and onto his knees. David still had stars in his eyes when he thrust the needle of the syringe into José's neck and pushed the plunger. Careful to be quiet, David eased his captor down to the floor.

"The scanner is saying that the Spencer Inn is being evacuated due to a bomb threat," Neal Black reported to their caller.

Even in his rush, David stopped unzipping José's winter coat to take it off him to listen.

"Threat?" the caller sounded disappointed. "But nothing about an explosion? Obviously Harlan wasn't as committed to Allah as he should have been."

"No," Ra'ees insisted, "he was very committed."

"If he was, then my news stations would be flying journalists out to Spencer, Maryland, to show a crater on top of Spencer Mountain." The man sounded frustrated.

"Kochar has a bodyguard," Black said. "Maybe he was too fast for Harlan."

"Harlan was a little green," Ra'ees said.

Keeping his ears tuned to track the conversation, David stripped José of his gun, a fully loaded nine-millimeter Glock semi-automatic, and two clips from his pockets. He found an LED flashlight in another pocket. A further search of José's unconscious body found a knife in a sheath strapped to his ankle, which David transferred to his own leg.

In José's coat, the police chief found more goodies. A disposable cell phone in one pocket, and cigarettes and a lighter in the other. David pocketed them all in case he needed them. The inside breast pocket held more hidden goodies—

several tiny bags of cocaine, which he kept in the pocket and zipped shut.

José, you have been a bad boy.

"Have they reported Kochar's murder yet?" the leader asked.

"Nothing on that," Ra'ees said.

Aware that José's hair and skin color were much darker than his, David yanked off his hat, pulled it down over his blond hair, and lifted the hood on the coat to conceal his face as best he could. Then he picked up José, placed him on the gurney, covered him with a blanket up to his face, turned his head so that he faced the wall, and tightened down the straps to hold him there.

"I'm beginning to think I'm not getting my money's worth," the leader said with anger in his tone. "Has anyone on the police channels said anything about O'Callaghan yet?"

"They aren't going to make the disappearance of a police chief public," Neal Black reported. "They're going to keep it as quiet as possible. We have nothing to worry about. All of my research indicates that Mac Faraday has a lot of pull with the local cops here. He'll give us anything we want as long as he thinks there's a chance that he'll get O'Callaghan back. I've read some speculation that they're brothers. We can pretty well guarantee that everyone around here will do what Faraday says. As long as we put pressure on *him*, we'll get what we want."

"There are no guarantees," Bauman replied with a knowing tone. "Where's Elder, your partner?"

There was silence from the passenger compartment.

Now to get off this plane without them seeing me.

Trying to appear as casual as possible, David moved toward the open doorway. He kept his hand on the Glock in his pocket. If need be, he was prepared to shoot his way out.

"Elder hasn't been answering his cell," Black reported.

"So that detective, Cameron Gates, got the better of him," Bauman said. "A common state police detective—a woman—fingered you and Elder, and now Elder is dead!"

"We don't know for a fact that he's dead."

"We don't know for a fact that he's alive!" Bauman raged. "Never underestimate your enemy! As soon as these local yokels found out that their police chief was missing, every cop in the state started looking for him. They're going to be looking for a plane to fly him out of the country, and it won't be long before they remember the airstrip on Sanders farm and send police out to start snooping."

The more he spoke, the more agitated the leader, who Ra'ees had referred to as 'Bauman,' became.

David could see that Neal Black's and Ra'ees' attention was directed at the cell phone, and that they had their backs to the doorway to the back room and the jet's exit. It would have been easy for David to slip off the plane without them seeing, but curiosity made him want to learn more about their plans.

Sanders Farm. Old Man Sanders had been an Air Force pilot. He had his own plane that he flew in and out of the area for trips to Florida and California all the time. But he died over ten years ago. How had they known about there being a private airstrip on the farm only a few miles from Deep Creek Lake?

"You were the one who directed us to use this farm and the airstrip," Ra'ees said.

"Even if they could wade through the paper trail to trace that farm back to me," Bauman said, "no one with enough gas to think of doing anything about it could touch me. What I don't want is anyone going in or near that barn."

What's in the barn? David held his breath. *I thought the Sanders Farm was deserted and a nearby farmer mowed the fields and cut the grass to keep it from being overgrown.*

"What's in the barn?" Neal Black had the nerve to ask.

"Hasn't anyone taught you yet not to ask questions?" Ra'ees asked the federal agent.

"Let's just say it's where the Easter Bunny is hibernating." Bauman laughed before he turned serious. "But he won't be handing out any presents this Easter if you morons don't get your hands out of your pants and get us those files. I paid good money for that formula, and I intend to get it. Ra'ees, make sure no one goes near that barn."

"I'll get one of my men out there to stand guard on it right away."

Bauman was on a roll. "I'm holding you personally responsible for getting that flash drive off Faraday and getting that plane off the ground. Ismail is preparing to rally the troops with a massive team-building exercise, and he needs our special guest there on time for the main event."

Keeping his head turned sideways so that the side of the hood covered most of his face, David stepped out of the cargo compartment and headed for the exit.

"Hey!" Ra'ees shouted.

Keeping his body sideways, David froze. He kept his hand on the Glock in his pocket.

"Did O'Callaghan give you any trouble, José?"

"Little," David said with a Spanish accent. "He sleeping like a baby now."

"Good," Ra'ees said. "Where are you going?"

"Cigarette."

"I'll bet," Ra'ees replied. "Go to the barn down across from the farmhouse and make sure it's locked up and secure. And I don't want to catch you snorting during your watch. We can't afford any screw ups on this job."

"Si, señor," David replied before grabbing the door's handle.

"Hey!" Ra'ees rose out of his seat.

Holding his breath, David tightened the grip on the Glock.

"You can't guard the barn without your weapon." After grabbing an assault rifle resting against the wall next to David, Ra'ees shoved it into the back of his shoulder. Keeping his face averted, David grabbed the rifle and hurried out the door to go find where the Easter Bunny had been hiding.

Mac stood among the hordes of resort guests clutching their winter coats close to block out the freezing wind and snow and checked the time on his cell phone.

It was closing in on ten o'clock. Time was ticking away. They had wasted a lot of time calling in the bomb squad to clear the hotel of any other devices and waiting for the state police to check for any other jihadists.

Even Gnarly was picking up on Mac's anxiety. Or it could have been the hordes of people milling around. On his leash, the German shepherd was pacing back and forth around Mac while eying everyone around them.

Mac felt a thin hand clutch his elbow. Forcing a smile to conceal his worry, he turned to his daughter. He saw the same smile on her face. "David is going to be fine." She hugged him tight. She was clad in a violet faux fur coat that matched her eyes.

Mac wrapped his arms around her. "I know."

He felt Spencer's leash tighten around his ankles as the pup circled them to bind all of them, including Gnarly, together. "When are you going to get that dog trained?"

"She is." Jessica gingerly backed away while untangling the leash that bound them.

"Here, let me help." Murphy knelt down and held out his arms. On cue, Spencer ran to him and leapt up into his arms. She licked his face while he rose to his feet and took the leash from Jessica.

"We need to find a base of operation," Mac said. "Spencer Manor has been shot up, and there's no telling when they'll allow guests in the hotel. And I'm also getting nervous with a bunch of strangers around. You saw how easily this jihadist walked in and went up to Kochar's room. I suggest we regroup at the Spencer police station."

"I'll text Tristan." Whipping out her cell phone, Jessica turned to Murphy, who was checking his phone. "Can I give you a ride, sailor?"

In the middle of turning to search for Bogie, Mac's head snapped around at the tone in Jessica's voice when she offered Murphy a ride. It's was more than flirtatious. It was even familiar. His eyes narrowed, he studied Murphy's reaction.

"I'd love to," Murphy responded, "but I need to meet someone first." With Spencer still in his arms, he made his way through the crowd.

"Who?" With a bounce in her step, Jessica fell in step behind Murphy.

There's something else for me to worry about. Well, at least Colt Fitzgerald is out of the picture. Murphy's got more than six-pack abs going for him.

With a sigh of exhaustion, Mac went in search of Bogie.

"It's business." With a grin creeping to his lips, Murphy noted that she was following right at his heels.

"Is this someone male or female?"

"To tell you the truth, I don't know."

"How do you not know?" she replied.

With a laugh, Murphy stopped so quickly that she ran into his elbow. He turned to her. "Don't you watch the news, surf the Internet, or watch television?"

"Not really." She stepped in close to him. *"I have a life."*

He leaned over to bring his face close to hers. With a deep breath, he tore his attention from her violet eyes, which threatened to pull him in and away from his current assignment. "Tell me about it."

"I'd love to." Daring him to kiss her, she brought her lips up to his.

"I'm afraid that if I kissed you now, I wouldn't stop," he said, "and we really don't have time for that. We're up against the clock, and some massive bad-asses whose motto is, 'He who gets the highest body count wins.'"

"So I'll help you save the world now, and you can kiss later. Sounds like a date to me."

"Seriously, I do need to go talk to someone." He continued to elbow his way through the heavy crowd of hotel guests to make his way down the street.

"I'm coming with you."

"I thought you were going to the Spencer Police Station," Murphy said.

"You said you were going to protect me and make sure I was safe until all this was over," she said. "Well, it's not over, and I need your body."

Murphy stopped and turned around. Even in the darkness of the night with only the outside lighting, he could see that her face was bright pink. Her fur coat hugged every delicious curve of her slender body down to her hips. From there down, her body was clad in black tights that eased down her hips to her shapely legs, where they disappeared at the lower thigh into black leather pirate boots with high heels.

Who needs whose body, buttercup?

With a giggle, she cocked her head at him. She peered at him through her long eyelashes. "To guard me ... I mean, I need you to guard my body. I need a bodyguard."

300

Saying nothing, Murphy cocked his head and flashed a playful grin at her. "You need *my body* to guard *yours*?"

"You *offered*."

"Well, I guess I have to," he said mockingly in response to the task at hand. "You did dump Colt Fitzgerald for me."

Murphy put Spencer down on the ground and took hold of her leash. He held out his other hand to her. When she hesitated, he tossed his head in a gesture for her to go along. "Come along, buttercup. I can't guard your body if it's all the way back there. I need it close by so that I can jump you at a second's notice when things suddenly get real hot."

After grasping his hand, she dared to wrap both arms around his arm and bury her face into his shoulder. "Oh, I love a man who knows how to talk dirty."

"I can't believe this is happening." Trying not to break down from worry and frustration, Mac turned around in search of a quiet place to catch his breath and regroup when he suddenly found himself face to face with Chelsea Adams, who had just stepped out of the crowd with her service dog, Molly. Her face was filled with confusion and worry.

"Mac ..." She glanced around at the police officers and security personnel directing the guests. She knew many of them from her relationship with David and her job as a paralegal to the county prosecutor. She didn't miss the concern and sympathy in their eyes when they caught sight of her.

Even Gnarly, who would have normally galloped over to Molly to lick her ears, was hanging back with his tail tucked between his hind legs.

"Where's David?" Her voice trembled. "What's going on? I heard there was a bomb threat here at the hotel. Why was rehearsal cancelled? Was that connected to this? Why can't

I get ahold of David? Has something happened to him? He was acting strange when he left the hospital …"

Mac took her arm. "Let's go over here." He led her over to a quiet corner outside the hotel that was sheltered from the wind, snow, and crowds of people.

Even without knowing for certain what had happened, she was sobbing before Mac could shelter her from crowds.

Leading Spencer on a leash, Murphy and Jessica walked hand in hand down the road from the Spencer Inn until they were almost out of sight of the street lights. In spite of the cold, their clasped hands kept each other warm.

Casting side glances in Murphy's direction, Jessica noted how perfectly her hand fit into his. The flutter she felt in her heart made her remember when she went on her first date in middle school. She tried to recall the last time she had felt that flutter and couldn't come up with a time. It had been long before her inheritance had thrust her into high society—before she had become immersed in a different class of friends.

This feels like it used to feel. Much different. Much better-er.

They had come to where the road started to decline down the mountain when Murphy led Jessica into a turnoff that she had never realized was there before. It was an unofficial overlook to the lake down below.

She found two black vans parked next to each other far off the paved road.

"Stay here," Murphy instructed in a firm tone. He handed her Spencer's leash. "Sit," he ordered the dog.

Spencer dropped her butt down to the ground.

"Stay." He held up his hand in the sign of a stop signal to her.

Gazing up at him, the sheltie waited.

While Murphy approached the closer van, Jessica observed an African-American man watching him in the rearview mirror. The driver muttered to someone in the van.

Standing still, Murphy waited with one hand on his weapon.

They heard a door slam on the other side of the van and footsteps approaching the rear. A short older man stepped around the corner and stopped. The only hair on his head was a white mustache that gave him a menacing air. He was dressed in military fatigues. He looked each of them up and down in turn. Finally, he turned his attention to Murphy. "Lieutenant Murphy Thornton?"

"Who's asking?"

"Colonel Glen Frost, United States Marines. Your CO sent me and my team to assist you. She says some bad-ass terrorists have one of my men."

The doors of the two vans opened. Four men and two women, all dressed in military fatigues, climbed out. They were each heavily armed and ready for battle.

"We have three more coming in from Washington via helicopter," the colonel said. "Just tell us where to go. When we're through, those desert rats are going to know they've been in a fight. We're all primed to do some serious butt kickin' from here to Iraq and back again. We're going to teach them about bringing their war over to our shores. Aren't we, Bravo Team?"

"Ooh-hah!" the rest of his team shouted in unison.

"Cute dog, by the way," the colonel said.

"Her name is Candi," Murphy said.

Sensing that she was being talked about, the little sheltie stood up and wagged her tail so hard that it looked like it was going to fly off her butt.

"Who's the princess?" Colonel Frost gestured at Jessica.

"That's Buttercup," Murphy said. "I'm guarding her body."

"Sweet!"

CHAPTER TWENTY-FOUR

In the middle of answering questions for her local, county, and state colleagues, Spencer Police Desk Sergeant Tonya paused to hold out a message sheet to Mac when he stepped through the door. "Archie called. She was in a lot of pain, so they gave her a sedative and she's going to sleep. I assured her that you'll be there tomorrow morning when she wakes up. So don't forget." She added, "I didn't tell her about David. I figured with everything else …"

"Did she say what she wanted to do about the wedding?" Mac asked.

"Only that she has no intention of going down the aisle in that designer gown on crutches."

Overhearing this, Hector, studying the computer monitor at which Tristan was seated, replied in a loud voice, "Jeff will have a stroke if you cancel!"

"If he didn't have a stroke when evacuating the hotel over a bomb threat during the high point of the holiday season, then he'll survive our cancelling the wedding," Mac replied. "Jeff's nerves are the least of my worries. Right now, we need to find David before they ship him off to Lord knows where.

After all this is over, I'll give Jeff a very generous bonus and extra vacation time to make him feel better."

Hector stood up. "You never give me bonuses and extra vacation."

"You don't throw hissy fits."

"We found where they're keeping David," Tristan shouted to be heard above everyone.

"We *think*," Hector said while patting the shoulder of a man who was sitting at the computer next to Tristan's. "Most likely it's where they have him."

The young man with long dark blond hair and black-framed glasses turned around in his seat to observe Mac looking down at him.

On the other side of the squad room, Bogie was pouring over maps with his other officers. Since the deputy chief didn't appear to be distressed by the visitor, Mac surmised this stranger had to be a friend rather than foe. "I don't believe we've met." He regretted his less-than-congenial tone as soon as the words came out of his mouth. His patience was wearing thin.

The rush of cold air behind him and the heavy pounding of combat boots on the floor signaled the arrival of more people volunteering to help their efforts to rescue Spencer's police chief. Holding her sheltie pup, Jessica looked like a brilliant purple flower oasis in the midst of military fatigues.

Upon spying Gnarly stretched out on the length of the sofa, Spencer squirmed and wiggled until, finally, the sheltie burst out of her arms and hit the floor running for the German shepherd.

Spotting the advancing twenty-five pounds of energy coming his way, Gnarly leapt from the comfort of his sofa and scurried as fast as he could for the confines of Tonya's desk. With the minimal amount of space through which to squeeze his large frame, Gnarly pushed the desk sergeant's chair on wheels out of the way in order to seek shelter from the yapping young dog.

"I think Gnarly has finally met his match," Tonya said upon noting the hundred-pound dog hiding from the fur ball that was one-quarter his size.

"I thought you said that dog was trained," Mac said to Jessica.

"She is," she replied. "You should see her beg."

As if to demonstrate, Spencer uttered a long pleading whine that ended in a high-pitched bark at Gnarly.

"Yeah, right," Mac said with a shake of his head before turning his attention back to the young man with the long hair and glasses who was looking him up and down.

"You must be Mac Faraday. Cameron Gates said that I could talk to you, but the other woman told me to report to Lieutenant Murphy Thornton."

"That would be me." Murphy closed the door behind him and elbowed his way through the throng of marines to make his way into the squad room.

"Lieutenant Murphy Thornton?" Tonya whispered to Jessica. "Any relation—"

"Son." A sigh escaped from Jessica's lips.

Tonya turned in her chair to admire the tall athletically slender man crossing the squad room to Mac and Hector. "I second that, girlfriend."

Hearing the swoon, Bogie muttered, "Yes, he is attractive."

"Way beyond attractive," Tonya said. "He's downright *dreamy.*"

The long-haired man at the desktop looked at Murphy Thornton, who was dressed in his black jeans and leather jacket. "Lieutenant Murphy Thornton?" He rose to his feet.

Doubtful, Murphy hesitated to respond.

After pushing his glasses up on his nose, he offered his hand. "Your boss told me to report to you." While the two men shook hands, he introduced himself. "Ethan Bonner. Computer expert extraordinaire. My late employer, Reginald Crane, had given me her phone number to call in an emergency. After I told her what had happened, she told me to come see you. I believe we're both looking for the same man. He was one of the two who killed my boss and good friend."

"What about the second man?" Mac asked him.

"Shot him this afternoon." Ethan looked over at Murphy. "He was trying to murder your stepmother because she had gotten too close."

"So my CO told me," Murphy said with a nod. "Cameron's with Dad now? Is she okay?"

"She's better than Reginald Crane," Ethan said. "Your boss had arranged a helicopter transport to bring us here. We landed at the Inn's helipad, and Hector was kind enough to take Cameron to the hospital to be with your father. Neal Black killed Crane in her jurisdiction. So she's claiming dibs when we capture him."

"Of course she is." Mac allowed a grin to come to his lips. "That's Cameron for you.

"I got a sense of that." Ethan turned back to Murphy. "I was told that you need someone to add something special to a flash drive."

Murphy dug a red thumb drive from his jacket pocket and handed it to Ethan, who examined it closely before saying, "I can work with this. Understand, I have no experience with explosives."

"That's okay," Murphy said. "I do."

"So do we," said Colonel Glen Frost, who had followed Murphy across the squad room to listen in.

Seeing Mac's and Bogie's questioning expressions, Murphy issued introductions all around. Colonel Frost offered his hand to Mac, and then to Bogie, to shake. "I remember both of you from the award ceremony a little more than a year ago. It's an honor to serve by your sides. I'm sick about what's happened. O'Callaghan doesn't deserve this."

"I have no military experience," Mac warned them. "I was a cop and detective—"

"You've still served on the frontlines," Frost said. "Just remember that these guys don't believe in telling you your rights—because they don't believe in anyone having any—nor do they take any prisoners."

"Shoot to kill. Got that." Mac held up his hand. "Obviously," he gestured at Murphy, Frost, and Bonner, "you're getting intel from some person—what did you say her name was?"

"We didn't," Murphy said.

"I don't like taking orders from someone whose name I don't know."

"Neither do I," Bogie said in agreement.

"*What* is it that they want?" Mac asked bluntly. "I thought about this after the jihadist attack at the Inn. This guy who called me said that I had something that belonged to him. He didn't specify *what it was*. Suddenly, you—" He poked Murphy in the chest, "correctly conclude that they sent someone to the Inn to kill this author, who we know had given something to your father, which I assume you now have. For all we know, that thumb drive isn't what they want. They could be after what Kochar gave to your father."

"You need to bring us up to speed." Bogie gestured at the squad room filled with local, county, and state police officers who had come in during the holiday season to help one of their own. "*We're all* putting our lives on the line—*we* deserve to know."

Coining a phrase he had heard often in Washington when dealing with cases involving national security, Mac said, "We *need* to know."

"They don't want what Kochar took," Murphy said. "They already have it. Kochar stole it off his brother's computer while visiting family in the Middle East."

"What is it?" Bogie asked.

"I don't know." In response to Bogie's doubtful expression, Murphy repeated his answer, and then added, "I was only ordered to collect it and deliver it to my commanding officer. Dad knows what it is, but I don't. I didn't ask. The less I know in this case, the better. But I do know that it is critical information that could assist our country in the war against Islamic terrorist groups."

Bogie and Mac exchanged expressions—each wordlessly asking the other whether to believe Murphy or not. On the one hand, he was the son of a trusted friend. But on the other, he was obviously a highly trained agent with the federal government and a military officer, and he was committed to serving his country. It had been Mac's experience that such agents were not above lying for the sake of successfully completing an assignment.

"David's on the phone!" Tonya shouted from her desk.

Everyone in the room moved en mass to the phone, where she pressed the speaker button so that they could all hear David talking to them in a whisper.

"David, where are you?" Mac dropped into Tonya's chair, which she vacated so that he could have access to her notepad. "Are you okay? Are you hurt?"

"I'm fine," David said. "They have a private jet parked at the end of the airstrip at Sander's Farm. It's a pretty good sized jet. The identification number on the tail is N666D."

"Where are you, David?" Bogie asked.

"I'm in Sander's barn."

They could hear him moving around.

"I don't think they know I escaped," he explained. "They think I'm drugged in the back of the jet. When I was sneaking off, I heard them on a conference call with a guy named Bauman."

Mac saw Murphy stand up straight at this information.

"He is obviously the main honcho in all this." They heard a crash and David curse. "Damn, that hurt!"

"What happened?" Thinking David had been recaptured, Mac's tone was filled with panic.

"I ran into a table," David groaned. "Hit me right in the shin. Ouch! Geez! That's going to leave a mark."

"David, can you get to the road?" Mac asked him.

"Garrett Highway is a mile away at the end of the lane, and they have a guy guarding it," David said. "If it wasn't so dark, I wouldn't have been able to get past them. I just kept telling them that I'm José."

"José?" a female African-American member of David's team laughed. "Major, you're the whitest white guy I know, and you're passing yourself off as *José*."

"It's really dark out—Bates? What are you doing there?"

"Saving your lily-white butt, that's what me and Matilda are doing here. She's waiting in the van to do some serious butt kicking."

"Who else did you call in, Mac? Did you go check Mom out of the nursing home?"

"I called no one," Mac said.

"We've all got your back, O'Callaghan," Colonel Frost said in a business-like tone. "Brief us on the situation."

"I counted twelve guards surrounding the jet and various other points around the farm," David said. "Some of them are trained professionals. Others appear to be hired guns from some drug gangs, I think. The guy I overpowered was obviously a small-time dealer, based on the amount of cocaine he's got stashed in the coat I stole off him. With all the coke, I'm carrying, I'm in big trouble if I get busted."

They heard silence, except for David's breathing on the other end of the line.

"This Bauman guy bought this farm through a bunch of shell companies or something, and he was paranoid about anyone finding out what he had in the barn—"

"So, of course, you had to go investigate," Bogie said.

"He said the Easter Bunny was hiber—what's this?"

"What is it, David?" Mac asked through braced breath.

"Maps."

"Of what?"

"Oh my God." David was breathing hard.

"What is it?"

"What's on that flash drive they want?" David asked. "I heard Bauman going ape about paying a lot of money for it. He used the word 'formula.' He wants it bad."

Ethan turned to Murphy before answering, "A man-made version of Ebola. There's no antidote."

"This barn is a bomb factory," David said. "I think to build dirty bombs. And these maps are of Vatican City. He was talking about the Easter Bunny hibernating here in the barn."

In silence, everyone digested the information.

David verbalized their thought. "They're planning to detonate a dirty bomb with Ebola at the Vatican on Easter Day."

Mac felt Jessica's hand grip his shoulder. The beat of his heart quickened.

"Damn!" David swore. "They're calling for me."

"They know you escaped?" Bogie almost grabbed the phone.

"No, someone outside is calling for José," David said. "I have to go. Text me at this cell with your plan. I'll be guarding the barn."

"David, don't go," Mac said.

"If I don't, they'll start looking for José and discover that I've escaped," David said. "Don't worry, Mac. I'll be careful. This is what I do."

Click.

"José? Estás aquí?" A young African-American man stomped around by the main door of the barn. "It's me, Raul." The young man started when he hear a thump in the dark woods followed by a curse in Spanish.

The hooded figure in the heavy coat limped around the corner of the barn.

"Está bien, José? Qué hacías ahí?"

"Hacer pipi." With a perfect Spanish accent, David said that he had been urinating behind the barn. He mentally thanked God that they weren't French terrorists. Then he would have had a problem. "Tropecé con una maldita roca." While rubbing his sore shin, David pointed over his shoulder to the dark shadows behind the barn where Raul could imagine a rock would be waiting for him to trip over.

Raul nodded his head. "Carlo and I, estamos viendo la ruta de acceso." He went on to tell David that they were very bored guarding the access road between the farm and the air strip. On the farm that was far removed from the main road, they had nothing to do. Then, they had seen José walk by, which had reminded them that they were planning to attend a major New Year's Eve party in downtown Washington the next evening. With the thousands of dollars that Ra'ees was paying them, they expected to score big with lovely prostitutes.

Exhausted by leaning over and keeping his face adverted from Raul's view, and from listening to him rambling on in Spanish while trying to keep up with his story, David was about ready to take out his gun and shoot him when Raul finally arrived at his point. "Tienes cualquier cocaína para comprar?"

He wanted cocaine for the New Year's Eve party.

Without saying anything, David reached into his inside breast pocket, took out two of the small packets, and offered them to Raul.

"Es eso todo? Nada más?" Raul sounded disappointed that he did not offer more.

David asked him how much he wanted, and Raul explained that they wanted to impress their "dates." Reminding himself that he was playing the role of a drug dealer, David reached back into his pocket. "Te va a costar." He told the desperate thug that it would cost him. "Cuánto dinero tienes?"

For his answer, Raul dug into his pocket and pulled out four hundred-dollar bills.

Uttering a sigh of disgust to show disappointment with the amount, David slapped a total of four bags into Raul's hand. "Tell no one," David said in English with a Spanish accent. "Don't want no one to know I am easy touch."

"Mucho gracias," Raul said before trotting up the road and leaving the police chief to count out and pocket the four hundred-dollar bills.

CHAPTER TWENTY-FIVE

"We know where David is," Bogie told the collection of police officers, sheriff and his deputies, and team of special ops marines.

Sheriff Turow had torn himself away from the hotel once it was cleared of the bomb and the guests were allowed to return inside. It was time to turn his attention to the international terrorists who had set up shop in his jurisdiction.

Bogie offered his suggestion. "I say we forget about that thumb drive—don't even risk it getting into their dirty hands. We've got an hour before the drop time. There's twelve of them, and three times more of us. Let's just storm in—"

"Not against these guys," Murphy said with a shake of his head.

"Why don't we assess the situation first?" Mac asked. "What do we know about this Sander's Farm?"

Tristan was hooking an HDMI cord to the back of the laptop. After plugging the other end into a portable projector, he directed the computer's desktop onto the wall. "Here, you can all see what we're talking about."

Everyone turned to the wall. The room fell silent. Jessica dimmed the lights so that they could more clearly see the image.

"That's the Sander's farm," Bogie said when the bird's eye view of the darkened farm appeared on the wall.

The farm consisted of a traditional two-story home, a detached garage, and an old run-down barn. To find it, one had to take a right turn off of Garrett Highway, the winding country road between Deep Creek Lake and Oakland, travel through a patch of woods, go down a small hill, and circle a pond before taking the road back up a steep hill to the farm-house. From there, the lane passed between the house and the barnyard along a thick strip of woods. At the edge of the backfield, the farmer's road cut through the woods, where it then opened into what appeared to be a field from a bird's view. This night, that field was plowed clear of the snow. Facing the woods and the farmhouse on the other side of the trees, a private jet rested at the far end of the field.

"This image is real time," Ethan said. "Unfortunately, with this satellite image, we're unable to get close enough to see how many terrorists there are. David reports a count of twelve."

"Is this a defense department satellite image?" Sheriff Turow asked.

"Google Earth," Ethan said. "Just as good. It's easier to access and legal to use. The man we are looking for is an FBI special investigator—"

"FBI!" Mac yelled. "David said they were terrorists." He whirled around at Murphy. "You said they were terrorists. Now he claims this guy is a federal agent!"

"Most likely a sleeper agent for an Islamic terrorist group," Murphy said in a matter-of-fact tone. "My team is getting together the background on this case to brief us all." He added, "Point is—this guy is not operating alone. Someone is backing them. The plane. The runway."

"David said they were on a conference call with someone they called Bauman," Mac said. "That could be a first or last name. Whoever he is, he has deep pockets. The death squad that hit my house. Plus the technology to fake a message to Agnes."

"They have money and people backing them," Murphy said. "That's why we can't go in there without a plan."

"Why would Americans be targeting Americans?" Tristan asked.

"It's not about patriotism," Murphy said. "This is about a twisted religion and a sick worldview that goes back to Genesis in the Bible."

"Not the Bible I grew up with," Mac said.

"Yes, the Bible you grew up with," Murphy said. "Remember Ishmael?"

In regards to Mac's questioning expression, Bogie said, "Abraham's first-born son. The older half-brother of Isaac."

"The covenant that God made with Abraham and Sarah was to be passed down to his son," Murphy said. "But Sarah got tired of waiting for them to conceive a child, so she had Abraham sleep with Hagar, her maid. Hagar gave birth to Ishmael. But God's covenant was not to be passed down through Ishmael. It was to be passed down through the son Abraham had with Sarah, who did conceive later. Ishmael's followers believe that God's covenant was passed down through Ishmael, not Isaac, and that *they* are the blessed people. Somehow, we Christians and Jews, descendants and followers of Isaac, have cheated them. *Ishmael is Islam.*"

Murphy waved his hand at the image of the plane on the wall. "Don't you get it? This is all about a sibling rivalry that has been going on for thousands of years!"

"Oh, so just because Dad let Tristan go to Florida for spring break in his senior year when I couldn't go," Jessica said, "my descendants have a license to go around beheading people who disagree with my worldview?"

"It's good to know you're not still bitter about that," Tristan said with a chuckle.

"It wasn't fair," Jessica said. "My grades were just as good as yours."

"I knew Tristan wasn't going to come back pregnant," Mac said under his breath. "Listen, I get it. This is a war of good versus evil. It's not Britain against France or Ireland against Britain. It's Satan masquerading as Allah in order to con an entire culture into destroying the rest of the world in the name of their god."

"And they're going to kill tens of thousands of Catholics on Easter day at the Pope's Holy Mass," Jessica said.

"We need to call in the FBI—" Sheriff Turow said.

"They're already here. We have reason to believe the guy making the ransom demand is a special agent with the FBI." Snatching his cell phone from his belt, Murphy slipped over to the door where he could hear better.

"How about Homeland Security?" Sheriff Turow asked.

"Do we have time for them to get here from Washington?" Bogie asked. "We need to get David out of there, and we need to blow up that barn."

"What if the barn already has toxins in it?" Jessica said. "We can't just blow it up. We could be spreading anthrax, or Lord knows what else, throughout the valley. As windy as it's been, it would spread all the way to Washington and up the coast in no time."

Murphy turned around from where he had been talking on his phone. "May I have your attention, everyone? My commanding officer is on the line. She's been involved with this investigation since it came to our government's attention, and she would like to brief everyone." He laid the phone down on the desk. "You're up, ma'am."

"Good evening, everyone." A throaty feminine voice oozed from the speaker. Via a remote hookup with Ethan's laptop, the absent leader of Murphy's team conducted the presentation for those in attendance. Ethan sat next to the laptop to operate the slide presentation.

"I'm sorry," Mac said, "I didn't catch your name."

"That's because I didn't throw it."

As an image of Special Investigator Neal Black appeared on the bare wall, she continued without missing a beat. "This is your target. It's because of sleeper agents like Neal Black—and believe me, he's not the only one—that we have been losing this miserable war against terrorism. He was able to escape detection, which allowed him to abduct Major David O'Callaghan, because he was born here and looks just like us. His mentors have taught him to fly below Homeland Security's radar."

Jessica gazed at the handsome, fair-skinned young man with reddish-blond hair. He looked like someone she would have shared a coffee with or taken home to meet her father. "How does someone like that become a home-grown Islamic terrorist?"

"Surprisingly easy," the voice answered from the speaker phone.

"Neal Black was born and raised in New York," Ethan Bonner reported. "His mother was a corporate lawyer who had no interest in being tied down to a husband—"

"But she wanted to be tied down to a child?" Bogie asked.

Nodding, Ethan said, "Neal Black was born via artificial insemination."

"Was that found in his background check?" Mac asked as a joke.

"Yes, it was," Ethan said. "When he applied and was accepted into the FBI, they did a thorough background check. Not only did he list no name for his father, but he also noted that he was conceived via a donation from a sperm bank. His mother never married and climbed to senior partner of her law firm. He was raised by a nanny."

"Neal listed no religious affiliation on his application, by the way," Murphy's commanding officer said. "We suspect that was at the direction of his mentor and handler, Jassem al-Bahdadi. Next slide, Ethan."

The slide showed Jassem al-Bahdadi as pictured on Homeland Security's ten most-wanted terrorist list.

"That's the slimy snake O'Callaghan killed summer before last," Colonel Frost said. "The major led the team that took out a terrorist training camp. In came al-Bahdadi with two truckloads of weapons. David called in and got the clearance to terminate al-Bahdadi, and he did." He puffed out his chest. "We each got the Bronze Star for that. O'Callaghan led the team."

"Somehow, word got out that O'Callaghan had fired the kill shot," she announced.

"How?" Colonel Frost demanded to know. His face turned red all the way up and across his bald head.

"Once we intercepted communication that they had Major O'Callaghan," she said, "we went digging through the records for that mission. The last person to check it out was a junior lieutenant in the records office at the Pentagon."

"Don't tell me that he's an ISIS spy," Sheriff Turow said.

"No," she said. "Upon questioning, he reported that he looked into the file at the request of Muhammad Muiz, special advisor to the President of the United States on Islamic affairs. He wanted to know the name of the shooter because the President wanted to issue that soldier the Medal of

Valor." She added, "The junior lieutenant says he had been instructed by Muhammad Muiz not to say anything."

"Then, this Muiz guy turned around and gave that name to his twisted friends so they could put out a hit on David," Mac replied. "What does the president have to say about his *advisor?*"

"He won't say anything until we give him proof that his advisor is a spy," she replied. "In the meantime, he and his staff are claiming the junior lieutenant must have misunderstood."

"Just like when David gets his head sawed off, it'll somehow be his fault ..." Colonel Frost muttered. In response to Bogie's questioning look, he replied, "I'm quite cynical about how management conducts its affairs." He added in a whisper, "I've seen it all."

The throaty voice from the phone said, "Fortunately, the lieutenant has provided us with copies of the emails from Muiz requesting O'Callaghan's name and instructing the lieutenant to tell no one."

"That's great," Mac said, "but by the time Congress gets through the president's attorney general and teams of lawyers to haul him out of the White House and before a special hearing, David will be dead."

"Along with every other red-blooded Westerner that he sets up while having tea and crumpets in the Oval Office," the colonel said with a nod of agreement.

"Surprisingly," Murphy's commanding officer said, "with just a little bit of digging into Muhammad Muiz's background, we found that he graduated from New York University with a doctorate in Islamic Affairs. You'll never guess who his academic advisor was when he was an undergraduate."

"Jassem al-Bahdadi," Murphy answered.

"Give the man a cigar."

"Was the president aware of this when he appointed Muiz to be his advisor?" Mac's eyes were wide with disbelief.

"Jassem al-Bahdadi didn't make the terrorist list until *after* the president had been elected and had already appointed Muiz to an advisory position," she said. "Nothing else in Muiz's background points to his being a spy. He was born in New York City to Muslim parents. He's a second-generation American. He makes frequent trips to the Middle East—all in the name of his position as advisor in Islamic affairs."

"And, of course, if he had meetings with the terrorists, then those were all in the spirit of diplomacy," Colonel Frost said.

"Exactly," she said. "Unfortunately, Muhammad Muiz does have the president's ear."

"If he's giving the president advice with the motivation of making our country vulnerable to the Islamic nation in order for them to take over …" Jessica shuddered. "That is the perfect position to plant a spy."

"Only if you have a president who's gullible enough to not see what the spy is doing," Colonel Frost said.

"His supporters say he's *open minded* to the beliefs of another culture," Hector said.

The colonel said, "He wouldn't be so open minded if it was the Southern Baptists beheading—"

"Look," Mac stood up to interject, "I'm not interested in taking down a president or exposing inadequate defense for our country and way of life. All I want is to bring David home in one piece and to marry the love of my life tomorrow. If we can save the world while doing it, then I'm all for it. Otherwise, I say call Homeland Security and have them shut down the bomb factory."

"That's what we're going to do," Murphy said in a quiet tone that served to calm Mac's rising temper. "But we can't go rushing in half-cocked. That's how we all—including the major—get killed. Before we make any moves, we need to figure out who exactly we are going up against and who or what they have backing them."

"Okay," Mac said with a heavy sigh. "This whole thing …"

"We all know how you feel, Mr. Faraday," Colonel Frost said.

No, you don't, Mac thought. *David is more than a friend. He's my bother. The only one I have. And if anything happens to him, I won't even be acknowledged as the brother he left behind.* He was startled out of his thoughts by Jessica's hand on his shoulder.

"Okay," she said. "So this Muiz guy, the spy in the White House, gets David's name and passes it on to the sleeper agent in the FBI …"

"Not exactly," Ethan said. "We believe it was a kidnapping of opportunity. Black and Elder were trying to obtain the formula for a man-made form of Ebola that one of their home-grown terrorists had acquired. Coincidentally, that formula ended up here on a thumb drive. While Black and Elder were hunting it down, they bugged Detective Cameron Gates' phone. She was investigating the murder of Reginald Crane, who they had tortured to death. They were trying to uncover information that would lead them to the thumb drive. As luck—bad luck—would have it, they overheard a conversation she had with Police Chief David O'Callaghan."

"They must have recognized his name as one of the ones on the terrorist hit list of American snipers who have taken out principal terrorist targets," she said. "That list was compiled from information Muiz had obtained using his position."

"So they decided to grab David *and* the formula," Mac said. "They have David, but they don't have the formula."

"That's the formula that this Bauman guy was going ape over," Murphy said. "Because he paid for it, but he doesn't have it and needs it for his Easter surprise."

"That thumb drive is the only thing keeping them in the country right now," his boss told them.

"This Neal Black guy comes from a good home, and his mother had money," Jessica said. "Why would he turn on his country like this?"

"When Neal Black was fourteen years old, his mother began dating Jassem al-Bahdadi," Murphy's commanding officer explained. "Jassem was very well educated. He was an adjunct professor in Islamic history at New York University. He came from money. Because Neal was young and vulnerable, Jassem managed to convert him to Islam."

"Jassem was a busy guy." Ethan switched the slide to a picture of Special Agent Leland Elder. "During the ten years that Jassem spent in the United States, which did include September 11, 2001—just saying—he volunteered as a counselor at a youth center mainly working with fatherless boys. That was where he met Leland Elder, who also became an FBI agent."

"It sounds like he was actively recruiting boys without strong father figures to convert to Islam," Jessica said.

"Exactly." the sultry voice from the phone explained. "According to our research, both boys became close to Jassem, who almost became a father figure to them. Yet, neither of them listed Jassem as a reference on their applications to the FBI."

"Then how do you know this is fact?" Mac asked.

"Homeland Security knows all about Jassem's background," she explained. "We know he lived in the United States for ten years and volunteered at the youth center. In 2008, he went back to Iraq, where he rose to a principal position in ISIS. A cross-check of the boys we could identify as members at the youth club turned up Leland Elder's name. Elder came to our attention this afternoon when he tried to murder Detective Cameron Gates."

"Black has been a little more difficult to track," Ethan said. "After he disappeared yesterday, agents from Homeland Security went to his mother. Since we knew that Elder had loyalty to Jassem, we asked her about him, and that was when we discovered that he was a family friend," he added in a significant tone. "Black's mother wanted him to go to Yale Law School. When Neal didn't make the cut, Jassem encouraged him to become a federal agent. Neal failed the psych exam to get into Homeland Security. But he was able to get into the FBI. At the present time, he has an application in with ATF."

"I guess he's lost any chance of getting that position now," Mac said.

She said, "Next slide, Ethan."

The next slide was of a black man with what appeared to be anger permanently etched into his face. His eyes were dark with hatred. "We believe this is most likely the man providing manpower and weaponry. Ra'ees Sims."

"Was he another boy who wandered into Jassem's Islam recruitment center?" Colonel Frost asked.

"No," she said.

"We found him through good old-fashioned detective work," Ethan said. "After I killed Elder, I found his burn phone on his body, and we traced the calls that he made with it. There was one call that lasted only a few seconds to a phone number in Texas that is registered to Sims Security. Less than five minutes after that call was made, Elder received a call from a burner phone that pinged off the same cell tower."

Mac and Hector exchanged glances.

"It was a signal," Hector said.

"Exactly," Ethan said. "The last phone call that was made on that burner phone pinged off a town right here on Spencer Mountain this morning. That call was to another burner phone in the same area."

"What kind of security company does this guy Sims run?" Jessica asked.

"Ra'ees Sims is trouble with a capital T," Murphy's boss said. "He is very active in the Muslim mosque there and hasn't been exactly quiet about his support for Islamic extremists. Most of his employees are members of his mosque. The ATF have been watching his company. They suspect him of trafficking weapons to drug gangs and protecting drug shipments for his customers. He then launders his profits from the drug cartels through his company, which we believe is a terrorist cell working under the guise of a security company.

"Here's another piece of the puzzle," she said. "When Sims started his company, he had a big down payment for an office in a nice location right in Houston. He had a lot of start-up money. We managed to track that money to—are you ready for this, Murphy?"

"I was born ready," Murphy replied.

"We followed the money trail to find that Sims' security company is in reality a shell corporation for NOH Bauman Technologies."

"Bauman," Mac said.

"NOH Bauman Technologies is a billion-dollar company that has been selling weapons to both us and the terrorists," Murphy said.

"Isn't it illegal for an American company to sell weapons to the terrorists we're fighting?" Mac asked.

"Only if they get caught," Murphy said, "and we can prove that they have been doing it knowingly and willingly. Without proof of that, a massive conglomerate like Bauman

Technologies can claim they are selling the stuff to a second party who is turning around and re-selling it to the terrorists."

"Bauman is so good at covering his tracks that he can make that claim," Murphy's commanding officer said. "He is a controlling stockholder of two major news networks, which is why even when journalists uncover things that are actually common knowledge to us in the military and intelligence community, they can't get that information out to the public. Journalists have told us that Bauman has been heard saying rather proudly that America will only know what he wants it to know."

"Which is why these slimy SOBs keep getting re-elected," Frost muttered. "If the people knew what we not only know, but also have proof of ..." He shook his head.

"Well, maybe we finally got that proof." Tristan raised his voice so he could be heard by everyone in the room. He yanked an earbud out of his ear. "I ran the jet's registration number through the FAA database—"

"How did you get in there?" Murphy's boss asked.

"Don't ask what you don't want to know," Tristan answered. "This plane is registered to Bauman Technologies. It was last seen taking off from Houston, Texas, and was supposed to land at Dulles airport. According to FAA, the pilot radioed that they had engine trouble and were landing at a private airfield outside of Morgantown."

"If the plane is registered to this Bauman guy, then we have a direct connection to David's abduction," Mac said. "Where is he? I want a few minutes alone with him."

"He's in Paris," Tristan answered. "I took the liberty of breaking into ... never mind. He's in Paris."

"Out of our reach and covering his tracks," Colonel Frost said.

"Nathaniel Bauman's conglomerate owns dozens of planes," Murphy's boss said. "He will claim that he had no way of knowing what Sims was doing with it."

"By the time all this is over," Frost said, "he'll be crying that he is as shocked and dismayed as the rest of America."

"Leave Bauman and Muiz to me," she said in a cold voice.

"What are we going to do about David?" Jessica asked.

"We're going to go get him," Murphy said, "and bring him home."

CHAPTER TWENTY-SIX

It had turned into a waiting game.

The state police and Colonel Frost's team went out to scout the layout of the farm and airstrip in order to plan their attack. Ethan Bonner, with Tristan's help, was working on setting up the thumb drive. Murphy would add his special touch at the end.

After calling Archie to discover that she was indeed asleep, Mac, with Gnarly trotting at his side, went to the police department's gym, located at the back of the station. He found Murphy Thornton already working out on the heavy punching bag.

Usually, one or two officers could be found working out. Even though the station was filled, at the moment the gym was vacant, except for the lone young man wearing black sweats and bare feet.

One punch turned into two, and then three. A series of three was followed by a side kick that sent the bag swinging. "As long as you're following me, why don't you be useful and hold the bag?" Murphy suggested with his back to him.

Still in the dark shadows, Mac was surprised that he had been spotted. Since their cover was blown, Gnarly trotted over and jumped up onto the bench. After making himself comfortable, he laid down, using Murphy's bag as a cushion for his head.

After wrapping his arms around either side of the bag, Mac braced himself and pressed up against it. "Jessica told me what you did for her in Grantsville. I wanted to thank you."

Murphy let down his fists. With a crooked grin, he shrugged. "You're welcome." He quickly added, "I didn't know she was your daughter at the time."

"Now you know," Mac said in a firm tone.

The two men exchanged long looks.

Mac finally broke the silence. "Exactly where have you been assigned in the navy, Murphy?"

"I've been assigned to work on special assignments for the Joint Chiefs of Staff," he answered before throwing a punch at the bag. "They're all classified, so I can't tell you anything else."

Catching his breath after the impact of the punch, Mac asked, "Are you a Phantom?"

Murphy stood up straight and stared at Mac. "What did you just ask me?"

"Murphy, are you a Phantom?"

Murphy chuckled. "Why would you ask me that?"

"Let's see," Mac said, "You have a boss with no name. You don't dress like your average navy officer fresh out of the academy. I was a homicide detective in Washington for over twenty years. I've met a lot of navy lieutenants and you are …" he searched for the right word "… different from any I've ever met before." He shrugged his shoulders. "Makes a guy wonder."

"Well, you met my father," Murphy uttered a laugh. "I haven't had an exactly average upbringing."

"You haven't answered my question, Murphy."

"That urban legend about Phantoms is relatively new," he replied with a shrug of his shoulders. "I frankly didn't know those rumors had made it to the general public yet."

"When did they start?"

"Right after Benghazi." Returning to the bag, Murphy said between punches, "According to legend, there are those in the armed forces and intelligence community who believe that America and her citizens need to be protected— a primary goal that appears to have been lost among the political infighting in Washington. Some higher-ups did some bureaucratic maneuvering to put together a highly secret team. Its members are hand-picked. At least, that's what the rumors say."

Murphy paused in his punching to catch Mac's eye. *"If such a team is real, their sole mission is to keep our country safe ... no matter how politically incorrect our actions may appear to the rest of world."*

"Is that legal?" Mac asked. "I mean, this team that acts on the orders of someone other than the president or Congress— isn't that operating beyond whoever's authority?"

Murphy stood up straight. "Major O'Callaghan has been abducted by a terrorist group that is being led by a special agent with the Federal Bureau of Investigations. Email chatter that my team has been monitoring, maybe legally, maybe not according to some folks, says that a massive terrorist group in Tehran is very excited about getting their hands on O'Callaghan. They plan to make him the main event at a special New Year's execution."

Murphy placed his hands on his hips. "Now, I can tell you exactly what will happen if we follow proper protocol. After a couple of hours of making phone calls up to the White House, who will then call Muiz, who gave this group O'Callaghan's name, a decision will be made that it will offend the people in Tehran if we ruin their New Year's party with a military attack on their party."

"I get your point," Mac said, "but I think you're being a little extreme."

"Tell that to the families of the victims of Benghazi who died after the military was told to stand-down because the administration didn't want to offend the very terrorists who killed them." Murphy leaned in to Mac from the other side of the heavy bag hanging between them. "When they're torturing O'Callaghan in their little preshow to the final execution—all the while streaming it live via satellite to all their terrorist cells across the world—with millions of Islamic extremists hooting and hollering to O'Callaghan's pain and humiliation—are you going to give a damn then about bureaucratic protocol?"

"It makes me wonder. Is it me or the times that are changing?" Mac cocked his head at him. "Secret military groups made up of phantom soldiers?"

With a chuckle, Murphy winked at him. "It's just the latest urban legend that has been making the rounds, Mac." He returned to punching the bag. He finished with a kick to the bag that almost knocked Mac off his feet.

Sweat dripping from his face, Murphy went over to the bench and picked up his water bottle. With his back to Mac, he took a long drink.

After releasing his hold on the bag, Mac turned around. "You still haven't answered my question, Murphy."

Murphy gave Mac a sidelong glance. "If I was, I wouldn't be able to tell you."

"*If* you were a Phantom, traveling the world on one deadly mission after another, I would have to ask why. I mean, if something goes bad, like is our country going to help you—"

"No, I would be totally on my own," Murphy answered. "The United States Government would deny knowing anything about me."

"What kind of man—"

Murphy whirled around. "If you don't mind my asking, sir, why did you become a homicide detective? Your adoptive father was an engineer. Your mother was a stay-at-home mom. You had the most balanced and normal childhood any kid could have, and yet you chose to go chasing after killers. Look at you. You have how many millions of dollars? You could play golf all day—"

"I hate golf and I stink at tennis."

"Travel."

"That I do like," Mac said with a shrug of his shoulders.

"So why, sir?" Murphy slung a leg over to the other side of the bench in order to face him. "Why do you put a target on your back and put yourself out there? You don't need the money."

Mac chuckled. "Considering what's in my gene pool, it was obviously in my DNA."

After flashing Mac a grin, Murphy reached across the bench to stroke Gnarly's back. The German shepherd stretched out to take in the petting. "Do you remember where you were when the towers went down on September eleventh?"

Stung by the question, Mac sighed. He eased down onto the bench on the other side of Gnarly. "Everyone who was alive then remembers that. My partner and I were on our way from downtown Washington to Springfield to question a witness. We were on the expressway coming up to where it passed the Pentagon when we saw the plane coming in. I remember saying to my partner, 'He's not going to make Reagan National,' when it hit the Pentagon. We actually saw it hit. My partner was driving and we almost had a collision." He lowered his head. "I was absolutely numb. I didn't know until later that it wasn't an accident, but an actual attack. All those people ..." His voice trailed off.

"Dad—we—lost three friends that day," Murphy said in a soft voice.

"How old were you then? Thirteen? Twelve?"

"Twelve."

Mac noted that Murphy was a year older than Jessica.

"We were living in Oakland, California," Murphy said. "Dad drove back—all the way cross country because the airports were closed and he wanted to get back here to help. He attended three funerals." He hung his head at the memory.

"I'm sorry, Murphy," Mac said.

"Three of my friends lost their mother," Murphy said. "She was a lieutenant like my dad was at the time. Their father was in the Army Corp of Engineers. The older girl, Aimee, was the same age as me. We had gone to elementary school together in Hawaii. Her sister, Joey, was the same age as Sarah. The boy, Troy, was Donny's age. Aimee had long thick dark hair and the darkest eyes." Murphy paused to take a long drink of his water. "She was my first crush."

"I can imagine how awful that must have been for them," Mac said.

Murphy slowly shook his head. "Turned out, their mother was the stabilizing influence in the family. When she was killed, their father couldn't adjust. He fell completely apart. He lost it. He became an alcoholic. Lost his job. While he didn't physically abandon the kids, I guess he did emotionally. I heard all that through friends. I tried to get and stay in touch, but I never got anywhere. Then ..."

After a long silence, Mac urged him to go on. "What?"

"I had just moved to Washington for my first assignment after graduating from the academy. I was riding my bike, my new BMW motorcycle, my present to myself after graduating. I was riding home late one night and I came to a traffic light in Crystal City. I'm sitting on my bike at this traffic light, and less than a half a mile behind me is the Pentagon, and I look over at the street corner, and I see this girl, only twenty feet from me, with long, dark wavy hair and these big dark eyes. She is curled up on a piece of cardboard. I still don't know how I was able to recognize her, but I did. It was Joey."

"Aimee's sister?"

Murphy nodded his head. "I took a side street and turned around and came back. She remembered me." He cocked his head at Mac. "Sarah is in her first year at the Naval Academy, and here is this girl, her exact same age, and she's living on the street."

"Where was her family?"

"She said her father had sold the house and moved away. He abandoned all of them. She had no idea where he was. She didn't know where Troy was either."

"If he was the same age as Donny, he'd be a minor," Mac said.

"I know."

Mac noticed tears come to Murphy's eyes when he took a drink. "I bought her dinner and put her up in a hotel for a night, but it didn't do any good. All she cared about was her next high. By the next day, she was out hooking."

"Aimee?" Mac asked in a soft voice.

"She had taken a bottle of sleeping pills," Murphy said. "Killed herself ... on September 11, 2011."

"Tenth anniversary of her mother's death," Mac noted the obvious.

"When those monsters killed Aimee's mom, they destroyed that whole family." Murphy turned to him. "Do you want to know the real irony?"

"What's that?"

"Aimee and her whole family were Muslim. Third-generation Americans from Indonesia." Murphy took another drink from his bottle. "Only complete and utter evil would destroy its own kind."

"And Bauman and Muiz? What role do they play in this war and conspiracy?"

"People like Bauman are in it for greed. Muiz probably hopes to become president or king after Islam conquers our country and declares Sharia law." Murphy laughed at the thought. "Can you imagine Jessica in a burka? She'd have to cut off her fingernails."

"Ain't gonna happen." Mac eased into the question. "You and Jessica seem to have hit it off."

Murphy shot Mac a sidelong glance. "Now we come to why you followed me in here. You want to know my intentions with your daughter. Are you apprehensive about your little girl getting mixed up with a *Phantom?*"

Mac turned toward him. "I like you, Murphy. A lot. I like how you don't beat around the bush. You're very capable of taking care of yourself. You're respectful. You're the type of man I have dreamed about Jessica becoming involved with. So, I have to ask. What are your intentions with her?"

Murphy locked his gaze with Mac. "I don't intend to have sex with your daughter, sir."

Mac was in the middle of a sigh of relief when Murphy added, "I intend to marry her."

Mac did a hard blink. He sucked in his breath and looked straight at Murphy, waiting for those dimples to flash at him before he burst out laughing. It didn't come.

"You're serious," Mac stated rather than asked.

"If she will have me."

When Mac said nothing, Murphy asked, "I hope I have your blessing to ask her."

"Murph—" Mac found himself stuttering. As the father of a lovely, bright, personable, and charming girl, he had envisioned having this conversation with a young man, but he hadn't envisioned having it in a vacant gym with a German shepherd snoring between the two of them. He thought it would be in a bar or a country club—over a very good cognac. "Do you know how many pairs of shoes that woman owns?" Mac was surprised to hear himself blurt out.

"No," Murphy replied. "How many?"

"I don't know," Mac answered, "but I do know she has a closet in her house dedicated just to them. That's a lot of shoes! Your whole year's salary as a navy officer will go toward keeping her shod."

"Is that a yes or a no to having your blessing?"

"Yes," Mac stuttered out, "you have my permission." Seeing a grin coming to the young man's lips, he added, "But I have to warn you, Murphy—"

"I know. She has a lot of shoes. I've been warned."

Turning serious, Mac reached for his hand.

"What?"

"Jessica …" Mac slowly shook his head. "My daughter is a sweet, vivacious, cunningly smart young lady who has a mind of her own. She gets it from me. Generally, she makes very good decisions."

"But …"

"Before her inheritance, Jessica was a hard-working college girl," Mac explained. "She had a hard time. Always broke. Had to do without a lot of things. Well, after becoming an heiress, she made friends and enjoyed the spoils of being wealthy. She loves the party circuit, high-society life, and the company of good-looking men who can wine and dine her."

"You think she'll say no?" Murphy stared at the far wall.

"I know she would sleep with you in a heartbeat," Mac said. "But give up her freewheeling lifestyle to become a navy officer's wife? I wish she would. If she did, your marriage would have my full blessing." He patted Murphy's hand. "But I doubt she will." Mac sighed when he added, "I'm sorry, Murphy."

Slowly, Murphy shook his head. "With all due respect, sir—"

"Someone recently told me that when someone starts off with 'all due respect,' they're about to say something disrespectful," Mac said.

With a laugh, Murphy sat up and flashed a wide grin at him. "Nah, I have nothing but respect for you, sir."

"Thank you."

"I have to respect you, because you're going to be my father-in-law."

Mac cocked his head at him. *Did he hear what I said? Jessica will say no.*

"I am going to ask Jessica to marry me," Murphy said. "She'll either say yes or no or tell me that she needs more time. I mean, we only met eleven hours ago."

"That is kind of fast," Mac admitted.

"I can respect her wanting to give it more time," Murphy said. "But if her answer is anything but yes, I will keep on asking because I love Jessica with all my heart. I knew from the instant I looked into those eyes of hers and saw into her soul ... I knew then that she was my soul mate. I can't imagine not having her and her shoes in my life."

Not knowing what to say, Mac stared with wide eyes at Murphy while he packed up his bag. He barely noticed when Murphy stood up and turned to him.

"So there you have it, sir. You followed me in here to ask about my intentions with your daughter, and that's what they are—plain and simple. I intend to marry her and to be the father of your grandchildren. Are you cool with that?"

Grandchildren? She's only a little girl! Speechless, Mac nodded his head.

"You don't look very good." Murphy bent over to peer at him. "Do you want some water, sir?"

"Maybe a little," Mac replied through a tight throat.

While Murphy raced off to get a cup of water, Mac felt Gnarly nudge him with his cold nose. "I'm not having a good week, Gnarly."

In agreement, Gnarly uttered a whine.

Jessica stared down the hallway where Murphy had disappeared to go to the gym. She did not fail to notice her father following close behind. The longer they were gone, the more worried she became.

What are they talking about? Me, of course. I swear, if Dad tells him about my closet dedicated only to my shoes I'll die—right here and right now. God can take me now.

Then, another thought crossed her mind.

Oh, Dad, please don't tell Murphy about the time I bleached my hair blonde and it turned bright orange instead.

"Hello, Jessica."

The low feminine voice behind her almost made Jessica jump out of her skin. She whirled around to see Dr. Dora Washington looking questioningly at her. The scent of a hot submarine sandwich reminded Jessica that none of them had eaten anything. The hotel had been evacuated before the food at the rehearsal dinner was served. "I didn't mean to scare you. Is Bogie in his office? I finished the on-scene examination of the two bodies at David's place and thought Bogie should eat something. So I brought him dinner."

Jessica swallowed down the growl in her stomach at the scent of food. "I think he is."

When Dora turned away, Jessica clutched her arm. "Can I ask you a professional question?"

"Is this about your application for med school?" Dr. Washington had offered to write a letter of recommendation for her. Jessica had yet to make a decision, even though she had already graduated with her master's degree in excellent standing at William and Mary University.

"I'm thinking of Georgetown Medical School," Jessica said.

"That's an excellent school."

"But what I wanted to ask you about is Russell Dooley's autopsy."

Dr. Washington frowned. "I can't talk to you about that."

"Dad didn't kill him."

"I'm sure he didn't—"

"I know he was stabbed twenty-nine times," Jessica said.

"I'm not confirming or denying that."

"Did you do a tox screen on Dooley?"

"That is SOP during an autopsy," Dr. Washington said.

"What was his blood alcohol level?" Jessica asked.

Dr. Washington crossed her arms and regarded the young woman. Her eyebrow arched. "Point one eight."

"Wow," Jessica said.

"Plus he had a very high level of acetaminophen."

"Pain reliever," Jessica confirmed.

"Several times the recommended dosage," the medical examiner said. "But I doubt if it did any good when he was stabbed to death." She turned around to head in the direction of the squad room and Bogie's office.

Not yet finished with their discussion, Jessica followed her. "He had to have been feeling pain, considering that he was stabbed twenty-nine times. Where were most of the stab wounds?"

"Chest and stomach."

"Not his back?"

"No."

"How about defensive wounds?" Jessica asked.

"He did have a couple of blade marks on his hands, yes."

"And his arms?"

Dr. Washington stopped to turn to her. "Arms?"

Jessica held up her arms and crossed them in front of her chest and face. "If you were being stabbed from the front, it is only natural that you would get cuts across your forearms when you tried to shield yourself from the knife. Did Dooley have any there?"

"No, but considering the amount of alcohol and painkiller he had in his system, he may have been too intoxicated or drugged to have put up that much of a defense."

"Maybe," Jessica said. "How many of those twenty-nine stab wounds were fatal?"

"One."

"One?" Jessica let out a squawk. "Out of twenty-nine, only one was fatal?"

"It was one plunged into the stomach and through the spleen," Dora said. "If he had received medical attention, he could have survived, but he bled out in the bathtub filled with water, which aided his bleeding out."

"And how deep were the other twenty-eight stab wounds?"

"They were only an inch or so deep," Dora said. "As a matter of fact, based on my experience and the stab wounds that I have seen in my career, I would suggest that the police look for a woman."

"Not Dad?"

Dora grinned at her. "Knowing your father, if he had killed Russell Dooley in a crime of passion, he would not

341

have had to have stabbed him twenty-nine times before killing him."

"He would have just shot him," Jessica said.

"I can't picture your father killing a man unless it was in self-defense," Doc Washington said. "But even though we all know him and know what type of man he is, until we can explain how his blood and DNA ended up at that crime scene, he's going to be under suspicion for killing Russell Dooley."

Jessica sighed miserably. "And I know that there are haters who will jump to believe it—unless we can find out who planted it there—"

"And how," Doc Washington said. "He does have one thing in his favor."

"He doesn't have a mark on him," Jessica said. "David said that all the blood there made it look like Dad had cut himself while stabbing Dooley."

"How does a man leave his blood behind at a scene without cutting himself?"

Jessica and Doc Washington stared at each other with the question in their eyes.

"Let me think about that," Jessica said.

"You got none of your information from me." Dora arched her lovely eyebrow at her again. "I need to get this sandwich to Bogie. He turns into a grizzly bear when he's hungry."

"Well, we can't have that." Jessica returned to staring down the hallway to the gym door where her father was alone with Murphy Thornton—talking about what?

Oh, dear Lord, please don't let Dad tell Murphy about the time I lifted my top on the bus to show all of my friends my first bra!

CHAPTER TWENTY-SEVEN

"I think that will do it," Murphy said in a low voice while carefully reassembling the flash drive. Ethan and Tristan watched from nearby.

Aware of the delicate precision in the work that Murphy was performing, Sheriff Turow, his deputies, Spencer's police officers, and David's team of marines were all hanging back while drawn in by their curiosity.

Each of them was well aware of the time ticking away on the clock on the wall. They were less than twenty minutes away from the time that Special Agent Neal Black had said he would call to set up the drop. They assumed it would be at Sander's Farm. A team of state police officers had already set up hiding spots around the perimeter to watch under the cover of the forest and darkness.

"Do we know if it's going to work?" Aware that the thumb drive contained a lethal amount of explosives, Mac was hesitant to take it when Murphy held it out to him. It appeared to be an average flash drive that people use every day.

"Unfortunately, there's no way to test it," Ethan said.

"It works on the same principle as bombs remotely detonated with a cell phone signal," Murphy said.

"Like the Boston Marathon bombers used," Tristan said.

"Only we're not using a pressure cooker," Murphy said. "We'll be using the processor of whatever computer or tablet they plug that into. The more powerful the processor, the more powerful the explosion."

Ethan explained, "They want that formula really bad. Therefore, we can safely assume that they are going to plug that thumb drive into something to make sure that the formula is on there as soon as they get their hands on it."

"Before they kill you," Murphy said. "Once they have the formula, they don't need you anymore. You're a liability. If the thumb drive doesn't have it, then they'll torture you to find out where it is."

"Is the formula on that drive?" Jessica asked.

"No," Murphy said, "we can't risk them getting their hands on it."

"Then—"

"I put a decoy formula on it," Tristan said. "They're going to get the formula for Leishmania instead."

"What's that?" Bogie asked.

"It's the epidemic that killed off the dinosaurs," Mac said with a tone that told the deputy chief that he should have known this piece of information.

"That's *believed* to have killed off the dinosaurs," Tristan said. "Actually, it's believed to be *one* of *many* diseases that killed them off."

"We're betting these guys aren't scientists," Murphy said, "and if one of them is, that he won't notice the formula is really from the Jurassic period."

"Actually, it's not—"

"Later, Tristan," Murphy said.

"Here's what's going to happen." Ethan took the drive out of Mac's open palm. "This little flash drive has a lot on it. When they plug this in, as soon as the flash drive connects, it's going to work like a virus and collect everything on that computer or tablet's hard drive. Then, all of that information will be sent via a satellite hookup to Murphy's team at the Pentagon."

"Isn't that risky?" Bogie asked. "I thought you just wanted to blow them up so that we could rush in to get David out of there, secure the barn, and arrest these terrorists."

"We can assume that whatever computer they plug the thumb drive into will have information on it," Ethan said, "Possibly information that could prove a connection between the terrorists and Bauman."

"So while they're waiting for the thumb drive to open up, it will be transmitting information to Washington," Mac said. "Aren't they going to notice—"

"The spyware is set up to work in the background," Ethan said. "They'll never notice."

"How long will all this take?" Mac asked. "When I've gotten a virus on my computer, it slows down. If this computer or laptop or tablet has a lot on it, it will take some time—time that we may not have."

"Suppose this system they plug it into has an antivirus program that'll detect it?" Jessica asked.

"It won't," Ethan said with complete confidence. "This is a very sophisticated and fast program. After all of the information is transferred, the explosive will detonate and the system will blow up." He told Mac, "You will need to be as far from that computer as you can be."

"How big of an explosion will it be?"

"Depends on the system and where it is," Murphy said. "It could just be big enough to get whoever is sitting in front of the laptop or tablet. The point is to create a diversion in order for us to rush in."

"Suppose this bandwidth is lousy?" Mac asked.

345

"Or they don't have Wi-Fi?" Jessica asked. "Didn't you say this farm was abandoned?"

"Not really," Murphy said. "According to the information David gave us, Bauman's terrorist friends have set up a whole dirty bomb factory inside the barn. That tells us that they have to have some means of communicating with their overseas partners."

"Which tells us that they have to have an Internet connection on site," Ethan said. "I'm going to get in there before the drop to hack into that connection and see what we can uncover about Bauman and his dirty dealings and send it on to Washington. David is going to get me into the barn."

"David said they have guards at both of the lanes coming into the farm from the main road," Mac said. "How are you going to get in?"

"Jessica and I are going to take him in," Murphy said.

Mac's eyes grew wide. When he turned to Jessica, he saw by the grin she was flashing at Murphy that it was true. His eyes narrowed. "No."

"It was my idea," Jessica said.

"No, no, no, and hell no!"

Murphy started, "It's a good—"

"You told me you loved her!" Mac raged.

There was a collective gasp in the squad room.

All heads turned to Jessica, who was equally shocked by the announcement. Her face turned various shades of color, from pink to white to red and then pink again.

"I do love her," Murphy replied.

Murphy's eyes flicked to Jessica to gauge her reaction and then back to Mac, who was the more immediate threat when he stepped up to bring his face to Murphy's. Anyone else would have backed up out of Mac's space, but the young man held his ground.

"You can put your own life on the line for your beliefs and convictions—which I admire—but there is no way in hell I'm going to let you risk the life of my only daughter! No way! And I can't believe that you would risk her life in the face of these monsters!"

Snapping out of her shock, Jessica rushed forward to push her way between the two of them. "Dad, stop it!" She grabbed his arm. "It was my idea! I volunteered! They need the element of surprise to get in close enough to neutralize them. I came up with the idea. I'll be protected. Murphy will be there right by my side, and I'll be armed. You taught me how to shoot. Plus, the state police and David's team and sniper will have them in their sights just in case they get antsy. It's a good idea."

"Find another way," Mac said in a low voice. "I don't want you near there."

"I *want* to be there." She glared up into his eyes. "I love David, too. I want to help. I can, and you can't stop me."

She could feel the heat from Murphy's body standing close behind her. "I won't let anything happen to her, sir."

"You can't guarantee that," Mac said.

"No, I can't," Murphy said. "But I can promise I'll do everything I can to keep her safe. I'll give my life for her if I have to."

Mac felt Bogie's hand on his shoulder. "He's Josh's boy, Mac. If he's anything like his daddy, he's a man of his word."

"We need a way to get to the end of the road that branches off to the airstrip and the barn and farmhouse." Murphy pointed to the map. "David says there are two guards hiding in the trees at the end of the road that forks off, and that they can see anyone approaching from any direction. They have radios and can communicate to Ra'ees Sims and Neal Black, who are in the jet, which has two pilots on board and three guards surrounding the outside. They are all part of Ra'ees's team—highly trained killers and jihadists. They can also communicate with the rest of the guards throughout the farm. If we can take out these two guards at the fork in the road and take control of their radios, then they'll all be blind when we make our move."

Bogie explained, "If we just drive up, then those two guards will contact their people, and we'll be dead as soon as we hit the fork."

Murphy was nodding his head. "But most likely, they won't kill us if they don't think we're a threat. We have to remember, these are Americans doing something very illegal. They aren't going to want to attract attention if they don't have to."

"Now how could those two terrorists ever feel threatened when they see a cute little thing like me come driving up in my purple sports car?" Wrapping her arms around Mac's waist, Jessica gazed up and batted her long eyelashes at him.

Looking down into her violet eyes, Mac was reminded of all the times she had managed to worm her way into doing exactly what she wanted. He unwrapped her arms from around him. "We're all taking a lot of chances. I don't like this. If you want all of this information off these computers to make your case against this billionaire terrorist, then sic the US Attorney General on him."

"The US Attorney General won't go after him because Bauman is protected," Murphy said. "I uploaded and sent the information my father got from Kochar to my CO. I took a look at them. They're financial records proving that Nathaniel Bauman, a United States citizen and a billionaire businessman, has been supporting and backing and supplying weapons to the very people trying to kill us—all while sleeping in the Lincoln bedroom at the White House as the president's personal guest."

"And if the United States Attorney General won't go after him, and if he is protected by the president, then what good is getting this further information going to do?" Mac asked.

"It will lead us to others who are involved," Murphy said. "It will supply us with ammunition to fight this war, even if we have to fight it alone." He arched an eyebrow at him. "If you don't want to do this, you don't have to."

"Thing is," Mac said, "they've given me no choice."

"Actually, we do have a choice," Murphy said. "We either fight, bow down to their god, or die. I'm a fighter."

"So am I."

"We all are," Bogie said. "I say let's go send them all on a one-way trip to meet their little black-eyed virgins."

Mac's cell phone rang.

"Let the games begin," Jessica said.

"Did you really tell my dad that you love me before telling me?" Jessica's attempt to sound annoyed didn't come off. The giggle gave it away.

Neal Black had ordered that the exchange take place at Sander's Farm, in the driveway between the barn and the farmhouse—exactly where Murphy had predicted. The farm was secluded, and the jet was located on the airstrip directly on the other side of the woods. Plus, the heavy woods provided a remote enough location for them to dispose of Mac's body after killing him once they got the thumb drive.

They had thirty minutes to gear up and clear out the guards at the end of the lane between the farmhouse and the airstrip in order to get their team into position—all before Mac arrived at the farm house.

Murphy passed out earbuds from his go-bag with a secure radio channel to the leaders and was finishing gearing up, which included hiding small-yet-lethal weapons on various parts of his body, when Jessica found a moment to be alone with him before they departed to set their plan into action.

Murphy's cheeks felt hot at the reference to the public announcement. "I envisioned a more intimate setting when I revealed my feelings—"

"To me or my father?" She cast him a sly grin.

"He asked," Murphy said. "I answered. I don't lie." He gazed at her. "Don't tell me that you're surprised. We have enough electricity flying between us to revive a dead man."

"Then I guess there's no use in my playing hard to get?"

"I'm not one to play games."

"Neither am I." She clasped his firm arms with both of her hands. "I love you, too."

They gazed deeply into each other's eyes. Aware of the various people in the police station trying very hard not to look in their direction, including Mac, who was having a long discussion with Bogie, Murphy cleared his throat and pulled back. "Well, I guess now would be a good time for me to give you something to show you how deep my feelings run for you."

Blushing, Jessica held her breath while watching Murphy reach into his black canvas bag. *This is so sudden. Idiot. Of course, it's sudden. He can't be carrying a ring around with him just waiting for the love of his life to show up. Maybe it's his navy ring. They get class rings, don't they?*

"It used to be my mother's," Murphy was saying while digging through the bag for a blue leather case. "My dad gave it to me, and I carry it everywhere with me. Since this is going to be our first night working together like this, it seems only right that I give it to you."

Murphy extracted a Coonan .357 Magnum semi-automatic handgun from the bag. It had a wood-finished grip.

Jessica's disappointment lifted when she saw Murphy's wide grin cross his face and the dimples flash at her.

As she bent over in laughter, he whispered into her ear. "I love a woman who appreciates my sick sense of humor." He gently pulled her closer, wrapped his arms around her, and tucked the gun carefully into the rear waistband of her pants. "This weapon has a longer barrel. It will shoot more accurately than that little pistol you used at the truck stop." He covered the gun up with the back of her top. "I fully intend to take care of you, Jessica Faraday."

She returned his gaze. "I love you, Murphy Thornton."

Even though they knew that time was limited, they held onto the moment to gaze into each other's faces—to commit every feature to memory.

"Hey," Mac called from across the room. "You two! Yes, I'm talking to you two lovebirds, we got to get moving! Let's roll!"

CHAPTER TWENTY-EIGHT

Murphy gunned the Ferrari that would take him across the bridge out of Spencer and onto Garrett Highway toward Oakland, Maryland. They were a couple of miles from the Sander farm when the state police car fell in behind him and turned on its lights and siren.

Instead of slowing down, Murphy pressed his foot to the gas pedal.

"That should get their attention," Jessica said while watching the lights of the police cruiser fall back, only to have another police car come up behind them.

Murphy switched off the headlights and turned the wheel to take them down the lane toward the fork. Their lights and sirens going, the two police cruisers sped on by.

"It's show time," Murphy said. "Are you ready for this?"

"I was born ready."

"That's a scary thought." He pressed his foot against the gas pedal to take them to the end of the lane. Then, gunning the engine, he threw the wheel to do a donut, bringing the sports car to a halt directly in front of where the two guards would be stationed.

Laughing gleefully, Jessica threw open her door and jumped out of the car. In her high-heeled pirate boots, her open coat revealing her low-cut top and abundant bosom, she was a sight racing around to the front of the car to give the guards a good look at her in the car's bright headlights. "That was totally awesome!" she squealed. "The way you burned rubber on the road and left those idiots behind like they were standing still!" She fanned herself. "I have never been so thrilled—my heart is beating so fast!"

Murphy had climbed out of the car and ran to her. "Exactly how fast is it beating, babe? Show me."

She pressed his hand to her breast. "Feel it!"

Murphy caressed her breast. "Oh, yeah," he breathed. "I can feel it, all right. You think that's fast … I can make it beat much faster."

"You got something more thrilling to show me?" she breathed while wrapping her arms around his neck.

"All you have to do is ask."

"Show me!"

He pressed her back against the car's hood. Pressing her down onto the car, he covered her lips with his mouth. The first taste of her lips made his head swim. He could feel her heart pounding against his chest so hard, that he felt like the two of them were going to combust.

Her taste, her scent, and the touch of her hands on his face and neck, it was all intoxicating—addictive. He felt a high like he had never experienced before—anytime, anyplace—with any woman.

He didn't want it to ever end.

When she lifted one of her legs and hooked the back of his knee with her ankle to pull him in closer, he thrilled to realize the feeling was mutual. Wanting more, he grabbed her hips and pulled them closer to him. Aroused, he pressed against her while she rubbed her leg against his.

"Time is running out," he suddenly heard the voice of Jessica's father announce into his ear from the earbud.

"Don't stop," Jessica said when he pulled back as if he had been struck by lightning.

"You two do know that I am listening to *everything,*" Mac said.

Murphy glanced over toward the woods. He could make out the silhouette of the two guards watching them. "We have company," he whispered into her ear.

"You have to slap me," she said.

"I'm not into that Christian Grey stuff," he said.

"Glad to hear that," Mac said.

"To make it work, you need to go ballistic," she whispered into his ear while caressing his neck. Abruptly, she pushed him away. "No! Not so fast!" She rolled out from under him and moved around so that he would have a clearer angle on the guards lurking in the trees.

"Oh, so that's the way you play it, bitch!" Murphy followed her. "Well, let me show you how we play that game where I come from."

He backhanded her across the cheek. She fell backwards onto the hood of the car. Grabbing her, he rolled her around so that she was bent over the car hood. She let out a loud whimper when he pressed up against her buttocks as if to pin her there.

"You want some excitement, sweetheart! How's this for excitement?" Murphy reached both of his hands down into his pants and yanked out a gun in each hand. Instantly, he aimed both guns, which were equipped with silencers, toward the silhouettes of the two guards in the trees and pulled the triggers simultaneously. The quiet of the woods was broken by muffled shots.

As soon as they went down, Murphy grabbed Jessica roughly by the back of her coat and yanked her down behind the car. "Stay here while I check to make sure the targets were terminated."

Wide eyed, she nodded her head.

"Don't move," he ordered in a harsh tone. "Wait for my report." Gripping both of his guns, he slipped around the back of the car and disappeared into the woods.

Alone, crouching in the dark next to her car, Jessica felt enveloped in fear. Even though she had known that Murphy was going to yank the guns out of his pants, when she heard the two men drop in the shadows behind the trees, the reality of the danger she was in—the danger they were all in—hit home. She had felt so safe when Murphy was there. Alone, staring into the darkness surrounding her, trying to distinguish each noise to determine if it was friend or foe, she felt her heart quicken, but not with passion—with fear.

"Targets terminated," she heard Murphy announce in a business-like tone across the earbud that she had stuck into her ear. "Jessica, release the geek and return to base. Frost, you're up."

"Roger that, Thornton," Frost replied.

Releasing the trunk release on her key ring, Jessica scurried around to the front of the Ferrari to help Ethan climb out of the trunk and put on his backpack. "About time," Ethan said. "the way you two were going at it, I had flashbacks to when I was nine and I was hiding behind the sofa while my babysitter and her boyfriend—"

"TMI, Ethan," Jessica said with a jerk of her head. "Barn is that way."

Ethan took off at a jog down the road toward the barn where David was waiting.

In the distance, she heard what sounded like another muffled shot.

"Last guard terminated," Colonel Frost announced. "Ethan, it's now up to you. You have eight minutes."

With one last longing look into the woods in hope of catching a glimpse of Murphy, she climbed back into the Ferrari and tore back down the lane to return to the Spencer police station and await word on the success or failure of their plan.

Glancing at the clock on her car console, she let out a sigh. The time was eleven fifty-three. Her father was due to meet Neal Black at twelve midnight—in seven minutes.

In a less than thirty minutes, it would all be over ... for better or worse.

PART THREE

One Day to Forever
Saturday, December 31

CHAPTER TWENTY-NINE

Having seen a picture of David O'Callaghan during the briefing at the police station, Ethan knew the description of the man he was to make contact with at the barn. However, David had never seen Ethan before. Plus, it was dark. With terrorists lurking all over the heavily wooded farm in the late hours of the wintry night, Ethan was hoping that David didn't mistake him for the enemy and shoot him.

Each member of the rescue team was equipped with a wireless earbud, which fit deep into the ear. Until Ethan located the police chief and gave him one, David was unaware of the location and identity of his rescuers.

Bogie had sent David a text stating that an IT agent would meet him at the barn close to midnight and to be watching for him. Even so, Ethan feared that one of the dozen terrorists would notice the tall, skinny Westerner, clutching a laptop case, stumbling through the thick woods in the deep snow in the dark.

If captured, how would he explain his presence? Would they even give him a chance to come up with a believable lie before torturing him to death like they did to his mentor Reginald Crane?

Clutching the handgun he had secured in the rear waist-band of his slacks, Ethan hid behind a tree when he neared the front door of the barn to find a man clad in a heavy winter coat pacing in front of the door. Seeing no one else in sight, Ethan uttered a stage whisper as loud as he dared. "Major?"

The man stopped and stood frozen still.

"Bogie sent me."

The man in the heavy coat with the hood backed up to the corner of the barn. "Ethan?"

"O'Callaghan?"

David hurried up the incline in the direction of the trees. "Follow me." He took off at a run around the back of the barn, which faced the tree line and was out of view of the farmhouse and the pond. With the full moon concealed by the barn's roof, they were in total darkness. Ethan broke out his LED flashlight to light their way to where David had found a window high up in the back of the barn. It was six feet from the ground. Using a stick, David propped it open.

"That's it?" Ethan asked.

"Climb on up," David said. "There's a table inside once you get in the window."

"Didn't you find a door that was unlocked?"

"The only two doors are in clear view of the guards." David bent over and clasped his hands together. "I'll give you a boost."

Ethan hesitated. "But—"

"You're a federal agent—"

"No, I'm not," Ethan said. "I'm an MIT graduate. I learned how to break through firewalls and bring government cybersecurity systems to a screeching halt with the stroke of a key. But nowhere did anyone ever tell me that I'd have to scale walls and climb through broken windows during a full moon."

Rising to his full height, David chuckled. "How about if you and I go back to the jet and ask for a key to unlock the padlock on the barn door—after which they will behead both of us?"

Grasping the side of the building with both hands, Ethan raised his foot for David to clasp. "Give me a boost, and I don't want to hear you laugh."

After receiving the signal from Ethan that he had tapped into the Internet connection at the farm and had control of their system, Mac muttered to the German shepherd sitting in the back seat of his SUV, "Okay, Gnarly, it's up to you and me now." He reached back to scratch the German shepherd behind the ears. "Remember, wait for my signal."

After reaching into his coat pocket to make sure he had the flash drive, even though he knew for certain that he had it, Mac turned back around and started the engine.

Oh, God, I know You're on our side, but please, oh please, really be with us tonight. Please have everyone who's working to help David ... and David especially ... come out safely.

Mac eased the SUV across the bridge and turned toward Oakland. Once he came into view of the lane, he turned right to take the rural road through the wooded area. A short distance later, the SUV emerged from the trees and the road dipped down to go around a pond and back up to a farmhouse. On the other side of the farmyard was a barn that was almost twice the size of the house.

"I see you, Mac," he heard Murphy's voice coming through the earbud. "There's a black SUV parked on this side of the farmhouse. Stay on the lane and round the farmhouse past the barn. You'll go around the farmhouse to the backyard. They're parked on the road between the backyard and an old garden."

"How many are there?"

"One SUV and four men," Murphy said. "They're all heavily armed with what appears to be assault rifles. I'm sure they have handguns, too. Ra'ees Sims is the leader—massive African-American."

"I remember his picture in the briefing," Mac said. "Owns a security firm under Bauman and is the leader of an extremist mosque in Texas."

"Exactly."

"He's extremely violent," David's voice came through the earbud to warn Mac.

"David …" Mac breathed. "You're okay."

"Of course, I'm okay," David replied. "They're planning to kill you as soon as they get the flash drive."

"Don't worry, I have my secret weapon with me."

When Mac rounded the corner of the farmhouse, the SUV came into view. The only reason he could see it was because the back door was open and the interior light was on.

Gnarly growled.

"Wait for my signal," Mac reminded him in a low voice.

Gnarly turned around in circles three times before plopping down in the backseat with a "humph" noise that signaled his impatience.

As soon as they saw Mac's vehicle approaching, two men emerged from the SUV and stood with their arms crossed. When the headlights hit them, Mac could see that they were dark skinned.

He brought the SUV to a halt several feet away. As he climbed out, they grabbed the door out of Mac's hand, yanked him out of the vehicle, and shoved him against the front fender of the SUV, where they patted him down for weapons.

Instantly, one found the flash drive in his pocket. With a grin like a child finding the prize in a box of cereal, he held it up to show the other man and turned around to wave it to the huge man waiting at the back of their SUV.

With his tall ears laid back flat against the top of his head, Gnarly sat up in the back seat to watch.

Mac slightly shook his head at the dog.

Even in the shadows, the dark-skinned African-American, who stepped into view from the rear of the SUV, looked menacing. "I told you to come alone, Faraday," Ra'ees Sims said in a low tone.

Grabbing Mac by each arm, the two men whirled him around and shoved him in the direction of their leader.

"I did," Mac replied after regaining his footing in the deep snow.

"Who's that?" Ra'ees pointed at the dog in the rear seat watching them.

"My dog," Mac said. "Your people wrecked my house, so I couldn't leave him there."

"He's a German shepherd."

"An *untrained* German shepherd," Mac said.

"Like he's not going to attack me and my men?" Ra'ees sounded doubtful.

"He's a certified coward," Mac said. "Let me show you." He turned to the SUV. "Hey, stupid! Come here!"

With a whine, Gnarly laid his ears flat back on his head, stood up, tucked his tail between his legs, and laid down in the backseat.

With a chuckle, Mac turned back to Ra'ees. "I'd get better protection from a cat."

"Or a woman." Ra'ees and his men laughed.

"He's clean." One of the gunman handed the thumb drive to Ra'ees.

"Close the doors to his car and lock it," he ordered. "I don't want Fido joining in our negotiations."

"Speaking of negotiations," Mac said while one of the men went back to the SUV. He heard the locks activate in his SUV, locking Gnarly inside. "Where's David O'Callaghan?"

"He's nearby."

"Where nearby? I want to see him and know he's alive," Mac argued while Ra'ees went around to the rear of their SUV. "The deal was the thumb drive for David O'Callaghan. You have what you wanted, now hand over O'Callaghan."

"You'll be with your friend soon enough." Ra'ees handed the flash drive to a young black man who was sitting cross-legged in the rear compartment of the SUV. "Make sure this has what we want."

Mac held his breath while the young man inserted the thumb drive into a small laptop. He heard the familiar ding of the flash drive connecting to the hard drive of the laptop.

Uncomfortably, Mac noted that he was sitting right on top of the SUV's fuel tank. Boxes next to him contained guns, rifles, hand grenades, and other ammunition. The kid was sitting among an arsenal.

This SUV is going to go up like a rocket.

"We've now got a connection," Mac heard Ethan announce in his ear through the wireless earbud. "We have lift-off, folks."

And some liftoff it is going to be.

Back at the jet, Neal Black was pacing up and down the aisle. There were three guards around the jet, a pilot sitting in the cockpit ready to start the engines on Ra'ees's command, and a co-pilot napping in the passenger compartment.

On one hand, Black wanted to go to the payoff, but his prisoner was such a valuable commodity that he didn't want to take the chance of letting David O'Callghan out of his sight— even if he was unconscious.

To arrive in Tehran with the man who had killed Jassem al-Baghdadi would be a personal, as well as a professional, achievement.

Jassem had been like a father to him. He owed it to Jassem to capture his killer and personally administer justice.

Jassem's murder had been a great setback for Islam. Now, by capturing his assassin within the very borders of the United States and taking him back to Iraq for a public execution, they could hold their heads high.

Islam would surely thank Neal Black for this triumph by quickly promoting him to powerful positions within the ranks of ISIS. To get paid a quarter of a million dollars for capturing O'Callaghan, who had killed the closest thing he had ever had to a father, was only frosting on the cake.

But I should be there to collect the thumb drive as well. After all, I am the one who tracked it down to Deep Creek Lake.

Periodically, Black would stop to peer out the jet's windows. Even though he could not see the drop-off point in the garden on the other side of the trees, he strained to see what Ra'ees and his men were doing.

How's it going with Mac Faraday? Did he indeed bring the thumb drive with the Ebola virus on it? Do they have it yet?

As a special agent with the FBI, Black had extensive training in negotiating with criminals—plus he was one himself. The victims always bartered, but a successful criminal never gives up control. Still, the victim and police would try to take control away by bartering. Okay, you want food and water? Then release one of your hostages. You want a helicopter? Well, we're working on it. We need time. How about a pizza while you're waiting?

Such did not seem to be the case here. When Neal had called with the drop-off time and place, Mac had taken the directions without question. Didn't ask where Sander's Farm was, nor had he asked to speak to David O'Callaghan again. He had the first time Black called …

Neal Black stood up straight and replayed his conversations with Mac Faraday, a retired homicide detective with a reputation for brilliance. He surely had training in hostage negotiations.

Yet, when Black had called to arrange the drop-off of the flash drive, Mac didn't ask for confirmation that David O'Callaghan was alive. He had during their second conversation, but not this last time, which was several hours later.

It doesn't matter. If Faraday had, he wouldn't have been able to talk to O'Callaghan because he's in a deep drugged sleep … or is he?

Neal Black turned around and shoved the pilot out of his way in his rush to the rear compartment of the jet where they had David O'Callaghan strapped down and drugged on the gurney. Black's pace quickened when he tore into the back room and saw the gurney up against the wall. The blanket was pulled up almost to his face, which was turned to face the wall. The straps held their prized prisoner down onto the gurney.

Neal Black ran across the room and yanked the blanket back to reveal José's dark-skinned face.

"Augh!" Neal Black screamed. Snatching the radio from off his belt, he shouted into it, "O'Callaghan has escaped! Repeat! It's a trap! O'Callaghan has escaped!"

Grabbing his gun from his holster, Neal Black, enraged at the escape, aimed his gun at the unconscious man's head and pulled the trigger.

"Damn it!" Murphy cursed and shouted into his earbud. "We're blown! They discovered David's gone! Mac, get out of there! Now!"

Colonel Frost responded, "We're taking the jet now! Go! Go! Go!" he ordered his team. "Don't let them take off! Move it!"

Hearing the announcement of David's escape, Ra'ees turned around to find Mac backing up from the rear of the SUV. The terrorist yanked his gun out his holster.

Grasping the remote on his belt, Mac plunged down to the ground. Burying his face in the snow, he covered his head with his arms just as the thumb drive exploded inside the laptop.

The blast ignited the explosives in the rear of the SUV, which went off in a series of blasts as each item ignited. Seconds later, the explosion hit the gas tank, which caused another great explosion to take out each of the men gathered around the back of the SUV.

Mac felt the heat wash over his body.

Beyond the explosion, he could hear Gnarly barking up a storm in the SUV.

"Infidel!"

Looking up, Mac squinted through the bright flames to see Ra'ees Sims stumbling toward him. He could see yellow and white-hot flames shooting up behind the black man who was flailing both of his arms.

As his vision cleared, Mac scrambled to his feet when he realized that the flames were moving toward him with Sims. Engulfed in flames, Ra'ees Sims was so enraged that he either didn't notice or didn't care.

Standing over Mac, Ra'ees aimed his gun down at him. Mac could make out the silhouette of the gun he had been holding when the explosion went off. "Allah!"

Mac heard a roar behind him.

The remote Mac wore on his belt not only unlocked each door in his SUV, but it also opened them. When he hit the button as he plunged to the ground, every door, including the rear door, had flown open to unleash Gnarly.

Launching himself from where he had leapt out of the vehicle after Mac had hit the door release, Gnarly flew over Mac to hit the black man with full force in the chest and knock him off his feet and back into the snow. The German shepherd clamped his jaws shut on the hand holding the gun. Upon hitting the ground, Gnarly shook his head to rip through Ra'ees' wrist.

Insane rage and hatred kept Ra'ees cognizant enough to reach with his other arm for his bayonet. "We know what to do with dogs!"

He threw back his arm to swing the bayonet, aiming directly for Gnarly's neck in order to cut off the head of the beast.

Two bullets from Ra'ees's own gun ripped through his head and terminated his attack.

At the sound of the gunshots inches from him, Gnarly leapt off Ra'ees Sims' lifeless body and hopped back to where Mac stood with the gun smoking in his hand. "You okay, Gnarly?"

Gnarly rose up on his hind legs to press his snout against Mac's cheek.

"You're welcome." After patting the dog on the head, he said, "but we're not done yet." Mac searched Sims' pockets for clips of ammunition and relieved him of the bayonet and the small handgun that he wore on one of his ankles.

Mac could hear gunfire and blasts that he had not experienced in years on the other side of the trees. In moments, the gunshots were reduced down to a spattering before he heard Colonel Frost announce, "Jet is secured. Pilots and guards are dead. None of them would let themselves be taken alive."

Sheriff Turow came through on the earbud. "Okay to send my people in, Colonel?"

There was a moment of silence during which Mac could hear the colonel speaking to someone in the background.

"What's wrong?" Mac demanded to know.

"Neal Black isn't here on the jet," Colonel Frost finally announced. "Mac, could he have been at the drop?"

"No." Mac cursed.

Murphy broke through on the earbuds. "He was trained by the FBI. He discovered that David had escaped. He had enough time to slip out while the team was moving in. Your people could have very well mistaken him for a member of your own team."

"He's going after David." Tucking his weapons into his waistband and clips into his pockets, Mac ran for the barn. "David, do you hear that? He's coming after you."

"Bring it on," David said.

Colonel Frost said, "I'm sending four men to assist you, Major."

Sheriff Turow added, "I'm sending two cruisers to the barn. The rest of my people are fanning out through the woods. We're going to get this guy."

"I'll try to intercept him," Murphy said.

Gnarly running ahead of him, Mac sprinted for the barn door. "David, I'm coming up to the door."

"It's padlocked from the outside, Mac," David warned him.

At the door, Mac shot off the padlock and threw open the door. "I'm coming in." Leading with his gun, Mac stepped inside. Upon seeing David braced up against the wall, Gnarly raced in to jump up on him.

Ethan was working away on a row of laptops. "I've almost got everything transferred. We hit the mother lode of information against Bauman and his whole operation. You wouldn't believe the stuff we got here. No way can the president and attorney general help him now."

Mac didn't care as much about what Ethan had uncovered as he cared about the fact David was standing before him in one piece. "You're sure you're okay?"

David sighed with disgust about his paternal attitude. "Mac, I'm fine."

They saw Mac fall from the shot to his chest before they heard it. He fell back against the wall and slumped to the floor while holding his upper chest.

With a roar, Gnarly charged toward the other side of the barn to where the shot had been fired. There was a door in the corner behind shelving that none of them had noticed.

Neal Black had noticed it, though.

Gnarly's attack was cut short when a whole shelving unit tumbled down on top of him. With a yelp, Gnarly fell, buried under boxes of heavy equipment.

Ethan drew his gun but could not locate the target before a shot grazed the side of his head. He jerked out of his seat and hit his head when he plunged to the floor.

Seeing Mac fall, David dropped down next to him to check his wound. Mac's hand and chest were already covered with blood. Gasping for breath, Mac gazed up at him. "I'm okay."

"No, you're not," David said. "Help's on its way."

"But not soon enough," David heard directly behind him. He felt the cold metal of the gun muzzle against the back of his neck. The click of the gun echoed throughout the barn.

"Turn around," Neal Black said. "I want to see your eyes when I put a bullet between them."

David gazed down into Mac's face.

Mac dropped his eyes. "It's okay," he whispered.

David held up his hands.

"Turn around, O'Callaghan," Black ordered. "Slow."

David rose up onto his knees. Making no sudden moves, he turned away from Mac.

A wicked grin filled Neal Black's face as he watched David turn around to face him—but he failed to notice the gun in Mac's hand.

As soon as David moved aside, Mac's hand shot up, and he fired three shots into Neal Black's head. The first shot went between his eyes. He was dead before the other two found their mark.

The special agent for the FBI dropped to the floor.

With a sigh of relief, Mac collapsed back onto the floor to the sound of police sirens and officers storming the barn.

"Mac, stay with me," David pleaded while patting his face. "I'm not through with you yet!"

"I am," Mac said, "I'm tired."

Finally, it was over.

CHAPTER THIRTY

"Did you get all of them?" The tone in Archie's voice betrayed her anger about the whole situation.

Everyone in her private hospital room agreed with her feelings. Bogie had awakened her at two o'clock in the morning with the news that Mac, the man she was going to marry in a huge wedding in twenty-two hours, was in surgery fighting for his life from a bullet to the chest that had been put there by an FBI agent.

They had awakened Archie's mother and oldest brother, Clint, so they could go to the hospital to comfort her.

Sheriff Turow was on hand, as was Murphy, who kept a protective hand on Jessica's shoulder. Even in the current state of affairs, his touch made her feel safe.

"Wasn't Mac wearing a ballistic vest?" was one of her first questions.

"Under his clothes, but these guys were serious," Bogie said. "It was an armor-piercing bullet."

Gripping Archie's hands, Jessica and Agnes stood on either side of her bed. "How bad is it?" Archie asked.

"He's lost a lot of blood," Bogie said.

"Dad's AB positive," Jessica said. "That's a rare blood type. Do they—"

"David is the same type," Bogie said. "He's giving them some of his blood as we speak."

"But …" Archie's voice trailed off. She shook her head. "Mac has blood here at the hospital. Because he's got a rare blood-type, he gave blood for them to keep here for him. I think he gave them four units."

"Maybe in the emergency they didn't check," Archie's brother said.

Jessica glanced across the room at Sheriff Turow. "You would think as soon as they saw Dad's blood type card that they would check the blood supply first thing."

"Was anyone else hurt?" Archie added with disdain, "besides the terrorists?"

"Ethan Bonner got a graze across the side of his head," Sheriff Turow said. "He was the IT guy. Gnarly was fine once we dug him out from the stuff Black pulled down on top of him."

"The military has taken over the whole facility," Murphy said. "No media is allowed in. Everything is very hush-hush."

"FBI is going ape about this," Sheriff Turow said. "I already got a call asking why they weren't called in. I told them because they were already there. When they get my full report about Special Agent Neal Black …" He shook his head with an evil chuckle.

"Don't forget his partner in terrorism, Leland Elder," Murphy said. "He tried to kill my stepmother. I take that personally."

"What about this billionaire terrorist?" Archie asked, "And this advisor to the President of the United States who gave up David?"

"They'll be taken care of," Murphy said. "Trust me."

Silence filled the hospital room. Uncertain of what to say in the circumstances, they each glanced at the others.

Finally, Agnes asked about what was on everyone's mind. "What are we going to do about this wedding? It's twenty-two hours away, and Archie, the only way you are going to make it down that aisle is in a wheelchair, and Mac may be dead anyway."

"Mom!" Archie wailed at the vocalization of their greatest fear.

"Mother!" Clint chastised her.

"It's the truth!"

"Frankly, that wedding is the last thing I want right now," Archie said. "It's given me nothing but heartache this entire week."

"I hope that isn't a sign of how your marriage is going to be," Agnes said.

"Mac's and my marriage is just fine, Mom," Archie said. "If you must know, we got married six months ago in the sweetest little ceremony with only a handful of friends at the church, and we were completely happy until we started planning this three-ring circus."

Agnes' and Clint's mouths dropped open.

Jessica and Tristan backed away from the bed while Agnes moved in. "Why in heaven's name are you sinking all this money into this fiasco of a wedding ceremony when you two are already married?"

"Because you always dreamed of my having a huge wedding, that's why," Archie said.

"Where did you get that idea?" Clint asked.

"Because that was all Mom talked about when I was a little girl," Archie said. "Finally, she had a little girl to dress in white to have this huge wedding with lots of flowers and—"

"That was you who said that," Agnes said. "Not me."

"Wait a minute!" Murphy yelled. "Whose idea was it to have this huge wedding?"

"Hers!" Archie and Agnes said in unison while pointing at each other.

"You're crazy!" Agnes said. "Kendra Douglas—"

"Who's Kendra Douglas?" Murphy whispered to Jessica.

"I'll tell you later."

"Why in heaven's name would anyone in their right mind spend good money on a big ole wedding for one stupid day?" Agnes had her hands on her hips. "Think about it. Your father and I eloped, and we were perfectly happy. Each one of your brothers took his woman to the justice of the peace and got hitched. A few of them had small church weddings with only a handful of family and folks, and then we went to the house and stuffed our faces, and we were all perfectly happy. What is it that makes you think that we wanted to drag our butts all the way out here for a big ole fancy wedding—especially with that hair?" She pointed at Archie's black locks. "Please tell me you didn't pay good money to the idiot who did that to you!"

Archie's oldest brother Clint joined in. "For such a smart girl, Kendra, you sure seem kind of stupid to me. Making us all dress up in those fancy monkey suits and standing up in front of all those people ... we don't know half of them. Harvey has been having panic attacks because he's afraid your friends are going to make fun of him when he eats with the wrong fork."

Tears came to Archie's eyes. "Why'd you all come out here for the wedding if you didn't want to?"

"We did it because we thought it was important to you," Clint said. "You're our little sister, and if dressing up in monkey suits and learning how to behave like civilized folks is important to you, then we were all willing to do it."

"Well," Archie said, "you don't have to do it. The wedding is off."

"If you want to know what I think," Murphy said, "coming from a big family myself, the fancy stuff doesn't really make a celebration a celebration as much as having those you love with you does. We're starting a new year. You and Mac are starting a new life together." He squeezed Jessica's shoulder. "New friends, new family. New loves. Forget the monkey suits and forks. Just spend this time together and be thankful to have each other."

Wiping tears from her eyes, Archie grasped her mother's and brother's hands. "He's right."

Agnes hugged her. "We'll all stay here as long as we can until you and Mac recover. We'll just forget all about that nasty wedding." She fingered Archie's dark locks of hair. "And get you a real hairdresser to make you pretty again."

"We'll bring in the new year on the ski slopes and chugging beer in front of the fireplace and eating with our fingers," Clint said. "The Inn is having a huge New Year's party on the outside patio. Tim McGraw is singing. We'll all have a blast."

"Dad will have a stroke and die if you call it off," Tristan said, "if he survives. Do you know how much money he soaked into this wedding—caterers, security, flowers? He won't get a penny back if we cancel at this point."

Jessica turned to Murphy. Her eyes meeting his, she sucked in a deep breath. "Can I talk to you for a minute?" she asked in a quiet voice. After taking Murphy by the hand, she dragged him out of the room into the hall.

"What is it?" Murphy asked her.

Keeping hold of his hand, Jessica glanced up and down the corridor.

A squeal at the end of the hall caught their attention in time to see Chelsea running to where David O'Callaghan had stepped off the elevator. She seemed to take flight before throwing herself into his open arms. Her joyful sobs echoed up and down the corridor. Speaking softly to her, David rocked her in his arms while stroking her long blonde hair.

Jessica blinked back tears at the sight.

"They have a lot to be thankful for in the New Year." Murphy squeezed her hand. "What do you want to talk to me about?"

Tightening her grip on his hand, she led him through a door that ended up being a linen closet. After closing the door, she turned to him, wrapped her arms around his neck, and kissed him full on the mouth.

With a moan of pleasure, he wrapped his arms around her and pulled her in close to plant another kiss on her lips. "I guess when the mood hits, it really hits." He nuzzled her on the neck.

"I really love you, Murphy," she whispered into his ear.

"I love you, too, Jessica," he whispered back. "I can't believe that we only met yesterday morning. Right now, I can't remember what my life was like before I met you, and I can't imagine living a day without you by my side."

She pulled back to gaze into his eyes.

He caressed her face. "I want nothing more than to have those eyes and that smile of yours be the first thing I see every morning."

"Do you mean that, Murphy?"

He said, "I mean it with every fiber of my being."

She eased down onto her knees.

He watched her with confusion while she clasped both of his hands into hers. "Murphy Thornton, will you marry me?"

Caught off guard, Murphy's mouth dropped open. There was a full instant of silence before he gasped out, "Are you proposing to me? Your father is in surgery and he may not make it, and you're asking me to marry you?"

"Are you saying the timing is inappropriate?"

"A little."

"Well, I'm sorry, but Tristan is right. Dad is going to have a stroke if he comes to and finds out that this big ole wedding was called off and that all that money went down the drain. But, you and I do love each other—"

"I'm not marrying you to save your father a bunch of money," Murphy said. "That has to be the lousiest reason I ever heard of to get married."

"I wasn't asking you to save money," Jessica said. "I was asking you because I love you and I want to spend every day of the rest of my life with you, and I want to do it now. Since this wedding is already planned and everyone we really love is already here, why not do it now? Archie and Dad put all the work into the ceremony. They're paying for it. All we have to do is take it and make it ours."

Murphy cocked his head at her. "That almost makes sense."

"It's like it was planned for us and us alone before we even met."

He took both of her hands into his. "When we get married—not if, when—divorce is not an option. When things get rough, and they will—I can guarantee it because every couple has problems—divorce is off the table. Can you commit yourself to us totally? Stick it out no matter what?"

"My parents were divorced," Jessica said. "I saw how much it hurt Dad. He begged Mom to stick it out and she bailed. I refuse to do that to you, and I refuse to go through a divorce."

Murphy brought his face close to hers. "That means that when we take our vows, for better or for worse, in sickness and in health, for richer,"—thinking of her wealth, he chuckled—"or poorer, we both need to mean it. There's no walking away on either side. I'm game for that. Are you, Jessica Faraday?"

"I was game the second I met you."

He cupped her face in his hands and kissed her on the lips. With a sigh, he covered her mouth with his and kissed her passionately. When he pulled away, he gazed into her violet eyes and melted.

"I love you, buttercup." He pressed his forehead against hers. "Now and forever."

The hiss and hum of the machines hooked up to Mac lulled David to sleep, which was a reprieve after two days and nights of chaos.

The doctors were very optimistic. The bullet had missed Mac's heart, but it had clipped a major artery, which made for extensive blood loss.

The quiet of the intensive care unit was not unlike the quiet of being on the lake in his father's fishing boat. In sleep, David found himself bathed in the warmth of the early morning sun, with the chill of the lake breeze raising the goose bumps on his arms.

After casting his line into the lake, David shivered before reeling it in. The bopper bobbed several feet out from the boat.

"Good cast."

David glanced over to see the man's silhouette in the seat across from him in the fishing boat.

His father came into view.

"Thanks," David said.

Patrick O'Callaghan picked up a coffee thermos from the floor of the boat. "Need something to warm you up?"

"I'm fine."

Setting down his fishing pole, Patrick poured some hot black coffee into the cup.

Watching him, David marveled at how much his father resembled Mac.

"I want to talk to you about Chelsea." Patrick brought the cup to his lips.

"I don't," David replied.

"Now I did not embarrass you by chewing you out when I caught you two in the boathouse—"

"Dad, we're sixteen years old," David said.

"I am well aware of that."

"In two years, I can go off overseas and fight and die for my country," David said.

"You're a boy in a man's body," Patrick said. "These are confusing times for you and Chelsea, and I don't want you two to end up making a big mistake and ruining your lives and your futures."

"I was using a condom," David said with a roll of his eyes that he knew infuriated his father, but try as he might, he couldn't help it.

"They aren't one hundred percent safe."

Keeping his eyes on the fishing line, David answered, "If she gets pregnant, I'll marry her."

"Oh," Patrick chuckled, "you have all the answers, don't you?"

David shot back with his fail-safe argument. "You don't understand."

"I completely understand because I've been there."

"Things are different now than they were when you were my age."

"No, they aren't," Patrick said. "The music and hair styles and clothes have changed, but young love is still the same. *I know.*"

"No, you don't."

"I was the same age as you when I fell in love—hard," Patrick said in a harsh tone that caught David off guard. "I had all the answers, too. She got pregnant. We were going to get married, but life intervened."

David sensed rather than knew that he was not talking about David's mother, his wife. He saw emotional pain in his father's face that he had never seen before. There was sadness in his eyes.

"How?" David asked in a small voice. "Why didn't you marry her if you two loved each other?"

"She was young," Patrick said. "It was easy to say that we would get married, but when push came to shove, she wasn't strong enough to stand up to her parents. They took the baby—your brother—and sent him away, put him up for adoption, and went on like his birth had never happened." He swallowed. "We both had deep regrets."

David's mind swirled. "I have a brother?"

Patrick nodded. There were tears in his eyes. "Not a day goes by that I don't think about him. Wonder if he is okay. Is he happy? Does his adoptive family love him?" He sniffed and picked up his fishing pole. "Does his adoptive father take him fishing like I take you?"

David looked long and hard at his father—and saw him as a man, a fellow man and a human like he had never seen him before. "You can find him."

"Maybe one day I will." Patrick O'Callaghan shrugged his shoulders. "I have a feeling I'll never meet him. Just something I feel in my heart. But my prayer is that one day, you will meet him and become good friends and brothers, and when you do"—he winked at David—"you'll bring him out here to our secret fishing spot and have nice long talks like you and I have had."

David watched in silence while Patrick re-cast his line.

The sun flickered across the water and blinded David.

Patrick O'Callaghan's image was in silhouette once again.

David felt his father's hand on his wrist.

"David …"

David jumped in his seat.

His cell phone dropped to the floor.

The clap of the water against the side of the boat turned into the hiss of the medical machines.

Blinking, David sat up. As his vision cleared, he realized Mac was staring at him. The oxygen tube was wrapped around his face, and the IVs were taped to his arm.

"Are you okay?" Mac asked in a weak and raspy voice.

"You're asking me?" David asked. "You're the one who spent four hours in surgery."

"You were muttering something about finding someone," Mac said. "Did Black get away?"

"You killed him. Don't you remember that?"

Slowly, Mac shook his head and laid back onto the bed. "Where's Archie?"

"Archie's fine," David said. "She's been coming in and out to check on you. She's in a lot of pain with her ankle. She ordered them to put off the surgery until we know you're out of the woods."

"What day is it?"

"Saturday." David took Mac's hand. "I don't think you're going to make the wedding."

Mac groaned. "All of that money … Archie's family …"

"They're okay with it," David said. "They're all planning to go to the Inn's big New Year's Eve party with Tim McGraw. As for the wedding …" He took a deep breath. "Jessica and Murphy Thornton have hijacked it."

"Hijacked it?" Mac jerked his head over to look at him. "Seriously? She's known him less than a day—"

"*She* asked him."

Mac sighed. "I hope that young man knows what he's getting into."

"Murphy knows how to take care of himself."

"That's what he thinks," Mac said. "He hasn't matched wits with my daughter yet."

They both laughed until Mac cried out in pain.

"Tristan is setting up a video stream so that you and Archie can watch the whole thing live," David explained. "The doctors released Joshua so that he can attend the wedding, and Murphy's twin brother and his sister from Annapolis look like they're going to get here in time to be in it."

"What about a gown for Jessica?" Mac asked. "She is not going to wear Archie's—"

David laughed. "She convinced the owner of a bridal shop in Oakland to open the store for her to pick a gown off the rack."

"Convinced? You mean bribed."

"And all of her bridesmaids are wearing the little black dresses that they all brought for your wedding," David said. "Murphy is wearing his navy uniform. His brothers will be groomsmen. They have it all planned."

Mac looked up at the ceiling. "I'm just thankful that we're all still alive." He grasped David's hand. "You're okay. You still have your head."

"Yes, I do." A slow grin crossed David's lips. "I don't have a smart TV anymore, but I do have my head."

Mac sucked in a deep breath while trying to decipher what David was saying. "TV?" He let out his breath. "Oh … yeah. David, I'm sorry—"

He clasped Mac's hand. "Forget it."

"But Chelsea spent a lot of money on that—"

"I hated it."

"But—"

David was shaking his head. "You have no idea how scary it is having a television that's smarter than you are."

"I'll get you a new one," Mac said, "one that's not quite so intelligent."

"All I want is to see the game," David said. "I don't need it to sync with my email or cruiser or toaster—just let me see the Super Bowl."

"Hey, we saved you from international terrorists." Mac's voice was getting raspier with exhaustion. "I think we can locate a television that can play straight football games without a bunch of bells and whistles."

"Don't worry about it right now." David squeezed his hand. "Get some sleep and get well."

Recalling his dream—or had it been a memory?—David stared at him, marveling at how much he resembled their father, until Mac, feeling his eyes on him, looked down from the ceiling.

"What's wrong?"

"Nothing." David cleared his throat. "Did your father, your adoptive father, ever take you fishing?"

"No, he took me bowling." Puzzled, Mac squinted at him. "Why are you asking me about that?"

"Dad used to take me all the time," David said. "I haven't been fishing since he died." Forcing an upbeat tone to his voice, he asked, "Will you go with me?"

After glancing around at the machines and IVs, Mac asked, "Now?"

David laughed. "After you recover. This spring. Dad and I had a favorite secret fishing spot that we used to go to. I'll show it to you, but you can't tell anyone where it is." Expecting Mac to readily agree, David waited for his response. Instead, Mac looked at him with hesitance. After a long silence, David offered, "I'll put the worms on the hooks for you."

"Okay," Mac replied, "I'll go with you … unless I'm in jail for killing Russell Dooley."

CHAPTER THIRTY-ONE

Jessica Faraday was on cloud nine. She loved nothing more than shopping—except for getting a real bargain when shopping. The bridal shop owner was ecstatic when Jessica paid her double the cost of the gown she had found in exchange for opening the store on New Year's Eve for her. Jessica was thrilled that the gown she had selected off the rack fit perfectly with her wedding.

No, it was not white. Yes, it fit with her style all the way. Plus, she happened to have the perfect shoes—she always had the perfect shoes for any occasion. She intended to keep it a secret that she paid twice for her shoes what she had paid for the gown.

She was almost up the mountain with her treasures when her phone rang. The caller ID identified the caller as David. With a tap of the button on her Bluetooth, she connected. "I hope you have good news."

"Two pieces of good news," David announced. "Your dad is awake, and they will be moving him out of ICU in a couple of hours. They're moving him into a semi-private room with Archie."

"Great," she squealed. "What's info number two?"

"Turow called to say that the state police picked up Gil Sherrard in Baltimore and that they're bringing him back to Garrett County. They found money—close to five thousand dollars—with blood on it, plus Russell Dooley's watch."

"Excellent," she said.

"Still doesn't explain the missing recording and how Mac's blood ended up at the crime scene," David said. "Sherrard's swearing up and down that he took the stuff. But Dooley was already dead, and he figured since the guy had no use for his cash and the watch, he'd help himself. With Mac's blood on the scene and no explanation, no jury will convict Sherrard, and there are people who will be more than willing to believe your father did it."

"Could Dad have arrested Sherrard at some point, so Sherrard set out to frame him?"

"We've looked into that already," David said. "No connection between any of them. The steak knife could have been stolen …"

Jessica was not listening. Instead her mind was rewinding to a conversation that she had overheard much earlier. When she almost missed a turn on the road, she pulled over and picked up the phone. "Why did you have to give your blood to Dad when he got shot?"

"Because he and I are the same blood type," David shot back.

"But Archie says Dad has blood on supply at the hospital, specifically in case there is an emergency and he needs it."

There was silence from the other end of the phone. Finally, David said, "No one indicated to me that they had Mac's blood here. They said they needed blood. His blood pressure was dropping. They had some but not enough, but no one said anything about him having a supply here."

"If Dad's blood is not there, but some was found at the scene—"

"Could be the blood that was supposed to be here at the hospital," David said. "I'm going to go ask some questions."

Jessica's mind was racing. "There was a witness who saw Russell Dooley going into his cabin …"

"Sherrard's son," David said. "He's being raised by Sherrard's sister. She and her husband own the motel. But he didn't see Mac. No one has placed Mac at the scene."

"Dooley was coming in from the woods?"

"Yes."

"I need to go to this motel."

"Jessica …." Before David could offer any more objections, Jessica hung up and was calling Murphy's phone number, which she already memorized and put into her phone with the ID 'Hubby.'

"Did you get a dress?" Murphy answered the phone.

"In my trunk," she said in a high-pitched voice. "It is gorgeous. I can't wait for you to see it."

"Not before the wedding," Murphy replied. "J.J. is on his way."

"Your twin?"

"He's going to be my best man," Murphy said. "They're going to release Dad from the hospital today. He insisted so that he can come to the wedding. Cameron …" His voice trailed off.

"What about Cameron?"

"She's got this thing about weddings," Murphy said. "She might not come. But that's okay. The important thing is that you're there. I've been working with Candi. She's going to be our ring bearer."

"The rings!" Jessica shouted. "I didn't think at all about the rings!"

"Taken care of, buttercup," Murphy said. "We'll have wedding rings. You got your gown and I got the rings. Sarah is driving out from Annapolis. Tristan is setting up the video streaming for your dad and Archie to see everything. Unfortunately, my sister Tracy can't make it from New York, but you'll be there."

"Oh, I'll be there," she gushed. "I went to the church and told them what's happening. The priest will be for me, since I'm Catholic, and the Protestant minister will be for you. The county prosecutor is a friend of Dad's. He'll bring the license for us." Suddenly remembering why she was calling Murphy in the first place, she added, "Can you do me a favor?"

"Anything for my buttercup."

"I need you to meet me at a motel—now," she said.

"Now?"

"Now."

"I thought we were going to wait until after the wedding."

"You need a warrant to get that information," the hospital administrator said when David tracked him down.

"I'm asking about Mac Faraday's blood," David responded. "He's a patient here down in ICU. Now if you would like, I could walk you to his room and he can ask you personally about the four units of blood he gave to this hospital for use in case he had an emergency. Early this morning, there was such an emergency, but according to the staff there was no blood here under his name—"

"There must have been some mistake," the sour-faced man with thick glasses and a bad toupee crossed his arms. "If Mr. Faraday had given blood to be kept on hand, a check of his records when he was admitted would have shown that, and it would have been brought up to the ER."

"But it wasn't," David replied. "I was there. I gave two units of my own blood to save him. Luckily, I was the same blood type. I heard them say that they used O negative for the rest of the blood. I want to know where the blood that Mac Faraday had given you went."

When the administrator glared at him, David said, "You don't have to tell me. We'll go downstairs, and you can tell him yourself."

The administrator lowered himself down at his computer and tapped some buttons. "What's his social security number?"

Prepared for the question, David read the number off from his notes. The administrator hunted through some screens. A hum came from deep in his throat.

David saw his eyes flick from one spot on the screen to another before he picked up the phone and called an office on the intercom. "Can you check on the blood supply for a patient for me?" He then read off a long patient number. "Faraday. Mackenzie. Our records indicate that there's supposed to be four units of AB positive in supply for him."

The two men eyed each other in silence.

"So your records do indicate that four units of his blood should be here?" David finally asked.

"According to our records. Maybe they just didn't— excuse me," he said into the phone. "What do you mean it's been misplaced? Where could it have gone? How do you misplace blood?"

The purple Ferrari looked very much out of place when it made its way along the long river road toward the motel. Seeing the assortment of rough-looking men and women eying her, Jessica was apprehensive about climbing out of the expensive sports car until she heard the roar of a motorcycle coming up behind her.

Murphy pulled up alongside the Ferrari and took off his helmet. "Slumming?"

Jessica climbed out of the car. "I have a theory, but in order to clear Dad's name, we need to prove it."

"What's your theory?"

"You'll think I'm crazy," she said.

"You're marrying a man you met only twenty-four hours ago," Murphy said. "Of course I think you're crazy. I'm not so sane myself."

Hand in hand, they made their way up to the porch of the cabin marked "Registration."

"I'm looking for cabin eight," she told the group on the porch.

"Are you with the police?" one of the women asked.

"I'm working with them." Jessica turned to the two boys. "I understand one of you saw Mr. Dooley coming in from the woods the night he was killed."

One of the boys nodded his head. "I did. Then after he went inside his cabin, I heard screaming. I heard him being killed."

"Where was he coming from when you saw him go into the cabin?" she asked.

The boy pointed toward the woods at the other end of the motel. "There's a path that takes you to the creek where you can go fishing."

Thanking him, Jessica and Murphy walked hand in hand past all the cabins to the path into the woods.

"The boy saw Russell Dooley coming in from the woods the night he was murdered," Murphy said.

"Time of death is between midnight and one o'clock," Jessica said. "It's been freezing cold this whole week—"

"That's because it's winter."

Shivering in the cold, they entered the dark, rough-cut path through the trees. The bright sun shone through the tree-tops and danced on the white snow.

"What was Russell Dooley doing in the woods that late at night?" Jessica said. "Not night fishing."

"Meeting someone?" Murphy suggested.

"He had a cabin to himself," Jessica said.

"But there are people all around that motel area," Murphy noted. "He was out to get your dad. You said he had a bunch of money on him. Maybe he brought it to hire a hit man to kill your father—on his wedding day."

"I have another theory," she said. "Russell Dooley always claimed my father framed his wife, Leigh Ann. That's what she claimed, but it was bull. He believed her because if he accepted the truth that she had committed murder, then he would have also had to accept the fact that he married a sociopath."

She stopped at a fork in the path. In the freezing winter, with the deep snow, it was easy for them to make out the one set of tracks that led down to the creek, which they could hear rushing toward Deep Creek Lake a few miles away. Tugging at Murphy's hand, Jessica trudged down the trail toward the water.

"What goes around, comes around," she said. "Russell Dooley told his daughter that he had proof that my dad framed Leigh Ann and that he was coming out here to confront him. He even hinted that my father might kill him to silence him."

Murphy chuckled nervously. "Do you believe that?"

At the creek's edge, she stopped. "No, because it's not true. But I believe Russell Dooley wanted people to believe that. He believed his wife was convicted of a murder that she had not committed because she was framed. Can you think of a more fitting punishment for my father than being framed for a murder he didn't commit?"

"The blood that they did not have at the hospital," Murphy said.

Jessica nodded her head. "Of course, he had to have it in something when he brought it to the cabin. If the police found the blood in IV bags, they would have known."

Murphy whirled around in the clearing at the creek. "So after planting the blood in the cabin, he had to put the bags somewhere the police would not find it." Spotting a rural trash can next to an outhouse, he removed the lid.

"The boy saw him when he came back after getting rid of the blood." She looked around him to peer inside. "What's in there?"

"There's a bunch of dead leaves." Murphy reached his hand down inside.

"Careful," she instructed.

He abruptly let out loud anguished cry that filled the trees above them, and then he dropped to his knees.

"Murphy!" she cried out while clutching him. "Are you okay?"

Heartily, Murphy laughed.

She slapped his shoulder. "How could you?"

"I couldn't resist." He continued to dig through the moldy, rotten leaves. "You should have seen your face."

"I'm going to get you for that."

"I'll make it up to you."

"How?"

With a wide toothy grin that showed off his dimples for all they were worth, he extracted four IV bags from the bottom of the trashcan. Three still had blood in them. One was empty.

"How's that for making it up to you?" he asked her.

Bishop Sullivan was having the best Christmas ever. For once, he had gotten everything on his list. A week after Christmas, he had barely come out of his room in his mother's basement, for he had yet to grow tired of his new computer with a touch screen, his games, and his smart television.

Of course, it would end soon enough when he had to go back to work on Monday.

"Bishop!" his mother hollered from the top of the basement stairs. "Some folks are here to see you."

In the middle of gulping his Red Bull, Bishop almost spit up the soft drink down the front of his Angry Birds T-shirt. "Huh!"

He gazed up the stairs to see two men in police uniforms—one from the sheriff's department, the other from Spencer's police—and a young couple. The man was dressed all in black, including a cool leather jacket, and the girl looked hot in black pirate boots, black tights, and a red sweater dress that fit perfectly in all the right places.

Licking the drool from his lips, Bishop released the control on his game mouse and wiped his hand on his shirt.

"Bishop," his mother said in that tone from where she stood on the stairs, "these people have a few questions for you."

His visitors were admiring the collection of new computer games and equipment that filled the man cave.

"Looks like Santa was very nice to you this year, Bishop," Police Chief David O'Callaghan said.

"Our question is," the sheriff said, "were you naughty or nice this year?"

"Why are you asking that?" Bishop's voice shook. His eyes were wide.

"We're sorry to hear about your grandmother passing away," Chief O'Callaghan said.

"She passed away eight years ago," Bishop's mother said. *"Bishop! What did you do?"*

"My father's blood disappeared from the hospital," Jessica Faraday said, "and turned up at a blood scene. Suddenly, a

393

week ago, Bishop, who works in that department at the hospital, took leave to attend his grandmother's funeral in Minnesota, and he obviously came into some money."

"He won five thousand dollars in the lottery." Bishop's mother narrowed her eyes on her son. "And he didn't spend one red cent on presents for the rest of us."

Bishop hung his head.

"Who bought my father's blood?"

"Tell them!" his mother ordered.

"I didn't get his name. He was just some guy. He offered me five thousand dollars for all of Mac Faraday's blood, and, like, what were the odds that this dude was going to need it, and what harm could have come from it?"

His mother was madder than Jessica. "And then you lied to the hospital, after selling that blood, and stayed here in this basement for a week and played games."

Jessica took an envelope from Murphy and stepped up to Bishop. She took a stack of photographs from the envelope and handed them to Bishop. "Here's ten pictures. Look through them. Is that man in any of them?"

"Jessica, I don't think—" Sheriff Turow objected.

"He's not under arrest yet," Jessica said. "We're just fact finding." She flashed a smile at Bishop. "If you help us, then we can help you."

Bishop looked at his mother, who had folded her arms across her chest. He didn't know which he feared more: going to jail or being left at home with his mother. He leafed through the stack of photographs. Three pictures into the stack, he picked out the man.

"That's him." He handed the picture back to Jessica, who handed it to Sheriff Turow.

David looked over the sheriff's shoulder to gaze at the picture. "Is that who I think it is?"

Sheriff Turow's eyebrows met in the middle of his face. "I don't ..." He turned back to Bishop. "Are you sure?"

"Positive," Bishop said. "What's wrong?"

"This man was murdered," Sheriff Turow said.

"I didn't kill him!" Bishop jumped out of his chair. "I haven't left this basement in more than a week. Just ask Mom."

"Don't ask me to be your alibi!"

Chapter Thirty-Two

In the hospital's intensive care unit, Abdul Kochar opened his eyes to see a vaguely familiar face. The wavy silver hair and closely trimmed jawline beard came into view as his vision cleared.

"The spy who couldn't put my book down," Abdul said through a weak grin.

"I have read your book, Abdul," Joshua told him. "I really couldn't put it down."

"So you didn't just say that as part of your cover?"

Shaking his head, Joshua observed all the tubes and needles. Abdul's injuries were more serious than his own. "You are brilliantly insightful, Mr. Kochar. Reading your novel about growing up in Afghanistan and the people and the way of life and—I've had assignments in the Middle East—"

"But I doubt that you had the opportunities to really see things from the viewpoint of the people whose roots are deeply buried in the sand and religion there." With sadness, Abdul shook his head. "I heard you were shot."

"It's not bad," Joshua said. "You got hurt worse than I did."

"Your son saved my life," Abdul said.

Trying to hold back a proud grin, Joshua shrugged. "It's what he does."

"For that—for both of you—I am eternally grateful."

Joshua patted his hand. "The information that you risked everything to bring back to our country has provided us with invaluable intelligence about shell corporations that are really fronts for terrorist cells operating here in our own country. We're now going to be able to identify powerful terrorists who have been living and operating right under our noses. For that, the United States is eternally grateful to you, Mr. Kochar."

"I am glad I was able to help you and your country."

Trying not to cringe with the pain from his wound, Joshua slowly stood up. "I wanted to come by to personally thank you for risking so much. I know it wasn't easy—especially since it is your own brother—"

Abdul grabbed Joshua's hand with both of his. "We're not all monsters."

Slowly, Joshua lowered himself back down into the chair. His eyes met that of the man lying in the hospital bed with tubes and machines connected to him. He was a man, just like him, who had taken two bullets while trying to help their country in a war against a religious ideology that had become horribly twisted.

Abdul Kochar had a much bigger stake in the outcome of this war. Much of it was being fought in his homeland, against many of his people, with his religion being at the center of all of it.

The anguish on Abdul Kochar's face was from more than the holes in his chest.

"I know you're not a monster, Abdul," Joshua said slowly. "Just like I'm not a monster. I don't know how much you know about American history."

"I have studied it."

"There was a period in the sixties," Joshua explained, "during the civil rights movement, where a lot of white folks fighting against giving African-Americans equal rights would spout scripture from our Christian Bible as evidence of how God did not create them equally and how it was wrong for us pure white folks to mingle with those lowly black folks."

Joshua paused to watch Abdul's face while he digested what he was saying.

"I'm a Christian, Abdul," Joshua said. "But I'm not a monster and I don't believe—I've never believed that any man was created less than equal to me. That small fraction of racists lifted scripture out of context and twisted it around to conform to their hateful views."

"Just like the extremists in my religion have done." Slowly, Abdul nodded his head while grimacing in pain.

"Unfortunately," Joshua said, "with all the media attention spotlighting those racists, a lot of people thought they represented all Christians everywhere. Even today, there are many who believe we are all racist monsters."

A weak grin came to Abdul's face. He reached for Joshua's hand. "Just like what is happening now with my people."

"I know that you are not all monsters, Abdul."

"You've seen the reports of what is happening in my country to my people," Abdul said. "The news won't tell even half of the truth about what Satan's demons have done to good—innocent people—whole families—in the name of Islam. How do you fight such evil?"

"With good," Joshua replied. "When good doesn't hide, stands up for what is right, and refuses to back down, evil will lose every time. Evil may gain a temporary advantage and may even think it is winning—but in the end—good always wins out."

"Evil has been around since the beginning of time, my friend," Abdul said.

"So has good," Joshua said. "I'm not giving up, Abdul. Are you?"

"And leave my number one fan to fight this war alone?" With a chuckle, Abdul clasped Joshua's hand. "No, we are going to fight this war together, my friend."

"What a way to spend our wedding night." Mac laid back onto the bed and looked across the room to where Archie was lying with her leg elevated. "I hope this isn't a preview of when Jessica and Tristan put us in the home."

Archie reached across to take Mac's hand. "At least we're together and we're all right."

Mac looked around the room at her raised leg and the IVs in his arm. "This is all right?"

"We almost lost you," she said.

"If we can't explain my blood at Dooley's murder scene—"

"We'll get an explanation for that." She cocked her head at him. "You're usually more confident than this."

"I've reached my limit." Mac tugged on her hand. "Archie, you know full well that I completely adore you. I love everything about you …" He raised his eyes to her hair. "Except your hair."

She stroked her dark locks. "Don't make me hurt you, Mac."

"You're the love of my life, Archie."

As best she could, Archie turned on her side to face him. "And you are mine, Mac. I love you, too." She smiled. "I'll even marry you."

"There's something that we never talked about …" He sighed. "Children."

"We have two. Which one?"

"I mean new ones. Our having children. You and me, together."

399

Her eyebrows came together in a furrowed brow. "I thought that was out of the question. You got a vasectomy."

Mac said in a soft voice, "I can have it reversed with surgery, and if you really want us to have a child of our own, I would be willing to do it … for you."

Her eyes tearing up, Archie kissed Mac's fingers. "Oh, Mac, that is the most loving thing that you could offer to me."

He held his breath to hear her answer to his offer.

"But no," she said.

"No? Are you sure?"

"Positive." She caressed his hand with both of hers. "Mac, I love our life together as it is." Taking in their surroundings, she said, "Well, not right at this instant, but generally—our life at Spencer Manor, and traveling, and Jessica and Tristan, and our friends. I don't want to change a thing—except my hair. I think," a wicked grin crossed her face, "when it comes to babies, we should be looking forward to grandchildren. Think of how much fun we can have spoiling Jessica and Murphy's children."

"Yeah." Mac's evil grin matched hers. "I like the way you think, woman. I think we should start with a German shepherd puppy."

Their minds reeling with plans for their conspiracy, they dropped back onto their beds.

The door flew open.

Her usually vivacious self, Jessica rushed in and stopped at the foot of their beds. "Well, look at the newlyweds!"

Envisioning the elegant, perfectly coordinated Jessica with a spoiled child and an unruly puppy, Mac and Archie laughed so hard that Jessica was forced to ask, "What's so funny?"

They wiped the grins from their faces and insisted that it was nothing. Not believing them, Jessica narrowed her eyes to violet slits and cocked her head. "I think you're up to something." She pointed a long fingernail at Mac. "You look evil."

"I wouldn't talk that way to the man who's paying for your wedding and doesn't even get to walk you down the aisle."

Tristan pulled a chair over to the television. "Don't worry, Dad, you'll be there." He climbed up onto the chair while Murphy held up his laptop. "You're going to see and hear everything live."

Jessica sat on the edge of the bed and took Mac's hand. "But since you can't walk me down the aisle, I asked David if he could do it in proxy."

Mac glanced up at David, who was waiting at the foot of the bed.

"Only if you agree, Mac," David said.

"Tristan can't walk me down the aisle because he's doing the video and audio streaming so that you and Archie and Cameron can be there," Jessica explained.

"Why can't Cameron be there?" Archie asked, even though she suspected she knew the answer.

"Cameron doesn't do weddings," Murphy explained. "But she thinks she could handle it if she's off site."

"Do you mind if David walks me down the aisle for you, Dad?" Jessica asked. "I really wish you could, but—"

"Only if you make the announcement that my brother is walking my daughter down the aisle for me," Mac told Jessica while eying David for his reaction. "I think it's about time we finally let this skeleton out of the closet. Don't you, David?"

"If we weren't blood brothers before," David said with a chuckle, "we certainly are now."

"What family skeleton are you talking about?" Murphy asked. "Am I marrying into a family of serial killers?"

"No," Jessica said. "David is my uncle. He's Dad's half-brother. They had the same father. Patrick O'Callaghan."

With a shrug of his shoulders, Murphy said, "Cool."

"You're not surprised?" Archie asked.

"I figured that out yesterday," Murphy said. "The way Mac lost it when David got snatched—"

"I didn't lose it," Mac objected.

"You broke his brand-new TV," Murphy said. "I figured you two were pretty tight. Then, when you flipped out—"

"You flipped out?" Archie asked Mac.

"When he found out that I was going with them to the farm to save David," Jessica said. "You should have seen him."

"I did not lose it or flip out," Mac insisted.

"You killed my TV," David said.

"I thought you were going to strangle Murphy with your bare hands," Tristan said with a nod of his head. "It was quite awkward."

"Point is," Murphy interjected, "when you were threatening to kill me, I saw the same spark in your eyes that Dad gets when he turns into a Papa Bear. Since it's never been publicly released who your birth father was,"—he tapped David in the shoulder—"I deducted that you two were brothers."

Jessica's smile lit up her face. "Okay then!" She hugged Mac and kissed him on the cheek before getting up and kissing David. "He's going to wear his marine uniform with all his ribbons and medals."

"She insisted," David told them.

"And what Jessica insists on, she usually gets." Mac called over to where Murphy was helping Tristan, "I hope you know what you're getting into, Murphy."

"I have an idea, Mac," Murphy replied. "Oh, thank you for the wedding."

"What about a honeymoon?" Archie offered. "I'm going to be laid up after my surgery next week, and we have a month-long honeymoon all planned for January."

"Have you ever been to Australia, Murphy?" Mac winked at the young man.

"No, I haven't." Murphy shook his head. "Thank you, but I can't do a month-long honeymoon."

Jessica's face fell. "Why not?"

"I've got two weeks holiday leave since I worked through the holidays," Murphy explained. "I have to report back to the Pentagon on Monday January sixteenth. We can go for two weeks, but not for a month."

David leaned in to whisper to Jessica, "You have to make concessions like that when you marry a man who works for a living."

"I still remember when I was grateful for a long weekend at the Outer Banks, sleeping in the back of a van with four of my friends because we couldn't scrounge up the money for a single motel room." Jessica wrapped both of her arms around Murphy. "Two weeks in Australia with my new husband will be perfect."

"That's the attitude to have," Archie said.

A sly grin crossed Mac's face when he asked, "And then after that?"

"After what?" Jessica asked.

"After you get back from the honeymoon?" Mac asked. "Where are you two going to live?"

Jessica and Murphy exchanged questioning glances.

David clarified Mac's question. "What are you two going to do after the wedding?"

Seeing Murphy's pink cheeks, Mac and David exchanged chuckles. Murphy blushed as easily as his father.

"*After* you consummate your marriage," Mac said. "Have you two discussed where you are going to live?"

"I'm not commuting from Williamsburg to the Pentagon," Murphy told Jessica. "I'm subletting a two-bedroom condo in Crystal City from a naval buddy who's stationed in Spain. I was planning for you and Candi to move in with me and Newman."

"Who's Newman?" everyone, including Jessica, asked in unison.

"My dog," Murphy said casually. "He came with the condo."

"What kind of dog is Newman?" Jessica asked.

Murphy shrugged his shoulders. "Basically, he's a Heinz fifty-seven ... a mutt ... a forty-five pound couch potato."

"Couch potato?" Tristan asked.

"Oh yeah," Murphy said. "Newman has his own chair and spends his whole day watching television. He *loves* TV Land."

Jessica smiled brightly. "Spencer will finally have a playmate."

"Yeah." Murphy frowned. "As long as she doesn't steal Newman's remote. He hates it when you touch the remote."

Mac and Archie exchanged knowing grins.

"Well," Archie said, "every marriage, no matter how much you love each other, requires some time for adjustment—even for your pets."

David turned his attention to Mac. "You can thank Jessica for clearing your name."

"You're just now telling me this?" Mac turned to Jessica, who was whispering into Murphy's ear. "You cleared my name ... of the Dooley murder?"

"It wasn't murder. It was suicide," Jessica said, almost as an afterthought.

"Doc Washington is taking another look at the autopsy results," David said.

"Wasn't he stabbed twenty-nine times?" Mac asked.

"The same number of times Harris Tyler was stabbed." Jessica plopped down on the bed next to Mac, who suppressed a grimace when he was jostled. "I found that to be quite significant. It was symbolic. I mean, the exact same number of times that Leigh Ann had stabbed Harris Tyler. Bianca even said she almost thought her manipulative mother had come back to kill Russell and frame you because she insisted she didn't commit the murder."

"All of the evidence said she did," Mac insisted.

"And everyone knew that she did," Jessica said, "except Russell Dooley, who was in complete denial. Plus, he was suicidal. He has a long history of suicide attempts."

"But he stabbed himself twenty-nine times?" Mac replied. "I was a homicide detective for over twenty years, and I never saw a suicide where the victim stabbed himself multiple times."

"I didn't either. That's why the thought never occurred to any of us ..." David grinned at Mac's daughter, "except to Jessica."

"Russell Dooley paid Bishop Sullivan, a clerk who worked in the records department, five thousand dollars for your blood," Jessica said. "He identified Dooley in a photo lineup."

"Five thousand dollars for my blood?"

"To plant your DNA at the scene," David said. "Jessica and Murphy found the bags of blood in a garbage can down by the creek. Dooley's fingerprints are on the bags, and they have your name on them. We just need DNA to confirm it's your blood in the bags."

Jessica's violet eyes were dancing. "After Leigh Ann Dooley killed herself, Russell blamed you. He totally bought her lie about you setting her up. He wanted to kill himself—he's been suicidal for years—but he also wanted to get even with you. So he planted the idea that he had uncovered proof

405

that you framed his wife. He totally made up this story about finding a recording of you admitting to planting evidence to frame Leigh Ann—"

"Even wrote a letter to his lawyer telling him about the tape and saying that if he was murdered and the tape ended up missing that you did it," David said.

"Of course, no tape would be found because none existed," Mac said. "It was all a lie to set me up."

"Exactly," Jessica said. "Before he came, he got his affairs in order, not because he expected to be murdered, but because he was going to kill himself and frame you for murder."

"I have to give the guy credit," Mac said. "Dooley came up with a pretty clever plan."

David nodded his head. "If you hadn't been shot and needed blood, we never would have discovered that your blood here at the hospital was missing."

"On the night of his 'murder,'" Jessica made quotation marks with her fingers, "Russell Dooley scattered your blood that he had bought from the hospital around the crime scene. Then, he took the bags out into the woods and put them in a garbage can down by the river. A witness saw him coming back to the cabin, which he wrecked to make it look like there was a fight. Then, he took a steak knife that he had stolen from the Spencer Inn and stabbed himself."

"Twenty-nine times." Tristan climbed down from the chair.

"Wouldn't that hurt?" Archie asked. "I broke two bones in my ankle, and I can't stand that. How could—he must have had a high pain threshold."

"Adrenaline," Jessica said with a shrug of her shoulders. "Determination. Conviction in what he was doing. I read of a case where a woman had been shot four times. The police arrested her ex-husband. He spent three weeks in jail before she came out of a coma and told the police that she had shot herself … four times."

"Russell Dooley had a high blood alcohol content and massive doses of painkillers in his system," David said.

"Most of the stab wounds were shallow," Jessica said. "Like he was working his way up to the fatal wound he had."

"Point is," David said, "between Bishop Sullivan's statement about Dooley buying the blood from him and Dooley's fingerprints on the bags that were found near the crime scene, you're in the clear."

Archie reached across to grasp Mac's hand. "Thank you, God! And Jessica."

"Hey, I'm daddy's little girl!" She hugged Mac.

"You certainly are," Mac breathed into her ear before kissing her on the cheek.

"You're all set up, Dad." Tristan handed the laptop to Archie. "We'll do a system test before the wedding."

Taking the remote, Archie turned on the television.

Murphy stepped over to Mac to shake his hand. "Congratulations, Murphy. I have to admit, I am pleasantly surprised that she asked you. Looks like my little girl is growing up."

"And thank you for your blessing, Mac. I'm going to do everything I can to take care of her."

"And you're taking on a big job … taking care of her, I mean." Mac jerked a thumb in Jessica's direction.

"She's worth the challenge."

"At the top of the news," a news journalist announced from the anchor desk, "a police chief from the western resort town of Spencer, Maryland, is missing. The FBI has been called in."

Mac and Archie looked from the portrait of David O'Callaghan on the television screen to the real person chuckling at the foot of Mac's hospital bed.

"You're missing?" Mac asked while the journalist went on to report that there was a scene of violence at David's home and that he appeared to have been removed by force.

"I wish they had used a better picture for that," David said. "I like my marine portrait better."

"It's all part of the plan," Murphy told them.

"What plan?" Archie asked.

"In other news," the journalist continued while a video of a private jet plane taking off played on the screen, "Billionaire Nathaniel Bauman notified the FAA last night that one of his private corporate jets was hijacked in Houston, Texas. Reportedly, the jet was stolen from Bauman's private airfield. According to the FAA, radar has picked up the jet leaving United States airspace early this morning and crossing the Atlantic Ocean in the direction of Europe."

"I thought we got control of that jet," Mac said. "Or was I mistaken about that?"

"We did get control of it," Murphy said.

"But it's left the United States, and Bauman has reported it missing," Mac said.

"Of course, he reported it missing," Murphy said. "It's called deniability for when his jet lands in Tehran and an abducted American is removed from it and beheaded. He can claim he had nothing to do with any of it."

"Like reporting a gun missing before using it to commit murder," Jessica said.

"So you have been listening to me all these years," Mac noted.

"But David's not on the jet," Archie said, "and he's not going to be killed in Tehran."

A sly grin crossed Murphy's lips. "But they don't know that yet."

Chapter Thirty-Three

New Year's Eve—Spencer Inn

"A guy could get used to this," Murphy said when the valet hurried forward to open the door for him to step out of the driver's seat of the purple Ferrari.

"Get used to it." Jessica took his hand and stepped through the front doors of the Spencer Inn. She glanced at the time on her cell phone. Seven o'clock. "In five hours, we're going to be married!" She clasped both hands around his elbow.

Spencer's high-pitched bark caught many of the guests' attention when she raced from the sitting area in front of the stone fireplace to leap into Murphy's arms. "How ya doing, Candi?" He rubbed the top of her head while she licked his face and squirmed in his grasp.

"Her name is Spencer," Jessica corrected him.

"I call her Candi."

"Wasn't Candi your first girlfriend?" Donny called from where he was sitting in the lounging area with Joshua, Cameron, and two other couples who Jessica did not know.

She instantly guessed that one of them was Murphy's twin brother. He looked exactly like Murphy, except that his longer hair fell in layers to the top of his worn leather jacket collar. He was clad in faded jeans and a sweater.

"She was," Joshua Junior said with a wicked grin that betrayed that he also had the same dimples as his twin. "Murphy dumped her after he found out she was doing the do with half of the basketball team." He stood up from where he had been sitting to offer his hand to Jessica. "I'm J.J., Murphy's older brother."

"By seven minutes," Joshua said.

"J.J. is going to be my best man." Murphy took him into a warm hug. "Thank you, bro, for making the road trip on such short notice."

"Hey, I've got your back as long as I get to kiss the bride."

Jessica reached up to give J.J. a kiss on the cheek. "It's a pleasure to meet you, J.J."

"And this is Destiny." J.J. gestured to the young woman who had been sharing the loveseat with him. "She's my date."

Jessica noticed a puzzled expression cross Murphy's face when the exceedingly slender young woman stood up. Keeping her eyes lower, a blush crossed her pale face when she came forward. She only shook Jessica's hand when she offered hers.

In complete contrast to Jessica, who was clad in a tiger-striped mini dress with a faux fur jacket in the same striped pattern and high heels, Destiny wore faded jeans and a worn sweater. Her long auburn hair was a thick mane of layered waves. Her makeup was barely there. When she did speak, it was in a soft voice.

"Sarah texted," Donny reported. "ETA is one hour, and she does have a little black dress that she can wear."

"Wonderful," Jessica said with a squeal. "Is she okay with being my maid of honor?"

Cameron said, "Sarah Thornton is game for anything."

"Sounds like my type of girl," Jessica said.

Joshua went on to introduce the other couple sitting on the sofa next to the fireplace. Only then did Jessica notice the baby carrier on the floor next to the man's feet. She spotted an immediate family resemblance between him and the Thorntons.

"This is Dr. Tad MacMillan," Joshua introduced him. "He's my cousin, and no Thornton wedding would be complete without him. And his wife, Jan, and little Tad Junior."

"How old?" Jessica moved across the sitting area to get a closer look at the baby.

"Eight months," Jan replied with pride.

"Too young to be the ring bearer." Murphy asked Tad, "Did you get them?"

"He got them," Joshua said. "I knew we could count on Tad."

"Get what?" Jessica asked while Tad reached into his coat pocket.

"The rings." Tad handed the ring box to Joshua, who stepped over to Murphy. "I got them out of your dad's jewel case."

"These rings signified many years of love and joy for your mother and me," Joshua said while opening the box to show Murphy. "I'm praying that they bring the same type of joy and love to you and Jessica."

Murphy swallowed. "I know they will, Dad."

Jessica rose up and wrapped her arms around Murphy while he showed her the two wedding bands. They were plain white gold, and, after many years of wear, were slightly scratched up, but they were gorgeous to the couple.

"They have a lot of history," Joshua said.

"And a long future," Jessica said tearfully while taking him into a hug.

411

"Welcome to the family, Jessica," Joshua whispered into her hair.

"I feel like we're already family."

Even if Cameron couldn't bring herself to attend her stepson's wedding, she did want to share in it. So, she joined Mac and Archie in their hospital room. Archie had slipped out of her bed to snuggle with Mac, leaving her bed for Cameron to stretch out on. She even rested both feet up in the sling.

The room ended up being standing room only with nurses, orderlies, and hospital personnel from all over crowding in to see the local social event of the year.

Expecting the big turnout, and not wanting Mac and Archie to miss out on the celebration, the Spencer Inn had food delivered to the dining room for everyone on the staff as a special thank you. The only thing missing was the champagne.

While waiting for the wedding ceremony, Tristan and Donny had set up a camera room in one of the church's Sunday school classrooms where guests could record special messages for the bride and groom. At the same time, via a webcam set up in their hospital room, Mac, Archie, and Cameron would be able to greet the guests who they had originally invited to what was supposed to be their wedding.

Tristan had just completed one last interview when, off camera, they heard a young woman's voice call out to him. "Hey, are you Tristan Faraday, the bride's brother?"

The camera turned to take in the long athletic figure of a young woman in a very short black dress. Her slender legs ended in a pair of black stiletto pumps with four inch heels.

"I'm Sarah Thornton, Murphy's sister."

Still, the camera was focused on her legs that went on forever.

"Tristan," Mac directed him, "raise the camera so that we can see her face."

The camera's formerly smooth movement jerked up to show that Sarah's face was as flawless as her figure. She didn't wear heavy make-up. She didn't need to. She was naturally pretty. Her dark silky hair fell straight, just past her shoulders, with bangs straight across her forehead.

"I know what you're thinking," she said to Tristan. After receiving no response, she continued, "This dress looks familiar."

"Uh-huh," Tristan replied in a choked voice.

"I left the academy so fast that I forgot to put my little black dress in the car," Sarah said into the camera. "Luckily, I'm the same size as Jessica and she lent me this." She grinned. "I had no idea she wanted me to be maid of honor. I hear you're doing the video and audio recording."

"Uh-huh."

A wide grin crossed Sarah's face. "I also hear that you own a pet tarantula."

Silence.

"Does it have a name?"

Silence.

"Answer her, Tristan," Mac prodded him.

"Monique," Tristan replied in a choked voice.

Sarah moved in closer to the camera. "I love spiders."

The camera shot trembled.

"You do?" Tristan's voice went up an octave.

"I would love to pet your spider, Tristan."

They could hear Tristan breathing heavily. "Seriously?"

Mac and Archie looked over at Cameron across the room. "Seriously?" they asked her.

Cameron was nodding her head. "Sarah is not like other girls. Josh says she used to put frogs down boys' backs."

"Seriously," Sarah said. "Do you have her with you?"

413

They heard Tristan gulp before answering. "In my suite at the hotel."

"Great! That's where they're having the reception. As soon as we get back to the resort, you can take me up to your room and introduce me to Monique."

"I should warn you," Tristan blurted out.

"What?"

"She's eight inches long."

Sarah giggled. "The bigger the better." She reached out to pat him on the cheek. "It's a date then. Don't forget. Right after the wedding, we're going to your room and I'm going to pet your spider."

Off camera, they could hear Tristan breathing so heavily that he seemed to be on the verge of hyperventilating.

At the door, Sarah stopped and smiled broadly to reveal dimples not unlike her brothers'. "I think it's so cool that you like spiders, Tristan. I never met a guy who had a pet tarantula before. I have a feeling you and I are going to be close friends." She trotted out of the room.

The shaking camera shot focused on the empty doorway for a long moment.

Finally, Mac intervened to ask, "Tristan do you—"

"I need to go outside and get some air."

"I think you should," Mac said as the screen went black.

"Aw, Tristan made a new friend," Archie said.

"It's about time," Mac said. "I was getting worried about him."

"You know," Cameron said, "this wedding thing isn't half bad when you attend it this way. Maybe I can convince Tracy, Josh's other daughter, to do her wedding this way next summer."

Archie sighed. "This is not bad at all." She smiled up at Mac. "I admit, it isn't as romantic as we had planned, and it was much more dramatic, but still, it's lovely."

"Except for running for my life for the last three days and getting shot and having surgery and being accused of murder, this week has turned out pretty good." Mac hugged her close.

The television screen came to life again with a view of the church sanctuary. At the sound of the organ, the nurses and orderlies shushed them.

With the groom in his dark dress naval uniform, Murphy, J.J., and Donny marched down the aisle to line up in front of the altar. Reverend Deborah Hess and Father James from the Catholic Church stood at the pulpit.

In the front pew, Joshua stood with Destiny, Tad, and Jan. Tad Junior was in his father's arms.

Each of Jessica's friends, clad in little black dresses of various styles, made their way down the aisle. The last one, the maid of honor, was Sarah Thornton. Her little black dress accentuated her flawless figure and long slender legs.

"Does she have a boyfriend?" they heard Tristan whisper to someone where he was operating the camera.

"No, she doesn't," Cameron replied into the mike that they had to communicate with Tristan.

"Sweet," Tristan replied. "Monique is going to love her."

"The bride is coming," one of the nurses squealed.

The wedding guests rose to their feet.

Tristan turned the camera angle from the altar and up the aisle to where David, in his full dress marine uniform, stepped through the doors with Jessica on his arm.

A gasp went through the church.

Jessica Faraday was a woman with a mind of her own. Anyone who didn't know it before discovered this fact when she came into view dressed in an exquisite gown that stopped three inches above the knee to reveal her long slender legs and her high-heeled open toed shoes. The scoop neck bodice and dress portion were decorated in the black and white pattern of the snow leopard—white with black spots. The floor-length white cape had a high collar. The white train wrapped around and attached to her waist, where it draped down her hips and around the back to trail behind her.

She wore a diamond-and-fiery topaz tiara and a necklace that had been given to her grandmother, Robin Spencer, for her sixteenth birthday. Before that, it had belonged to another ancestor who had been of some nobility in England. The fiery topaz in her drop earring brought out the violet in her eyes.

The bride carried a bouquet of red and white roses, which Archie had selected to decorate the church. In keeping with the snowy theme, Jessica's fingernails and toe nails were painted white with a snowflake design.

On their way down the aisle, David paused to wink at Chelsea who had taken a seat in the front pew. Formerly one of Archie's bridesmaids, she had quickly shifted to the role as the date of the father-of-the-bride-by-proxy. Even if she was no longer a bridesmaid, it did not stop her from wearing the red strapless gown she had purchased for the wedding.

Chelsea's service dog, Molly, was seated at her master's feet. The red bandana tied around her neck matched Chelsea's gown.

Not to be excluded from the main event, Gnarly sat next to Molly. He wore a black bandana with red trim. Things had worked out well for the German shepherd. With Mac and Archie in the hospital, he ended up with his own holiday getaway. He'd be spending time at Chelsea's home with his favorite gal pal Molly.

David handed his niece off to Murphy and took his position in the front pew next to Chelsea. As if she feared that once again, someone would try to take him from her, she wrapped both of her hands around his arm and held on tight. Patting her hands, David whispered into her ear before kissing her on the cheek. Laying her head on his arm, she clung to him throughout the ceremony.

At the altar, Murphy kissed Jessica's fingertips, which emitted an "ah" from the ladies in the church and the hospital room.

"Murphy is so much like his father," Cameron said while refilling her bowl of popcorn from the giant bowl brought in by an orderly. After toasting them with a Big Gulp that she had brought to the hospital, she took a big sip.

Before they knew it, it was time for the vows. In a choked voice, Jessica vowed to love, honor, and cherish Murphy.

Archie glanced up at Mac to see a tear form in the corner of his eye. "I, Archie Monday, take you, Mackenzie Faraday, to be my husband," she said in a soft voice, "to love, honor, and cherish, from this day forward, in sickness and in health—"

"You better," he murmured.

The nurses and orderlies in the room stopped watching the wedding to take in the scene between the couple in the hospital bed, the couple for whom the wedding they were watching had been planned.

"For richer or poorer, for better or worse, 'til death do us part," she finished.

Mac clasped her face in his hands. "And I, Mackenzie Faraday, take you, Archie Monday, to be my wife, for better or worse, in sickness and in health," he patted her injured leg, "for richer or poorer, 'til death do us part."

Blocking out the room filled with guests watching the wedding on the other side of town, they kissed passionately.

Then came the exchanging of the rings.

"May I have the rings?" the minister asked.

Murphy and Jessica turned to look up the aisle. The guests turned around. The ushers opened the doors to the sanctuary.

417

Bogie stepped into the doorway with Spencer on a leash. The dog's whole body quaked with excitement. At the altar, Murphy gave Spencer a hand signal and mouthed, "Sit."

Spencer sat obediently.

Bogie knelt and released the leash from Spencer's collar.

"Candi, come," Murphy called.

Spencer shot down the aisle like a rocket. Several feet from the couple, the pup launched herself to jump into Murphy's waiting arms.

The guests cheered while Murphy held the squirming pup so that J.J. could untie the ribbon to the pouch in which they had put the wedding bands. In theory, it seemed to be a simple and cute part of the ceremony that would emit an "ah" moment from the guests.

But Spencer was not content to rest nicely in Murphy's arms while J.J. untied the pouch. She wanted to kiss her man all over his face and squirm while doing so. After several minutes of waiting for the dog to be still in order for the rings to be produced and exchanged, the guests began to titter with laughter, which seemed to excite the sheltie even more, which made her wiggle harder.

Finally, Murphy thrust Spencer into J.J.'s arms. He practically ripped the pouch open and emptied the contents into his palm.

Not done with kissing her new master-to-be, Spencer twisted in J.J.'s arms and thrust her snout in Murphy's direction at the same time that the rings hit his palm. With a jerk of her head, Spencer hit the underside of Murphy's outstretched hand and sent the wedding bands flying.

A roar of laughter went up through the church and the hospital room while Murphy tried to catch them in midair. He succeeded in snagging one, but the other bounced off his knuckles and dropped right down the front of the bride's gown and landed perfectly between her breasts.

Gasping, Jessica clutched her bosom with both hands.

Silence dropped over the church sanctuary as the guests awaited the bride's reaction to the mishap.

While everyone held their breath, Murphy opened his palm to study the wedding band he had caught. "I believe that one is mine." He pointed at her bosom.

Without missing a beat, Jessica planted both of her hands on her hips. "Well, if you want it, big boy, come and get it."

The church erupted with loud laughter.

In the hospital room, Mac laughed so hard the nurses were afraid he would pop his stitches.

At the altar, Murphy made a show of pushing up his sleeves. "Don't be nervous."

"Be gentle," she replied, "this is my first time."

Murphy and Jessica doubled over with laughter. After they finally dried their eyes, he retrieved the ring and placed both of them in the minister's hand.

After the exchanging of the rings and the lighting of the unity candle, the minister pronounced them husband and wife. "You may kiss the bride."

Jessica threw her arms around Murphy's neck and planted a passionate kiss on his lips that brought cheers and laughter throughout the church.

The church bells chimed to signal midnight.

"Happy New Year, Lieutenant and Mrs. Murphy Thornton," the minister said.

"Happy New Year, Mr. and Mrs. Mac Faraday," Cameron said from the next bed over.

"This isn't just for the new year," Mac said while gazing into Archie's face, "this is forever."

PART FOUR

FOREVER
SUNDAY, JANUARY 1

EPILOGUE

**Eighteen Hours Later - Desert Outside Tehran, Iraq
Secret Islamic Terrorist Training Base**

From the air-conditioned comfort of the back of his limousine in the jeep convoy, Nathaniel Bauman surveyed the rows and rows of new and old recruits training to take over ranks in their battle for superiority over first the Middle East, and then over the world.

It would all be his.

Yes, Ismail Kochar and the rest of them believed he was supporting their cause because of their ideology.

In reality, it came down to power. He who controlled it all won. As long as they depended on his dime to support their crazy cause, then he controlled them. Once they controlled the world, then he would control them, and as a result, the world would be his empire.

It was really quite simple.

He already controlled the most powerful man in the world, the President of the United States. Nathaniel Bauman owned Muhammad Muiz, the president's special advisor on

Islamic affairs, which meant Bauman controlled precisely how the United States fought, or rather didn't fight, this so-called war.

With his conglomerate owning two major news sources, Bauman had strategically placed himself in a position to keep the truth about the realities of the war on terrorism out of the public eye. As long as the news stifled stories about the growing number of terrorist incidents taking place on American soil, or labeling them as less scary crimes like car-jackings or workplace violence, then the American public would never realize the gradual enemy invasion.

Ignorance can be bliss—especially when you're the enemy.

If things went as Bauman planned, by the time America discovered what was really at stake in this war, it would be over and Islam would already be the victor.

Everyone's success or failure rested in Nathaniel Bauman's hands.

It's great to be king.

The limousine rolled to a halt at the end of the red carpet.

Various members of the group had video cameras set up. Bauman's bodyguard climbed out and opened the door. Hastily, Bauman climbed out, and, careful to not be caught on camera, scurried into the cinderblock building where he found Ismail Kochar smoking a thick cigar at a table.

"Where's the jet and O'Callaghan?"

"Black radioed that they got held up in Dulles," Ismail said. "They will be here in the next fifteen minutes." He checked the time on his cell phone. "Time is slipping. I want this execution to be done today. New Year's Day. It will make a bigger impact if we bring in the New Year with the triumph of executing Jassem al-Baghdadi's murderer."

"Well, since we have time before the plane arrives, we can discuss that matter of importance—"

"What matter?" Ismail asked with a cocked head.

The door opened and a guard led Muhammad Muiz inside. "Bauman, what are you doing here?"

"Important meeting to discuss the president's decision to fire you and replace you with Jared Hasem," Bauman said.

Ismail jumped out of his seat. "Hasem is completely against our movement. He is against violence of any means or matter. If the president listens to him, why—"

"Who told you this?" Muiz asked.

"You did," Bauman said. "When you called and begged me to meet you here so that we could discuss this matter and other changes happening in the American government."

Sucking in a deep breath, Muhammad Muiz backed away from the two men. "This must be a trick. *You* called *me*."

"No, I didn't," Nathanial Bauman insisted.

"It's a trap," Muiz said. "To bring us all together to prove our conspiracy. What are we going to do? They know."

"Even if the Americans know, they can't touch us," Ismail said. "Allah is on our side."

"And I control the American government," Bauman said. "I own the major news networks. The American people only hear what I want them to know about our government. Those other news journalists, they call our president gullible—I tell the people that he's open minded. They say that Islam is a tyrannical religious movement run by madmen—I tell them that we are about peace, love, and happiness. Those who say otherwise are simply paranoid."

"But those who lured us here could be recording what you are saying." Muiz fiddled with his tie. The sweat was pouring down his back.

"But no one will believe them," Bauman said with a grin. "They can record anything and everything they want. No one who can do anything to us will see or hear it."

"By the time anyone does believe them, Islam will have complete control of the United States, and Sharia law will be in effect," Ismail said, "and anyone who does not bow down to us will be exterminated."

With a roll of his eyes, Nathanial Bauman chuckled at the terrorist's insane quest. "Calm down," he said to Muiz. "Just go back to the United States and keep whispering the pillars of peace, love, and happiness to the President. And tell him that anyone who says otherwise is participating in hate speech—"

"Which hurts our feelings," Ismail said in a mocking tone.

"And we can't have that," Bauman said.

Muiz said, "It will be very hard to convince them not to hurt your feelings when you kidnap a celebrated marine in America and bring him here to execute him."

Above them, they heard the roar of the jet plane coming in for a landing. Cheering, the young recruits outside rushed toward the field and waved their weapons.

"Our special guest is here." Ismail Kochar scurried out of the building. Upon his appearance, the crowd of hundreds of terrorists parted to allow him, Bauman, and Muiz to make their way onto the airfield.

The jet plane rested on the tarmac. The stairs popped open and slowly lowered to the ground.

They waited for Neal Black to make his appearance with their prisoner of war.

Silence fell over the men.

"Where is he?" Ismail asked.

No one had an answer.

Cautiously, Ismail, Bauman, and Muiz, followed by several other guards, made their way to the jet. Ismail pushed two of his guards up the stairs. After a couple of minutes, one of them came to the doorway to report that no one was on the jet.

"Someone has to be on it," Bauman yelled. "Someone had to fly it." He charged up the stairs and into the travel compartment. As the guards had reported, no one was on the jet. He rushed up to the cockpit to find it empty.

When he came out, he found Muiz staring wide-eyed at him. Wordlessly, he pointed at the two seats at the back of the jet. A white box rested across the seats.

A note was written across the top of the box. It said, "From the citizens of the United States."

"What the—" Nathanial Bauman shoved Muhammad Muiz out of the way and threw open the lid of the box to reveal the heads of Neal Black and Leland Elder. There was an envelope taped to the underside of the lid of the box.

Bauman ripped it off and opened the letter.

"What does it say?" Muiz wiped the sweat off the back of his neck.

"It says," Bauman reported, "This letter is to inform you that your sleeper agents got the ax." He chuckled. "What type of sick …"

His laughter was interrupted by a loud beeping sound within the plane.

Muhammad Muiz grabbed Bauman's arm and pointed at the two heads. All four of their dead eyes glowed red.

A feminine voice came from inside the box. "Prepare to be exterminated in t-minus thirty seconds."

"No!" Wailing, Muhammad Muiz ran from the jet plane. In his haste, he tripped and fell head over heels down the stairs before landing in a heap at the bottom. Screaming, he clutched his shattered leg.

Thinking it was an attack from inside the jet, the army of terrorists stormed the tarmac.

"You can't do this!" Bauman raged at the box. "I'm an American citizen."

"We apologize if this hurts your feelings."

Dropping to his knees, Bauman tearfully pleaded for the bomb to change its mind. "No, no, no, no, no," he said repeatedly.

"Allah!" Ismail grabbed the gun from his holster and shot at the box.

The massive bomb that encompassed the luggage compartment of the jet exploded on the tarmac. The explosion was magnified by the jet plane fuel that filled the tanks, which had been topped off during a fueling stop in Israel.

The world news reported that the bomb, built with parts that traced back to NOH Bauman Technologies, which had been sold to a drug cartel in South America, took out the whole camp and the terrorists who had journeyed from several countries away to take part in a defining moment in the terrorist's war.

Spencer Inn

Dipping low in the sky behind the mountains in the distance, the sun was out of sync with Murphy's body clock. According to his internal clock, the sun should be rising instead of setting.

The sun had just started to rise to greet the new year when Murphy and Jessica had slipped away from the wedding reception to go up to her penthouse suite.

Correction: *Their suite.*

He was still getting used to "hers" and "his" being "theirs."

Spencer's whine at the bedroom door awoke Murphy to realize that the pup had not been outside for close to twelve hours. After kissing his new bride on the cheek, Murphy threw on his clothes and hurried Spencer down the penthouse elevator, through the lobby, and outside to the scenic hiking path to take in the breathtaking view of Deep Creek Lake down below.

All was quiet. Murphy could almost hear the snow icing up while the temperature dipped with the night's approach. The scenic overlook was vacant as if everyone else in Spencer, like Murphy and Jessica, decided to spend the day recharging their batteries from the days leading up to the new year.

The black stretch limousine took up several diagonal parking spaces of the turn off at the overlook.

Murphy and Spencer slowed down their jog to a walk. The rear window of the limousine slowly lowered a few inches. A slender hand encased in a black leather glove slipped out of the opening. Murphy extracted the red thumb drive and blue and gold pen from his inside breast pocket and deposited them into the outstretched palm.

"You're late, Lieutenant."

Through the open window, he could only see that she was wearing a black fur trimmed hat on her head and black sunglasses.

"I got married last night," he replied.

"Congratulations." He could make out the tug of a smile at the corner of her plump red lips. "I guess you haven't seen the news then," she said. "There was a huge explosion in Tehran. Last report I heard, well over a hundred terrorists were killed in the explosion."

"Any Americans?" Murphy asked.

"Officially or unofficially?"

Murphy did not answer her question.

"Nate Bauman was on the plane," she said. "He's dead. His official cause of death will be an accidental plane crash … in France."

"Why not the truth?"

"Because the board members at Bauman would have to

explain to stockholders what their CEO was doing visiting with Ismail Kochar, a known terrorist leader, during what was planned to be a public execution of a United States Marine." She tilted her head. "They may be able to pull the wool over the eyes of their stockholders, but the Joint Chiefs of Staff know the truth. If your bride has any stock in Bauman, tell her to sell immediately. By the time we're through, there'll be street people living under bridges worth more than a share of Bauman stock."

"And Muiz?" Murphy asked.

"The White House press secretary is preparing a statement. Their story will be that Muhammad Muiz, special counsel to the president in Islamic affairs, was the victim of a kidnapping by extremist terrorists and died in an explosion during a botched military rescue operation."

"That's a lie!" Murphy replied. "Did you show the president the evidence?"

She nodded her head. "He also heard our recordings of a conversation between Muiz, Bauman, and Kochar that pretty much outlined their conspiracy."

"Then why is the president telling the country that the military botched up rescuing his adviser, who was really a traitor, instead of admitting—"

"Because he would have to *admit* that he appointed a *traitor* to be his *adviser*," she said, "which would be an admission of his own poor judgment."

"And if he had an ounce of integrity he'd step up to the bat and take it like a man," Murphy said. "Major O'Callaghan is going to have to spend the rest of his life looking over his shoulder because he's on a terrorist hit list! He's a celebrated United States Marine and a *presidential* appointee sold him out! But all they care about is covering their butts—even if it makes this *traitor* look like a *martyr*."

Calmly, she shook her head. "*That's* why we have Phantoms."

Murphy gritted his teeth.

"Somewhere along the line," she explained, "our country's leaders have gotten their priorities screwed up royally. The security of our country and its people has dropped down the list below getting votes wherever you can get them and covering your butt after screwing up."

"And telling the truth about what really happened wouldn't meet that priority," Murphy said.

"Politicians with agendas are bureaucratic farmers," she said. "They're experts at spreading manure." A smile crossed her lips. "But we did win this battle in the war, Murphy—thanks to you."

"I didn't do it alone," Murphy said.

"No one ever does. Men with integrity realize that." The window rose up. "*Try* to get some rest on your honeymoon, Lieutenant. Enjoy Australia. It's lovely this time of year."

"How did you know we were going to Australia?"

The limousine was already pulling away.

Murphy and Spencer arrived back up in the penthouse to find Jessica, clad only in the Spencer Inn signature bathrobe, signing for room service.

"It's about time you got out of bed," he said after holding her tightly in his arms and giving her such a deep kiss that he feared they would end up sweeping the trays of food to the floor.

"I got lonely." Stealing a strawberry dipped in dark chocolate from a plate, she grinned. "And hungry." She took a bite from the fruit. "I ordered our first dinner as husband and wife." She swung out her arm to show him.

He saw two bottles in an ice bucket. One was a bottle of champagne, the other a bottle of cranberry juice. There were also two champagne flutes. She went on to list the menu as two salmon dinners with whole grain rice, a huge salad with a balsamic vinaigrette dressing, and a dessert of strawberries dipped in dark chocolate.

"Is the salmon wild caught or farm raised?" Murphy bent over to study the fish on their plates.

Jessica's violet eyes were wide with confusion. "Is there a difference?"

"Farm raised is injected with artificial colors and toxins," Murphy said. "Studies show a connection between eating farm-raised fish and a higher risk of cancer."

"Are you telling me that, less than twenty-four hours after marrying you, I tried to kill you?"

As if to make an attempt to save him, Spencer leapt up into a chair and snatched the salmon from the plate directly in front of Murphy.

"Spencer!" Jessica rushed to chase the pup making a bee-line behind the sofa.

Grabbing her arm, Murphy pulled her back. "Let her go."

"But you just said it was toxic," she argued.

"I don't think one piece is going to kill her." Murphy flashed his dimples at her in a broad grin before wrapping his arms around her waist to hold her tight. "We have a lot to learn about each other and adjustments to make, but as long as we see this journey as one big adventure, then we have nothing to lose."

"I love adventures!" She wrapped her arms around his shoulders.

"I figured that already," he said with a laugh.

Her eyes met his. "I'm truly committed to making this work."

"Oh I know that, buttercup," he said. "Hey, we got engaged and married in less than forty-eight hours. If anyone deserves to be committed, it's us." He covered her mouth with his. When he let her up for air, he whispered into her ear, "I love you, Mrs. Thornton."

She buried her face in his neck. "I love you, too, Lieutenant Thornton."

With her masters otherwise occupied, Spencer, aka Candi, gave her all to protect them by scurrying back to the table to steal the last piece of toxic salmon.

The End

LAUREN CARR

ABOUT THE AUTHOR

Lauren Carr

Lauren Carr is the best-selling author of the Mac Faraday Mysteries, which takes place in Deep Creek Lake, Maryland. *Three Days to Forever* is the ninth installment in the Mac Faraday Mystery series.

In addition to her series set on Deep Creek Lake, Lauren Carr has also written the Lovers in Crime Mysteries, which features prosecutor Joshua Thornton with homicide detective Cameron Gates, who were introduced in *Shades of Murder,* the third book in the Mac Faraday Mysteries. They also make an appearance in *The Lady Who Cried Murder*.

Three Days to Forever introduces Lauren Carr's latest series detectives, Murphy Thornton and Jessica Faraday in the Thorny Rose Mysteries. Look for the first installment in this series in Spring 2015.

The owner of Acorn Book Services, Lauren is also a publishing manager, consultant, editor, cover and layout designer, and marketing agent for independent authors. This year, several books, over a variety of genres, written by independent authors, will be released through the management of Acorn Book Services, which is currently accepting submissions. Visit Acorn Book Services' website for more information.

Lauren is a popular speaker who has made appearances at schools, youth groups, and on author panels at conventions. She also passes on what she has learned in her years of writing and publishing by conducting workshops and teaching in community education classes.

She lives with her husband, son, and three dogs on a mountain in Harpers Ferry, WV.

Visit Lauren Carr's website at www.mysterylady.net to learn more about Lauren and her upcoming mysteries.

CHECK OUT
LAUREN CARR'S MYSTERIES!
Order! Order!

All of Lauren Carr's books are stand alone. However for those readers wanting to start at the beginning, here is the list of Lauren Carr's mysteries. The number next to the book title is the actual order in which the book was released.

Joshua Thornton Mysteries:

Fans of the *Lovers in Crime Mysteries* may wish to read these two books which feature Joshua Thornton years before meeting Detective Cameron Gates. Also in these mysteries, readers will meet Joshua Thornton's five children before they have flown the nest.

1) A Small Case of Murder
2) A Reunion to Die For

Mac Faraday Mysteries

3) It's Murder, My Son
4) Old Loves Die Hard
5) Shades of Murder (introduces the Lovers in Crime: Joshua Thornton & Cameron Gates)
7) Blast from the Past
8) The Murders at Astaire Castle
9) The Lady Who Cried Murder (The Lovers in Crime make a guest appearance in this Mac Faraday Mystery)
10) Twelve to Murder
12) A Wedding and a Killing
13) Three Days to Forever
15) Open Season for Murder (May 2015)

Lovers in Crime Mysteries

6) Dead on Ice
11) Real Murder

Thorny Rose Mystery

14) Pull Over for Murder (April 2015) (featuring the Lovers in Crime in Lauren Carr's latest series)

KILL AND RUN

A Thorny Rose Mystery
(featuring the Lovers in Crime)

Chester is in the throes of preparing for what promises to be the social event of the year—the wedding of Joshua Thornton's little girl to Hunter Gardner.

While the Thornton family is busting with excitement about the big day, Cameron is struggling with pain-filled memories of another wedding day so long ago—followed much too soon by an even larger funeral.

All hope to push her grief far into the past is dashed when the FBI arrives with news about her late husband. A recently arrested hit man has confessed to killing her husband as a contract hit.

The identity of who had arranged the hit, and why, is unknown—but whoever it was had to have deep pockets to hire this assassin.

Determined to learn the truth about her late husband's death, Cameron sets out for Washington, DC.

Worried for his wife's well-being, Joshua, who is stuck at home due to wedding and professional obligations, reaches out to his newly married son Murphy Thornton (who is up to his ears in his first official murder case) and his bride Jessica Faraday to keep Cameron safe, catch a killer, and get her home in time for Tracy and Hunter's wedding.

Coming April 2015!

(former working title *'Til Murder Do We Part*)

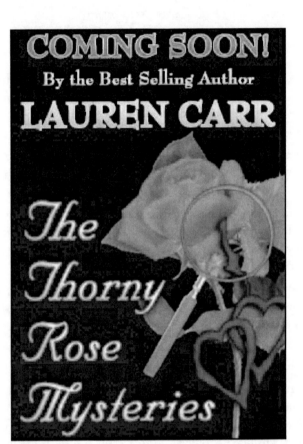

COMING SOON!
By the Best Selling Author
LAUREN CARR

The
Thorny
Rose
Mysteries

CPSIA information can be obtained at www.ICGtesting.com
Printed in the USA
LVOW08s1439210115

423772LV00020B/722/P

9 780692 353844